THE DAILY GRIND

BOOK 3

THE DAILY GRIND

BOOK 3

ARGUS

To Raven and Quetz, whom I love very much.

All rights reserved. No part of this publication may be reproduced, stored in a retrieval system, or transmitted in any form or by any means electronic, mechanical, photocopying, recording, or otherwise without prior written permission from Podium Publishing.

This is a work of fiction. Names, characters, places, and incidents are either products of the author's imagination or used fictitiously. Any resemblance to actual events, locales, or persons, living, dead, or undead, is entirely coincidental.

Copyright © 2023 by Forrest Taylor

Cover design by Paul Ghezzo

ISBN: 978-1-0394-4389-1

Published in 2023 by Podium Publishing
www.podiumaudio.com

BOOK 3

CHAPTER 1

The car rolled through an arid, dusty desert. James was fuming while Alanna was rocking out to whatever James was playing on the radio. It was, all things considered, exactly what their last few weeks had been leading to all along.

"I just hate . . . how much of a waste . . . of time this has . . . been." James hashed out his sentence between Alanna belting out the lyrics to some kind of sci-fi rock anthem. "I know Anesh felt like he'd found a bunch of leads, but with the exception of that actual, literal serial killer, not a single one of those was a dungeon."

Alanna cut herself off midchorus, clearing her throat and slipping back into conversational tone. "Ah, come on. I mean, at least we stopped some murders. And we got to eat at that ridiculously good burger place back on the border of Texas. That's not nothing!"

Sighing as he shifted lanes to pass around a fuel tanker, James kept grumbling. "I just wanted to find another dungeon," he griped. "We fucking know they're out there now, and it's possible that most of them aren't nearly as friendly as ours."

"Friendly?" Alanna choked on the water she was sipping, keeping hydrated under the October sun. "James, do you remember when it sent an army of the largest, and also sharpest, things it had to murder all of us?"

"Yeah, but it didn't leave the borders," James responded, explaining his logic. "Karen did. Monster Karen. We need a better name for that. But anyway, *that* kidnapped people, but the Office just kind of . . . was a dangerous place?"

"Are you coming around on my point of view?" Alanna asked, not having to put in much effort to hide her smile with how surprised she was. "I remember we had this conversation back when we were considering if we'd have to kill the dungeon."

James shrugged, glancing over at her briefly before looking back to the road. "I mean, evidence sort of holds your theory up, right? The dungeons are the Grand Canyons of mystical bullshit. They're dangerous, obviously, but not hostile. Or! Or. The one we know of is."

"We *know* of one other one. Just not . . . where it is. Or anything important about it." Alanna matched James's shrug as she turned up the AC. "What's actually bothering you?" she asked her partner.

The question wasn't out of nowhere. The level of annoyance that James had been radiating for the last thirty miles was way above what he normally projected, especially around his friends. Alanna knew James well enough to know more or less how he operated—at any given moment, James would have one thing that he was worrying about, and as time went by, he would either remove that worry by fixing a problem, or he would slowly go insane. And all that worry and anxiety and annoyance would spill over into other related conversations. Like this one. Until James had rolled the problem over in his mind long enough and found an opportunity to discuss it.

So, the question. "What's really bothering you?" It wasn't out of nowhere. It was Alanna's way of providing a crack in the dam for James to make use of.

The silence stretched on for a while, sudden and oppressive in its appearance. Even the music seemed to join in, James's eclectic playlist choosing now as a good time to introduce some quiet saxophone jazz. But eventually, he had to respond. "What if we can't go back?"

It wasn't a question, not really. It was a statement, a lot of thought in a small number of words. What if those colossal beasts were the norm now, what if their entrance into the place was guarded, what if it was too dangerous, or too angry, or simply too aware of them to make it possible to go in and live? What if, what if, what if.

What if this was it? Their lives had held some magic, and now they didn't anymore. What if, eventually, Rufus and Ganesh would leave, or worse. Pendragon would starve slowly, the magic items would lose their charge, the skulljacks would become normal. And they'd be left with a few random skills that they never trained in but didn't make them stand out at all. And Alanna would be basically superhuman, but what else was new.

And the magic would fade out.

"Not gonna happen," Alanna promised him.

James snatched the flare of annoyance in his heart and slammed it down before it could make him say something he'd regret. "But how do you *know?*" he asked.

She just shrugged, a gesture that he caught out of the corner of his eye. "I don't know anything," she admitted, shifting in her chair to try to find any position comfortable for her long legs. "But, worst-case scenario, we can always sell it and get jobs as guides to people with tanks." She let the humor out of her voice and stuck a hand on James's arm. "But we're not done. Not even close, got it?"

James tried to smile as he replied. "Yeah, I got it. It's just . . ."

Alanna nodded back. "It's just . . . there's a lot of risks, and not many chances, yeah? But don't worry. We'll get through this. You're not one guy fighting staplers anymore, man."

And just like that, James felt the tension that he'd been holding in for weeks seep out. Because his partner was right. He wasn't alone. Not anymore. He had friends and companions and a roommate in his own head, and all of them cared.

And right now, as he drove through tan and red rocks and endless dirt, as the music played and Alanna reclined in her chair to fiddle on her phone, that was enough.

"I feel like every time there's an internet argument about . . ." Alanna started in before James groaned and cut her off.

"Mia? Is Mia trans? I cannot remember." Alanna looked over at him, tilting her phone down. "Uh . . . are you okay?" she said, raising her eyebrows at James's expression.

James nodded, rubbing at his chin. "First off, we haven't talked to Mia in . . . months? A year? But also. What about the dungeon?"

". . . The *dungeon*, James, is not a gend . . . well, actually, I don't fucking know what gender the dungeon is. Sure, fuck it, why not. The dungeon is trans." She rolled her eyes, fluttering a hand in the air.

"No, you dork. Be serious." James paused for a second, then cracked a warm smile. "Okay, no, don't be serious. But this is a real thought—we should keep an eye out in the dungeon for something that could help with this kind of situation."

"I'm not sure how okay I am with you calling being trans a 'situation.'" Alanna poked at him playfully.

James flinched, still smiling, though. "Stop that! And I'm just saying, D&D has a *cringingly* proud history of magic items that force a change in gender. I'm not expecting to find a perfect fit, but if we could find something like that . . . well, fuck, we're already trying to give people skulljacks, right? We're not pretending that the status quo is the best possible option. We should just, you know, do that thing you always talk about—use our power to shape the world into something better."

"Fuck, I didn't think you were listening." Alanna grinned wolfishly.

"I always listen to you," James said with perfect sincerity. Out of the corner of his eye, he saw Alanna's eyes widen as his words connected. "Okay, less sappy. What other massive social issues should we be on the lookout for easy fixes to? Global warming?"

"I feel like we should ask Anesh about this for some reason. I feel like he's going to yell at us for something if we overcommit to *another* sweeping worldwide magical improvement project," Alanna mused, getting a laugh out of James.

The car rolled on into the Arizona afternoon, air-conditioning and good company the only thing keeping the inhabitants alive. And even as the desert around them baked in the sun, the two of them jokingly hashed out the future of humanity, only half joking.

"I found another dumb internet argument." Alanna spoke up from the back of the car, where she was lying across the seats and flagrantly disregarding seat belt laws. Secret had taken the front seat, the shimmering blue serpent sitting with his myriad eyes closed and snoring. James was pretty sure Secret didn't need to snore. He didn't know what had happened to his life to make it this silly, but he was rolling with it.

James tried to catch Alanna's eye in the rearview mirror, but she was just holding her phone over her head. "How are you not getting carsick? Stop that." She did not, and James tried not to smirk as he refocused on the road. The kind of plants that could endure the end of all life on the planet covered the sides of the road, with towering stone cliffs to the right that looked like they had been cut into straight lines with some massive, ancient laser.

"It's about water rights," Alanna continued. "And specifically if people should have water rights."

"... Yes?" James ventured.

"Yeah, obviously, yes." She practically snorted the words. "And we think that because we're humans who don't have the power to reshape the terrain of the world. Corporations, on the other hand..."

"Is this where we find out you're an anarchist?" James asked excitedly.

Alanna stuck one finger up in the air, the digit framed in James's rearview mirror perfectly. "That word doesn't mean what you think it means!" she declared. "I'm just kinda pissed at people again. I really should stop reading the comments."

As James tried to suppress the urge to facepalm while driving, he had a thought that he wanted to share with his girlfriend. "Okay, so, go with me on this journey..."

"I'm in the back seat of your car. I have to."

"... dungeon things," James said simply, ignoring Alanna's interjection.

She rolled onto an elbow, tossing her phone into the front seat and neatly into Secret's coils without waking the semimaterial creature. "That can't be your answer for everything."

"Why not?" James asked. "The green orbs make places better. We can . . . get some of them? Do a thing? Alanna, every single contemporary problem you've been pissed off about this trip, I cannot help but think that we can solve it with magic. We need more magic."

"We need to find another dungeon," Alanna stated. "Get more orbs. Get *better*. Rip into every issue we can get our hands on."

"Reshape the world, just a bit?" James said with a worried grin. "Everything still feels so huge. Even now, I'm thinking about how many green orbs it would take to fix just . . . just *water*. A hundred? No way. A thousand. Ten thousand. How many tumblefeeds are we gonna have to kill? This isn't just a full-time job we're signing up for."

The world rolled by outside. A few other cars flew past in the oncoming lane, while someone in a battered old pickup prepared to sprint ahead of James when it was clear. He let the guy; the old dude driving looked like he had somewhere to be, and honestly, James was just impressed that a car that looked like it came from the fifties could still *move* like that.

Eventually, Alanna spoke up again. "Got anything else you're doing?" she asked.

"Nah, guess not." James chuckled. "Maybe I'm just tired from all the driving."

"Pull off up ahead. Let's get something to eat. You'll feel better."

Secret snapped to attention, strange purring snore forgotten and no longer doing whatever his version of sleep was. "I would like a hamburger!" he declared to them. Outvoted even if he would have protested, James nodded and steered for the off ramp.

"Hey. I miss you guys," Anesh started to say, in defiance of normal conversation order.

James gave a quiet smile to the face on the other end of the video chat, his mouth moving in accordance with his wiseass instinct rather than the spark of love he felt in his chest. "Ah, you just miss having sex now that you're used to it." Alanna snorted out a choked laugh next to him, holding up the back of her hand to cover her mouth.

"Oh, hey, James!" Anesh spoke loudly, tipping his eyes up to stare at the ceiling. "Yeah, good to see you, too! What's that? Who's in the room with me? Oh yeah, say hi to your sister, you arse!" On James's end, he saw Anesh tilt the camera of his phone down to show Kayle sitting on the couch, spoonful of cereal halfway to her open mouth.

"Oh, whatever," she yipped back, putting too much emphasis on the "ever" for James to not think of his sister as a dumb teenager. "It's not like I don't know you guys are fucking. All the time. Besides, James pays me not to tell Dad."

Alanna raised an eyebrow at him, and when Anesh got the phone back into place, he did, too. "What?" James defended himself. "My dad is, as Alanna has mentioned before, kinda sorta super homophobic."

"That's really sad," Anesh said with a frown. "I was hoping to meet your parents at some point."

"First? Ow, too real. Second, I've *told you* about my parents. Why would you want to meet them?" James questioned.

Anesh shrugged, still a little down. "It's just something that's important to me in a relationship."

"Oof," Alanna said from the passenger seat. "We'll have to figure that one out later. My mom is . . . oof."

"Big oof, indeed." James nodded. "Anyway, Arizona is both hot and normal, as far as we can tell, and we're probably going to fly back in the next week or so." He delivered the report to Anesh, who was currently acting as command and control for the various projects their new team had going on.

It was, James mused to himself, basically exactly what he'd always wanted. A real-life guild of adventurers. Only secret, which was kind of annoying, since he had to not tell the whole internet how cool his life had gotten. And also just a *lot* of work, which was exhausting.

Exhausting in a good way, though. And he had not one but two Aneshes (Aneshi?) to help him out. In theory, they had a nearly unlimited number of Anesh-based life-forms to help out, actually. In the aftermath of the great escape, it had taken James almost two days to finally get around to actually *asking* Anesh why there was a backup of him running around. As it turned out, it was pretty simple, in the kind of way that dungeon nonsense was ever simple.

Anesh had, over the week while they were in the dungeon, managed to figure out how to absorb an orange orb. The single one that he'd kept in reserve for almost a month. According to him, the secret was understanding the concept of them. Just like yellows were time and blues were tools, oranges were the dungeon's avatar of complexity. And after absorbing it, he'd gotten himself a . . . well, calling it a power would've been kind of off, in a few ways.

A job, maybe? A task, perhaps. Or, to the mind of someone like James, who played a lot of card games, a triggered ability.

Point was, Anesh now had his own personal side quest. Once a week, all he had to do was remove six license plates from separate white four-door sedans that had functioning radios, and boom. Reward granted; ability activated. In this case, the outcome was pretty simple: an extra Anesh.

As he was the first and only person to absorb an orange, they were unclear on whether or not this would be a similar effect for anyone else. Would the quest change? The reward? Both? Probably both—hopefully both. Did it work like the blues, where you could only absorb so many at a time? What did it mean to be two copies of the same person? How did the *copy* feel? Could they even tell anymore which was which? The philosophical and moral questions this posed were absolutely mind-boggling and could have astounded humanity for *decades*. Hell, those questions *had* astounded humanity for almost as long as we'd had stories about magic and the future; this just took those hypotheticals and made them very real, pertinent issues. So, of course, Anesh used it to double up on his university classes.

The skulljack technology that James and the other survivors had smuggled out of the dungeon was critical for this whole process, allowing the two Aneshi to resync with each other every few days, to keep themselves as the same person and not diverge too far. But even without it, they were both just . . . Anesh. Maybe an Anesh who sometimes didn't remember a conversation or a plan, but Anesh, nonetheless.

They alternated duties these days. One of them always available to report in to or request assistance from. They had a roster of volunteers to keep exploring the dungeon when the time came to check if it was safe; they had people keeping in touch with the survivors who didn't want anything to do with the dungeon ever again; they had a few people making contact with possible assets to the guild, including trying to find reputable doctors and researchers to help publicize the skulljack technology in a safe way. There were even a couple people whose job was specifically to stress test the orbs and try to find applications for them. Last James had heard from them, they had determined that the orbs weren't real, and that was when he'd gotten a headache and stopped listening. They had a lot going on was the point.

And all that information flowed through Anesh.

The money flowed through him, too. And he was careful to manage what they had, because even though James and Alanna had pulled out what felt like a small fortune to them, a huge chunk of that had gone to repairing the lives of the survivors, especially in the immediate aftermath of the escape. Which was why James and Alanna found themselves driving cross-country in an old rental car instead of flying to all their stops.

At least James had convinced him to let them fly first-class on the way home. Small victories.

James pulled his mind back on track as Alanna said something to Anesh, and he realized he'd zoned out of the conversation.

"Damn," Anesh was saying. "I didn't put high odds on Arizona, but I was almost certain about the mall." He rubbed at his nose on the other end of the video. "You're sure?"

"Yeah, we—" Alanna started to say before James jumped back in.

"I'm not sure," he cut her off, weathering a sharp glance. "I know, we didn't find anything. But we're not exactly the best detectives around. Even so, I'm almost certain that at least one person was hiding something." He pinched the bridge of his nose, mimicking Anesh. "Look, we just don't have the time or goon power to search a whole shopping mall. We don't have the ability to search *anything*, honestly."

Alanna let out a long groan and shifted in her seat, kneeing the dash in front of her. "It's the fucking time compression," she griped. "We don't even know if that's a requirement, either! Every one of these fuckers could be different. Maybe it just opens on a full moon, or maybe you need more than two people. Who knows?! Every day's an adventure!"

James snorted. "Alanna's whining aside"—she bonked him on the forehead with her first two fingers—"Alanna's legitimate concerns aside, if we assume a door is open for a few minutes a week, we . . . we cannot find that. We will not find that on purpose. We *need* to find the people who've already stumbled across it."

That got a nod of understanding from Anesh. "Well, we can always send more people down to check it out later." He paused. "It's weird saying that, huh?" The young man shook his head, video compression turning his face into a blur for a second on James and Alanna's end. "Okay. Call it. Come home. I'm getting lonely here, anyway."

From the background, a shouted "I *bet* you are!" rang out.

"Goddammit, Kayle." James sighed at his sister's words and Anesh's blush while Alanna burst out laughing.

"Please come back and kick your sister out," Anesh begged, cheeks copper-red even through his darker skin. Clearing his throat, trying to recover some composure, he settled on repeating himself to his friends on the other end of the conversation. "But yeah, even if you didn't recover any fancy new magical toys, come back. Need me to book your tickets?"

"Nah, we got it. Also, we may not have found dangerous magic, but we *did* find a place that sells awesome pie." James perked up as he started talking about lunch, seeing a small nod from Alanna next to him as she fiddled with her own phone. "The diners down here are insane. They put cheese on apple pie, and it's kinda good? And the filling was, like, crisp and gooey at the same time, and it was delicious."

"Pie is the best dessert," Alanna added. "It's sugar and fruit, which is more sugar, but it *feels* like you're eating something mildly healthy."

Anesh blinked slowly a couple of times, face caught in a look of puzzled curiosity. Eventually, he stopped his train of thought and replied, "Well, if nothing else, you figured out how to make me want pie from across the country. That's *like* dangerous magic. Some kind of memetic weapon. Oh, how's Secret doing?"

"Sleeping." James shrugged. "He's enjoying being more physical, but he needs to sleep a lot. Also, we're in Arizona. *Hardly* across the country."

"All right, we can catch up when we get home," Alanna chimed in. "We gotta get going." She held up her phone to show something on the screen to James.

He nodded back at her. "Right." James spoke to Anesh. "We love you. Enjoy your pie!"

"What . . ." Anesh paused as there was a knock at the door. His head snapped around to look over at it before turning back to the phone as he stood up. "Did you guys really—"

James hung up, cackling. "Oh, that was good timing!" he congratulated his partner in pie.

"Fuckin' perfect," Alanna said through her own laughter. "I'm tipping the delivery driver like a . . . a . . ." They both paused. "Yeah, that sentence had a lot more potential when I started it." Alanna smiled, and James let out a small grin, still caught up in the great mood. "Whatever, he's getting a tip."

"Unquestionably!" came the agreement from James. "All right. I'm done with this fucking desert and its hateful sun. Ready to go home?"

It didn't even take Alanna more than a heartbeat to decide. "Please," she declared, tired conviction in her voice.

Three weeks of flying and driving to a half dozen potential dungeon hot spots, pretending to be FBI or DEA agents, or in one case, lawyers. Talking to almost a hundred different people who lived and worked in areas where an Anesh and his statistics team had found things that just didn't add up. Missing people, missing time, missing buildings in one case. That last one, it turned out, was actually just an unlicensed and illegal demolition; James had wanted to take the bribe—Alanna talked him out of it.

Three weeks away from their new cabal of those who were in on the secret of the dungeons. Those places outside of space where impossible creatures and even more unlikely treasures waited, along with danger to match. And those people, almost fifty of them, that James and his friends had pulled out of their prison in the middle of one. Many had simply wanted to rebuild their almost-forgotten lives, but more than James had expected had asked to join them. Maybe for revenge, maybe for curiosity, maybe because a lot of them were like him and really did believe in the idea of using whatever weird technology they could find to advance humanity. James was looked to as a savior, and a leader, by those people, and for all that he didn't think he was worth it, it hadn't taken him long to find his footing and find himself looking forward to being back at the "home office."

Three weeks away from his boyfriend. That was something new for James, honestly. He'd never really had a relationship, except for one girlfriend back in high school who lasted a week before she got annoyed with him. James had always sort of assumed he was bisexual; it was just something unique for him to actually experience it. At least their girlfriend was here with him, stuck in the same overheated car. That was *also* something new, but somehow not that much of a speed bump for any of the trio. They were, if nothing else, open-minded millennials. James had a suspicion that if they weren't, they never would have made it out of the Office alive.

Three weeks of a series of moments of "wait, why didn't I think of this before" from both himself and Alanna. And Anesh, and Dave, and Sarah, and everyone, really. Texts sent in cryptic wording just in case anyone was listening in, hinting at possible things to check at some future date. They didn't dare get a Slack—that would just be too easy of a target if the Wizard Police *were* real, as James was increasingly suspecting. And so those ideas built up, buzzing in the back of everyone's heads until the moment they could have one big meeting and figure out their next plan of action.

Three weeks of anticipation. Of waiting for the next move. Of fearing that life was slowly sliding back to "normal." Of fast food and motel rooms, of not having the energy to do anything but fall into bed at night, of growing more and more bored of the road. James was, he'd learned, not a road-trip kind of person. He wanted to be. Maybe he needed less of a goal. Less of that ember of hope that they'd find something *weird*, that little ember constantly crushed out with every failure.

Three weeks of letting the one dungeon they *knew* was real sit and stew and wait for them to return.

Well. Three weeks ended today. Time to head back now.

They shouldn't keep their friends waiting.

CHAPTER 2

The first thing James did after stepping off the airplane was almost trip over a child. The *second* thing he did, sore, ears filled with the muffled sound of rushing water, tired, and absolutely prepared to just kick the next toddler that ambled in front of his path, was make his way to the baggage claim.

And when he and Alanna got there, the third thing he did was forget everything awful about that flight, break into a grin, and give Anesh a crushing bear hug when he spotted his boyfriend in the crowd.

And for just a moment, there was no press of humans around them, no impatiently waiting for luggage to be dispensed, no airport PA system telling him to be on the lookout for unattended luggage or suspicious behavior; there was just the warm feeling of dry skin against his own and a pair of arms returning the hug as best as was possible when someone was being smothered.

Out of the corner of his eye, James saw Alanna giving a similar, if slightly larger, hug to another iteration of Anesh, and he smiled. A real smile, this time, that came naturally and without thought or question.

"Oooooh, fuck, it's good to see you again," James rumbled.

"Arrgmuph!" Anesh agreed. Or, well, probably agreed. It was hard to tell what exactly the tone was when he was pressed against James. With lips in a small, guilty smile, James released him from the crushing hug and let Anesh catch his breath. "Yes, good to see you, too. Glad to be home?" Anesh asked him after some theatrical panting to recover his breath.

James nodded empathically. "Unbelievably," he said. "Let's get our luggage and get the hell out of here. You brought my car?"

"I did. Did you know this place charges more than Heathrow for parking?" Anesh asked with a thin veneer of curiosity.

"I did not need to know that!" James replied cheerfully. "Alanna. Alanna, please, let Other Anesh go—we only have so many backups."

Alanna laughed and released her Anesh, letting him drop a couple inches back to his feet as she did so. "Sorry, sorry. Hey, is it really okay for both of you to be here?" she asked them, suddenly realizing how weird it might seem to the average person.

Anesh shrugged, and Anesh mirrored the gesture. "It's probably fine," one of them said.

"Everyone's just going to assume we're twins, anyway," the other continued.

"How the hell do you decide who talks first?" James asked as he scanned the luggage conveyor for any sign of his bag, and also any sign of a break in the wall of people. The flight back had been packed, and the baggage claim wasn't any easier to navigate for it.

"We pick one of us to be first every time we resync," Anesh said. "And then that one goes first every time, and we alternate on sentences," Anesh continued. "It's surprisingly easy to get used to—when you know what's being said anyway," first Anesh finished.

James pressed his eyes shut and rubbed at his forehead. "Oh, wow, it's like listening to you in stereo. How did I not get to experience this before?"

"One of us was always in class, and you two went hunting after a few days." The Aneshes shrugged. "So you only really saw one of us at a time, except... ahem." Both Aneshes blushed a bit as the second one let the sentence trail.

"Except when we were *not talking*." Alanna leaned in and winked at James.

James felt his air-travel headache escalate. "You guys are on two completely opposite ends of the innuendo spectrum and somehow can't just say *sex*," he muttered, his voice swallowed up by the crowd around them. "Okay!" he opted to say out loud. "I see one of my bags. Let's grab that and get out of here before Secret gets mad!"

"Where is Secret, anyway?" Anesh asked.

"We don't see him on you, and normally that's where he sits," an Anesh commented.

At that question, James had the good grace to look sheepish. "Well, I did tell you he's been spending more time physical, yes? And it turns out that the more time he spends solid, the more people can start to see him. And he can't just swap back and forth between what body style he's using, and we couldn't reschedule our flight last-minute, so . . ."

"So?" both Aneshes prompted.

"So he's in the luggage," Alanna answered dryly. "We should really grab that duffel bag before he decides he's done waiting for us."

"I am not a piece of baggage!" Secret insisted loudly from the tubular duffel bag he was currently sitting in as James carried him up the stairs to the apartment.

"For someone who's not baggage, you sure do weigh a fucking ton," James muttered, his aching shoulders still sore from being seated in either a car or an airplane for most of the last week.

At the front door, James stopped to pet a Welsh corgi and tell it that it was a very good doggo, while Anesh slipped behind him and propped the door open so that Alanna and Anesh could carry the other bags inside. As the dog bounded away, fuzzy tail shaking in satisfaction, James turned and followed them in.

The living room was an absolute mess. This, on its own, didn't honestly surprise James. Five humans in six bodies lived here, along with three fabrimorphs—a term James still wasn't sure on—and one particularly sturdy Maremma sheepdog that was one of the most well-behaved dogs James had ever met, even if it did seem to have developed a taste for cardboard. And at the best of times, none of the humans were that interested in clearing off the massive table that they all used for meals, for games of D&D, and as a storage spot for whatever they needed to be set down in the moment. And ultimately, this was only a three-bedroom apartment, even if one bedroom *did* have an extra closet that shouldn't fit inside the building and was also occupied by over half of the population of the structure.

Still, that didn't explain why most of the noncouch seating had been rotated around to be in the way of anyone walking through the door. Nor did it cover the reason that one of James's bookshelves had been turned to be against the wall by the kitchen—a terrible place to store anything that was susceptible to damage by rogue food.

No, those things were explained less by their overcrowding problem and more by the massive whiteboard and pair of cork panels that now sat across the back wall, covering most of the sliding glass door to the patio and firmly blocking access to the fireplace.

It looked like a conspiracy theory gone awry. Scribbled notes in different colors of pens, dozens of photographs and news clippings tacked up, grouped together, and connected by lines of red string. The original Wikipedia—going down any one rabbit hole was sure to cost you an entire afternoon on a madman's board like this one.

"What," James asked, tone flat, "in the hell. Is . . . all this? All of it. Also, hey, JP. Why are you here?" He looked down at the feeling of something thudding into his ankle and saw a certain red-and-black stapler looking back up at him from one slitted central eye, pen legs making scratching noises on the strip of hardwood floor. "Aw, hey, Rufus! I missed you, too!"

"I've got a lot to keep track of," the Anesh behind him muttered guiltily, while the one farther down the hall yelled it back with the same level of guilt in his voice, just a bit louder.

"Hey, James," JP said from the couch. "I'm just hanging out. Anesh wants my help trying to find a dungeon he thinks might actually be online later, but until then, I'm just working on this Shadowrun character. Did you know your rule book is falling apart?"

James dropped his luggage and almost let it hit the floor before remembering Secret was inside it and catching it, lowering it the last foot or so and unzipping it to let the multieyed, multifanged concept of a secret inside drift out and, with practiced flicks of his tail in the air, float lazily over to his place on the couch, where he curled up next to JP. "Yeah," James replied smoothly, as if this were normal. "I took out all the sample characters when they started falling out and then figured that as long as pages weren't going to stay in, I'd sort them in order of use for character creation. If you're wondering where the skills are, they're after the bit on starting points for mages."

"I was not wondering that, but thank you." JP bobbed his head. "I was more wondering why some of these pages look . . . different."

"The rules for hacking are stupid and I fixed them." James betrayed no emotion as he answered, then pivoted back to a more human tone. "Also, what's this about an internet dungeon?"

JP just leaned back and tapped the mess of lines and details behind his head. "Ask Anesh. I just work here."

"Oh. Cool. I actually wasn't sure if you were still part of the team; I haven't seen you in weeks."

"Well, you've been on the road. And I've been driving Dave around every day, since he's taking care of Pendragon now and still trying to keep a normal day job." JP didn't get defensive. He was a remarkably calm guy; where some people might see a personal attack or an angry comment, he just found a question to answer, politely and accurately, with a smile on his face. It was what made it so easy to get along with him. It was also why James didn't bother getting mad at him when he hadn't wanted to go on the rescue delve with him and Alanna. He knew JP was just being true to himself, and blaming him for it wouldn't accomplish anything, even if it did sting a bit.

"Dave does have a great job, though," Alanna said, coming back out of their shared room with a fresh T-shirt on her torso and Ganesh on her shoulder. "Where's Anesh?" she asked, maneuvering through misplaced furniture to climb into the most comfy chair at the head of the table, reaching out a bare foot to poke at Secret's tail.

"Bathroom," answered James's sister, Kayle, walking into the living room like she owned the place.

"What about the other Anesh?" James asked, at this point more or less having fully accepted that his sister was apprised of everything that was going on around here, as long as she was using his couch as a bed.

"Also bathroom. They're the same person, bro. I dunno why you think they'd drink different amounts." She rolled her eyes at him, a gesture that actually did manage to cause a burst of anger in the back of James's head. Sure, she'd helped Anesh save his life a month ago, but ultimately, his sister was still an enormous pain in the ass to him, with a lifetime of petty annoyances in his memory to remind him just how much he disliked spending time with her.

And she'd been staying here for almost a month now—more than enough time for him to get sick of her presence.

"Why are you still here, anyway?" James asked, as nonbitter as possible.

It didn't work, and his sister sneered at him. "Mom and Dad are still on vacation. They decided to go to *Arizona*." Kayle inflected the word like she was talking about a sewage treatment plant. "So I'm here for another week, with all the insane stuff you do."

James tried to divert away from her hostility. "Arizona? That's cool; we were just there. Maybe we crossed paths?" He glanced at Alanna, who gave a friendly shrug.

"Bet they're checking out the Grand Canyon. Oh, man, what if there's a dungeon in the Grand Canyon?" Alanna commented.

Kayle sighed in that way only a teenager could when the adults in the room were being boring. It never ceased to amaze James just how quickly she'd come to terms with the existential threat to humanity and then turned it in her head into something boring that wasn't her problem. He'd suspect a hostile infomorph at work, if he hadn't had verification from Secret that such wasn't the case, and if he didn't know his sister was just the kind of person who didn't . . . care. Not really. Not in a way that he could empathize with. "Well, whatever," she announced to them. "I'm going out."

"Have a good afternoon," JP said politely, while Alanna went with a hearty "See ya!" matched by Secret's "Fare you well." And James settled on "Dressed like *that*?"

She paused at the door, sliding sandals onto her feet. "What's wrong with *this*?" She gestured to her jean shorts and tank top, mockingly matching James's tone.

"Nothing," James said, trying and failing to position himself out of the way without falling over badly placed chairs. "I just like giving you a hard time."

With a huff, she slammed the door behind her.

There was a long breath of silence as everyone watched the door, some with eyebrows-raised amusement, and others with concern that she might come back.

It was actually *very strange* that Kayle didn't care. About the dungeons, about the Anesh clone, about *literal, actual magic*. She could acknowledge it, but it didn't engage her interest in any meaningful way, and James was actually legitimately uncertain if it was because she was under some other abstract dungeon spell, or if she was a contemporary teenager, or both. He was pretty sure being a teenager didn't exempt you from caring about things like Secret; he liked to think that if he'd known Secret when he was younger, he would have had a vastly different childhood.

Eventually, Alanna spoke. "Well, *that* was fuckin' awkward!"

James laughed, and JP joined him, as did both Aneshes coming down the hall. "Okay, so, hey, Anesh. Before I relax and take the world's longest shower, JP said something about a Wikipedia dungeon? What's up with that?"

"Wait, he found a Wiki dungeon?" Alanna interjected, carelessly leaning half her upper body over the back of the chair, balancing with both hands upside down on the seat of a less plush, more wooden seat behind her throne. "Like, a dungeon inside Wikipedia?"

Anesh sighed and started to answer, but James cut him off. "No, that would be silly."

"Really? More silly than . . ." Alanna gestured around at the maybe-copy of Anesh, at Rufus trying to make himself a cup of coffee, and at just generally everything else in the apartment.

James sniffed. "Sillier, then."

"I thought I found a dungeon that—" Anesh didn't get far in that sentence before Alanna spoke up.

"So, like, you find it through certain links at certain times of day, right? Like, you have to go from the page for Cheshire County, England, to the page for trains, to the page for the history of obsessive behavior, all at 12:06 in the afternoon?"

"Okay, I can see it," James said. "And then you get into this sorta back-hallways part of Wikipedia? So, like, there'd be even weirder random articles that distort the farther 'in' you get, you can only travel via links. Threats?"

"Memes, right? But, like, the cognitohazard kind. Things that make you black out or forget your eleventh birthday if you see them. Or just kill you, maybe." Alanna shrugged. "Maybe other digital ones, too, like just straight-up viruses. Virii. Or maybe certain words are traps and try to eat your mouse cursor!"

JP didn't miss his chance to contribute, either. "What if the loot drops are edit privileges? Maybe you could lock actual wiki pages for X amount of time or something. That's probably a power none of us should have."

"This would make a fun game," James stated, draping himself back over the couch. "We should make this."

"Can I finish?" Anesh asked, half growling.

James and Alanna looked over at him as if surprised he was still putting up with them. "Oh! Right! How do we get into Wikipedia again?"

He sighed, but with a smile on his faces. "Okay . . ." Both Aneshes rubbed at each other's shoulders, a gesture that made James suddenly realize just *how* convenient it would be to have an extra body that was fully equipped with the knowledge of exactly how tense your friends made you. "It's not even close to anything you wankers said. I think."

"You think?" Alanna quizzed.

JP slid a folder across the table to her by way of explanation. "There *might be* a hostile chain of links on Wikipedia that eat people."

"That's *kind of* like what I said," James rebutted, leaning on the breakfast counter and coming to the new realization that he still hadn't taken his shoes off. "How did you find this alleged dungeon? I mean, not that I'm . . . okay, this is gonna sound dickish, but none of the eight places we checked out panned out. Why this one?"

"To be fair, and in your own words, it's more likely that we just couldn't find the entrances than that they weren't there," Alanna pointed out. "But I'm also curious how you found this."

Anesh shrugged, not sure how to explain the tenuous chain of coincidences and logical leaps that he'd put together to form a rough outline of this picture. Thankfully, he had JP for that. "It's that skill of his," their friend exposited. "Pattern recognition, it turns out, is very useful, especially when we have fifty people to serve as examples."

"Examples?" James asked. "Fuck, I know we haven't been talking much while we've been on the road, but I feel out of the loop. Can we please get a Discord or a Slack or something? I know it's a security thing. I don't care anymore."

The decision to keep things mostly on paper had been an early one. Hell, it'd been James's own insistence that they limit use of their smartphones when it came to recording dungeon stuff or even keeping notes. It was why JP was handing Alanna a folder full of paper, and it was also why at least one Anesh had seen fit to reorganize their very limited living room space to make room for whiteboards instead of a more stable TV stand or something.

Fundamentally, none of them trusted the dungeon. Or whatever wireless carrier they were using. Or the possible existence of the Wizard Police.

Honestly, as far as James knew these days, any government mass surveillance that might have caught onto their bullshit was either not real or defeated by the baffles that were the antimemetic defense grids the dungeon employed. The real problem that had emerged was that now he *knew* things in the dungeon could mess with electronics, like Monster Karen constantly screwing with their radios. It was a looooong jump from radio to an iPhone, but considering the dungeon had actual sentient iPhones, it probably wasn't so far that any of them wanted to risk it.

Still, the line at which healthy paranoia started being too inconvenient was approaching fast.

"The examples are the survivors," the Anesh in slightly green shorts said. White-shorts Anesh picked up the thread of conversation without a pause, adding, "It's the specific way that the Office tried to erase them from reality."

"There's kind of a weird... I guess we'd call it a rough edge?" The Aneshes shared a glance and a nod. "It's a hard end to documentation, just a bloody big hole in the world."

"The dungeon wasn't really that precise."

"It left a crater of information, and the size and shape of the crater is... recognizable."

James made a strangled noise in the back of his throat. "It is... really hard to keep up with you talking in stereo."

"You get used to it," JP reassured him in an absolutely non-reassuring voice.

"Okay, so, that's how you find stuff like this?" James asked, legitimately curious. He saw Alanna roll over in the chair, paying real attention now and not just playing off her casual lounging as a nap. "You look for... what, places where police investigations start and then vanish?"

"Basically," Anesh said. "Police records are hard to actually get ahold of, and we don't know anyone in the service that we can talk to for it. Also, houses that are long-term empty and not for sale. Businesses with constant hiring advertisements but no turnover. That sorta thing." He graciously spoke with one voice to be nice to James. "It also helps that Secret's back. I've been wanting to talk to him about his, for lack of a better term, vegan habits."

James eyed Anesh suspiciously. "I'm going to have questions if you tell me that my snake-son only eats artisanal, free-range memories."

"What, like that one?" Alanna snarked at him.

"No, no, because he . . . doesn't eat memories. He sort of skims off the top. Secrets, catharsis, dreams. I suppose we couldn't prove it if Secret was taking a whole hell of a lot more from us, but I trust him, and it seems like he's not actually consuming anything," Anesh explained.

Alanna raised her hand. "Question! What about the actual meat Secret eats? Does that make him not vegan?"

"The what now?" JP looked down at the leviathan on the couch next to him and tried to scoot a few inches away as inconspicuously as possible.

"He eats burgers," James explained. "He says that he can truly savor them."

"Fast food burgers?" Anesh asked, eyebrows raised.

James bit his lower lip, showing off teeth in a worried expression that said he knew exactly where this was going. "Yes?" he answered tentatively.

"Yeah, don't eat at those fast food places," Anesh told him.

"Ever, please," the other Anesh emphasized. "Anyway, the point is, we're going to keep doing research. But it's hard without a network of contacts to draw on. We need to be able to place or bribe people, or just buy our way through some problems. And for that, we just need more resources than we have. The money's running out."

James nodded, already knowing what the answer was. "And for that, I'm gonna need to cut this vacation and go back to work." He looked around at the mess that his apartment had turned into and smiled. "I feel pretty good about it, though. Anyone wanna take bets on if Theo wants to come in with me to check it out?"

No one wanted to take bets.

CHAPTER 3

"So, I've got this friend." James sat on a tan leather couch, surrounded by comfortable pillows and a couple stuffed animals. Through the two boxy windows, sunlight streamed in, tinted green from the leafy trees waving in the gentle autumn breeze outside. "Okay, friend is the wrong word. She's . . ."

The woman sitting in the chair across the room waited patiently for James to find the words. Her name was Lua Margman, and if the long brown hair, circular glasses, and floral print dress didn't give away her chosen role in life, the sign on her office door that said "Talk Therapy" certainly did. It was a space that she'd reclaimed fairly easily, having only been missing in action for about a month inside the Office.

"Perhaps it would help if you simply described your relationship," she prompted James, who was the latest of the survivors to agree to let her try to help them cope. Many of them were getting by on their own, or at least faking it well enough, and still more were helped by the support group. But Lua was all too aware of how the trauma of the Office wasn't going to fade overnight. So she was here for people, with a summery voice and no lies or half-truths to get in the way of healing the mind.

Admittedly, the young man on her couch right now was perhaps the last person she'd actually expected to see.

Regardless, James nodded at her prompt. "Okay, so, we were friends since high school. Middle school, actually. We sort of went to college together, lived close enough that we were walking to each other's houses every day. We had what a younger version of me would call 'adventures,' before I . . . you know."

Lua nodded politely at him. She didn't *know*, but she could infer. And she believed him.

"So, when we both had jobs and were sick of our parents asking us when we were gonna get married, we moved out. Together, of course, because why not. And it was, I am told, great."

"You were told." Lua rarely put question marks on her sentences when talking to a patient. Too easy for them to feel like she was questioning them instead of clarifying for herself.

To James, it felt like she was reading him like a Wikipedia article, and her every statement was just clicking another link. It was a weird but not unpleasant feeling. "I was told. And I've learned." He took a deep breath, feeling all the held-back panic and anger brewing at the edge of his mind. "Her room is still in my apartment. I see her again all the time now. But I don't . . . I don't remember." His voice cracked slightly. "For the last year, I haven't remembered her. Never thought of her, never missed her, never even noticed she was gone."

And Lua made the connection. "She was one of . . ." A small pause, to compose herself. "She was one of the captives."

"Yeah." James wiped at the corner of an eye, trying to be inconspicuous, which was a failing move around someone as experienced as the woman on the other side of the room. "Sarah. She runs the support group for everyone now, and she's . . . I mean, I have this external image of who she is. We sorta stumbled across it almost by accident; it's part of what got us to come in and pull everyone out. But I don't *feel* it."

"Months, you said." Lua held up a hand, lightly, while she thought. "It must have affected you quite a lot." It took her longer than normal to figure out what to say, how to keep James talking.

"That's the thing," he said with a self-mocking laugh. "Actually, that's sort of what I wanted to talk to you about." James waved at himself in general. "So I'm depressed. It's not bad enough that I've gotten on an antidepressant for it, but it's there. And it sucks. But I'm trying to figure out if . . . if . . ."

If he was always like this. James didn't say it, but Lua heard it. The desperation in his voice, the worry that he was out of line.

"Your friend," she said. "Sarah. She was important to you."

"Apparently." James snorted. "I'm trying to reconnect with her, but it feels like I'm not catching up, and neither of us knows what to do about it. Sometimes we fall back into routines that *I don't recognize*, but she clearly does, and I see what we *were*, and I don't know what to say."

"When a relationship ends," Lua told him, staying matter-of-fact while still showing him a warm empathy, "it takes part of us with it. That's not just me being a spiritual weirdo, either," she said with a knowing smile and got a small, amused response from James, who was now balled up around one of the larger pillows on her couch, knees tucked up on the cushions. "Humans have a negative reaction to a breakup, to the death of a family member, to a friend moving away . . ." She looked at him meaningfully. ". . . the reaction comes in many forms, but a common one is sudden lack of dopamine production in the brain."

"Wait, we go into withdrawal from breakups?" James interjected, curiosity overriding pain for a moment.

Lua nodded, pursing her lips. "Not exactly, but that's not entirely wrong. So, yes. We do. Perhaps not from a weeklong fling, but if you've been with someone for a year? Certainly. And your relationship with Sarah, well." No lies, she reminded herself. No half-truths. "You don't recover from the loss of a decade-long support in your life overnight. Some people may never recover from it at all. But *you*, James. You were robbed of the chance to heal."

"I didn't know," he muttered into the pillow. "But I don't want to just . . . blame the depression on this. It just feels . . . it feels . . . I didn't . . ."

"You didn't know." Lua nodded back at him. "But you do now. I don't think anyone will ever know if you can undo the damage, now that Sarah is a part of your life again. This kind of mental health isn't, you can imagine, a frequent branch of study." He laughed at that, still guarded but a little more real, and Lua smiled at him. "But if nothing else, we can try to help you heal from the loss." She leaned back in her chair and folded her hands in front of herself, watching James as he stared out the window at the rustling trees. "Why don't you tell me about your friend?" she asked.

And James did.

The evening was one of those ones that got cold too quickly, given how sunny it had been just a few minutes ago. Night sneaking up and mugging those poor souls who had forgotten, or opted out of, a coat. Which was why Anesh was rubbing his arms and hurrying from the car to the front door when he got home.

Similarly, he blamed the cold for why it was so hard to parse what he was looking at when he stepped into the apartment that had rapidly become his heart's home.

"What are you doing," Anesh asked, in a way that made it clear that it wasn't a question at all, and also that while he didn't exactly disapprove, he was going to ham up his scorn.

"I'm infiltrating," James said, his words slightly slower than normal as he puppeteered two bodies at the same time. "It's a delicate situation."

Anesh looked over at the kitchen, where the drone—nonsentient; James had just gotten it today—was currently trying to open the freezer. Next to it, another drone, this one green, with sharply angled panels of plastic and metal and much more flexible rotor mounts, looked on; Ganesh was either curious or maybe just making sure his potential brother wasn't about to get launched into the ceiling. Again.

"I thought the skulljacks didn't really let you connect this well." Anesh raised an eyebrow as he watched the scene unfold, coming into the kitchen to grab a soda out of the fridge.

"Turns out, it's *people* I can't connect with. Well, won't connect with. Or maybe just the people in the support group. I . . . man, I don't know how to open myself up that way. It's very cool and deeply terrifying." James shrugged, and the drone mimicked the motion as best it could with a small twitch of its manipulator. "This slick little toy, though? Oh, man, it's cool. I can't feel through it, but I can absolutely enjoy having a sense of presence in two places at once."

Anesh looked back at James, his mouth set in a thin line that was almost, *almost* a well-hidden smile, which his boyfriend wouldn't appreciate at all, since James had his eyes closed. "You're trying to steal Alanna's ice cream."

"I am not!" came the protest.

"Well, I mean, you're not trying very hard. Or very effectively, anyway—this actually looks like you're trying super hard," Anesh said with a laugh in his voice. "Why the *Mission: Impossible* music?"

James opened his eyes, the drone stilling where it was now perched on top of the freezer. "It sets the mood. Makes it easier to focus."

"Really?"

"No, but I was hoping if I answered fast enough, you wouldn't question me."

Anesh tossed him an ice cream sandwich. "My way was faster."

"Your way is traceable. Alanna's gonna be mad."

"The ice cream is for all of us, James," Anesh told him patiently. "That's the perk of being in whatever kind of relationship this is. We share things."

James unplugged the impressively jury-rigged string of adapters that led to the back of his skull. "It's a poly triad—it really isn't *that* confusing."

"Well, remember that I've never had a date before, or ever really thought about my sexuality, so any of this is going to confuse me." Anesh scratched idly at the back of his own head as he tried not to feel awkward about that.

His parents had been traditionalists, for all that they spoke with South London accents and had only spent a combined total of maybe a year or two in India. They'd had an idea in their head of what was "moral," shaped by family traditions passed down from their parents, by British culture, and by popular media in general. And that, in turn, had passed down to a confused son, who had at some point shrugged and decided he was more interested in numbers than snogging and gone to the colonies to pursue that passion.

Ironically, that was where he'd met his boyfriend. And girlfriend. And a whole *new* patch of confusion. But it was something he wouldn't trade away.

"Anyway." He spoke a little too loudly, trying to cover his awkward embarrassment.

James did notice, and started to say, "Hey . . ." to reassure his friend, to tell him it was okay, that he didn't need to be perfect.

But Anesh actually did have a pretty good distraction. "You know what else confuses me?" he said, trying to regain his footing. "What in the *hell* is that cabling? How does that even function?"

"Oh! This . . . nonsense. Yeah." James clicked his tongue in disappointment. "So, I needed to convert the drone's signal to standard Ethernet, right? But it uses Bluetooth. So I had to get this wireless adapter and then plug that into my head and then use that to get into the laptop that's running a Bluetooth program to control the drone. Except I needed an extra thing for the wireless dongle, because, it turns out, not every skulljack is identical, and some of them are missing pins."

"This is a mess." Anesh shook his head at the table as he came over and took a seat on the other end of the couch, back pressed against the arm so he could face James. "There has to be something easier. Especially if we plan on using this tactically."

"Oh, absolutely. This is me hammering out something that worked out of extra cables around the apartment. I'm sure we could just get a drone that has a Wi-Fi access." James shrugged himself. "Frankly? I'm fuckin' amazed this works so *well*. I can almost *feel* the drone body, and there's practically no lag. And there *absolutely should be lag*."

Anesh actually had a good answer to that. "Didn't we agree that 'it's magic' was an okay explanation here?"

"Magic might explain how the skulljacks are transmissible, or how they seem to be able to translate perfectly from binary to brain," James conceded. "But it just seems to start to stretch disbelief when they also ignore, like, the speed limits of the hardware they're attached to, you know?" He pointed at the wireless broadcaster. "This thing has a pretty weak signal strength, and a bandwidth of maybe a single Mbps. That is absolutely not enough for a human consciousness. I'll admit, I could be wrong about the drone, because, like, I dunno if my pitiful human reflexes would even notice if there was some kind of lag. But no one who's actually playing with these things talks about there being lag between *people*. That's weird."

"Maaaagicccc," Anesh enunciated, which provoked a loud laugh from his friend. "Look, it's probably just one hypercomplex blue orb or something. Just take the win!" He bit down into his ice cream with a mock glare at James.

"Okay, okay!" James lay back into the couch and just relaxed for a second, enjoying the feeling of closeness with Anesh. The two of them had, over the last month, gotten a lot more comfortable with being near each other, with casual moments of touch and affection. And it made James happy, in a passive way that was always there, under his skin and in his smile.

Then he noticed the time and swore as all that pleasantly lingering happiness got swallowed up. "I gotta get to work. Fuck. You have a good night. Say hi to Alanna when she gets back from her mom's."

"Will do," Anesh said, feeling a similar amount of emotional whiplash as James hopped off the couch and went to find a work shirt. "Why are you so concerned, anyway? Aren't you basically unfireable?"

"Yeah, but I promised Theo I'd help her train the new people," James said as he balanced on one foot against the kitchen counter to slip a shoe on. "For the first time, we have a chance to restock our roster without half of them getting eaten by the monster behind the curtain, and I'd really like to be able to show up for work and not have to actually do so much job."

"I'm confused," Anesh stated. "Are you a manager now? What even is your work anymore?"

James gave him a sad look. "I'll be totally honest with you, man. I don't have a clue," he said before closing the door behind him.

Two more days, he thought. Two more days and he'd be trying the door again. He'd told Anesh and Alanna and everyone else that he wasn't going to risk it just yet and that he just wanted to get back into the swing of things at work. But that was, of course, a fiction.

His hands itched; his heart sped up just thinking about it. There was a whole world out there waiting, assuming it wasn't going to kill him the second he stepped through. And even that would probably be pretty exciting.

A month of recovery, victim relief, and a road trip through a beautiful but ultimately kind of mundane autumn had left James feeling a little trapped. Like the walls of reality were suddenly visible to him, and he couldn't just put them out of his mind anymore. And while he loved his partners, cared deeply for Secret and Rufus and Ganesh and everyone else in his apartment, and was really, *really* trying to reconnect with Sarah . . .

He was restless. Looking forward to that moment that he could once again wager his life against the dungeon and walk away feeling victorious with a fistful of orbs and weird technology.

For that, it was worth a lot. Even helping Theo train new people.

Maybe. Probably. Almost.

CHAPTER 4

Eleanor Elias Chase sat in the passenger seat of a semitruck cab and wondered how the fuck her life had gotten to this point.

She was tired. Exhausted. So sleepy at this point that the dark highway outside and the rocking of the vehicle as it powered through the cool night were making her eyes heavy. She'd been tired for a couple weeks now.

That's how long it had been since she'd deduced that the Wizard Police were real.

El really needed a better name for them, she decided. But not now.

Two weeks of shitty motels, of glances over her shoulder, of shaking fear as she went into her bank in a makeshift disguise to close out her account and get the last of her money. Almost two weeks of crappy road food, hitchhiking with whoever didn't look like an axe murderer, and not ever enough sleep.

Two weeks since they'd come to her work, innocuously looking for "anything out of the ordinary." Fuckers.

Eleanor couldn't take the risk that they were after her, though. Because she really did have a secret, and really did have a reason to distrust the Wizard Police.

It had been six months since she'd found the Gate. Since she'd slipped into a world she didn't think she was supposed to see and started dredging it for personal gain. Since she'd begun exploring those endless roads where day and night were arbitrary, delving those towering spires of parking structures where no one ever came to collect their cars but the security cameras were always watching, and running for her life from the nightmarish things that lived in gas stations and rest stops.

But oh, how she'd thought it was worth it. It was her own private secret. Just her, and her car, and an eternal road that she had a whole twelve hours on, every week. And the magic she'd dragged out had let her blackmail her way into college, motivated her to push her art into new styles, and shown her a side of the world that was wondrous and broken all at once. And she'd ignored the risks, that the government might be watching, that The Man didn't take kindly to citizen wizards, that someday, someone would show up at her door and she'd disappear forever.

And then they had, and she'd run like hell and never looked back. Well, never turned back. She'd miss her mom, even if the woman was overbearing as fuck. And her absolutely-not-girlfriend Izzy. Fuck, poor Izzy. El would have to find a way to rob a bank and send the money back for her. She'd miss her car. El hadn't ever *gotten* why anyone was that into project cars and the minutiae of engine specs and tire contact points until her car had turned into her personal sword and shield against the small patch of paradise she scavenged in.

Well, that, and when she'd found a fourteen-cylinder engine that you had to count by rolling your hand across the top, since half the gaskets weren't there unless you scrolled to them across the surface. *That* thing was weird and wonderful and more than enough to kick-start her interest in the mechanical mind-set.

And that car was gone now, ditched at a random parking lot, just in case the license plate could be tracked. One more casualty of her life.

The truck rocked as it went over a small hill, and she let herself float just on the edge of sleep. There was so much to do tomorrow. She needed to get to a town, find short-term work, or get back into pickpocketing. Buy food, maybe steal some fruit from a grocer. Find a place to sleep. Just thinking about finding a place to sleep made her . . . so . . . tired.

El's eyes closed as she let her mind run, and she never noticed when she drifted off.

Someone else noticed, though.

"Interesting," the driver next to her intoned, his voice deep and rumbling. "This is not what I was expecting."

Eleanor, halfway between asleep and awake, cracked her dream-eyes open and glanced over at the man. He was best described as burly, in a way that almost made her laugh. Thick arms, a scruffy patch of facial hair that showed he only shaved once a week or so. Flannel shirt, of course.

Outside the truck, there was nothing. No road, no stars in the sky. Not even darkness. Just an empty abyss.

"I'm dreaming," Eleanor muttered.

"Yes. So am I." The driver nodded without moving. "I have never had a dream before." He blinked without closing his eyes. "Have we met?" the driver asked her.

El glanced over at him again and tried to focus through the fog of dream logic. She'd always been good at dreams, kept a journal and everything—one of her favorite journals, now left behind with all the others. There was something wrong with the driver. Something off about his voice.

She answered as honestly as she could. "I've never met a dream that talked to me," El told him.

"Oh, you mistake me. I am no dream. Leastwise, not in the manner that you mean." He spoke like a poet, like someone who was absolutely unselfconscious about using fancy words, and yet, somehow not coming across as pretentious. And it was then that Eleanor placed the voice, the sound and tone and speech.

She'd only heard it once, but it had been two weeks ago, and it had been kind of a big deal for her.

Outside, heat and sharp rocks rippled across the reality of the dream as fear started to settle into her heart. "You . . . you're . . . I know what you . . . you . . ." She tried to speak but lost her words in that sleeping feeling of running forever and never gaining a step.

The trucker turned to her, and the disguise sloughed off him like water. There was no flannel, only endless scales. No scruffy beard, only a thousand eyes. And a persistent sense of the color blue and something hidden, hanging haunting in the dream with her. "I would ask you not to be afraid, but I worry we are past that," the monster said. It pondered her for what felt like weeks before tilting its massive head and musing, "You must have seen me at some point, for us to meet here. I wonder . . ."

"Get away!" Eleanor screamed, voice catching in her throat before bursting forth.

And just like that, the monster was gone. Her eyes snapped open, again, and for real this time. She was pressed back against the door of the cab, back painfully wedged into the handle. No eternal blue leviathan in sight. There was only an old trucker, worriedly looking at her out of the corner of his eye as they rolled down the empty road.

"You all right, girly?" he asked her, voice rough from a lifetime of cigarettes, and oh so perfectly human. "You were screaming a storm in your sleep."

"I'm fine," El told him, short of breath. "Just . . . just a nightmare."

He nodded. He'd seen enough runaways to know about nightmares. "A'ight. Well, I'm stoppin' for coffee in the next town, if anywhere has the lights on. You want anything?"

Eleanor wanted anything with caffeine, yes. She didn't plan to sleep for a long time.

"You're back!" a surprised Daniel greeted James as he strolled into the lobby of work. He was seated behind the security desk by himself, leg propped up on the chair of whoever was probably out on patrol right now.

It was weird, to James, to see someone actually in a normal context whom he'd previously only seen running for their life. Daniel was no longer covered in scratches and stains, his uniform wasn't torn and was actually clean, and his leg . . . well, he still looked like he was healing, but he wasn't in danger of bleeding out. Also, he was a lot more energetic, which was both a blessing and a curse.

"I am back," James agreed with a solemn nod, politely not mentioning that he'd been back for days and Daniel just hadn't noticed. "Is that surprising?" he asked, grinning.

Daniel shrugged. "No? I dunno, maybe you just wanted to get as far away as possible. I did." He waved his hand around the lobby, the same place that Secret had once defined as "imbued with cynical suffering," as if to indicate his will to escape.

"Wait, dude, you of all people had a pretty traumatic experience. Like, you almost got eaten, twice. Why *are* you here? Everyone else didn't wanna come back to work at this building," James asked, curious and concerned in equal measure.

"I still have to pay rent," Daniel explained with a sad shrug. "And I missed almost a whole week of work. Is it weird that I got more sleep on our adventure than I did the week before in the real world?"

"Yes." James didn't have to think before answering.

"Yeah, well. Are you going back in?" Daniel looked almost . . . excited? Was this the same person who'd almost snapped from exhaustion and fear in the Office?

James raised an eyebrow. "I'm here for my shift, man. My vacation is over. Also, maybe, but there were monsters, remember? Why are you so . . . eager?" he inquired.

That got a sheepish look from Daniel, the kid glancing down at the security desk in embarrassment before answering tentatively. "I . . . I wasn't kidding about not having time to sleep. I was hoping I could take a nap in there if you were going in."

"Are you kidding me," James flatly nonasked. "No." He crushed Daniel's attempt at dreams before thinking on it for a second. "Not tonight, at least. Honestly, that's not a bad idea. We should maybe try to capitalize on the time dilation more, actually, now that you mention it."

Deflating slightly at James running off with his idea, Daniel nodded in resignation. "I get it," he said with a sigh. James was about to bid him good night and walk off, but Daniel cut him short. "Anyway, before you go up, we've got a new policy. Gotta check your bag." He gestured toward the duffel that James was carrying.

"Um . . . why?" James asked, adjusting the bag to be slightly farther from Daniel.

"New policy, like I said. Dunno why. But I need to check. It's on camera." Daniel motioned upward to where several black domes dotted the ceiling like ever-watching warts.

This put James in an awkward spot. On the one hand, he didn't want to cost Daniel his job, and he was pretty sure that his laissez-faire interactions with Frank had led to this policy in the first place. On the other hand, the duffel bag really wasn't filled with gym clothes.

"How . . . um . . . what's the resolution on those cameras?" James took a second to figure out how to phrase it.

"Not perfect, but I can see, like, face details." Daniel checked the monitors on the other side of his desk before looking back to James. "Why?"

James plopped the bag up on the desk for Daniel to check. "Look, just, um . . . don't dig too deep in the main bag, okay?"

"Wh . . ." Daniel started to ask, before realizing that his question was kinda silly and stopping. "Yeah, sure." He unzipped the bag carefully before shuffling around some of the notebooks that James had in there for cover. His eyes briefly widened as he spotted the matte-black hard plastic case filling the bottom of the bag, this one much larger than the handgun case that James had purchased what felt like a lifetime ago. "Um . . ."

"Please don't look up at the cameras," James said in a friendly tone, stopping Daniel's worried motion. "I'm just borrowing it from Anesh. You know, to check."

"Right," Daniel said, swallowing hard. "Yeah, of course." He zipped the bag back up and slid it across the counter to James. "All right. Well, I'm here all night. If you need anything . . ."

James nodded to him. "I know," he said. "But . . ." He hesitated to say the next part but ultimately settled on being up front with the younger man in front of him. "Look, I know you did your best. But I dunno if it's safe to bring you in as backup, you know?" There was one person James had in mind as backup for tonight, and it really, *really* was not Daniel.

For a split second, Daniel looked like a kicked puppy, and James's heart wrenched. Maybe it was the wrong choice, maybe he shoulda just lied and run with it and dealt with the problem later. Maybe, maybe . . .

But then Daniel's expression squared up, and he shrugged, a little dejected. "Ah, you're right. I ain't the right person for that." He sighed and looked like he was really trying to be tough and not quite succeeding. "Well, if you have teams with a slot for a new guy with a good map, let me know, okay?" He smiled weakly at James, like he was giving him an out to just ditch Daniel altogether.

That, of course, wasn't what James meant, either. "Dude, the magic map is huge. And you're not *bad* at this; you just aren't the person I want for backup if I'm going to fight a dragon. Of course there'll be a spot on a team later. Just . . . not one with Theo or Alanna. Or probably Dave, either. I actually haven't asked if he's mad about anything, if you'd believe that? Anyway, I gotta go. I'm gonna be late, whatever that means these days." James slung the bag into his grip and waved over his shoulder as he walked off toward the elevator bank.

"Thanks . . ." Daniel said softly, smile a little more solid.

"This is just a stupid idea," Theo said bluntly.

She was not, in her defense, *wrong*.

James, in *his* defense, had actually worked most of his shift tonight, and he felt like that more than earned him the right to having backup that didn't sass him.

"Come on," he said dryly, a little anxiety in his veins. "It's almost time. Get ready."

Theo still worked here, which James had been aware of when he'd come back. It was important to his plan. She hadn't been in the clutches of the dungeon, or Evil Karen, long enough for the antimemes that kept information about the place secure to really dig their claws into her. And so getting her old job back had been pretty easy. She wasn't too happy about the revelation that the only reason she'd been *able* to take the job was that the person who'd had it before had already been carved out of history, but after a small bout of existential dread, she was back at work and more than willing to screen for James while he did his thing.

She was also bucking to get James his own management position, so he could start ignoring or making up rules like she did. Something down in production, maybe.

It had been a bit of a revelation to James to learn that the building had basement floors that were actually used for production of some of the specialty connectors and circuits that the company sold. So, as far as he was aware, this place was every tier of a company, from design to manufacture to marketing to tech support. And some of those departments also rented services to other companies. And no one could accurately tell him where the business made its money. It was deeply unsettling, and now that he knew that the dungeon was rooted here like some ancient and vaguely unpleasant tree, he was more than ever suspicious of why he got amazing dental insurance and a three-hundred-dollar voucher to classes at the local parks and rec department.

"What exactly is this building *worth*?" James had asked her. "Because at this point, I could probably scrounge up the money to buy the company outright and we could just take this place over. If nothing else, we could move manufacturing into the dungeon and really save on carbon emissions."

Theo had only shrugged. That was above her pay grade, and she wasn't gonna send emails to upper management snooping around.

She was totally willing to back James up on revisiting the dungeon, though. Well, "back up" in the specific way he asked. And "willing" was also a bit of a stretch.

"This is insane and suicidal," she reminded him as they stood outside the door, her holding her phone out and counting down the minutes.

"Working here was always those things. I'm seriously concerned about the whole building at this point." James covered up his own nerves with irreverent banter; despite their near-death experience together last month, Theo still didn't know him so well that she could see through his emotional smokescreens yet. "Has anyone ever actually met upper management? Is this place just another layer of the dungeon? The more I learn, the less *real* it seems."

"Shut up and get ready. You have two minutes." Theo scowled.

James was already ready. Or, as ready as he could be without unneeded risk. He was wearing his old, heavy leather coat, crouched on the floor next to the duffel bag. Inside the gun case was popped open to reveal one of the alarmingly legal P90 bullpup rifles that Anesh had purchased, somehow, without being arrested, from a legal vendor, who was apparently allowed to sell these things.

It was absolutely illegally modified for fully automatic fire. And from what James had seen, even the more worrying dungeon life wasn't prepared to withstand sustained fire from it. One of the terrorbytes probably could. A tumblefeed might be at least resistant because of what a mess they were. But anything else?

He was just waiting for the door to open.

"I'm serious here," James said, clearly not serious here. "*I've* never seen the CEO. Or any management above you, actually . . . Theo, are you a conspiracy?"

"One minute." She ignored his rambling. "James, are you sure about this?"

James snapped to serious in a heartbeat. "Yes," he said. "We need to know. And we need to know if it's not just calm at the entrance, and then a death trap thirty feet in. And I . . . am not going to risk Anesh or Alanna on this. Ever." He looked at Theo, and she met his eyes with a hard frown. "You remember what we agreed?"

"Yeah. Ten seconds. Ready?"

"Ready," James said and slung the gun up to a firing grip, rising to a low stance, prepared to move.

They'd agreed, with only minor coercion on James's part, that if the door was guarded, Theo would close the door. If the door was clear, and James got a little ways in, Theo would give him time to get back, but if it looked like a threat to everyone in the building, Theo would close the door. And if James went in, and five minutes passed, and he didn't come out . . .

Theo would close the door.

Of everyone James knew, Theo was literally the only person he trusted to not do something stupid. To prioritize keeping everyone else safe over his stupid ass.

But right now, Theo was here to open the door in the first place.

And among the endless cubicles, the eternal beige and gray landscape, the smell of printer ink and the glow of fluorescent lights . . . James didn't see a thing moving.

So he swept forward, gun up, checking his corners, and, for the first time in a while, set foot on the ground where he belonged.

CHAPTER 5

James came home to an unusually empty apartment, considering it was four a.m. the day after a dungeon opening.

When he walked in, the lights were out. Bedroom doors were closed, and he swore he could hear light snoring from the room he shared with his partners. If Rufus or Ganesh were around, they were probably napping themselves, something James had been moderately surprised to learn was a thing they could do.

A steady wooden clicking and a thump against his shins informed him that Aberdeen, the shaggy white ball of a dog that had apparently decided she was enough of a good doggo to stick around, was still awake. And James gave her some head pets while he leaned over and flicked on a living room light.

"You smell like gunpowder," Sarah commented blandly from her seat on the couch.

James barely bit down the panicked urge to shriek as he spasmed backward, bitter adrenaline pumping through his heart unasked for and unneeded. "Why would you *do that?!*" he hissed at Sarah, keeping his voice down so as not to wake those sleeping.

She smiled at him. "I'm conducting a scientific experiment to prove the existence of the element of surprise. Did it work?"

"Little bit," James admitted. "Why are you still up?"

"I wanted to make sure you didn't die in the dungeon," Sarah answered.

James flushed a little and rubbed at the back of his hand. "Why would you . . ."

"Please." The word was flatly amused. James had expected angry, though. But the changed tone didn't do much to make him think there wasn't an awkward sword of Damocles hanging over his head.

"Okay, fine," he said. "The entrance is clear. Unless the place is *really* playing the long con and waiting for all of us, we can go back in whenever we're ready." James turned his head away and mumbled, "I was going to tell everyone, eventually."

Sarah gave him a sad look. "I know. *I know*. It just sucks that you felt like you had to lie in the first place. I feel . . ." She shook her head, trying to force the uncomfortable words out. "I don't feel great about feeling like an outsider in your life, you know? Even if you'd fudged it to Anesh and Alanna, you never would have lied to *me*." She looked up at him, her normally bubbly personality dampened by the harsh time spent imprisoned in the dungeon, and more so by her feeling of alienation afterward, but it was still a surprise to James to see tears in her eyes. "I'm not used to not . . . having you here."

It was all too much for James. And before he knew it, he'd followed the pulling on his heartstrings and was sitting on the couch next to Sarah, arms around her as both of them silently let tears roll down their faces.

It was a solid five minutes before they pulled apart, and she gave him a sniffing, weak laugh that he returned to her.

"In the interest of being honest," James started mildly, "I should let you know that my therapist thinks my depression may be, in whole or in part, because the Office ate my memories of you."

"Seriously, that is so wonked up!" Sarah yelped.

"That's what I said!" They shared a weak high five. It was flimsy and dumb, but it was spontaneous and neither of them had even thought about it before slapping hands together. "Some kinda dopamine thing. Did you know you can go into withdrawal from other people?"

She held up a number of fingers. "I've had this many exes, my dude."

"Riiiight," James drawled. "So, hey, vaguely related question that I thought of the other day off something Anesh asked me. Have you been using your skulljack?"

"No." Sarah almost choked on the word but tried to keep her voice from turning too dark again. "The support group is good for a lot of people, and I know some people have actually enjoyed them. But it's just . . . it's too scary for me."

"The deep irony here," James casually tossed out, "is that if neither of us was terrified of these fucking things, we could undo the damage they caused."

There was a long silence. The kind that ate language and layered the colder darkness onto a room. Eventually, Sarah spoke. "Well, darn."

James couldn't help it. His laugh probably woke up *someone*. It certainly got Aberdeen to raise her head off the floor and glare at him as if in reminder that it was four a.m. and stop making so much noise, please.

"Someday," she promised James. "Maybe someday soon. But I'm still afraid."

"It's okay!" James reassured her. "I'm in no rush. And . . . you're here now. And I know you remember, and I don't, and that hurts. But we were friends for a *reason*, and I can feel it. It's like a current that I can just dip into whenever you're around. If I were less tired, I'd probably not say out loud that this is what I always imagined magic felt like."

Sarah felt herself tear up again, but this time with a smile. "You've said that before. When you were very tired," she told him.

"Oh, that reminds me!" James suddenly shifted gears, pulling his discarded coat over and riffling through the pockets.

"That reminds you? *That*?"

"I have a bad memory and my brain is finicky—you know this. I am *positive* you know this." He rooted around and eventually found what he was looking for.

Out of a coat pocket, James pulled a small, shimmering emerald orb and handed it to Sarah with a smile. "I picked up gifts as an apology for obviously lying to everyone and risking my life in a fairly stupid way. Do you want first crack at it?"

"Was that a pun?" she asked, already reaching for the orb. And then, speaking in time with James as he said, "I can't prove anything, right," with a roll of her eyes, Sarah clamped her hand down on the green ball.

[Local Area Shift : +26 PSI Maximum Water Pressure]

[+3 Skill Ranks : Cooking—Recipe—Coffee—Siphon Brew]

"Anything good?" James asked.

Sarah relaxed back into the couch with a sigh of satisfaction. "I can take a real shower again!"

"Wait, *again*? We've lived here to . . . together . . ." James managed to not stumble on his words too much. "Since we got this place, though. Did you forget how to shower or something?"

"No, our water pressure's just sucked the whole time." Sarah stuck her tongue out at James. "Not that you'd know."

"I feel like I should be offended." He smirked back. "Well, anyway. I kinda want to get to bed. Anything else you wanted to talk about since you took the time to ambush me?" James maneuvered himself to keep giving pets to the dog while also freeing up a hand to give a quick back pat to Rufus, who had climbed up onto the table. Or maybe he'd been there the whole time and only just now made his presence known. Rufus would be the best damn infiltrator ever if he could talk about what he spied upon.

Sarah shrugged at James. "Nothing, really. You *should* tell them, though. Oh, and . . . this might be a weird question, but do you guys still do a weekly D&D game?"

"Of *course* we do. Look at me. I'm a caricature of someone who plays tabletop RPGs. Long hair, pale like a fucking vampire, *this* . . ." James went to gesture at his absolutely not-work-appropriate T-shirt and beat-up leather jacket but was stopped by two irritated companion animals demanding more scratches.

Another shrug in response. "You're kinda deep into responsibility, my dude. Maybe you all stopped. Maybe you had enough fantasy adventure in Officium Mundi."

"I'm not sure we should be naming it. It seems like names are special around the dungeon, somehow. Look at how much smarter Rufus is than the average strider." James poked at the stapler, currently upside down and wiggling his pen limbs in an attempt to entice more belly rubs.

"Uh-huh," Sarah muttered dryly.

"Okay, but really." James smiled. "We still play. And you're absolutely welcome. I hope. If my sister can get in on it, I'm *sure* Anesh would be up for ... oh my god ..." He trailed off.

"You just realized that two Aneshes means two GMs, huh?"

"It's fuckin' brilliant!" James slapped his forehead. "How did I not see it before?! We need to get him to clone himself more." His intense stare made Sarah *almost* unsure if he was kidding or not.

"Pass. One Anesh is enough Anesh. Two is also enough Anesh, but please, no more Anesh," she told him. "I'm pretty sure it's bad for him somehow."

"Oh, fine. Spoilsport." James stood, stepped around Aberdeen, and promptly rammed his shin into a chair. After about fifteen seconds of swearing loudly inside his head, he spoke out loud, trying to keep his voice down. "We need to fix this. This is too much."

"Well, there's always just cracking greens until we get more rooms," Sarah volunteered. "That's what ... what one of my old squad mates did. He tended to keep all the greens for himself. Said his apartment was like a palace."

"Oh, fuck. I never actually talked to you about that, did I? What happened?" James stopped hamming up the damage to his leg and addressed his friend as reassuringly as he could.

Sarah smiled, the thin line of her mouth looking quite small and fragile. "I'll tell you later. We should maybe try to figure out where he lived, though. Rent the place before anyone else does. If we're being mercenary about it."

James winced. "That seems a little too cold. Maybe we just rent some office space and put all the 'work' stuff there? *Nonhostile* office space, which I am amused that I have to specify."

"I know a lot of people in the support group don't ever wanna be in a conference room again," Sarah told him. "But then, if we just get a small chunk of a building for our own use, it wouldn't really be for them, huh?"

"Right. A place for us to meet up with the other two new teams and anyone else we recruit. Make plans, a central location for backups of maps and stuff. Place to store *chairs*." He glared at the offending furniture. "Also, we won't have to keep cracking greens here."

"Why don't you want them here?" Sarah asked with a raised eyebrow.

James blushed a little in the dim light of the lamp. "Okay, this is gonna sound dumb . . ." She nodded at him, partly to say, "Go on," and also partly to say, "I've seen worse from you." James felt his heart skip as he recognized and reciprocated the ancient gesture that he didn't remember ever making himself. "I don't want the dogs to stop being a treasure," he told her.

"Buh?"

"The dogs. Like Aberdeen here." James gave the dog more ear scritches. "They're so . . . unique. Special. They're a personal treasure to me. I don't want to fill this place with so many things like that that I forget how cool the dogs are."

"That's . . . very you," Sarah agreed.

"Thanks!"

"We're gonna need another briefcase to pay for everything," Sarah informed him, jumping back to talking about their potential workspace.

"Yup. We'll prioritize it next week." James paused. "Um . . . are you . . ." He let the question sit in the air until Sarah caught it.

"Oh! Um . . . maybe. I don't know. I don't think I ever could match you guys at this point. But I'd like to come along?"

"Of course!" James answered without hesitation. "Fucking of course you're welcome. If you can play D&D with us, you can come to the dungeon with us."

"That doesn't even begin to make sense," she riposted.

"Look, I'm tired," James muttered with a roll of his eyes. "It was hard enough to think up enough wit to say the thing about the dogs. Let me go to beeddddd."

Sarah giggled and waved him away. But as he started to walk down the hallway, she stopped him with one last thing to say, her voice somber enough to make James really listen. "Hey. Tell them" was all she said before James started walking to the door of his shared bedroom.

She sat there, just taking in the calm and familiar atmosphere of the living room for a little while. The little things you don't appreciate until a three-month captivity forces you to stop taking stuff for granted.

Down the hall, Sarah's orb-enhanced hearing let her pick out bits of a conversation.

"Hey," James said softly to his sleeping partners. "I'm gonna take a shower first. I smell like gunpowder. And I'm preemptively sorry. I didn't want you guys to worry."

On the couch, Sarah smiled. Patting the cushions and prompting Aberdeen to jump up and turn her furred bulk into a pillow, she laid her head back on the doggo and let the knowledge that her friend was still *there* for her lull her to sleep.

She did have to make some effort to tune them out when they started having sex, though. The weird echo effect on the moans from duplicate Aneshes usually required the use of headphones or burying her head in a very fluffy and understanding dog.

Secret was dreaming.

Dreaming, for him, was a much different experience than it was for a human, though he was only vaguely aware of that fact.

As an infomorph, Secret didn't really exist in his physical shell the way James or Alanna did. He lived, for lack of a better term, inside the thoughts and minds of those creatures that hosted ideas. James, mostly. But a host of others as well.

Much like a human gradually made a living space more comfortable for themselves, so too did Secret. He gradually rearranged things to better suit him, pushed certain concepts forward, and, over time, revealed more and more of his complexity to the person thinking about him. Or, alternately, he took in complexity from that person.

From James, he had absorbed a personality, a sense of self, a love of speaking like a character from a trashy high-fantasy novel, and a *deep* pride and sense of protectiveness for his family. From Alanna, he had taken in shards of responsibility for the whole of humanity. From Anesh, it was a will to grow in knowledge.

To each of them, he would give his life if asked. Or, more likely, if needed. They would never ask, which was part of why he would so willingly die for them. That part also came from James.

Anesh and Alanna were new homes to him, compared to James, where he had been "born." But again, it was a cycle. As he spent more time in their heads, they learned more about him, which meant more of him was there, which meant . . . and so on. Until eventually, they would understand his whole self, and then he would wholly *be* with them, as he was with James.

Then, of course, there were others. Those people who were aware of Secret, whom he had a metaphorical toe dipped in. He didn't really bother to try to influence them, to reveal more of himself to them. Not that he didn't want to meet new people, but more that they might not want to meet him, and he was nothing if not polite. And there were *so many* of these others now. Secret had, in defiance of his own name, revealed himself in front of a whole crowd of humans and didn't regret it for a second.

But now, when his physical shell slept, it dreamed. And when he dreamed, he felt himself start to drift, unmoored by the confines of a mind. An idea, unthought. It was horrifying the first time it happened, but when a fearful start had brought him back to wakefulness, Secret had learned there was no real danger to it. James was always there, an anchor to drag him home.

And so he began to take pleasure in snoozing in the back seat as James and Alanna drove down those southwestern highways. Letting himself be thought of by rocks and birds and cacti and the occasional hiker who would think, for just a second, of a flash of blue and a vault of information kept hidden.

And then, one day, he dreamed and found himself pulled to one of the others. They had also been dreaming, though human dreams were familiar territory for Secret. And he'd said hello, and his partner in slumber had responded!

The man's name had been Ethan, and he'd been fascinated by Secret. Though, upon waking, Secret had been dismayed to learn that none of the things learned in the dream had stuck with Ethan. Very little of it actually stuck with Secret himself. Only a lingering sense of something just out of reach.

It wasn't the first, or last, time that Secret had drifted to another dreaming mind. Each time getting a little better at leaving his mark on them, letting them hold on to the knowledge of their meeting when they woke. He started making friends with people, some of whom had only barely glimpsed him hidden under a blanket in the back seat of a car or poking a dematerialized snout out of the back of James's shirt to try to grab a piece of fruit off a store display. It seemed, to him, harmless, and it turned out, for all that he was a minor god-thing of secrecy, he *loved* the meeting of new persons.

And then, he'd encountered Eleanor, though he didn't know her name himself. Not yet.

She had almost instantly seen through his mask, though he'd only put it on to be polite. It was rude to go into someone else's dream in the nude. But more than that, she had been *terrified* of him. Not just of what he was, but of what she *believed* he was.

She had believed something about him. Something dangerous, and incorrect, and Secret couldn't quite sniff out what it was.

So he marked the time. And every night, he made sure to find himself asleep and broadcasting across the continent, searching.

And tonight, again, he found her.

"Hello there," Secret said. He was wearing a mask, but one that was entirely his own. Fewer teeth, fewer eyes. Those unsettled humans in great numbers. *She* was driving this time, a car that hummed and thumped and burned in the dream world in glorious mechanical unity. The dream was the feel of the car, the whip of the wind. Secret had become part of it in the passenger seat and found himself already wearing sunglasses.

Secret was cool. He could *feel* it thrumming through the dream.

"You're not really here!" the girl screamed over the noise of the engine and the road. "You can't hurt me!"

"I also *won't* hurt you." Secret nodded at her. "I am simply present to apologize. I frightened you on our last meeting."

The girl slammed her foot to the floor, ten miles of distance covered in one martial stomp that shook the seats. "I'm free. I'm on the road, and I'm free," she howled.

Secret was confused. And then he realized she wasn't talking to him. She was either ignoring him or too deep in the dream to notice.

This was her dream. The place she went when she truly slept, where her mind rebuilt itself and perfected its self-image. He felt like an outsider, an intruder, but he didn't leave.

Instead, he spoke a few soft words to her. "You should be free," he whispered as the wind roared around them. "You should be safe," he murmured as the road signs blurred by.

Secret was, fundamentally, different than a human. But while he and James had conspired to make himself human enough to be a person, he still retained many blessings that humans missed out on. And one of them was the ability to *see*, with eyes unblinking, the shifting of the sky as this young woman's heart internalized and began to echo his own words.

You should be free. You should be safe.

The road was a little less red, a little less angry. The car hummed under them, engine kicking, but it was in excitement, not fear.

Secret added one last sentence that he hoped would take root as he felt the woman begin to wake.

"I wish to be your friend."

The cliff approached. The tires screeched. The dream ended.

Secret woke up with a start.

He shook his head lazily, looked around the closet that he'd claimed as a personal den. Something in that dream had been important, he thought with a tired nod. He was tired a lot these days.

Oh, well. He'd remember later.

He laid his head back down and sought out a new naptime companion.

"I've bloody got it!" Both of the Aneshes slapped the table in their living room, causing a brief stutter in the morning routine.

Well, perhaps *morning* was a bit too strong of a word. It was two p.m., and things around the apartment were just starting to get moving.

Anesh, despite his sleep being disrupted by James's coming home from work, had woken up at roughly ten a.m. and promptly gotten back to his own task. On days like today, when neither of him had class, it was especially helpful to have an extra set of hands and eyes for research purposes. He'd spent the last six hours organizing his notes, trawling Wikipedia and various occult forums—some of them potentially useful sources of information, some of them *insane*—and wondering whether it would be advantageous to purchase corkboard and note cards in bulk off Amazon.

At around noon, JP and Dave had showed up, and Anesh had been reminded that D&D had been moved to today, and half of him shifted planning and research goals while the other half worked with JP to keep in touch with the two nascent teams that they were now fully committed to bringing into the Office next week.

At around one, James had staggered out of bed, taken a shower, been joined in the shower by Alanna, and been reminded that shared showers weren't sexy, as his access to hot water was conquered by the one person in the apartment taller than he was. Then, once he'd properly equipped himself with pants and a Hawaiian shirt, he'd sauntered casually out into the living room like he owned the place.

Which he kinda did.

After asking if anyone had eaten anything today and getting guilty looks from his boyfriend(s), James had scowled and started making pancakes.

Rufus had tried to help. Then James started remaking pancakes while Rufus cleaned himself in the sink. They were blueberry pecan, there were enough for everyone, and they tasted like the perfect complement to this mid-October day that felt like it was trying to disguise itself as late August.

When Alanna came out, still blinking sleep out of her eyes, it had been with a chirping iLipede clinging to her bathrobe, getting a fix of static electricity. She'd simply taken a stack of pancakes and plopped down in a chair next to Dave before beginning to discuss character creation. For the first time, James recognized the value of Alanna's ability to compartmentalize. To shift from throwing him in a choke hold over lying about his plan to go into the dungeon to quietly cuddling as they slept. To jump from, on a larger scale, a solid month of plans and schemes and detective work and travel to . . . conspiring with Dave to make a party of all bards. James had a feeling he'd be approached about this later.

Sarah was out walking Aberdeen. Kayle was taking advantage of this long pseudovacation to spend more and more time sleeping over with her boyfriend, a fact that James had chosen *not* to poke fun at her for. Ganesh was taking advantage of the city's currently lax drone laws to simply feel the joy of flying under the sky. And Secret . . .

James looked around before noticing a coiled blue tail sticking out from under a chair. A quick check showed that Secret was, apparently, also in on the plan to roll a party of bards.

For the first time, in a *very, very long time*, James felt like he was truly at home.

Then Anesh slapped the table like he was a used car salesman about to start a pitch and just fucking *shattered* the mood.

"Okay, I'll bite!" James announced, sparing everyone else the job. "What is it this time? Is it Wikipedia again?"

"No!" James could tell when Anesh was excited, because both of them talked in unison as they did here.

"Internet in general? I'm not making fun of you here, bee-tee-dubs. I'm legit just going to try guessing."

Anesh almost *sneered* as he answered, but in a way that James knew wasn't aimed at him. "It is not the internet, though I have suspicions about the dark web."

"National landmark? Does the Washington Monument actually act as a backup teleport to the shadow zone?"

"What?"

"It's a comic reference, you uncultured—"

"No," came the interruption.

James flipped a pancake in a perfect arc, caught it on the spatula, and neatly dropped it onto the plate beside him. "Some kind of . . . oh, I dunno. I haven't had coffee yet. Someone make me magic coffee while I cook and come up with ideas to throw at Anesh."

As Dave utterly failed to stand up to make James coffee, he raised a hand to ask, "Can we just know? I'm actually curious. And James is too tired to make this funny."

"Ouch!" James exclaimed from the kitchen, more hurt by the words than any kitchen mishap.

"It's Tracy, California," Anesh announced dramatically.

There was not a word spoken. Even Rufus stilled in scrubbing his carapace for a second. The only noises in the apartment were birds and cars passing outside.

And then, from JP, "Anesh, no one has a clue where that is."

"In California, I guess?" Alanna asked with a smug smile.

"All right, all right. Shut up and listen." Anesh went back to his now-practiced method of alternating which of him spoke between sentences. "It's a town in the middle of California. It has one of the highest homicide rates in the US, which was the first hint. But more than that, it also has generally just a slightly sideways feel to it."

"Explain," James said, leaning over the kitchen counter, arms crossed as he absorbed what Anesh was saying.

"Like the dungeon. Our dungeon, anyway. James, don't take this the wrong way, but your company is bloody strange sometimes," Anesh said.

Around the table a few people nodded. JP started listing points on his fingers. "They pay for you to take martial arts classes, they don't seem to have a management structure, they put several disparate parts of an industry in one building, a building that is *constantly under remodel*, and they seem to uniquely hire people who were capable of either finding, or surviving, a dungeon. It's either a bizarre coincidence or something is up."

"That . . . is a lot of things, yeah," James admitted. "Theo and I actually talked about this last night. She's noticed a few more weird bits, though I can't remember them now. To be fair, I think a lot of the stuff they do is just some executive reading a random memoir from a more successful executive and implementing policies that don't fit together. I honestly don't think it's magic; I think it's just corporate America."

"Right!" both of the Aneshes said with enthusiastic confidence, ignoring James's counterargument. "It's like the normal way of doing things got buggered up around that building. Probably, if I'm right, around the door itself. Normally, people wouldn't notice, or they'd be made to forget, by the things like Secret living around it. But now we have a clearer picture because the bigger one is dead, and we can use that to find places that don't have the same kind of defense."

"So, Tracy?" Alanna asked, genuinely curious now.

"Tracy." Anesh nodded. "JP, do the list thing again."

JP sighed and smiled and started counting off points again. "All right! We've got the missing-persons rate, the homicide rate, and the general crime rate. Not too weird so far, just sad. Then we have the secret military weapons cache, the oddly placed extra postal routing station, and a *very* out of place, well-funded hospital."

"Hang on, what was that about the secret—"

"Then there's the small quirks that every small town develops, like how their slogan is 'think inside the triangle,' or how they don't have a single pawn shop despite the high rate of military personnel *and* drug use." JP ignored James's question as he kept going.

From under the table, Secret spoke up in a deep and vibrating voice, "I, too, am interested in this underground . . ."

"And, finally, MC Hammer lives there," JP finished, continuing to ignore everyone until he was done. Not to be a jerk, just to make sure that he got through the whole list properly.

Alanna was the first to react to that. "I mean, he has to live *somewhere*."

"But he doesn't. He lives here."

James tapped the counter in thought. "I think . . ." he mused, "I think that if we treat the dungeons as able to warp causality like that, then we will never be able to sleep well again. If they can, that's a real shame, but we *need* to proceed as if Hammer is there by coincidence."

"That's fair." Anesh nodded. "And was largely the conclusion we came to as well. It was mostly just a fun factoid."

"So, it's a weird place, and not just because of the murders and military base and bed-and-breakfast?" James asked as he went back to pouring discs of batter into the heated pan.

"Right. And I want to go check it out." Anesh nodded. "I'm on break from a couple classes, so one of me can be spared for a little while, and we don't have any big projects after next week's delve."

James and Alanna froze. "Are you . . . sure?" Alanna asked, tension in her voice.

"Yup," Anesh replied, oblivious to it. "It shouldn't be hard. JP can come with me. He doesn't have any obligations, anyway."

"It's true!" JP told them with overplayed cheer. "I am adrift in life, with no purpose. A puppet with no strings or girlfriend!"

Before just how depressing that sentence was could catch up to James, and before he could express worry at Anesh going off alone, his friend shuffled around the table and headed down the hall to the bathroom. "It'll be fine, guys. Now eat your pancakes and roll your characters. I'll be right back."

James sighed and shared a look with Alanna. "I know that we're only, like, three days more combat-experienced than he is, but I'm still super worried."

"Right?" Alanna replied, moving closer and keeping their conversation quiet while the others gave them some space. "I don't wanna be super codependent or anything, but I want him to be safe. James, we went on a simple road trip and ended up slugging it out with an axe murderer."

"Knife murderer, and you know there wasn't any actual punching involved, but yeah. But, still, we gotta be cool about it. Support him, help where we can, but we can't be overbearing. We aren't parents, we're partners."

Alanna raised her eyebrows so high they threatened to leap off her forehead. "Did you *hear* the thing about the three percent murder rate?"

"No?"

"Right, that was on the dossier he had. *Three percent*, James!"

"Okay, so we support him and also send Aberdeen along to maul anything that looks at him funny. And Ganesh, too, for the snooping."

"And Hyades, for the same reason."

"Who?"

"I named my shotgun Hyades, after the false stars from that one Robert Chambers book."

". . . I have so many concerns about everything you said, but I'm a huge nerd and a supportive partner and so I am on board."

The two of them nodded, and Alanna leaned in to give James a quick kiss before the two of them turned back to the living room. At least, they reasoned, they could do the absolute best they could to support their boyfriend if he was going to be out of their sight for more than two seconds.

Anesh stood, almost right next to them, arms folded on his chest. "You two forgot there were two of me, didn't you?" he asked, after

Alanna's yelp and James's dropping of a pancake had passed. "Seriously, I . . . I . . . love you, too. But come on, at least have coffee before you start conspiring. You two don't pay attention to your surroundings at *all*." There was a brief pause, while James considered bribing this iteration to not tell the other one, before Anesh cut that line of thought off with "I'm absolutely sharing this, you ass. Besides, it's hilarious. And it's cute that you care. Now come make your characters and pretend our lives are normal before I give you my list of questions on skulljack drone piloting."

With a grin, James took the threat seriously and sat down to make the best bard he could.

CHAPTER 6

There were hurdles to clear, of course, before any good dungeon delve could begin. It wouldn't be daily life on Earth if there weren't a whole host of petty injustices between an objective and the righteous. Or, in this case, between it and the easily amused, the thrill seeking, and the mildly desperate.

As it turned out, though, when James and Alanna tried to offer to help, many of those hurdles had already been bulldozed by their teammates back home while they were on the road. It had really taken the gusto out of them both for about ten seconds, until they both came to the unified realization that they now had less work to do, more of the fun adventure ahead, and that James personally wouldn't be pressed to act as some kind of guild leader for at least another week.

Gear had been purchased and prepared for transport. Neatly packed and perfectly weighted duffel bags containing survival gear, armor padding, and usable weapons set up near flawlessly thanks to an old skill Anesh had acquired on one of their prior delves. They were back to being on a budget again; the costs were stacking up as they burned money taking care of those who had been cored out of reality by the dungeon's memetic defenses. So, the armor wasn't full-body riot gear, but instead sports padding and military surplus helmets. And the weapons were mostly sledgehammers, more durable hatchets, and the old standby the crowbar.

There wasn't much in terms of dungeon weaponry on offer, sadly. Their experiments trying to totemize their supply of blue orbs hadn't borne fruit yet, so they'd mostly been finding people who could absorb them and searching for powers that were exploitable. That had led to James picking up about eighteen charges of "Schedule Meeting," which was useful but annoying. As it turned out, you couldn't replace an absorbed power. Nor could you just burn all the charges; they tired you out and, after a certain point, hurt you. A long time ago, Dave had told James that his "remove half of" ability could have cut the abstract concept of suffering in half, but that he'd probably die from it before it finished working. Now, James wasn't sure Dave could have even gotten that far before he'd just found himself unconscious.

Which sucked, because it made it harder to constantly search for new opportunities with the blues.

All this boiled down to an amount of firepower that was, sadly, kinda lacking. That said, there were, this time, going to be no fewer than thirteen humans and at least one or two dungeon Life making the delve. And even though emergency firearms were already boxed up and ready for combat, those were distinctly *emergency* guns.

James had learned in his expeditionary romp that the noise curfew was back on, and gunfire absolutely attracted the wrong kind of attention. Not every time, but *any* time. Enough that it just wasn't worth the risk unless you wanted to get a good, reckless sprint in.

But thirteen people solved a lot of problems that one or two would fold under. And James and Anesh alone had survived some pretty nasty situations. So he wasn't too worried about it. And on top of that, they had a few other offensive options to try out as well. Someone had put a set of wrist rockets into the pile, and James remembered from a high school misadventure that those things could pack a hell of a punch. Whether it would be enough to hurt anything in the dungeon was up in the air, but it was worth trying, even if only as a distraction. Also, another someone—James suspected it was JP—had put one of those oversize Super Soaker water guns that only seemed to have existed for a brief period in the nineties into the gear collection. James hadn't asked what it was filled with, but it was apparently finally time to figure out if the stuffed shirts were waterproof.

What had really surprised James was that the money had gone this far. There was a *lot* of gear in those bags. And even given that Anesh had bought as much at the military surplus store as possible, trying to keep his Amazon account from being *too* suspicious, that kinda cost added up. What had surprised James more was when he'd been informed by JP, their now-official guild treasurer, that money was actually coming *in*.

Not everyone they'd pulled out had been fully erased from history. And many of the ones who'd gotten some of their families, their jobs, their *lives* back were more than a little thankful. It wasn't much, and James would never *ask* for it to be much. But fifty or a hundred bucks poured into the hat, from twenty or thirty people? It added up to something. And that something came in the form of bribing a chemistry grad to look the other way—and maybe lend a hand— with putting together some more thermite weaponry that was slightly more shelf-stable than grenades with a single button as the trigger. In retrospect, James was actually astonished that he hadn't hurt himself with one of those things.

The other thing the last bits of the money had gone toward was a pair of fire extinguishers, one class A, one class C. "Just in case," Anesh had said. He hadn't specified in case of *what*, but it was pretty clear from the size of the locked metal box he loaded into the trunk that the amount of fire he intended to bring to the party was significant.

"I feel like we may be violating our own rule about not burning the dungeon down." James bit his upper lip in an expression of concern. "I mean, I've had to tell both other teams now that Molotovs aren't acceptable, but here we are, letting you bring . . . this much . . . thermite in?" He held his hands out to gesture roughly the size of the box Anesh had packed. "I mean, that's a lotta fire. We're honestly kinda lucky we haven't torched the place already—isn't this just a bit overkill?"

It was JP who chimed in as he walked by checking things off on a clipboard. "As far as I know, setting things on fire has only ever worked out for you guys," he calmly told them as he triple-checked the date tags on the bright-red fire extinguisher cylinders.

"Please don't encourage us," James monotoned. "We're enough of a problem as is."

He was only half joking.

The rest of the week passed in a blur for James. His weekend came and went with minimal impact; he still spent all his time rushing around and running errands, picking up last-minute ideas for equipment, giving rides to people who were still rebuilding their lives, going to his cooking class that he'd stubbornly continued taking, and trying to figure out how to induce a power outage.

That last one he actually did a lot at work. Wikipedia was sorta helpful on that front, but it was idle speculation, and James was pretty sure they could come up with a better plan. The second-to-last thing was because, even after dozens of orbs, he *still* hadn't really gotten a level in cooking. He knew precise recipes for some foods, he could use a knife blindfolded, but he didn't have the whole *pattern* of it down. He was learning it, slowly, that casual and ingrained way of moving and thinking in a kitchen that divided someone who cooked dinner from a chef. But it annoyed him that sometimes the orbs gave components without the links between them.

The power outage was so the newly installed security cameras would be off so they could sneak in. Ever since Frank had been arrested and had apparently also been stealing one metric fuckton from the company, there'd been heightened security. Daniel still worked the front desk on Monday nights, so James had an easy in there. Maybe one or two other people could slip by, too, without too much suspicion.

But they didn't plan to slip one or two people by. They were bringing twelve. Thirteen, depending on how you counted. And some bags. And boxes. And a hand cart. And some bicycles. And a gurney, just in case.

Anesh and JP had collated a lot of ideas into their group loadout. Drained their bank account to do it, but they'd *planned*. No matter what caught them off guard, they had the foundation to recover from it.

Of course, it made it a pain the ass to carry it all in. And they might have to rebuild Fort Door in its entirety.

So James ran errands. He went to work, pretended everything was normal, and shared knowing nods with Theo and Daniel. He listened to Anesh share increasingly convoluted theories on the locations of potential dungeons. He went on walks with Alanna, the two of them both kinda hoping something dangerous would happen out in reality that they could burn their nervous energy on.

They were champing at the bit. They were ready. He'd been ready for months. His little trip in last week was nothing compared to what he really wanted.

There was just one more thing for James to sort out.

On Sunday, he found time to talk to Theo.

He opened with, "I need the security cameras off tomorrow," before pretending to attempt diplomacy. "Also, hey, how's it going? Nice skirt."

Theo looked up from the emails she was answering at her desk to where her coworker and/or underling had barged into her office. "Thanks, my gran and I went shopping. I dig it." She kicked her leg out and plopped her foot up on a low filing cabinet to show off the long black-and-red skirt, rose patterning with thin gold lines looking equal parts majestic and casual. "Also, no?"

"It's so we can bring people into the Office. Like, the other Office. The one I pronounce with a capital letter," James explained.

"Still no," Theo deadpanned. "Also, Secret was way better at that than you. The capital letter thing."

James cracked his knuckles idly. "He's literally talking inside your head, partly. So of course he's good at it. Also, would it help if I bribed you, or said please or something?"

"Bribe might help," Theo conceded. "But dude, you can't go back in there. That place is lethal, and I'm not gonna let you get yourself killed. You almost died saving me. And everyone else. And Daniel, I guess," she reminded him. "Your friend practically *did* die, until he magically didn't. No *way* I'm giving you an easy way into that shithole again."

It had never seemed to James that Theo was a particularly protective person. She was aggressive, like a particularly irate badger. She played rugby, she went skydiving on her vacations, she had taken to combat situations in the dungeon better than any of the other survivors. She was, frankly, the *last* person James had expected to want the place off-limits.

Of course, James had wanted the place *killed* for a bit there, if such a thing was even possible. So who was he to judge?

Regardless, Theo just didn't seem like the kind of person who would cross her arms and say, "No, too risky" to anything. Even if it was fighting monsters for candy.

"I'll be honest, I kind of expected you to want to come in with us," James admitted. "We got you a crowbar and everything." That was not, strictly speaking, true. They did have a number of crowbars, but it wasn't like James had earmarked one for Theo's personal use. She didn't need to know that, though.

His boss glared at him, turning in her chair to slap the palms of her hands against the desk. "It *eats people*, James!" she yelled at him, ignoring that the door behind him was open. "Do you know how many employees have wandered in there and *not* been jerked out by you and your pals?" She demanded the information of him, and when he didn't have an immediate answer, she gave him one. "More than zero." Theo raised her voice again. "We've had staffing issues for so long, we kinda take it for granted, but there's a reason, and it's that we're working on top of a big fucking monster. And it's killing people. And I'm not letting you go back in there." Her voice almost broke as she finished saying her piece, though she held it together until the end.

James could see real concern in her eyes. And also real fear. She was wary of the dungeon as a whole, afraid that they'd die, or that they'd aggravate it and maybe send a wave of tumblefeeds sprawling out into the building to paint the carpets with blood. And maybe that was something to be worth being afraid of; maybe it was something that they should address before they started poking around in there again.

But...

"Just because you're keeping us out doesn't mean that people aren't falling in," James said softly. He made eye contact, and it was Theo who eventually looked away. "There's more than one door. We know that, for sure. And there might be more people like Frank—combination high priest and hit man, dragging people in and selling them to the highest-bidding dungeon creation." He was reaching, but he wasn't *wrong*, and she knew it. Now it was James's turn to put his hands on the desk and lean in, Theo raising an eyebrow at this transformed version of the previously socially timid employee she knew. "There's a chance we can help people. And, failing that, there's a chance we can pull wonders and miracles out of that place." James stood up and smoothed his work shirt like he was brushing off dust. When he spoke again, it wasn't a question. "We need the security cameras off tomorrow. Three to four a.m. Maybe some kind of maintenance routine, I dunno."

It was strange, Theo thought, to go from being someone's boss to being part of their team. Or maybe that was the wrong word. She should get into the habit of thinking of it like they did. Of being part of something new.

There was a silent, tense minute where Theo had the urge to go back to answering emails from other managers and shift leads, to read memos and tactically ignore James and make her will known—that the dungeon was *off-limits*.

And then she nodded at him. "I'll talk to the . . . well, you don't need to know. It'll happen," she said.

"Thanks," James told her. He didn't smile; it didn't feel like a friendly conversation. He just nodded, let her know he appreciated it.

As he was walking out, about to close the door, he heard Theo mutter from inside, just loud enough for him to hear, "I better get that fucking bribe . . ."

That was worth a smile.

At three a.m. Tuesday morning, James Lyle put his call log on hold, set his headset down on his desk, and stood up with a silent arch of his back. He stood over his workstation, one of six in this little cluster of half cubicles, none of the others of which were occupied, and unbuttoned the dress shirt that had been confining his throat all night. A quick look around showed approximately three overworked techs on the floor, none of them paying attention to him as they tried to explain through low-quality connections that the company that had contracted them as tech support didn't have a responsibility for the warranties the customers had assuredly already voided anyway.

Thirty seconds ago, James's boss had walked by and given him an uncomfortable conspiratorial nod and a solid frown. Her part was done; the security camera maintenance cycle was running, and she now washed her hands of this endeavor.

James walked with long steps to the elevator, waited patiently with his arms folded behind his back for it to arrive, and stood in much the same position as it took him down to the lobby. The two security guards on duty at the front desk looked up as he walked over to the door, the eyes of Daniel and Tyrone, the previous night guard whom Daniel had replaced after he was fed to the dungeon by Frank, following James as he swung the double doors open and locked them in place.

He stood at the top of the concrete steps that led down into the parking lot. To either side of him, manicured lawns and flower beds gave off a wet, earthy scent in the rapidly chilling night air. And at the bottom of the steps, in an otherwise mostly empty parking lot, a cluster of a half dozen parked cars killed their engines.

As doors opened, trunks were popped, and people launched into motion to start unloading, it was JP who walked up to James. He stood at the bottom of the steps, his leather jacket a more stylish mirror to the one that James used to use as armor, and made a gesture that was almost a salute before he turned it into a casual brush of his already immaculate hair.

"Reporting for adventure, sir!" He grinned up at James. "Permission to come inside?"

James grinned back. From either side of him, the two kids working the front desk hustled down the steps to assist in unloading heavily laden backpacks. He watched for a second as, with an almost mechanical precision, everything came together. The people, the *team*, assembled in front of him holding their bags, extra stashes of survival gear, a hand truck stacked with bankers' boxes that hid gun cases, and their own good-luck charms and personal touches. They all stopped at the bottom of the stairs first, though.

Anesh and Alanna moved to flank JP, each of them with either Rufus or Ganesh on their shoulders and smiles on their faces. Fanned out to the left, Other James stood with his own partners close at hand, their group clearly loaned some of Momo's extra studded leather, and with a rainbow magnetic distortion crouched patiently in front of them. On the right, Karen and those who had flocked to her pragmatic and calculated logic stood almost to attention, dressed like they were going to just another day at the office. Karen herself stood with one hand on a hip, the mother-turned-adventurer representing the oldest member of their group and wearing a stoic, determined expression on her face. Even Dave, who normally didn't go for theatrics, stopped where he was helping Daniel pull one of the carts forward and looked up at James; time and near death had not done much to diminish the fervor now found in his eyes.

James looked down at all of them and felt his chest burn. There was a riot inside him; the accomplishment to get this far, the curiosity at what lay ahead, and the pride in everyone assembled here. There was a host of larger purposes alight in the people before him, but all of them were looking up at *him*. And in that moment, he could feel all of them.

The drive of adventure, the promise of a prize, the need to safeguard humanity, the opportunity to advance the world. All of it resonated in his heart.

His smile grew a bit wider, and he saw the lips of everyone in front of him tug upward as well.

"Permission granted," he finally replied to JP. And then, to the larger crowd, "Stop standing around! We're wasting time! Let's get this stuff ready to move!"

There was a brief moment when everyone started moving at once and almost tripped over each other in the rush to climb the stairs. It was, to James's almost surprise, JP of all people who started casually tapping shoulders and directing people in an ordered way. Funneling the small crowd toward the elevators while he wheeled the bike he was carrying into position to be on the second trip up.

When James stepped into an elevator, flanked by Alanna and Anesh, everyone else gave them space, and the quiet ride up gave James a little time to think on something that had been bothering him.

After a month or so away, and a lot of conversations with Alanna, James had come to the conclusion that he had grown an amount of resentment for JP. He didn't want to, really. But that desire didn't have much of an impact on the bitter voice in the back of his head that told him that JP was kind of . . . something unpleasant. Not untrustworthy, certainly. He'd proven that he could keep the dungeon secret well enough, just like the rest of them. He hadn't broken and run at the first sign of danger. And it wasn't unreliable, either. James could quite honestly say that he could rely on JP to be JP, one hundred percent of the time. It was never a question of him backstabbing or lying. It was just that, when James had called his friends to action, two of them had said yes with no strings attached, and two of them had said no. And of the people who'd said no, Anesh had admitted that he was *afraid* and asked for James to forgive him for it. Either in spite of that, or perhaps because of it, James hadn't felt like forgiveness was even needed; Anesh was being *reasonable*. No matter how things had turned out, they hadn't walked into it as superheroes, and being afraid was totally justified. But JP? Well, he just sort of declared "nope" and didn't participate.

And maybe he had been afraid. Maybe he had been judging the risks and chosen a pragmatic path. Maybe he had simply not trusted James, in a cruel plot twist. But that wasn't how JP explained himself.

In Shakespeare's *Julius Caesar*, there was a moment where the Senate calls Caesar before them. And, for whatever reason, Caesar simply says, "No." He does not provide them a reason; he says, "The cause is in my will. I will not come." It was one of James's favorite scenes from the play, and he knew it was one of JP's as well, given that JP was secretly a drama kid who had been the one who'd dragged James to see the amateur production he'd played good old Julius in. More than simply play the part, though, JP had taken that line to heart, in a serious way. It was something James had found admirable about the man over the years—that he was firm and determined in how he stated what he wanted, and then chased it.

But when he'd said, "No, I don't want to die on a fool's errand," it had set a seed of annoyance in James's own heart. This little thought that maybe their goals didn't line up enough to even be friends anymore.

And now here JP was. Back again for casual adventure. Because he willed it so. And James knew that if it turned into a situation where their lives were in danger, JP would be the first one to want to leave. To pack it up and quit the group for good. Because he would will it so. But right now, his friend was making sure that everyone was standing in good order while James counted down the seconds on his phone.

3:43 a.m. Tuesday. One minute to go. The people around him suddenly and without prompting ceased their whispered conversations, voices kept low to keep the few people left on the call center floor from hearing them. It was in this moment that James remembered that his life was still grounded in some kind of reality. There was a normal, beyond the dungeon, and it existed down thirty feet of eggshell-white hallway that wasn't going to try to kill him for walking down it. He had a choice, ultimately, to just cut his losses at any time and walk away.

He could also choose, as he did now, to step forward toward the double doors of the stairwell and turn to address everyone behind him. Out of the corner of his eye, he caught sight of Theo, arms crossed, standing off to the side of the elevator landing. Watching them, seeing them off. He gave her a small nod.

"All right, guys, we've talked this over a million times, more or less. The first part's the hardest. We're in, first, to make sure it's not a trap. If we don't come out in ten seconds or so, everyone else follow on our heels. Pile the gear up, we'll start setting up, and then we'll figure out what our short-term goals are." He looked around at the faces, some eager, some determined. "We aren't all here for the same things," James told them, "but that doesn't mean we're not a team, got it? Take care of each other, no matter what happens."

Then he turned, brushed his jacket out behind him and adjusted the collar, and yanked the door open. And with a grin that only Anesh and Alanna were privy to, he led his friends into elsewhere.

The gray and beige of the Office welcomed him home like an old friend, albeit an old friend who sometimes tried to murder him. The small area around the door that James had checked out last week remained unchanged, but it was a far sight from what it had been before.

Fort Door was gone. The dungeon had paved their little fort and in its place rebuilt cubicles and carpet. There was no sign of the final stand at the exit from the great escape, nothing left to show where humans had bled and almost died to save themselves from creatures that defied basic biology. But what there was wasn't simply the same flat slope of cube walls that James had encountered in his first adventures here.

Near the door itself, there was that small open gap that there always was near structural walls in this place, about fifteen feet of hard-carpet floor space with almost nothing breaking up the monotony. Then the cubicles started. Many of them were now structured like the pods in the office outside—clusters of six or eight desks with minimal privacy, all with their backs facing each other in geometric boredom. Beyond that, though, it began to get more familiar, with the walls getting higher, the geometry warping, and trappings like paper vines and creeping cables providing the atmosphere of an ancient temple.

Except for one major variation this time.

A few hundred feet in, past dozens of the desk pods, some of the cubicle walls jutted out of the ground at harsh angles. They rose taller than the rest, and just when it would look like they couldn't sustain any more weight, another wall would be there to brace it. It looked a whole lot like what James and Alanna had dubbed an apartment tower during their deep dive—fully enclosed cubicles layered on top of each other, the walls bowing out or forming jagged ledges on the outside, with only a few windows or potential points of entry. Unlike the one they'd found, though, this tower rose well over two hundred feet into the air, a commanding tower that dwarfed the area around it and gave off an ominous shadow in the fluorescent lights.

"That's new," Anesh muttered. "Wait, James. It's doing the vending machine thing." He gestured up the spine of the building, his hand moving to indicate distance but crossing no visible space. "The ceiling isn't that tall here; where's it *going?*" Ganesh launched off his shoulder, taking to the air in low circles and keeping his head tilted toward the tower, curious and alert in equal measure.

"Up." Alanna cracked her neck as she peered up at the heights of the tower in front of them. "Same place we are, I bet." Rufus clacked in acknowledgment on her shoulder. The place felt like a challenge, even to his small frame.

James smiled at them. "I believe," he addressed his friends and lovers, "that we've been provided with a replacement fort." He cleared his throat as he caught sight of a tumblefeed perched on a ledge ten stories above the ground. "Provided we prove we earned it, that is."

Anesh looked around, the two of him scanning the area before moving off to the side and dropping the duffel bags somewhere out of the way of the impending crowd from the door. "All right, mates," he said with an excited vibration in his voice. "It's not a trap, or it is a trap and it's big and obvious and just our thing. So let's get everyone in here and get this show rolling."

"Fuck yes," James said quietly. "Let's see what wonders lie waiting for us."

In the still, dead air, the three of them shared a moment of intimate anticipation before their backup caught up to them.

CHAPTER 7

First floor.

James and Anesh went first.

No matter how much combat experience he and Alanna had together, no matter how eager the others were to get into the thick of things, no matter how much James wanted to *see* the others in action, there was no question that it was going to be him and Anesh. It wasn't even a selfish thing. It was simple tactics and safeguards. The two of them had a connection that let them do this on a level that no one else could match. And no, it wasn't the connection from the skulljacks, though Anesh had brought up that it would be a massive tactical advantage. It was more that the two of them had spent so much time together, both in and out of this place, that they could act almost without thinking about the other.

It was more than trust, it was more than skill, and it was more than friendship. They were *the* two-man team to aspire to; they maybe even could have been without the Office. And this place had served only to sharpen their bond to something razor edged.

All that added up to them being the best people to throw into unfamiliar situations, for now. And the tower was nothing but an unfamiliar situation. Maybe it was the dungeon's awkward attempt at a thank-you, or maybe it was a giant baited death trap. Or maybe it was just random, and they were overthinking it.

Either way, until they knew better, James and Anesh would check it out.

The first floor was dark. The only illumination came from their flashlights, the entry point, and the desk lamps that would flicker to life intermittently. The base of the tower was probably the widest part, but it still wasn't a huge amount of ground to cover—six-by-six cubicles, with two hallways running parallel to each other and a third small corridor crossing their path in the middle. Despite the chaotic layout of the outside, the ground level was surprisingly structured. In the gloom, though, it was hard to figure out if that simple pattern held any secrets.

James pursed his lips as he looked into one of the enclosed cubicles. Behind him, an Anesh held a pair of heavy Maglites, one of them angled over James's shoulder and into the room. On first glance, it looked basically normal. Or, rather, as normal as this place ever got. Desk, shelves, filing cabinet, garbage can, chair. No computer here, not even a laptop. Though there was a keyboard on the desk that didn't connect to anything, so James made a mental note to keep an eye out for a shellaxy in case one of the computers had wandered off on its own. It just didn't feel like it was complete, somehow, no matter how average this space seemed.

He stepped inside while one Anesh waited patiently out in the hall while the other scanned another cube on the other side. Sweeping his own flashlight beam around, it occurred to him suddenly that there weren't that many trappings here. Not that much stuff on the desk, no extra pencils or more than a couple folders full of paper. No coat hung on the filing cabinet or bagged lunch sitting behind an inconspicuous shelf. He frowned and leaned over to open the desk drawer, confirming what was bothering him. It was mostly empty. No snack stash, no hidden wallet or purse, no personal electronics.

If this place *was* meant as a reward, it certainly wasn't the kind that provided wealth. Or food, which was arguably worse.

Before he had time to process that thought, the tape dispenser hopped to life on bird claws formed from staple removers and lashed out at him with a gooey tongue. James let out an awkward squawk as he reflexively caught the tape in the palm of his gloved hand, snatching it out of the air in front of his face, but feeling a sudden and surprisingly strong yank toward the whirling, bladed maw of the tapir on the desk.

The light shifted around him, sharp shadows leaping upward, as James leaned into the pull, took a half step forward, grabbed the small monster by its back, and flung it out into the hallway. It slid to a stop, leaving gouges in the carpet, and let out a sticky hiss in James's direction.

Then Anesh slammed a crowbar into it hard enough that the sticky sap that made up its insides splattered up the interior wall of the cubicle James stood in.

James stepped out as Anesh stooped down to grab up the two small orbs, one yellow, one orange, and pour them into a belt pouch, just as they heard the noise of a strider cracking in half from the other side of the hall, and the other Anesh stepped out, dropping the carcass and pocketing his own yellow.

"Okay, well, we know this place is . . ." James started to say before, from down the hall, from the cubicles surrounding them, from a dozen different small places, they heard noises. Rustlings, hisses, soft clatters and clangs as a whole host came to life, angry.

Both Aneshes turned to James with a pained look. The kind of look that told him that he really should have known better than to deliver a dramatic line like that so low and over the plate. ". . . Occupied?" both of them finished for him, sarcasm in their unified voice.

"Yeah." James sighed, setting his flashlight on the floor to give them some light and pulling his trusty and notched hand axe off his belt. "All right, let's get to work."

"All right." James stood over a series of desks that had been pushed together into what he could only describe as a war room table. In front of him was a sheet of paper onto which he'd sketched out the floor plan of the bottom of the tower, which had been passed around a couple times, and a pile of orbs. "So that's the deal. Somewhere between ten and twenty life-forms, all of them instantly hostile. Nothing new, but some are types that we only ever saw deeper in before, like the tapir. Be *real* careful with those. There's a sort of slanted wall bit *here*"—he tapped the map—"that's a ramp up to the next floor. We peeked up but didn't see anything, and it's a lot darker than the bottom. No windows on that one." James looked around at the team leaders who had joined him here, the main group of delvers still unpacking and organizing gear a little ways away to avoid too large a crowd. "So, questions?"

"Who can go in?" Momo asked. Her team, three people and one magical dog strong, didn't have an official leader, so James had gotten to meet all of them over time as whoever was available came to their meetings or therapy sessions. This time, she'd been the one to come over while the two boys tried to figure out where to clip their radios onto the hockey pads.

"Part of me wants to just say 'anyone' and be done with it," James admitted. "But no. We're thinking that we'll rotate through, go floor by floor with different teams. That way no one starts to get exhausted, and we have backup if anyone gets overwhelmed." He pointed up at the tower that dominated the view of the entrance. "I'd like to clear this out before we go too much farther in. It's a huge risk to have a potential nest of hostile things at our backs, especially this close to the door to Earth."

"So, who's first, then?" Momo pressed.

James sighed. "Fine, it's you guys. Happy?"

"Yup!" the young woman agreed. She'd had to flatten her short mohawk with a helmet, but that hadn't stopped her from expressing her goth self by stenciling tiny skulls on the shoulder pads of her armor and spray-painting the rest of it black.

"All right, any *other* questions?" James asked with an eye roll, while Anesh patted him on the shoulder reassuringly.

"What about the door?" Daniel asked. He was here in his role as a guard, along with Tyrone. Not because they were both employed as security guards, but because they'd decided that the door itself, if it couldn't or wouldn't be closed, was a problem and should be watched.

"If we keep teams on rotation, there should always be someone watching the door," James said. "We'll sort it out so you can actually spend some time exploring, too, so that you're not tethered here all night as backup. If you want?"

Daniel paused for a second, then nodded. "I actually need to do some exploring," he said, saying the phrase *do some exploring* in the same way most people said "feed the cat." Because for the memetic life that shared his head, exploration was quite literally food.

"All right, cool. And that will also help us find more resources that can be put to use." James had almost said the word *exploited* there but pivoted at the last second. It didn't *mean* anything negative, in his head, but it was harsh language and he didn't want people thinking of him as a tyrant. Yet. "Next?" He looked around the table.

"My group and I are here for a specific reason," Karen stated. She was the oldest person here, by far, almost fifty years old. It was hard for James to not mentally default to thinking of her as the "adult" of the group, but he had to keep in mind that she just didn't have the experience that his friends did when it came to this sort of situation. It didn't help that Momo apparently had started thinking of her as a backup mom, which made it harder to veto any of her firmly worded suggestions. "We need to be able to pay to repair everyone's lives, and we can't do that if there isn't anything in there." She raised her eyes sharply to the tower.

James had been prepared for this and nodded. Karen's goals didn't exactly run contrary to his, but she wasn't interested in the orbs that much, although the team she represented might be. "I agree," James said. "But fortunately, there's enough of us that we can cover both. Momo, you guys will be on tower duty with us. JP, you and Dave will go with Karen and start exploring out a little bit. That way, we'll always have at least one group here on rearguard in case of emergency."

He closed his eyes and winced briefly as he realized that that one team would only ever be able to cover one emergency. It was very annoying to know that as their numbers grew, the number of problems went up along with it.

"So, how are we splitting the loot?" JP asked pointedly, cutting to the root of the mild tension in the air as he pointed at the orbs, one of which Rufus was casually rolling away.

"Well, first priority goes to feeding the familiars." James poked Rufus with a gloved finger. "Though they should *ask first*, you dink." That got a laugh from the table, and even a small twitch of a smile from Karen. "After that, I think now more than ever our method of shares is appropriate." James took a breath and looked around at everyone, making eye contact to show he wasn't just goofing around this time. "There is literally nothing to stop teams from pocketing cash or cracking orbs in the field. I get that. And hell, if you have a few dozen yellows, go ahead and treat yourself. Same if you need to use blues or purples to get out of tight spots."

"That's not fair," Karen flatly stated.

"It doesn't have to be fair," James said. "We just have to agree to it." He spread out the orbs on the table, knocking down the pyramid that Alanna had carefully constructed and earning an annoyed exclamation from her. "Anesh and I earned these, but we're putting them into the pool. I trust everyone else to do the same, because I want to. If we start arguing over who deserves more money, or more orbs, or whatever? We are fucked. We will *never* survive this place, or each other."

There was a blanket of silence as even the others within earshot stopped rustling with their gear and making quiet conversation to listen in. The point James was making was solid. If they didn't work together, then they might as well just quit now. There was no point in specializing or having backup if that backup would be bitter about not getting paid as much.

"That said," JP contributed, "we should also set aside a percentage of the physical cash toward the group fund."

Perfect timing, James realized. JP shored up the one thing that had *actually* been Karen's complaint, which James himself had totally forgotten to address. "Yes." He nodded at his more socially apt companion. "As our self-elected treasurer so astutely brings up, we do have dependents out there in the real world who are counting on us. So we take care of them first."

Karen leaned back, mollified. "That's all we want," she said. "We'll take turns in the tower in that case."

"Appreciated," James told her, not quite smiling, but much more relaxed than normal when talking to her. "But I actually do think we should be exploring. If we can find, and unlock, even one more briefcase, we can pay for a month of operations. So that's your primary goal. Well, that and getting acquainted with the tactics of this place."

JP nodded again. "And we can help with that. Well, Dave can. I'll also be learning as we go."

"Dave is a good squire," Alanna agreed.

James grimaced. "Sorry, squire?"

"You'll figure it out eventually." Alanna patted him on the shoulder. "So, anything else?"

No one had any more questions.

Fourth floor.

Simon clicked his radio twice as he knelt in position, signaling as quietly as possible to his friends. Two clicks was yes, three was no, and right now, he was looking at a big old yes.

They'd crawled up the stairs with Alanna and Anesh as backup, while a different Anesh had bandaged up Leader James's arm down on the ground. He'd ignored his own warning about the tapirs, and it turned out that his favorite coat was no match for a few dozen spinning, gnashing blades. So this might be the last floor they cleared tonight, which was strangely disappointing to Simon.

He hadn't really understood what was going on when they were first cut loose from the monster's network. His chest had hurt, and it had later turned out that someone—probably Alanna, really—had hit him hard enough to crack ribs. He'd stumbled from camp to camp, brain still catching up to being an individual again. And then, after either two hours or a whole day, a different James than the one who had helped bail them all out had talked to him. Just some random guy who'd sat next to him and taken the time to make conversation, no matter how tired he was. And Simon had started to wake up. Momo, too, had been pulled in. And before they knew it, the three of them were friends. And then companions. And then had made out of a computer monitor a dog that looked like a rainbow distortion in the air. Then, somehow, he was *back in here*.

Only this time, they were predators, not the prey. And when he looked up at the motivational poster on the wall that seemed to just be a blocky image of a printer with the equally blocky text of "copy" underneath, it amused him rather than creeped him out like it would have a month ago. It was a liberating feeling.

James—Simon's James, that is—was on the other side of this enclosed hallway with Momo, waiting on just the other side of the vending machine. This was the first floor where they'd found a spatial warp, with this hallway that only went one direction. So Simon had backtracked, looped around, and made his way carefully through the dim hallways in the light from his camp lantern and the two windows on the floor until he could see what had been concealed from them by the towering form of the vending machine at the end of the intersection.

Two clicks meant yes. Yes, there was a potted plant on the other side. Yes, it was waiting to ambush you. Simon couldn't see that well, having turned off his light to sneak up on it, but he could make out two long bulbs facing at an angle toward the vending machine's corner. Waiting for anyone to poke their hands or heads around that obstacle.

He crouched, waiting for a reply from his friends. He had more weapons on him than he ever thought he'd own, and he took the time to quietly draw the machete that he'd been given by the organization. Leader James had given him a weird look when he'd handed it over and promised it was "better quality," whatever that meant.

His radio came to life briefly. Two clicks of static in reply. Simon nodded to himself, got into a runner's position, and after a deep breath to steady his nerves, took off in a sprint toward the head-high potted plant. He made it to within maybe five feet before the thing started to turn toward him, and by then, it was too late. Simon wasn't a swordsman, but he did know how momentum worked, and his swing took off one of those ominous pods and left the machete buried halfway through the stalk of the other one before he stumbled past it and into Momo and his James, who were already moving past him.

Momo practically howled as she came around the plant's hiding spot. They'd tried to convince her that alerting everything on the floor to their presence was a *bad idea*, but she'd said it was important to keep morale up. Simon had banded together with the other two members of their group to haggle her down to only doing that when they were pretty sure most of the floor was already dead, just so they didn't have to deal with another swarm. The first one wasn't too bad, but they'd been less tired then. None of them, they had agreed, fancied trying it again, but harder.

None of this was relevant to Momo swinging her own blade at the plant and chopping into the thick stalk that made up its trunk before several of its broad, waxy leaves flicked upward from the pot and shoved her away. Hard. Hard enough that she tumbled back down the hallway intersection, head over heels. Momo hadn't needed to borrow a machete from the group's armory; Momo was, Simon had learned, *exactly* the kind of person who already owned functional swords.

Then James stepped in, with his wrestler's build and heavy armor, just in time for the half-severed pod to burst into a spray of thorns. Many of them bounced off the plastic plating, some of them caught on the cloth parts. One carved a thin crimson line down his cheek. None of them stopped him from grabbing and snapping important parts of the plant, even as it resisted and rained down solid, heavy hits onto his shoulders and chest with its branches and vines. While he held it, a shimmering rainbow waver in the air roughly shaped like a dog lunged in and gnashed vibrating teeth at exposed vines and flowers.

Then Simon and Momo caught their balance, looped back around, and hit it again. And the three of them kept hitting it until it stopped moving entirely and a trio of yellow orbs dropped, one the size of a golf ball and the other two the smaller versions.

"Yeah! Fuck you, plant! That's what you get for not being a mammal!" Momo triumphantly yelled, jamming the blade of her gladius into the dirt of the pot. "No offense, Mags," she followed up to their dog, running a hand through his back in a friendly pet.

James gasped for air, rubbing at the soon-to-be bruises from the multiple hits he'd taken. "I'm really worried that you're way too into this," he told her. "Maybe you can wear the armor next time."

Simon just shook his head and smiled as he collected the orbs into the pouch. Friends, companions, and now weird teammates. The three of them felt ready for anything as they got ready to check down the last hallway.

"Ow." A brief pause, and then, again, "Ow." Same tone, same volume, nothing changed. "Ow."

"Stop that!" Anesh tapped a finger against James's lips in a gesture that he didn't realize was strangely intimate until after he'd done it. He was, even after months, still getting used to this. "And sit still. This is hard."

James made a childish groaning noise at his boyfriend. "But I wanna complain!" he whined before Anesh poked at his cut flesh again. "Ow!"

"Look, don't blame me. You're the one who should be doing this—you have the first aid training," Anesh muttered as he stitched closed the spot on James's arm where the tapir had rent a series of tears in the skin.

"You have the ranks in sewing, though," James countered. Which was true, but for Anesh's money, it didn't really make him feel any more comfortable sticking a needle and surgical thread through his boyfriend's skin.

But fortunately, he was almost done. "Okay, antiseptic, which is gonna sting, and a bandage, and you're done," he told James, who continued his whining until the bandage was firmly in place. "Now what have we learned?"

James sighed dramatically. "Don't get cocky. Actually, seriously, don't get cocky. I feel like the worst example right now." He flexed his arm, getting a feel for the range of motion he had and seeing if he could move without popping the stitches. Anesh actually had done a good job, though, so it would be okay for the time being, and it wasn't bleeding anymore. "I think, being weirdly introspective, that I may have tried too hard to impress everyone," James admitted.

"You know you literally saved a lot of their lives. I don't think you—" Anesh tried to console him, but James cut him short.

It wasn't that he didn't appreciate that Anesh instantly jumped to trying to cheer him up, it was more that he really did want to be more honest with himself. "It's not about what they actually think," he told his friend. "More about what the voice in my head tells me they think. Anxiety's kind of a shit, sometimes."

"Ah. I don't really understand, but that makes sense."

"Good enough for me! And I do appreciate you trying to be supportive," James said. "Also for the medical aid. Think I'm good to give it another try?"

"No!" Anesh gave him a shocked look.

"That's a firm maybe. Got it." James smiled. "Okay, where's our other half? Still sweeping the area?"

"Yeah." Anesh nodded. "Me and Alanna were gonna get some cash looted while I took care of this. Because neither of us knows how to take a break, I guess." He shrugged a bit.

James grimaced. "Okay, we're inventing new pronouns for you. Or stealing some from a language that future proofed for cloning. This is getting difficult."

"I admit, it's a challenge." Anesh finished packing away the first aid kit after disposing of the bloodstained gloves and needle and eased into a chair next to James at their makeshift map table. "Want to see how the tower group is doing?"

"You just said I shouldn't be running around." James gave a disapproving frown to Anesh.

For his mockery, he got another irritated flick on the forehead. "No, you wanker. I sent Ganesh to keep an eye on them in case they needed saving. Here." He pulled out a phone and the two of them watched from a dark perch as a trio of humans plus one other thing dismantled a potted plant.

"They're not bad," James admitted. "My namesake there needs to get hit less, though."

"Is that your professional opinion?" Anesh smirked. "Besides, it's not like we did any better the first time we found one of those."

James bared his teeth in a grimace. "Thaaaat was a surprise, yes. And technically, I *am* a professional at this."

"'Don't get hit' is not tactical advice, my friend," Anesh informed him in an aloof tone, making quote marks with his fingers as he said the first few words.

"Don't sass me" was the only reply. "How long until the check-in with the away team, by the way?"

They had, of course, brought radios in. With the monster that had been messing with the dungeon dead, they seemed slightly safer to use without threat of interference, though everyone was made firmly aware of the fact that electronics of any kind could be compromised. It was why James had insisted on handing out notepads and telling people to not just make notes on their phones. Still, radios were useful tools, even with the potential for tampering, and they had a schedule for check-ins to make sure everyone was still alive and kicking.

"Thirty minutes," Anesh answered him. "And we've got about five hours left before we leave, counting our buffer time. What do you wanna do with it?"

"Well, that's only about two hours of actual adventuring, because we're gonna have to divide up loot and do debriefings and stuff. And

I'm realizing that I don't . . . I don't . . ." James's voice caught for a second as he struggled to catch his breath. "Man, I don't know if I wanna do this. This feels like a responsibility I didn't ask for, again. What happened to the two of us just wandering around and having fun?" As soon as he said it, he felt guilty. Fun? Fun was for places that didn't have kidnapping victims and death traps. Not to mention the potential ways to upgrade the world, or humanity as a whole. James didn't get to have fun, he got to—

"Yeah, I miss that, too." Anesh derailed James's panicked train of thought like the end of the tracks. His boyfriend shrugged. "We picked up all these extra people, and now I'm doing all this organizational work because I'm good at it, but I don't really *want* to. I guess kinda like you with the leadership thing." He sighed and leaned back in the chair, tilting his head to look at the tower behind them. James turned to see what Anesh was staring at, twisting in his seat, before Anesh spoke again. "Want to see if we can call dibs on taking the next floor? Just us, maybe Alanna too if she's not tired. Oh! We could get Daniel and . . . um . . . other guy. They're probably bored."

James almost cried. Without even really thinking about it, or meaning to, Anesh had just shattered about a month's worth of guilt that had been building up in his chest. And then, casual as can be, asked James out on a dungeon date.

"Fuck, I love you," James told him, quietly. Then he rolled forward onto his feet as Anesh gave him a surprised glance. James stood from his chair, swinging his good arm around. "I'm gonna go see if we've got a box of glow sticks anywhere. I'm sure *someone* brought some!"

Anesh grinned and shook his head as James walked away. As he watched Rufus fiddle with the growing pile of orbs on the table, he wondered if he was having fun with Alanna looting cubicles. Outwardly, he looked idle and calm. But in his chest, Anesh felt that little spark of excitement at being in a literal dungeon flare to life and start to grow into a fire. And when he cast his eyes up the tower that stood as a challenge over their doorway, that fire *burned*.

Ninth floor.

They weren't pushing the time limit yet, but they were getting there. Two hours left, with a small safety margin, and they had only made it this far.

It occurred to James, as he and a single Anesh made their way carefully up to the ragged hole in the side of a cubicle wall, that he and Anesh *had* technically had a dungeon adventure together today already. But he decided that one didn't count, on the grounds that it was official business and not just this kind of messing around.

Not that they were messing around, really. They *were* here to clear the floor, to secure the tower, to establish a base, all that jazz. But they were also here after handing command over to Alanna and other Anesh, who were both kind of tired and fine letting them abdicate responsibility for a little while. The away teams had checked in; everything was fine, and there were no disasters to solve. And so, James and Anesh got to have some fun.

Right now, that fun came in the form of ducking from jagged door to jagged door, avoiding the patrols that plagued this floor.

Those patrols were 2.0s, armored white shells that came up to knee height, waddled around on geometrically precise tentacles, and had lasers for eyes. And they were both strangely active compared to some of the occupants of the lower floors and also strangely inattentive relative to same. They lurched down the hallways, stopping at not-quite-random spots to check inside cubicles or under desks, their eyes occasionally glittering with light as they shot low-intensity lasers through the gloom. But, for all the fact that they were patrolling here, they also didn't all instantly react when James and Anesh killed one the first time, not until one of them stumbled across the wrecked hull, anyway. And so it had become a game of picking off isolated patrols one at a time.

This floor had more space to it than most of the others; James had already suggested and everyone had agreed that if they found the oranges powering the spatial warps in here, they would leave them alone. If this *was* going to be their staging area, he wanted it intact. The other thing it had that had started showing up the closer they got to the top was windows. *Reasonably speaking,* they should be well above the line of Officium Mundi's ceiling, given how far they'd climbed. But reason didn't always apply here, and so, there were chunks of bright white light beamed in from outside, giving parts of the outside edge of this floor a bit more visibility.

James leaned just far enough to get a sight angle down a hallway, saw it was clear, and tapped Anesh on the shoulder. His partner rose from his crouch to move with a few calculated steps across the gap between this cube and the next, briefly illuminated clearly in the sharp light beamed in from outside. They were up against the outside wall, here, as they snuck into position, and right near the window on this side. The two of them had been at this for half an hour now, not counting the minutes that it took to climb the tower. Fortunately, this place didn't seem to have a respawn timer, so the floors that were cleared stayed cleared, but that didn't mean it magically got an elevator. So, legwork it was.

Across the hall, James saw Anesh hunker down in the shadows of the doorway, pulling a folder stand into place to give himself a little extra cover. He shot his friend a thumbs-up, and the two of them settled in to wait.

They didn't have to wait long. By this point, between an old perception skill of Anesh's, James's lasting love of stealth games, and liberal use of the nonalive drones that had been brought in as scouts, they'd more or less mapped out all the guard routes. So it came as no surprise to either of them when a 2.0 turned a corner and started making its way down the corridor toward them.

It had an off-white shell, smooth and opalescent. The tentacle cables at its base moved it with precision and pattern, not haphazardly like the lesser shellaxies. The illuminated ring on the front that they suspected was its eye glowed a muted blue, with blinks of red occasionally betraying the weapons hidden there. It wasn't the first one they'd fought today, and the wealth of green orbs they'd collected was a testament to their improving tactics. No more fair, head-on fights for them, no. If these hostile machines were going to play by rules and mappable routes, then James and Anesh were going to exploit the hell out of that.

The upgraded shellaxy came closer, and James counted down in his head. He was a little off, hitting the count of two and not zero when it stopped, made a ninety-degree turn, and swept its glowing eye over an uninhabited cubicle. It was unclear to James what the shellaxy was actually looking for, since the warped geometry in the cubes meant it was staring at a flat wall and not the expected door. If it wanted to see in, it just had to shuffle a foot to the right and look through one of the semicircular holes near the base of the cube wall. But that wasn't really relevant. What *was* was that after this set part of the thing's route, it would turn—just like that, yes—and walk down to the end of the little dead-end hallway and pause for ten seconds.

The instant it stopped, James and Anesh burst out of their hiding places, took a series of bounding steps down the hall, grabbed the suddenly confused and furious shellaxy by the underside of its case, and threw it out the window.

"Kobe!" James yelled as they lobbed the flailing mass of cables and toothy ports out into the open air. It seemed to hang there for a breath, and Anesh almost had time to worry that these things could fly, before gravity took hold and it plummeted out of sight.

When you ran a dungeon delve on a budget, and you didn't want to further damage your favorite axe or have to replace any more expensive 5.7 ammunition, you found ways to get the job done for cheap. Bandages weren't free, and neither was burn gel, and every one of these things that had been subjected to the harsh mistress of gravity was one less that they had to actually get hit by.

"All right!" James rubbed his hands together, running a finger over a small scrape he'd gotten for forgetting his gloves. "That should be the last of them. Wanna go see what slim loot this floor has?"

Anesh peered over the edge, looking down to the base of the tower to try to see where they'd cratered their latest target. A quick check showed that everyone had moved far enough away thanks to a well-timed radio warning earlier, before the shower of shellaxies began. "Yeh, sounds good," he responded cheerfully. "Also, Kobe?"

A single energetic nod from James. "For accuracy!" he unhelpfully explained.

"No, I mean, I don't know what that means," Anesh said as they started sweeping the cubes. They weren't being as careful as they had been—this floor had shown no signs of any non-2.0 life, but they still kept an eye out all the same.

"Impossible!" James called back from one cube farther in where he was going through the drawers of a storage cabinet. "You have access to the internet. There is literally *no way* that you don't get that reference!"

"I mean, I know it's a basketball player," Anesh told him as he came to stand in the door of the cube where James continued to go through cupboards in a futile attempt to secure something of value. "Well, *he's* a basketball player. Thanks to either constant exposure to JP or one of the skill orbs, not sure which. Are you done here? I really don't think that this place has anything worth taking, unless you need scrap paper."

"It's for accuracy," James reiterated, again unhelpful. "And yeah, I don't . . . hang on." He shoved aside a pile of unmarked manila folders in the bottom drawer he was looking in to reveal something that actually stood out in this place. "Score! Coffee!"

"What, like, a cup of coffee?" Anesh asked, puzzled. The tower had, so far, been stingy with the loot, but not totally devoid of it. It was more like it was . . . unfurnished rather than spiteful. But the idea of a cardboard cup of espresso in the bottom of a desk drawer was . . . worrying. Especially since Anesh's brain chose that moment to make the connection that sometimes coffee cups in here exploded.

Fortunately for James, Anesh had a pretty good reaction time. And while he'd already started moving to dive-tackle his boyfriend out of the way of any potential molten blast of caffeine, he was also fully capable of pulling up short and stopping before contact after James held up a brown paper bag of ground coffee.

"No brand name," James mused. "Suspiciously corporate green branding on the front. Smells okay?"

"Stop sniffing the coffee!" Anesh complained. "Every time, this thing! We can't trust the food in here!"

"Oh, stop freaking out. We can absolutely trust the food here. Almost everything in this place has, at some point, been a trap and tried to kill us, *except* food," James retorted.

Anesh frowned. "What about the actual coffee? The coffee cups, you may recall, *explode*."

"I don't think coffee over a certain temperature counts as food." James rubbed a gloved hand over his mouth. "There was that one McDonald's lawsuit about that a while back. Or maybe the coffee itself is perfectly safe to drink, but it's the cups that explode." It was an interesting thought experiment. If food was safe, where exactly was the line for what counted as food? It must be human food, otherwise half the stuff in here that some dungeon life could eat wouldn't count. Hell, the plants wouldn't count, since at least *some* of them were organic, and goats could totally gnaw through those.

"Are you okay?" Anesh asked, breaking James's train of thought.

James twitched a bit as he stopped puzzling over the food question in the middle of a hostile dungeon. "What is food, anyway?"

"Nope. We're not doing this here. Grab your beans and let's go," Anesh said with a smile.

"All right, all right." James laughed. "Up or down?"

Anesh slowed his walk briefly, and James did the same to avoid bumping into his friend's backpack. Both of them knew what they *wanted* to do, obviously. No matter how tired their legs were from hiking up nine stories, or how much James's hand hurt. Despite having expended half their ammo, long distances to any support, and a clock that was pushing them to play it safe. Despite *all that*, well . . .

They still wanted to try just one more.

They stood there in silence for a couple seconds, thinking. Responsible, or exciting?

James sighed and knelt, unzipping his backpack to check inside. "Okay. I've got room, for sure. We haven't used the medkit too much. Stitches are still holding—good job, by the way." He slung the rifle strap around his chest to check the gun, perhaps unnecessarily, as they hadn't actually fired either of their backup weapons yet. "Yup. Still here," he joked idly.

"Is this leading up to you trying to justify going up another level?" Anesh asked, amused. "Because I'm already willing to agree, but we should be quick about it. Also we've got all these melted parts of the armor now, which is a problem."

It was a problem. The parts of their shell plating that had taken sustained hits from the 2.0 lasers had melted and then reset in sometimes quite jagged formations. They took the time, with imprecise use of James's axe, to trim back some of the worse ones that might trip them up or stab them if they made a particular dodge, but it wasn't a clean repair job.

Still, though.

"I want to keep going. One more," James said. Anesh wavered a bit, and James took the chance to make his case. "Look. We've got so many greens out of this. And we didn't even get seriously hurt, aside from"—he rubbed at the small cut on his cheek where a piece of plastic shrapnel had nicked him—"small things. The rewards are piling up. We should keep going."

"Thaaaat"—Anesh pointed an accusatory finger at him—"is *exactly* the greedy mind-set that I would expect from the person who once turned around to fight a plant while being chased by a tumblefeed." James winced at having that memory of stupid behavior brought up. "But still!" Anesh continued. "Even if we are on an adventure date, you need to remember a lot of people are counting on you. I might be expendable, but *you* aren't." He jabbed his finger gently into James chest plate.

"You are in no way expendable," James replied softly, the quiet words doing very little to hide how suddenly *angry* that thought made him. He looked away awkwardly after realizing how dramatic that had been. "But still. I mean, we're here for the orbs and the money, mostly. It would be kinda silly to not do the efficient thing and take another floor without making someone walk all the way up here."

"James," Anesh said, ignoring the second half of the explanation, "there's two of me. Not two people who are very similar, two of *me*. If one of me dies, I'm still alive, and I can make more of myself. It is an objective fact that you cannot be replaced and I can." He leaned in and laid a hand on James's arm. "I don't know much how to think about it yet, but it's there. And it would just help . . . you know."

James did know. Thinking about stuff like that alone never helped. He turned back and looked down at the face of his partner. Anesh was, against all odds, smiling at him. A quiet confidence that he knew James wasn't trying to be an ass in any way and was prepared to wager anything on that.

James leaned forward and the two of them shared a small kiss, the feeling electric on James's lips. "Yeah. I'm sorry," he said with his own smile.

"Good. Now pack up your coffee and let's see what the next floor has," Anesh said, slinging his own bullpup around for easy access in case something jumped them at the top of the stairs.

After doing as ordered, James joined Anesh at the foot of the stairs. "Dark up there," he said calmly, unclipping a flashlight from his belt clip and flicking it on. "Ready?" he asked Anesh with a glance and a smile, light in one hand, axe in the other.

His friend nodded with an equally excited grin. "Yeah. Just one more, right?"

"One more," James agreed.

When JP, Dave, and Karen and the rest of her team came back, it was to the sight of Alanna and Anesh piling up small armfuls of shattered plastic shards and components in an otherwise empty cubicle on top of the much larger wrecked hulls of a half dozen shellaxies.

"Are those Macs?" asked one of Karen's followers, the young nursing student by the name of Deb who'd probably kept a good handful of survivors alive on their escape.

"We don't call them that, for legal reasons," Alanna told her without missing a beat as she dumped her armful of collected scrap into the graveyard.

"Were you attacked?" Dave asked with the kind of concerned voice that said that he was more interested in the tactical information than if they'd actually been hurt. Alanna didn't take offense, though, because she was aware that he had probably already come to the conclusion that if they were doing this, they weren't dead or hurt, and jumped to the question he found actually important.

She dusted off her hands as Anesh came back with another cleanup load. "Nah. James and Anesh hucked these things out of the tower and let gravity do their job for them. We already got the orbs out; they're on the table with the others. If you guys wanna just pile your stuff up there, too, we'll probably divide it up after the boys come out of the tower." She looked over their group as they moved back into the cleared area around the tower itself and noticed that Deb was actually supporting a limping JP. "Are you all right? You guys have any trouble?"

"Team Four learns quickly," Dave said with a hint of smug amusement. "JP doesn't! He sprained his ankle, possibly hurt his knee, and now he knows how it feels," he said as he strode past them and dropped the brown leather briefcase he was holding on to the same table that held the pile of orbs.

Alanna and Anesh both sighed in unison. It was kind of fun, to them, to establish this level of closeness. While Anesh and James got on perfectly, and James and Alanna had a kind of warrior-poet romance going on, Anesh and Alanna themselves hadn't really felt like they'd exactly clicked quite all the way. Which was a problem, if they were going to be in a relationship together. So, the two of them had been sitting around and just talking to each other, enjoying the downtime while James and the other Anesh were in the tower, and Daniel and his teammate were mapping out the immediate area. With no one left to watch the door, the two of them had been in a kind of enforced proximity to each other, and they *did* care about each other, so they'd talked.

And now, they rolled their eyes together as each shot the other a knowing glance that said, "Yes, I am aware that JP is kind of . . . this . . . but we are friends with him, yes? So let's not tease him. Too much."

"JP . . ." Anesh started hesitantly. "We brought you here in the confidence that . . ."

"I know" came the response.

"It's just, *last time* . . ." Alanna said, spreading her hands in front of her in a helpless gesture.

"I know!" JP restated, getting laughs out of a couple people, and even the ghost of a smirk from Karen. "Well, mock me all you like. *I* got the arm of a beautiful lady on the way back." He comically stuck his tongue out at Dave, who didn't even notice. The comment elicited a hint of a blush from Deb, who was still supporting him. It was hard to remember for their friend group, sometimes, that JP was actually startlingly good when it came to flirting, his confidence and cocky grin lending him a hidden strength in the field.

Alanna and Anesh grinned and dropped it. "All right!" Alanna said. "We're low on time, so everyone start stowing your gear and we'll get ready to move out. Daniel's due back in ten minutes, and if someone . . . um . . . Deb? Deb. Can you radio up to James and tell him to get his cute ass back here? Use those words, thanks. I'm needing to talk to Dave. Everyone else have fun." She momentarily tapped Anesh on the shoulder as the group, fresh off their first actual success, moved around them. Some injured, some remembering close calls, but all of them abuzz with the energy of a win. "Hey, Anesh, can you get the details from Karen on the briefcases? I'm gonna go talk to Dave and see how they did."

"Got it." He nodded at her. "I'm looking forward to them getting back. It's always a bit knackering to combine experiences," Anesh said with a wistful glance up the stacked pillar of cubicles that his other self was currently in.

"I'm gonna assume that's good," Alanna said, patting him on the shoulder before they split off. "No one says that," she grumbled to herself good-naturedly as she waited for the group to pass by, leaving her at the mouth of the cube farm with Dave as he walked back over to her. "Okay, debrief me," she said when they were more or less out of earshot.

Alanna hadn't known Dave for very long, but she knew how to talk to him. Or, more specifically, she knew what it meant when someone behaved the way Dave did. Alanna had a younger sister who was on the spectrum, and she recognized the same traits in Dave—no pleasantries or small talk, no wasting time, not out of malice but just because it was hard for him to see the point. While she could, and sometimes did, find it kind of exhausting to deal with, Alanna still felt like she frequently got less annoyed by Dave than everyone else did. So, when she asked him about how Karen and her crew had done, she did so in the least number of words possible. He already knew that she wanted him to keep an eye on them and let her know what she needed to know, and so, "give me the info" was pretty much enough.

Dave nodded, sloughed his backpack to the floor, and answered her. "They're pretty all right. They all hesitated when they might get hurt, which got some of them hurt. Including JP, who probably shouldn't actually be going that deep." He nodded back at the table where he'd left the briefcase. "We found two of those. One of them had a camera snake on it, so we left it but brought this one along. I kept the work order for it—it's also on the table—but I don't know how we'll find the place we're supposed to deliver the box of pencils to. The numbers here don't go in order."

"Find anything good? No, wait, find anything weird?" Alanna asked.

"We found a bottle of aspirin that no one wants to test, and also Karen brought back a few dress shirts that she suspects are special.

I found a paper clip that bends in more directions than you think it would. Also here." He tossed over a USB stick. "It converts files."

"Into what?"

"Good question," Dave said blandly.

"Okay, worrying. How far out did you guys get?" Alanna asked.

"Not that far. Karen is . . . meticulous. She also sort of started giving orders to people. But she's smart enough to not try to counter commands that are about safety." Dave shrugged. "Eh. It just took us a lot of time because she wanted to check everything. Like, *everything*."

Alanna shrugged. "Frustrating. But what's wrong with checking everything? It's not like we'll run out of dungeon to explore." She looked back over her shoulder at the group. "I dunno about you, but I know James and I both find it weird that someone almost twice our age is here. I know I *shouldn't* find it awkward, but . . ."

"But she acts like everyone's disappointed mom," Dave finished with a little half shrug. "And her being older means some of us might listen on reflex, even if it's wrong. We should tell her so she knows that might be a problem."

"Ugh. Yes," Alanna agreed, tilting her head back in frustration and noticing that she needed to cut her hair down again to the point it wasn't getting caught in the armor slots. She had no idea how James handled the ponytail in these things. "All right. Well. No one died, and it's not critical. Did you guys have fun?"

Dave wrinkled his lips for a second, slightly opening his mouth before closing it again. Alanna gave him an expectant look with raised eyebrows and amused wide eyes before he eventually decided, "Yes. Yes, I did."

"Good enough!" she exclaimed. "Let's go see if James is back yet, and we can start dividing up orbs."

Tenth floor

There was, absolutely, some kind of sound and light dampener between the floors. James had a fairly reasonable suspicion that if they ever just threw this place piece by piece into a wood chipper instead of using it as a home base, that the number of orange orbs to come out of it would be enough to eventually make him a five-star general or something. It felt kind of weird to *not* go with Plan W for Wood Chipper, really. But then, what would the point of that be when the only uses for oranges were getting certifications—and potentially responsibilities—that they didn't need, or absorbing them? And so far, no one had come close to the understanding that Anesh had to absorb one, and Anesh already had one and couldn't take in another.

Besides, this place was rad, and James wanted to make it *his*. A grimly fortified tower rising over the surroundings, stretching taller than it could physically fit or support? How could he *not* want to own a piece of that?

Regardless, the reason he'd decided there was a noise filter was that, as soon as they'd ascended the spiral set of sideways wall chunks laid out like a staircase and poked their heads through the floor of the top level, James had instantly been able to hear what was going on here.

"Meeeetttiiiinnnngggg!" howled a chorus of wailing voices.

"Oh, good," he whispered to Anesh, who was grimacing beside him. They both had bad memories about these mask things. Sticky notes shouldn't have bone claws inside them, they agreed with a shared look of frustration.

The other thing James noticed, as he turned off the flashlight, was that this floor was lit. There were ceiling tiles above them, complete with their own fluorescent lights, much like the main ceiling of the dungeon itself. It probably wasn't the *same* ceiling, given how warped this place was in space; James didn't know how hard it was for the dungeon to line up non-Euclidean structures with each other, but he was prepared to cut it some slack here.

The lights were dim, only half of the white bars of illumination actually on. And in the open space they lit up, the whole floor devoid of any walls except the exterior, a strange scene played out. In the middle of the floor sat one of those wide conference room tables, though this one was mercifully devoid of emaciated humans sitting around it. Instead, it had eight chairs. And on its surface, the smooth greenish wood paneling was empty of anything except for one of those old overhead projectors that James remembered from middle school.

Sitting on the surface of the projector was one of the masks. Its normally wildly fluttering sticky note form was instead still, and on the wall behind it, somehow, despite not being made of polystyrene, a vision of it was projected against a cloth backdrop. It was only barely visible from the angle that James was at, still half in the floor, but that wasn't even the weirdest part.

While the one on the projector was still, the *others* weren't. Too many masks to count floated in lazy loops around the table, the chairs, the projector, everything. It took James a second look at the prompting of a nudge from Anesh to notice that they were trailing something with them; lines of some substance poured onto the floor or table as they passed. Their movements might have been sluggish, but they weren't random; whatever they were doing, they were drawing specific circles on things with . . .

"Is that coffee grounds?" James asked Anesh quietly, with a little concern in his voice.

His friend squinted into the dim light and tried to make out what was going on before finally making an unseen shrug. "No idea. What do we do?" He kept his voice low as he asked James, not wanting to alert a whole swarm of the masks.

But James didn't answer. He was distracted by the sudden stillness of the brightly colored masks in the air over the table. They'd all come to a stop, facing the projection on the far wall. And below them, small grains of matter floated upward, smoldering. It *was* coffee grounds, James was certain now; he could smell them burning in the air.

Then there was a flash from the projector's surface, and a split second later, so fast that only Anesh really caught the difference, a similar blaze of light from the screen.

And then the mask that was projected wasn't anymore. It was sitting there, floating in the air. The one that had been lying flat righted itself and went to greet its copy, a howl of "hiiiiriiiinnnnngg!" echoing through the floor.

And then another mask took its place, and the rest of them went back to redrawing their circles of coffee.

James pulled Anesh back down below the floor level, and the two of them turned and sat on one of the wide steps. "Okay," he said, nervously clipping his axe back into its small belt sheath. "That is clearly a problem. There's, what, thirty of those things in there?"

"I estimate there's forty-six," Anesh said with a shaky calm.

"Um . . . that's a specific estimate." James momentarily forgot the massed enemy formation above them.

Anesh looked over at his boyfriend with a wry grin. "James, please. Just trust me when I say that I can do math in my head."

James thought about that for a brief second, then nodded. "Yup. That checks out. Okay. Forty-six masks. And they're making more. That's a problem."

"And we want the projector," Anesh said, nodding along.

"We do?" Anesh silently arched his eyebrows at James's question. "Okay, yeah," James relented as soon as he thought about it. "We do. So, how do we deal with that? Call for backup?"

"I keep forgetting we can do that," Anesh said. James agreed with him; it was hard, after so many days of independent adventure, to remember that they had a whole squad to call up if they needed help. "But I was actually thinking of something simpler." Anesh pulled up the PS90 in his hands, keeping a grip on the compact little rifle. "Why don't we just shoot them?"

James looked at him like he'd grown an extra head. Well, *another* extra head. "I hadn't thought of that!" he exclaimed. "Which is weird, since I totally thought of that when we got jumped by the first batch of 2.0s."

"I feel like you're just better at reacting in combat than planning for an ambush." Anesh shrugged. "Either way. We've still got, what, eighty bullets left?"

"I like that you can apparently create complicated geometrical estimates to count batches of flying tentacle monsters, but you can't keep track of ammo use," James said. Waving away Anesh's protests, he popped the magazine off his own gun and checked before he continued, "Okay. I'm ready if you are. On three?"

"On three." Anesh rose to a crouch, rotating on the step alongside James, the two of them dropping their backpacks to the floor below them, leaving the stairs clear in case they needed to run. He smirked back a bit of annoyance and James reached over and adjusted his firing grip, pulling his elbow up and the rifle back into his shoulder a bit harder. "I'll take the left. Don't hit the projector," Anesh told him.

"Duh," James responded. "One. Two." They stepped up, legs tensed to move. "Three!"

They exploded up the stairs in perfect unison. For once, just for *once* in this damn place, they weren't the ones being ambushed. It took four earsplitting cracks, followed by the metallic *tings* of the firing pins slapping back into position, before the masks realized they were under attack.

James was already moving when the swarm turned toward them. Steadily planting his feet one over the other as he swept out to the right of the room, heading toward the wall with the screen on it and keeping the projector itself out of his firing arc. Anesh, less experienced in this, simply planted his feet and kept shooting. Both of them sighted down their guns, pulling the triggers as fast as they could line up new targets.

It wasn't hard. There were a *lot* of targets, and once the masks started swarming toward them, missing became difficult. Shreds of paper and chunks of bone sprayed into the air as James knocked targets out of the air, twisting his shoulders in short, precise jerks if any of them got too close. A bullet might not do much structural damage to a cluster of papers, but the masks weren't exactly normal biology, and a hole through one of their "hair" strands or a shot to one of their riblike bones was more than enough to drop them from the sky.

Clumps of them fell from the sky as they wasted time trying to form up into an overwhelming wave. James felt sharp pain in his ears with every bullet he fired, smelled the burning gunpowder with every 5.7 round that got sent into the aerial crowd. But given the masks' lack of strategy, their numbers were thinned rapidly before they started breaking. Ones and twos started lunging toward them, their teamwork clearly not at the same level as James and Anesh as their disorganization, confusion, and perhaps even fear drove them to try to close in for their spiny attacks without the swarm as back-up. And that, above all, was what let the two men methodically gun down their enemy.

By the time James ran out of ammunition, he'd had to take two firing breaks to drop his rifle to hang by the sling and grab a mask out of the air that got too close. In frontal attacks like this, they were nothing. Just paper and a few brittle bones, easily torn apart. When James's rifle clicked empty, the surviving masks didn't even notice. Anesh was still shooting into them, taking careful shots as long as none of them were charging him, and slightly more frantic shots when they were. But it didn't matter, James realized, as he drew his axe and used it to unsatisfyingly smash one of the masks down to the floor, where his boot finished its screaming face. Their foe was *running*.

Out of the windows they fled, and the boys let them. Their screams about hostile work environments and poor management trailed into the distance as their diaspora sent them fluttering into the well-lit air outside. And then, they were left alone, ears ringing, in the mostly empty room. Nothing but the brass on the floor around them, pockmarks of bullet holes in the walls, and the table and projector that they had deliberately, but still miraculously, avoided shooting.

"Well, that worked pretty well!" James yelled to Anesh.

"*What?!*" Anesh yelled back.

James blinked at him. "Yeah, we need to get earplugs. Earplugs!" he repeated loudly, motioning to his ears.

"Yeah, I can't hear, either!" Anesh shouted.

James laughed and shook his head as he set his hatchet on the table and pulled his radio out of a pocket. "Hey, ground floor. Be on the lookout for some masks in case they head down there. We're fine and alive up here, and . . . uh . . ." He looked over at Anesh, who had a notebook out already and was making careful notes of the patterns of coffee grounds spilled on the floor, some of it clearly scuffed up by the masks crashing to the ground en masse. "Well, we found something kinda cool. Tower's cleared now, anyone who wants to come up and take a look should. Over."

The radio in his hand lit up, and he jammed it to his ear to try to hear more. A dim, tinned facsimile of Alanna's voice came over it, but James still couldn't make out the words. He checked his watch and shook his head to no one in particular. "All right, didn't hear any of that, sorry. Kinda deaf right now. We're just gonna head back down. See you in a few. Over."

Now for the real challenge, James thought.

Convincing Anesh that it was time to leave.

Alanna rolled her eyes at the radio as James responded loudly enough that she had to turn down the volume. "All right, guys, let's get this started." She turned to the actually quite large crowd surrounding the desks they'd pushed together. "They'll be down in a second. Anesh can speak for Anesh, and James can just go last." There were smirks at that, after the confusion played out on some of their faces.

On the makeshift table was a pile. A *large* pile, Alanna noted with some satisfaction. She'd added to it, but it wasn't all her. And she knew some of the people here would have snuck themselves one or two yellow orbs, but she didn't begrudge them that. Because the stack here had a lot going for it.

Over a hundred yellow orbs of varying sizes, one of them as big as a grapefruit. Maybe two dozen blues, some of them even acquired on purpose. A smattering of magical items of varying useless effects. A big-ass pile of greens from that whole business with the rain of

Apple products. Even a few small oranges from the tapirs that had them—surprisingly not all of them; maybe it was a maturity thing, and older ones grew the extradimensional space?

And then the still-locked briefcase, set aside for a later delve. And the absolute harvest of petty cash funds. Alanna had directed their newer guild members to sort it out into stacks of five hundred each, figuring that was worth a share of loot, but even then the rubber-banded piles still occupied a decent chunk of real estate on the surface.

No purples, because that would be too good to be true. Especially since everyone was explicitly told not to go in too deep, so there shouldn't be any chances to encounter a decision tree. No reds, either, because James had made it incredibly clear that if you encountered anything on his list of "this explodes," you were not to touch it. No really powerful magic items, no life-changing phenomena. But still, for a handful of hours, even if it did involve risking your life, this represented a life-changing amount of power to any one of them.

Now they got to split it. Which didn't feel quite as good to Alanna, who mostly looked at the orbs as a way to focus potentially useful knowledge into a single, incredibly capable individual. But the aura of the room was one of excitement, and there were more than a few proud grins around the table.

By the time JP, at Alanna's prompting, had finished explaining their loot-share system to the people who hadn't been in contact with them over the week, James and Anesh had actually gotten back to the ground floor. Their return coming just in time for them to enter into the ongoing argument.

"You're saying the loot system is dumb," James said, nodding. "I get that; we certainly need something better for a larger group."

"I am *saying*," Karen emphasized, "that this is childish."

JP winced, quietly talking half to himself and half to those seated near him. "Ah, she said the C word."

"Childish?" James replied, his voice seeming torn between iron-cold anger and shocked amusement. "Lady, I didn't invite everyone to the extradimensional infinite office Dyson sphere thing so that that we could fuck around with accounting spreadsheets!" he exclaimed.

While that got laughs, especially from the younger delvers, Karen wasn't deterred. "You're treating these like toys, not tools!"

Around them, the others awkwardly cleared throats, shifted chairs away, and desperately tried to not get caught up in the escalating argument.

"They're both!" James retaliated. "And a lot more besides! And I already agreed that we need a better system, so maybe don't belittle the one that worked for us before *you* joined!"

"Well, if you've been doing this professionally, you should know better!" Karen practically yelled back.

"Okay, hang on." Anesh laid a hand on James's shoulder. His voice, in contrast, was still calm. James wasn't sure which Anesh this was, which small part of his life he'd shared with that one and only that one. But he was still Anesh, and James would trust him, no matter what. As James fell silent, his friend spoke again, voice calm, his accent coming through heavily as he enunciated. "We *have* been doing this more than you, but that doesn't invalidate your point. But it also doesn't make it not rude when you act like we're idiots."

JP chimed in as well, taking the opportunity to add his opinion. "James *did* agree with you that we need a better division, too. Twice, actually."

"Yeah, that's mostly what I'm mad about," James said. "It kinda feels like you're treating me like a kid, instead of . . . I actually don't have a title in mind, but *anything* else."

Their debate shifted away from any heated words after that, as everyone calmed down and apologies went around. But it still left one big problem.

"Okay." James got them back on track. "We've still got this *massive pile of treasure*." He gestured to the table in front of him, where Alanna had been helping Rufus carefully stack up orbs in pyramid formations. "Do we want to split it now, or do we figure something else out and do it later?"

There was a chorus of voices, all at once, and a room full of hungry looks that told James the answer right away. Even with everyone talking over each other, the intent was clear.

"I think they want the money," Alanna stage-whispered to James, who rolled his eyes.

"Okay! New plan!" James declared. "Until we can think up anything better, we split everything more or less evenly, with someone deciding if anyone has earned extra, okay? Then you can figure it out personally if you want to trade." When the crowd started demanding who would figure it out, James simply dragged Dave in front of himself like a human shield, Dave awkwardly flapping his arms like he wasn't sure if he should be resisting. "Does anyone here distrust Dave? No? Great, it's Dave!" He pitched his voice lower. "Congrats, Dave, you have a new job for today."

There was more to it, of course. Karen and Daniel, who it turned out was an accounting student before he'd had to drop out of college, got into a discussion about attribution of wealth. They had to figure out what to set aside for group expenses. There was another argument about feeding Rufus, which James stomped down with zeal. Some people complained they got the "bad orbs," whatever that meant, but James was almost certain that was just good-natured grousing.

It felt weird, and wrong, to him. This was supposed to be the fun part, and Karen's interjection left it with a blanket of tension and annoyance.

But eventually, with about twenty minutes before they all had to be out the door, Dave had found James while he was hauling crates of stuff into the ground floor of the tower, pressed a pile of stuff into his hands, and told him to go nuts.

And by the end of the ten minutes, when people started stashing their own delving tools in the tower themselves and began exiting the dungeon, James had made enough strategic trades to feel happy again. Well, *strategic* may have been a strong word. Mostly he'd given up anything that wasn't a green for a green.

"Why," Anesh asked, rubbing his forehead as James showed him the eight lustrous emerald balls. "I mean, I get it, but why?"

"Oh, I also kept this paper clip that bends in weird ways," James said cheerfully as they finished securing and inventorying their stuff. Everyone else was gone now; it was just James, Anesh, and Alanna. The entrance felt quiet, peaceful. Like it *should* be when they came here, James realized. The crowd distracted him from what was important—the people he loved and the dungeon he lived for.

"Right, but you traded away blues. Those literally save lives," the other Anesh said. This one had a slightly less judgmental tone, and James realized in a flash that this was the one he'd taken the top of the tower with.

"I feel like the greens provide more long-term economic benefit, since I'll be using them in my . . . our . . . bedroom." James shrugged. "Also, I kept some of the money, so we can go get dinner. Hey, wanna see if the cool kids want to go out to get pancakes? Four a.m. pancakes, anyone?"

"You should use them in a rented business space, so we can have a place to conduct operations that isn't our house," Anesh told him.

Alanna, dumping the last hand truck full of MREs on the ground, glanced at Anesh. "Wait, why didn't *you* get any greens?"

"I did, I just want James to use his so I can use mine on a college campus."

"Oh my god, you two are selfishly adorable." She threw her arms around their shoulders, then shot an apologetic glance at the other Anesh. "James! Add him to the chain!" she commanded, and James complied, wrapping that Anesh in a half hug. "Good! Now, I heard pancakes. Are you paying?"

"Wait, am I the only one who took money? Where did it all go?" James asked, concerned.

"Karen traded for a lot of it, and a big chunk went into the survivor fund and the operations budget," Anesh answered instantly. "And I would like to nominate Karen to be our group accountant, since apparently that's her actual skill set?"

Alanna scowled. "I'm still mad at her."

"Mad enough to make her do spreadsheets so we can go adventuring?"

". . . yes," she said stoically.

"Okay." James steered them toward the door. "Fifteen minutes before this closes. Rufus and Ganesh are in the pack and everyone's out, so let's go see if we can discreetly invite Team Two to dinner without anyone catching on. And Dave. And, I guess, under duress, JP. Happy?"

Alanna stopped smirking at him. "Yup!" she said cheerfully, entirely unaffected by James's weirdly soured view of tonight's dungeon delve.

It wasn't until an hour later, after everyone had gotten to their cars, after he'd reassured Theo no one was dead, after he'd texted Sarah that no one was dead and invited her to pancakes, after the cameras were back on and the dungeon sealed and their scavenged candy and orbs and whatever else packed away, that James's brain clicked on what the problem was. Sitting in a large booth at their local twenty-five-hour diner with a few chairs pulled around for the people who didn't quite fit, JP had just commented to Sarah that it was a pretty good haul for six hours of work.

"Oh, fuck," James said, tossing his ensyruped fork down.

"What?" Alanna and Anesh instantly looked over to him, concerned.

"This turned into a *job*."

There was a silence that seemed to stretch through the entire building. Even the waitstaff taking orders a few tables down seemed to pause.

Then the laughter hit him like a waterfall.

CHAPTER 8

"James!" The call went out through the home. Alanna's voice startled Anesh and Ganesh, who were absorbed in some project on the table, woke up Sarah, woke up *Secret*, who apparently slept now, and then made its way to James. Sarah just rolled over and pulled the blankets over her head like a cocoon, while Anesh blinked twice, realized he wasn't implicated in this, and went back to work. Which left only a dog that didn't care and an oblivious boyfriend to pay attention to Alanna's call.

A boyfriend who was wearing headphones and ignored it. Or rather, didn't hear it.

"James," Alanna repeated, having stalked down the hallway, past the new batch of salvaged motivational posters that covered up the fist holes from that time a stuffed shirt raided the apartment—"Embrace the Efficient Totality," this one said—past Anesh's old room, which was now Sarah's room, past Sarah's old room, which was now empty, and through the door to their shared bedroom. She stood behind James, hands holding his headphones perfectly hovering near his head. "James," she repeated.

"Yeeeees?" James drawled out, rotating in his chair and promptly getting his ponytail tangled in the headphone cord. "Ah, fuck, dammit. Why?!" He struggled for a second as Alanna handed him back the headphones and he took a second to pull his hair out of it. "What's up?" he asked while extricating himself.

Alanna smothered the wide grin she was wearing as she watched him. "Oh! There's, like, fifteen damn greens on the shelf out there?"

"Um . . ." James bit his lip, eyebrow raised. "That isn't really a question? You said it like one, where it goes up at the end, but I don't know what you want."

"*Why* are there fifteen greens on the shelf?"

"Oh! I'm saving them." James honestly hadn't made the connection, so he was relieved to have an answer to give. Unfortunately, that wasn't actually the question that Alanna wasn't asking.

She rolled her eyes. "No, I get that. But *why* are you saving them? Just use them on the apartment!"

"We're getting an office soon, though. Or, well, no. We're getting industrial-commercial flex space, which is actually just a fancy way of saying that we're getting a warehouse with some carpet and a bathroom. But still, I was gonna use them there and see if we could get, I dunno, training perks or something," James explained.

Alanna sat down on the bed, letting her muscles relax as she transformed a sit into a sprawl. It had been a few days since their delve, but she'd still exerted herself a lot more than normal during it. Hauling, running, occasionally punching, all of it strenuous work for a person, no matter how many muscles they packed on. And all of that took its toll in sore arms and legs and a desire to lay down on anything with enough cushions. "Training perks?" she eventually asked, staring at the ceiling.

"If we're lucky." James shrugged, having fully disentangled himself and tossed the headphones on the desk. "I'm thinking something like, I dunno, faster muscle mass development. Or maybe a percentage buff to learning martial arts!"

"Does it ever do percentages? I don't think I've seen one, and you guys' notes don't have any, either." She spoke with confidence, because Alanna was the kind of person who read the notes. Twice. Maybe more if she needed to be sure. "Also, that first one, wouldn't that just cause more damage from using muscles? You know that's how your body builds muscle mass, right?"

James stood, stretched, and then flopped face first onto the bed next to her. The collective upgrade to a king-size mattress was, he decided, one of the best uses of their ill-gotten loot so far. "Yes, I am aware of how muscles happen. Also, you have absolutely seen percentage buffs. The reduced entropy in the apartment is one. And so far, we have *no fucking clue* what that actually did." He tried to shrug, but it got absorbed by the pile of thick blankets instead. "I'm assuming it's fine, though, since it's not killing us."

"As far . . ."

"Yes, as far as we know, *thank you!*"

"Just making sure you have a healthy fear of anything that might be prepared to murder us," Alanna said cheerfully.

James snorted into a pillow. "Thanks. Just what I need. Anyway, I'm still saving the greens. I talked to Sarah about this the other day, actually; I kind of like where our apartment has ended up, you know? And I'm afraid that if we pile too many things on, it'll lose its magic."

"You talked to me about this, too, ya know." Alanna smiled at him, turning to face James as the two lay side by side. "You keep forgetting stuff like that."

"Ah, but I might forget ten percent less while I'm here!" he countered with a grin and an energetically raised index finger. "That's the other thing. It'd be easier to move to a new base space than it would be to move our home. At least, I think it would. In case an orb does something actively problematic."

"Fair enough." Alanna nodded. "Anyway. It's almost two p.m. I know it's your weekend, and I don't have a job anymore. What're we doing today? I'm not spending my whole Friday trying to make the living room functional, especially not when Anesh is out there doing some kind of Frankensteinian experiment with delicate electronics."

"I want to know," James said sagely. "But I also don't want to know?"

"It's a weird feeling," Alanna agreed. "Want to see if Sarah wants to go get dinner? I could eat Thai."

"You say that literally every time." James laughed.

Alanna tapped her fingers against his forehead. "I'm keeping my options open!" she said. "Also, seriously, I need to do something not dungeony today. Just something normal."

"We tried that once. It didn't work. But I suppose I could postpone my plans of watching hour-long video essays on deep reads of the themes in Fallout to get some food and walk around a bit, sure." James rolled off the bed, coincidentally rolling over Alanna in the process, who let out a peal of laughter and tried to turn the motion into pinning James to the floor as both of them fell off the end of the bed in a tangle of limbs. James had a sudden appreciation for Anesh's presence in the room, because a few months ago, his floor would have been covered in random assorted stuff that could easily have broken, or broken him, as he toppled to the ground. But his new, more literal roommate was the fastidious sort. And so, instead of a random CD case or a discarded fast food bag, he got his nose rubbed into vacuumed carpet.

The two of them froze as the sound of clapping filled the room. Looking up sheepishly, they saw a sleepy-looking Sarah and an amused-looking Anesh standing there in the doorway, watching their antics. Well, Alanna looked up; James did what he could and raised his eyes. "Mmet me uff," he muttered at Alanna, who seemed to suddenly remember she was holding him down and obliged.

"And Alanna wins by pin and count out!" Sarah announced, voice groggy. "The crowd goes wild!" Next to her, Anesh made hushed cheering noises. "You two done?" she asked with a smile.

"Never!" Alanna responded, followed shortly by, "Except for right now. Do you feel like curry?"

"I feel like a shower," Sarah replied. "Dunno why I slept so long."

"Nonsense fatigue," James said, and then explained to the group of people throwing huhs his way. "Like, when your life is too weird, there's this actual thing that happens to humans where our brains just stop being capable of caring and just tell us to take a nap and wait for it to all blow over."

"That is super weird," Anesh commented. "Also, why do you know that?"

James scoffed at him. "Please. I have access to Wikipedia and a lot of free time at work. It's also not called that, but I forget the real name. Now! Let me up, and let's go get food."

For a brief period, the mundanity of the life of friends getting ready to leave their apartment took over. James flopped on the couch and poked around the internet on his phone while Anesh got changed and Sarah showered. Alanna fiddled around trying to do minor cleaning of their kitchen while they just waited a bit and only gave James a *little* bit of casual ribbing for the pile of green orbs still sitting on the shelf. One Anesh, then the other one, petted the dog and reassured her that they'd be back. But in short order, the five of them—both Aneshes needed to eat, after all—were out the door and on a short walk to the nearby Thai place. Then two of them, who wished to remain nameless, ducked back inside to grab coats, because even though it had been a hot year, mid-October had still decided it would be a chilly day. Bright, but windy.

And for that short twenty-minute walk, James was a normal person again. They talked about books they'd been reading, or conversations they'd had on the internet, or, if they were Alanna, somewhat broad plans for a large-scale political system that took advantage of modern technology. Because Alanna.

Despite the fact that it was only for a few hours every week, and not even most weeks for the last month, James had been feeling like he'd had armor on almost nonstop. He could still feel the weight of it, even now, which was frustrating. And this last delve had been *exhausting*. Not just because it came at the tail end of a day at a job he still hated, not just because he had all these other people to take responsibility for, not just because he hadn't really . . . slept . . . at all. But just because he felt like he had fully committed his life to this one hole in reality, and that was all he was now. Like a unit in a tactics game, his hobbies and relaxation and comfort had taken a back seat to being deployed across the country to hunt for dungeons, or being sent out to buy bulk road flares and football padding, or, you know, actually getting into fights with bizarre monsters that were trying to kill him and turn him into orbs.

So he savored this pleasant evening of just being with friends.

Right up until they got seated at the table, and Sarah segued into, "So, what are you working on that has a whole engineering department covering our table, anyway?"

"No, no!" James protested weakly. "One dinner! Just one dinner without dungeon stuff!"

One Anesh patted him on the arm reassuringly, while the other turned to answer Sarah. "Sorry, friend," the first said to James, while his counterpart started explaining. "It's a drone interface for the skulljacks. James gave me the idea the other day, and I wanted to see if I could build one that had a little more flexibility to it."

"Wait, this is my fault? Again?" James peeked over the menu he was hiding behind.

"Yeah, sorry, mate." Anesh grinned sheepishly. "It was the whole ice cream thing. I had wanted to have this for the delve the other night, but we didn't have the capital for more scout drones. Honestly, scouting is the biggest thing we need to worry about, and it would really help, especially if we could have people literally able to see through the cameras."

"That big of a deal?" Alanna asked, the traitor.

"Well, James and I were talking about mapping as much as we could the other day. Since the dungeon changed its landscape, we want to be able to cross-reference for more changes," Anesh answered.

James sighed and leaned back in the chair. "Okay, okay, I'm resigned to this. Yeah, the problem is that it stuck that tower right in the middle of the entry." He gave a brief explanation to Sarah, which turned into a round of storytelling from all of them as they went over small highlights of the ascension. Culminating in him and Anesh getting really excited about the potential of the clone machine.

"We can copy ammunition," James pointed out. "No more paying for the overpriced bullets for the guns Anesh got!"

"We could copy better guns . . ." Alanna suggested dryly. Alanna was, out of all of them, the best defined as a gun person. She didn't really like guns, but she knew how to shoot. Her dad had been a cop, after all, and he'd taken his daughter's interest in his job seriously enough to take her to the shooting range with him fairly often. Alanna had just enough of a developed sense of taste in firepower to be annoyed with the choice of PS90s from Anesh. "Also we could copy something *reasonable*? Guns and ammo are . . . We can just buy those, guys."

"Well, you *obviously* need to see if it can clone dungeon items," Sarah offered. "Is that on the list already? I assume you have a list." Anesh absolutely had a list.

"We could make copies of people!" James excitedly said. "Like, I dunno about you guys, but I'm enough of a transhumanist that I'm into the idea of having backups of myself." Sarah and Alanna made tight-lipped eye contact with him and then slowly and silently raised their hands to point at the pair of Aneshes sitting at the table with them. "Okay, okay, fine, yes. But that's different. That's an Anesh thing. I'm talking about a thing for all of us, mostly me. Something reproducible."

Alanna sipped at her water, looking around to see if a waiter was planning to come by. The restaurant wasn't too busy, but so far, no serving staff had prowled across the hardwood floors to see if any of them were ready to order. "What's it like?" she casually asked Anesh. "Being two people. I've been meaning to actually ask you for a long time. Like, I'm pretty sure James and I are cool with it?" A raised eyebrow to James got a nod in return. "Yeah, we're cool with it. And I know you can make more of yourself, too, but what does it actually *feel* like?"

"Like being me," Anesh said. They were on what James's nerd brain had automatically labeled Twin Protocol, where they took turns speaking in paragraphs instead of one sentence at a time or occasionally saying things in unison. "I mean, I'm still the same person, right? It's just that there's two sets of experiences. Kind of. Not really. Okay, I'm a bit bad at this but . . . how much do you remember about yesterday?"

Yesterday, for James, had been a weekend. When prompted, he could easily remember sleeping in, having a noonish breakfast of mostly bacon, getting roped into browsing Amazon for an hour looking for wireless cameras, and then taking a walk to the coffee shop at around eleven p.m. "A lot of it," he ended up telling Anesh.

"Great. How about two days ago? Or three?" Anesh pressed.

"Oh, easy! Three days ago was dungeon stuff." James almost laughed, until his brain caught up to what he'd said. "Ooh ho! No, wait! That was four days, wasn't it? I . . . don't have a clue. I guess I was at work?"

"Exactly," Anesh said. "You don't remember what specific day we climbed the tower, but you remember that we did it. As evidenced by the exhaustive detail you just dumped on poor Sarah." He shot her a pair of sympathetic sets of puppy eyes.

Sarah swatted at him. "Oh, shush, you dork. I don't mind."

Half the table laughed, and Anesh grinned as he wrapped up his point. "Thing is, you might remember what you did, but our brains don't usually categorize things by days. It's why James can't tell you what chapter anything happens in in whatever book he's reading, but he can recite the whole plot word for word. It's the same thing. When we reconnect, we basically just update things we've done, and the fact that the timeline doesn't line up . . . doesn't matter. Because it doesn't matter anyway. I'm just living twice as many days."

"This would be a literal nightmare without the skulljacks," Alanna told him bluntly.

"Oh, probably. We'd drift over time and eventually be different people. But that wouldn't be too bad. I can't see any future where I'm, like, a villain." Anesh stroked his chin. "I'd need a goatee."

"Can you grow a goatee?" James smiled as he tried to imagine it. "That could be kinda hot. You'd look like a Bollywood actor!"

"What in the world would you even pretend to know about Bollywood?" Anesh rolled his eyes at James.

James cracked his knuckles over the table, stretching out his arms with a low groan at the lingering soreness that he turned into the reply of "Ohhh, I dunno. What do *you* pretend to know about it? I'll steal that."

"So, Anesh!" Sarah chimed in, cutting off James's satisfaction at his cultural appropriation burn. "Any luck finding a new dungeon?"

Anesh swirled the chunks of ice in the bottom of his cup before idly trading for a full cup from Other Anesh, who was more hydrated than he was. The version not currently drinking spoke up to answer Sarah. "Turns out, it's awful and I hate it. I think so far, the biggest argument against the idea of the Wizard Police is that it would be bloody impossible to spot any of this stuff. I did a second sweep of older spots that I was *sure* about, and I'm still pretty damn sure that shopping mall in Tennessee is either a dungeon or haunted, but it's so hard to pin them down."

"Doors!" Alanna exclaimed. "Time limits! Weird conditions we don't know about!" She slapped the table, briefly drawing the attention of nearby diners. "We need interns. An army of interns! No, what's the plurality for interns?"

"An internment? No, too close, and horrible. An exploitation?" James mused.

"A café," Sarah said and giggled while everyone else caught up to the joke.

"We have interns, though," James said. "We have, like, thirty people who didn't fully get their lives back that we're employing. Use them."

"We really don't have the money for that." Anesh winced. "We need briefcases. Badly. Like, I was hoping for at least one this week. We didn't even meet our operational expenses, if we count support for the victims."

"Shit." James grimaced himself. "We could . . . and I hate to offer this, but we could go through the vent again. Fight our way to the door, collect enough cash that way?"

"Hard pass," Alanna told him. "Not unless you can convince me there's someone to rescue again. And *last time* that put us more in the red, not out of it."

"Okay. We need to make money, then," Sarah said, shrugging. "I'm sure we can do that."

"How?" several people asked at once.

She looked at them in surprise. "Haven't you all been cracking orbs this whole time? Sooner or later, you hit a marketable skill that you can use to make some extra cash."

There was a round of slow blinks as everyone thought about what they had access to.

"I'm not sure my sweet snowboarding tricks will get me cash," Alanna commented. "Or Anesh's . . . longbow skills? Am I remembering that right?"

"Yeah, that's me. I've also got a huge chunk of high-level math and furniture appraisal. That seems like a dead end." Anesh frowned. "James? Anything you can remember?"

It was actually kind of hard. The skills given by the orbs were always ready to kick into high gear, but they were almost always divorced from context. For a normal human who'd learned how to fish, the thought of fishing might be tied to memories of going on road trips with their mom, of the smell of the bait shop, of dirt roads and paddle boats. But with an orb, you *knew how to fish* and nothing else. If you weren't fishing, it wouldn't come to mind. So it was hard to keep a mental inventory.

Which was, of course, why Anesh had a written one. Somewhere. For now, James just had to think. "First of all, I think you're selling short how much money you can make off snowboarding tricks." He pointed at Alanna, and then at Anesh. "Or off going on *Antiques Roadshow*. Or, you know, *being a math tutor*. I just thought of that, though, so maybe I shouldn't say it in that tone that's accusatory, sorry." He let the words loll out of his mouth. "As for me, um . . . card counting? Cooking could get me a job, but I already have a job. I could be a very specific car mechanic, or I could manufacture LSD. Oh! That reminds me!"

"*That* reminds you?" Sarah gave him an incredulous look.

"Yes! That orange I got on the exodus run gave me a military rank. I wanted to see if it was possible for me to get paid for that." James nodded.

"Okay, first of all." Anesh steepled his fingers as both of him leaned in, lowering their voices. "I feel like maybe you shouldn't talk so loudly about making drugs in a restaurant. Even if we do seem to have been forgotten." He glanced around, trying to grab the attention of a waitress.

James had a stray thought hit his brain. "Is this . . . are we forgotten? Is this Secret being mad at us for leaving him alone at home with Aberdeen?"

"No. This just happens when the bar here is busy," Anesh reprimanded him. "Probably. Anyway. You're in a military?"

"Yup. US Air Force." James nodded. "Not really sure how to use that, though. I also haven't gotten deployment orders or anything, so I'm pretty sure that they don't think I'm AWOL."

Alanna facepalmed. "James," she said slowly. "I'm pretty sure active military members can buy restricted firearms. You may need some checks first, but I'm almost certain that you can."

"What, really?" He looked surprised. "Honestly, I was pretty busy, so I kinda forgot to check."

"Yes, really." Alanna sighed. "Also, you really need to check in with . . . I actually don't know, but somewhere. Before you *do* get arrested. Assuming that can happen. Does anyone know if the oranges give responsibilities along with legal status?" She directed that question at Sarah, who just shrugged and made a low noise of uncertainty in her throat. "Great."

Sarah interrupted with a question that James had brought to mind. "Hey, why *do* you still work there? I quit as soon as the dungeon started paying my bills back when I was a delver."

"That makes you sound super old," James said. "Like a scarred veteran adventurer. Holy shit, you can be our cloaked figure in the corner of the tavern!"

"Nah, I don't look good in a cloak." Sarah smiled at him. "Anyway. Job?"

"I feel like I owe Theo a lot," he explained. "And also, it's extra income. And also, it's kind of . . . okay, have you ever heard the line 'my job would be great if I could leave whenever I wanted'?"

"Sort of. Where's that from?" Anesh asked him.

James pointed to himself. "Me. I say that. Anyway, it's that. I can quit literally at my leisure, and the dungeon will still be open to us. Though the enhanced security is a bit of a pain. But we've got the skills and resources to just . . . ignore it, mostly. But I see no reason to bother quitting. What would I do? Lounge around all day and get mad at RimWorld mod conflicts?"

"I don't know what that means," Alanna told him. "But you could have some time to yourself. Worry less about being caught up forever in dungeony things."

James just shrugged at her. "I mean, it also keeps the money coming in," he restated. "Which we *do* need right now. Though there's a horrifying gap between my hourly wage and what we need to support the dozens of people that need us. And speaking of things we need money for, does anyone want to split an appetizer when we finally get noticed? Maybe some pot stickers?"

"Can we back up," Anesh said. "To the part where James can make LSD?"

"Oh, yeah! Super good at it, too!" James gave a wide smile. "Can't believe we haven't tried being drug dealers yet." He sat back in his chair with a smug look on his face.

Alanna let out a low hum. "Honestly, why not? LSD isn't actually that harmful to people. And it's shown to be pretty effective in combating depression in the right dosage, which . . ." She cut off as she made eye contact with James.

"Yeeeah," he said, letting out a huff of breath. "I'm still not super okay with the idea that depression might actually be a knock-on effect of dungeon antimemes. But that . . . actually, hang on!" He snapped his fingers, and Alanna figured out where he was going at the same time, sitting forward with wide eyes.

"Holy shit, LSD is a mnestic!" she burst out.

"Wat," Sarah and Anesh said simultaneously.

"A mnestic is something that makes you remember," James explained. "So, if LSD fights depression, what if it does so by causing 'hallucinations' that are actually memories of people they know?"

"That is . . . a bloody *massive* logical leap," Anesh said diplomatically. "I'm not willing to buy it. And not enough to get me to entertain the production of absurdly illegal controlled substances."

"It's the fact that they're mostly harmless that makes me okay with it. *Though* Alanna did say 'mostly,' and I don't know enough to say otherwise," Sarah said. "Also, if it does work the way Alanna thinks it does . . ." She trailed off, and everyone already knew what she was going to say.

"Yup," James said casually, breaking the awkward quiet. "So! What now? Plans for world domination? Anyone get anything good from their orbs?" Alanna and Anesh both dodged eye contact with him. "No, no. You did *not* give me crap for saving mine when you didn't even use yours!" he accused Alanna.

"I'm saving the yellows to trade to the first tree we find!" she argued. "I just . . . think the purples are better." Alanna crossed her not-insubstantial arms in front of her as a conversational shield. "Fight me."

"Nah, that's a good reason." James grinned. "What about you, oh auspicious boyfriend? What's your reason?"

"I got distracted," Anesh muttered. "I thought I found a new dungeon and then I had classes and . . . I just got sidetracked."

"Okay, now *that's* funny," Alanna said.

Sarah ruffled Alanna's hair. "Oh, be nice," she said with a grin, playing peacemaker. "Besides, it's easy to forget some of the smaller ones. I actually just found one of the level ones in an old pair of jeans the other day."

"Get anything good from it?" James asked, as Anesh also leaned forward with interest, tapping up his note app on his phone.

Sarah just smiled. "Chemical composition of shampoo. Bad news! Shampoo is weird!"

"See, that's what happens when you just use 'em right away." Alanna stated it like it was a concrete fact, even though she was mostly talking out her ass.

Sarah snorted in reply. "All right, laugh it up. You guys can all get to use your toys on your own time."

"Toys?!" James exclaimed. "I will have you know these are the hard-won spoils of war!"

"And?"

"And don't mess with my toys."

The collective laughter at James's indignant face finally got the waiter to show up.

CHAPTER 9

Lorian Bulregard was, above all else, a bit of a prick. At least, that was what James had decided about the Phi Delta Theta brother seated across the table from him. He was almost a comical stereotype of a prick, really: slicked back hair that was a little too greasy, a generic tough-guy tattoo visible on his arm, a weasel grin that made James think the dude was constantly mocking everyone else in the room. He'd insisted everyone call him Tyr and claimed it was a middle name, which another brother had privately informed James was a bald-faced lie. He also kept insisting he *totally wasn't racist, you guys* but that he'd never date anyone who wasn't the right bloodline. Just a real piece of work. And he was *exactly* the sort of asshole that attritioned other players out of the semipublic house party poker game every Saturday night with his mom's money.

Which was actually sort of relevant to how James had come to be sitting across from him with roughly five thousand of his dollars in a neat pile.

As it turned out, James's previously acquired skill at card counting was almost impossibly powerful. Like, he was what Hollywood thought card counters were. The only problem was, it didn't give him any actual ability to bluff or even understand poker that well. He'd gotten a crash course from JP, who *of course* was a card sharp himself, before they'd come here.

JP knew people. James had been vaguely aware of that for a while; he knew JP was outgoing, that he was involved with multiple different social circles. But he didn't really understand that JP was networked like this. When James had casually mentioned funding operations through gambling, and specifically cheating at gambling, it had taken JP two phone calls and ten minutes to get the two of them an open invite to a party and knowledge of the buy-in to the game going on in the basement.

It had taken him less than that long once they arrived to introduce James to four people, all of whom James had already forgotten by the end of the sentence, before sweeping James down the stairs to where their quarry waited. And under a minute, with a couple quiet comments and a smile that just oozed "trust me" to get James and himself seated at the table, their buy-in arranged before them in chip form.

"My buddy here," JP had told them, "is better at this than I am. And I am *tired* of letting you all walk away with my money unscathed!"

He'd laughed, they'd laughed, and even James had broken his nerves enough to give a sociable chuckle. And then, the game had begun.

It didn't take long for James to realize that this really was a game to these people. They were, mostly, rich kids. Having fun with their parents' money, not really concerned about the fact that the cost to be at this table was a half year of rent for someone like James. But they'd never think that, because JP had James in disguise as the kind of person who wore a blazer everywhere. The worst part, to James's eyes, was that many of them weren't even *bad people*. Just these perfectly insulated dorks who wanted to have friends and be respected and thought that money was just one of those things people had. It was kind of impressive to him that JP could be friends with people like this, but then, JP also took a break after the first few hands to go talk to literally anyone else, so maybe they weren't best buds, anyway.

None of that made it a challenge for him to take their money away from them. Tactically or emotionally. Oh, it took him a few hands to get his feet under him, to remember the tricks JP had taught him. But once he had that most basic groundwork, he also had a skill burning a conceptual hole in his mind as it churned on overdrive. Card counting, he'd learned, was easiest with blackjack. But they weren't playing blackjack; they were playing Texas Hold'em, and that made it more complex. Not *harder*, but just more lines of light in his thoughts as his rank in card counting blazed answers to him.

He'd been dealt two aces. There were six cards left in the deck, because they weren't really playing that seriously. Mike, to his right, had raised hard, which probably meant he had a pair himself. There was a limited number of pairs left available. Only three of the options had a third or fourth mate left in the deck to be revealed. Aces were one of them. The odds that someone else had an ace were about forty percent. The odds that Mike had an ace dropped dramatically when he raised, and James's odds went up. Five of the six remaining cards left would be flipped over. That was a greater than eighty percent chance of the last ace, assuming it was there, and an assured victory. If, that is, no one was holding it. James let himself approximate. His skill gave him the odds, but putting them together took math he had to do himself, and social deduction that he fed into the engine of his magic. Twentyish percent chance someone had it, multiplied by eighty percent of it being on the table, meant sixty-four percent of an unbeatable hand. His card-counting skill also informed him that roughly twelve percent of the other available outcomes favored his victory but were dependent on what random chance had dealt his foes.

He raised a thousand dollars. Every other person at the table laughed and matched.

The ace hit the table in the flop. And that was it. No struggle, no tricks. Just pure math, rolling the dice, and the win was his. Of course, now, James had a whole new game to play. And that game was called "bait Lorian Bulregard."

He didn't have a skill orb for it, but he liked to think that this was more of a personal calling.

"So, Lorian!" James cheerfully puffed his breath to clear some of the heavy cigar smoke out of the air over the table. "How's it feel to be about to tap out?"

"Ha! As if I'd just walk away. There's always the option to buy back in, my boy," the pompous prick replied.

James nodded sagely, ignoring being called "my boy" by someone who was younger than him. "Right, right. After all, I've got *allllll* your money here"—he circled his hands over his growing stash—"it would be such a shame if it got lonely, away from its friends. Especially since this is gonna be my last hand, and it'll be gone forever."

"I do believe he's trying to taunt you," one of the other frat brothers said in a New England accent that was weirdly out of place on the West Coast.

"Oh, absolutely!" James told them. "Is it working?" The three players who weren't fans of Tyr-No-Really-It's-a-Middle-Name laughed boisterously, a sound that came across to James's ears as weirdly hollow. The one guy who seemed to be Lorian's friend just glared at James. A look with so much blatant disgust in it that he was feeling a serious longing for the dungeon and the much more honest combat therein.

But it was working. Loath to let any of his money go to someone like James, Lorian raised. James matched it, and the fourth card was flipped. It changed nothing, James had already won.

"Is that all?" James mocked the pot. "You won't even win back what I've already got from you! Come on, man, go big! You can do it!"

Lorian eyed James's reckless smile for a few seconds, perhaps thinking himself the dramatic hero at the climax of the night's story. "You're *bluffing*," he accused.

"Maybe," James said, showing teeth.

"What do you have? Total." He leaned over for a quick count, and James had to give him an unfortunate amount of credit. He might have been a gross, racist asshole, but he wasn't stupid enough to not know how to count. "All right. I'll be *nice* to you." He let the word drip off his lips like sludge. "Raise everything you've got left. Twenty-eight thousand and four hundred."

James froze briefly. Just for a second. But it was noticed, and it put an almost cruel smile on Lorian's face. He was, for that moment, the predator who had just sprung his trap.

Of course, again, James had already won.

Still, that didn't always get through to his brain. And the prospect of having not just the night's winnings taken away, but also the money that he'd borrowed from the delver fund, from JP, and from his own savings account, made him hesitate.

Then he remembered. But he decided to play it out anyway. "You don't have that many chips," he pointed out, aiming to make his voice sound just the right level of desperate.

"I'll buy more," Lorian said with a flip of his hand. "Or just write you a check. If my credit is good to you?"

James eyed him. "Check. If that's allowed." He glanced around at the others at the table, who just shrugged. Most of them had already folded anyway. They didn't care about the rules; rules always took a back seat to a good show. And no matter how this show went, it would be funny.

It didn't take the slimeball long to pull out his checkbook—who kept their checkbook *in their coat pocket?*—and write it out with long, looping script from the personalized, etched-gold pen he carried. Every single detail of this guy that James had seen tonight just made him hate the man more.

"Is that to your satisfaction?"

"Yup," James said simply, shoving his whole pool into the center of the table. "At the risk of being a casino-movie cliché, all in."

They flipped the last card. Lorian gave a wide, sneering grin. "Ha! Two pair! Kings and sixes. Now, let's see what you bluffed with."

"Three aces." James didn't hesitate. He *was* having fun, but something about the way this guy and his goon were acting had him on edge. "Sorry, friend," he said with a pitying look. "Bluffing is hard to do when you're busy counting all your money." *Dammit, brain, keep the zingers inside for just five minutes,* James chastised himself.

But for all that he was worried about someone trying something, no one did. There was a round of cheers and jeers as he swept his swollen pile of loot toward himself, both for and against him. But mostly, just because it was a hell of a show for the rest of the people at the table and those watching the game. James politely excused himself, cashed out the chips with the person running the whole night, stacked the neat bundles of hundreds into his messenger bag, lied a promise to come back next week, found JP, and rushed them the hell out of there.

"Well, that was fun!" JP said with a grin.

"Of course you had fun. You sipped knockoff champagne with rich kids while I had to do aggressive math at people who could destroy my credit rating by asking nicely."

"Ah, but did it work?" JP asked, suddenly serious for a moment despite his present tipsy feeling.

James didn't respond until he'd glanced around and made sure no one was within earshot as they made their way out the front door of the house and down the street to where they'd parked. "I have sixty thousand dollars in my bag," he said flatly, his heart hammering in his ears. "And it wasn't even a challenge. How the hell do people play this game professionally? I'm terrified that someone's going to come out and shoot at me."

"James, this isn't a mobster movie." JP refrained valiantly from rolling his eyes.

"Tell that to the guy leaning on my car smoking," James commented, causing JP to whip his head forward before relaxing with a disgruntled huff as he realized there was no one there and James was messing with him.

"Don't do that," he said as they climbed into James's beat-up old Subaru, a harsh contrast to all the Teslas lining the city side road. "Besides, you're underestimating these guys. The ones that play here aren't the normal frat guys. They're the kids of tech start-up gurus and investment bankers, and they literally do not understand money. These are people who have family members abusing the 'the first twenty-eight thousand in gifts has no tax' law. You don't need to worry about fleecing them for a little bit."

"Is *this* why I've never seen you work, but you always pay for your own food? Wait, hang on, are you a con artist?" James blinked, clicking his tongue as he navigated them onto the highway to head back home to suburbia.

JP grinned at him, answering without words.

"All right. All right, that's insane. How long has this been going on? Wait, wait, no, I remember back in high school, there was that time someone just brought lunch to you, and you never explained it. Have you ever paid for anything in your life?" James mused. "Never mind, don't answer that. Also, speaking of twenty-eight thousand, who the hell is that Lorian guy? He was way too easy to bait into the double-or-nothing deal."

"Ah, Tyr. Yeah, he's . . ."

"Noooo. Don't call him that."

JP snorted a snicker. "Right. Well, his dad's an oil exec, and his mom's a political lobbyist. I don't think he's ever had contact with reality. He's not even from here; he's a member of the fraternity's chapter at Princeton. He comes by because he likes the big fish, small pond thing."

"And he's a Nazi." James nodded knowingly.

"What? No! He's . . ." JP paused, then tapped his chin with a single finger, staring up at the ceiling upholstery. "Okay, in some ways . . . no, goddammit, you're right. Does that make you feel better about taking his money?"

"I took a *lot* of his money." James smiled toothily. "That's sorta what worries me. Like, when the skill kicked in, I knew, *knew* that it was just a matter of time, and my estimated value was positive. No matter what, I was going to win more than I lost in the long run. And some hands, like that last one, I just could not lose. So I ended up winning—maybe enough that I was worried he might try to murder me?"

"Nah. He wouldn't do that. He might be rich, but he can still be arrested."

James gave JP a sideways look with pursed lips and raised eyebrows.

"Okay, fine!" JP relented. "Your anarcho-socialist worldview is probably accurate, and he could have you murdered! But he *won't*, because this was me calling in a few favors, and even if he's mad, it won't happen again."

"Aw, I don't get to do this next week?" James pouted.

"Sorry, my dude," JP told him. "A few people owed me, which is how you, an unaffiliated rando, got a seat at a moderate-stakes backroom poker game. And while I make a point to collect favors, that only goes so far. So next time you need to make some quick cash, you're gonna have to go get kicked out of a casino."

"Got it," James said. "So, you're the group's Face, then."

"What?"

"Like from *The A-Team*. Or Shadowrun. Or . . . lots of things, probably. I'm the bard, Alanna's the paladin, Anesh is the rogue, and Rufus and Ganesh together form the wizard. You're the face, and Dave is inexplicably the lead character from *Beastmaster*." James ticked off fingers on the leather of the steering wheel as he ran through the group.

JP pressed his eyes closed in exasperation, rubbing at his forehead as they made their way down the dark streets toward the apartment. "I want to be mad at you for this, but now all I can think of is Dave with shoulder-length hair and pecs, and it's really throwing off my game."

"You're welcome!" James smiled.

And that was how his weekend ended. With a small joke, and a bag full of rolls of cash.

Alanna woke up at the normal human hour of nine a.m. And so, out of vague guilt and bleed-through motivation, so did James. Anesh had already left for classes, one of him going to sit in a small room for a summer class with six other people and a teacher who knew more math than James knew existed, the other one going to tutor students in trigonometry as a favor for a different professor. Neither of them was worried that anyone would figure out they were the same person, though James had his concerns.

The affair of waking up had changed dramatically for James when his relationship had begun. Once they'd sorted out exactly what they were doing and made sure in the weeks following the Big Rescue that they actually wanted to be *together* together, there had been some modifications to their living situation.

Alanna had moved in, for one. Even with Secret sleeping in the bonus closet that there physically wasn't room for in the apartment, there was still enough extra space in there for a dresser and some personal effects. And Alanna lived light, so fitting her into the place wasn't a problem at all. Anesh, similarly, had kept most of his room intact, but shifted his sleeping spot from his own bed to James's. The idea had been floated of selling or storing his bed and just using that extra room as an office of sorts. Or, at least, a place to put all their desks and computers. But they'd been busy.

"We were busy" was kind of their unofficial relationship motto, really.

The real change had been the small, quiet moments. Waking up wasn't something to groan at and roll back into the covers for anymore—at least, in a nonjoking way. Now, for James, waking up was a gradual thing that started when his partners began to stir, and was . . . warmer, was how he would describe it.

Small touches exchanged with them as they got out of bed, or he did. A small rub of the shoulder, a ruffling of Anesh's hair or scratching the back of Alanna's neck as they rose. Or, in Alanna's case, grabbing either of their butts when James or Anesh tried to get up. Short, quiet sentences exchanged about what they were planning for the day, or when they would be home. A kind of mild coordination that kept any of them from worrying about each other too much. And then, dozing back into a pleasant snooze, with a lingering feeling of skin contact and love.

Or, sometimes, instead, it was getting up with Alanna to go jogging.

"Uuuugggggh." James arced his arms overhead and managed to avoid the critical error of letting himself fall backward into the blankets and pillows. "How do humans get up this early?"

"Well, most of us don't go to bed at three a.m.," Alanna told him with the hint of a grin on her face.

"First off, I work night shift," James reminded her. "So having my eyes open at all is kind of impressive right now. Admire me."

"Oh, I am." She wiggled her eyebrows at his shirtless self while James hunted for clean socks.

James flipped an absolutely-not-clean sock over his shoulder at her. "Bah. Also, I was up late last night because I was busy taking candy, and money, from rich college students. That should earn me a pass anyway."

"I wasn't judging you anyway. You don't actually need to come with me, you know," Alanna told him, giving him a hug from behind while he stood at his dresser.

"Yeah, but it's a thing. I wanna have more things with you guys, you know? Shared routines and stuff. I can be tired for that. Also, the apartment has extra time for sleeping, so I'm not actually *that* tired." He reminded her of the green orb he half remembered from what felt like years ago, which had added an hour to the apartment's timeline that could only be used for sleep. No one was really clear on when that hour occurred, though, so James just chose to believe he was waking up more rested than otherwise possible, and it seemed to be working.

The two of them finished their wake-up routines in companionable quiet, getting dressed, grabbing a piece of fruit or a fig bar for breakfast, brushing teeth for Alanna and scoffing at the taste of toothpaste this early for James. And then, the weird part of what was becoming their morning-jog routine, a cup of coffee.

The coffee machine was magic. This much was beyond reproach. And it showed, amazingly, no signs of deteriorating or losing its touch. A single cup of its miracle juice could push a human's reflexes to the edge of the possible and make their speed match. More, and you could cross that line into something that shouldn't realistically be a thing a human could ever do. *Too* much coffee and you passed out until the mystic caffeine burned out of your system.

This was probably their greatest dungeon-delving tool, but they hadn't been using it properly at all.

So, James had suggested, and Alanna had agreed, that their morning jogs should be under the influence of the coffee. Both to get into the habit of remembering it existed, and also to acclimate themselves to how they could move while it was in their blood.

Because, yes, it made you faster, and sharper. But it didn't give you the experience that came from a lifetime of moving in your own body, normally. So, they trained themselves to feel not just powerful with their buff but comfortable. For James, especially, this was important, because one of the purple orbs that James had acquired toward the end of their Big Rescue was one that boosted his acceleration.

And boy, was that one vague.

What it *meant*, he'd eventually figured out with some math help from Anesh, was that his acceleration in a given direction had a sort of curved average applied to it as a buff. The modifier of per second squared wasn't just the normal physics notation but a measure of how long he had to sustain movement to actually start to flex the new "muscle" that let him start pulling anime ninja moves. And while it was a muscle he could flex harder, it was also one he couldn't really turn off; getting used to a whole new pull of force in all his motions was weird, but James was adapting. Basically, it meant that if he were jumping, or trying to pull himself up a ledge, he wouldn't be sustaining enough acceleration over enough time to actually get the full benefit of an extra G's worth of momentum. Not that he wouldn't get any benefit at all, but there was certainly a lot more of it when he started running.

James could run. It was the one thing he was good at in gym class in high school, because he'd been in band, and playing the trumpet for three years gave someone a hell of a good lung capacity. James, after months of going to the gym and pursuing life-or-death adventures, could really run. His muscles were more solid, his poise more balanced. James on coffee could *run*. His legs blurred and his mind followed suit as he launched himself down the black asphalt path that ran behind their apartment. And James, built on adventure, burning coffee, and imbued with a number of purple orbs?

James could fucking *run*.

Alanna could also run, to her credit. But for her, it was less about bursts of speed and an irresponsible top speed and more about endurance. She could run forever, because she was toned for it. Alanna didn't get tired; Alanna got bored. But it did mean that she had to give James a minute to run back to her before the two of them started jogging side by side, after he got excited by the initial speeds he could pull.

"Two more days," Alanna said between heavy breaths as they beat feet down the cold road. Around them, an unkempt network of blackberry bushes and small trees provided a tunnel of foliage against the houses and apartments the path ran near. "You have any plans for next delve?"

"I'm gonna . . ." James panted out, unaccustomed to speaking while running, and not holding the same endurance. "Gonna go with the new teams. Explore a bit. Just have some fuh . . . fun. Guh. Slow down a minute," he panted as Alanna smiled and sped up.

"I want to find a decision tree," Alanna said, saving her breath from laughing out loud as James put his head down and pushed to catch up to her. There were cracks in the pavement here, and the occasional stick or rock on the path, but that was part of the fun. The coffee made their reflexes hum, letting them pick out and ignore obstacles like that as if it were second nature. And at this point, it almost was for them. They were both more in tune with the magical effect than before. "I've got a lot of yellows saved up that I want to trade."

"Good plan," James huffed, shooting out words between heavy breaths. "Anesh. Wants. To. Make the copier. Work."

"It's not really a copier . . ." Alanna started, but James just flailed a hand at her as he pumped his arms to run.

"Bah!" he exclaimed. "It copies! You come up with a better. Name."

She already had one percolating in her head. Something about overhead, maybe—it was an overhead, and it could reduce costs; that seemed like the way to go. But before Alanna could take James's challenge, she noticed something off to the side of the path and threw an arm in front of him to call a halt.

They both stopped about half a block later. It's not easy to stop on a dime when you're moving at ten miles an hour. Humans, unlike bikes, don't really have brakes.

When they stopped, Alanna almost instantly turned around to go back to what she'd seen by the side of the path, while James, catching his breath in great gulps of air, shook his head theatrically and stumbled after her.

There, by the side of the path, sitting in a patch of purple and blue wildflowers still holding on in the rapidly cooling October morning air, was a shoe. It lay in the rough gravel and soil, wrapped slightly around a larger rock that lay in the dirt with it.

"It's a shoe," James said, master of the obvious.

"Yeah . . ." Alanna muttered, kneeling down.

"Someone musta lost it. Wait, no, that doesn't make any sense. How do you lose a single shoe? Is there another one around here?" James scanned the bushes. It wasn't a sandal or a sneaker or something; this was a businessman's shoe. Thin black laces, the kind of shoe that you got someone to polish for a nickel while you waited for the streetcar. Classy. This wasn't the kind of shoe you lost on the side of the walking trail. "Hey. There's another one," he said, stepping past Alanna and pushing into the waist-high grass that formed a thin barrier before the thicket of trees and thorny vines fully took over. He grabbed the shoe off the tree branch where it must have been thrown. "Hey, what . . ."

He turned back to Alanna, who was similarly holding up the other shoe, examining it. James caught her eye and turned the shoe over and shook it, sending out a spray of dust and shredded paper.

Instantly, both of them were on guard, and Alanna rose to her feet. Months ago, something they'd done had attracted the attention of an agent from the dungeon that had been lurking in the real world.

A stuffed shirt, most likely under the control of Monster Karen, had kicked in their front door and nearly killed James. The incident had put their hackles up for a while, but it hadn't happened again, and they'd started to forget about it and assume it was a one-off.

But now, this. Business shoes and paper blood? Near where they lived? Not a coincidence. Couldn't be.

They were unarmed, but they weren't defenseless. They were buzzing with the coffee, which had previously let James go toe-to-toe with the stuffed shirts in limited ways. And there were two of them. And, if need be, Secret was just one personal revelation away.

The two of them silently fell into step, James taking the lead, Alanna two arm spans to his right and a few steps back. And they pushed through the bush together. Twigs and thorned vines pulled at James's legs, making him wish he'd worn longer pants than the running shorts he'd started the jog in. The two of them shoved aside branches, some of the leaves still damp from where the cold sun hadn't yet dried out the dew, as they moved forward.

"Half a suit coat." James tapped the piece of cloth hanging on a tree as they passed. "Edges look like wet cardboard. This is absolutely a paper pusher."

They moved forward. Deeper into the vegetation. Until, all of a sudden, there was a gap in the green. A small circle, fairly wide if you weren't worried about being scratched up by blackberry bushes, fairly cramped if you were. It wasn't dark, but there were only a few gaps in the trees overhead that let any of the morning light in.

Toward the back, in the circle of dirt and trampled leaves, sitting with its back against a tree, was a man. Or rather, the shape of a man. Its mask, that oh-so-clever symbiotic organism that too perfectly mimicked a human face, must have slipped off long ago. All that was left was a blank slate, taut construction paper, eggshell white. It was missing its shoes, showing only normal feet, which actually surprised James. He'd assumed they'd be less . . . human. One of the feet was split in half from between the second and third toe, all the way to the heel, though, so maybe that counted. It still wore the other half of its suit over a dirt-stained white shirt and black pants that had more than a few rips.

There was a thin puddle of dust around it, seemingly undisturbed by the elements.

Alanna sucked in a sharp breath as the two of them entered the clearing, and James could practically feel her tensing up to fight if the thing moved. But his mind jumped to something stranger rather than focusing on that. As soon as he saw the employee, he felt a thought cut through his mind. *Look away*, it said. But it said it all wrong. It shouted it; it rang bells and launched fireworks to get your attention so it could tell you how you shouldn't pay attention. It was bold, and obvious, and it left the scent of rot in James's brain.

A quick glance at Alanna and shared raised eyebrows showed that she'd thought it, too. And as James thought about it, a few puzzle pieces started to click together. They'd known for a long time that the employees often carried purple orbs and they could use them to make thoughtforms like Secret. Hell, that was where Secret had come from. They also knew that the monster that had been kidnapping people had sent agents out into the world to protect its interests, and that against all odds, those inhuman things hadn't aroused mass suspicion. They also knew that they'd run past this part of the path at least a couple times over the last week—sometimes twice a day—and yet they hadn't noticed the torn parts of the employee before now.

And now, with that one too-obvious thought drifting in his perception, James realized that he now knew what the rotting corpse of an antimeme looked like.

Shaking off the strange sorrow of seeing this thing that would otherwise be their enemy lying here in repose, James stepped around its side while Alanna knelt down next to it.

"No orb," she said clinically. Like she wasn't looking at a corpse, or *was* looking at a corpse but had some kind of CSI job. "If it died here, then it must have run out of energy. No orb for the infomorph, so, same."

"If an infomorph gets killed, where does the orb drop?" James asked, suddenly struck with a thought. "Didn't Secret help us kill the one that was covering up Sarah's room? Shouldn't that have dropped an orb somewhere?"

"Different rules, maybe." Alanna shrugged. "Doesn't look like it got in a fight. It just . . . lay down and died. Maybe it stopped receiving orders. Or maybe its last orders were to wait and watch or something." She looked up at James. "We should take it back."

"To our apartment?" He stuttered out a low "uhhh . . ." before Alanna cut him off.

"No. To the dungeon. If for no other reason than that we can't easily deal with it here." She ran a hand over the blank face. "Huh. That's weird," she said, turning the head sideways and motioning for James to look in. "Check this out."

It was a port, at the base of what would on a human be a skull. It looked an awful lot like the one that James wore on his own neck.

"Ah." James wrinkled his nose. "That's anxiety inducing. Now I can't stop wondering if this is what people turn into if they're plugged in long enough." He scooted back a couple half steps from the body.

"I think it's more likely that this is what the Karen thing was supposed to be puppeting," Alanna told him. "Which makes me wonder if there's more of them. Or maybe if the skulljack technology isn't unique."

"That's *more* worrying!" James informed her.

"Well, is it as worrying as me asking you to grab the legs?" Her partner gave her a blank look until Alanna got a grip under the corpse's arms and started lifting. "We can't leave it here. Not now that literally anyone could see it."

James grunted acknowledgment and dusted off his knees. "All right, all right. And yes, it is more worrying than that," he said, looping his hands under the thing's shoulders. One of them crumpled like wet cardboard as they lifted, and James had to make an effort to not just rip the arm off by accident. "Okay, this is gonna sound bad, but . . . why don't we just burn it?"

There was a pause, and Alanna wrinkled her nose in thought. "Doesn't seem disrespectful, I guess. Fireplace?"

"Sure. Get the legs."

***

"Welcome to our new digs," Anesh said, throwing open the doors where James was waiting, grin plastered on his face. "As a heads-up, I've still got a few people coming by in a bit here, so no talking about the dungeon in front of the contractors." Anesh himself had been here for a few hours by the time James arrived, unloading stuff from their rented moving van that Anesh was *absolutely* certified to drive, a distinction that had not gone unnoticed by James as his friend had gone out the door.

Still, both the building and the truck were intact, and Anesh had been happily working with Momo and Alex to pull in tables and lockers, as well as all the white- and corkboards that they'd had hanging on their walls for the last several months. James had to do a small double take on that last name. Alex was someone he vaguely remembered from their mass escape, but she hadn't come to the delve last week, even as part of Karen's group. He'd have to talk to her later, and he made a mental note as he looked at the progress. Under Anesh's direction, the open interior of the warehouse was quickly turning into something straight out of a low-budget spy thriller student film.

And it was a warehouse. It had a nice facade out front, a decent-size parking lot off a secondary road, bushes and exterior lighting left over from the last people who had leased the building. But for all that the paint was fresh and the leasing agent called it a "commercial-flex space," there was no real hiding the lack of any kind of ceiling panels to cover all the ventilation overhead or the fact that there were really only three interior walls breaking up the fairly massive square footage of the interior.

"Do we actually need this much space?" James asked, standing in the middle of a barren carpeted floor. It was that same kind of hard carpet that places used when they didn't want to pay for actual tile or hardwood floors but still didn't want to let any of their employees make the mistake that comfort was anywhere on the list of priorities. Tightly woven green and dark-red fibers made triangular patterns underfoot. The smell of drywall hung in the air, almost overpowering the lingering scent of bleach. "It just seems like it's . . . huge? Especially given the size of our, and I hesitate to use this word, 'organization.'" He emphasized the last word with air quotes, fingers cocking in lighthearted sarcasm.

"Sure do!" Momo butted through their conversation, figuratively and literally, as she hauled a pair of gym mats between where James and Anesh stood talking in the middle of the open floor. "We're making a fight club in the back!"

"Wat," James croaked out, much to Anesh's amusement.

"She's being hyperbolic. We're setting up a place for people to get used to fighting, maybe a firing range, too, if we can get enough soundproofing. It's important that people be able to actually know how a fight *feels*."

"Like we didn't." James nodded.

"Like we didn't. Exactly." Anesh gave his boyfriend a soft smile before shaking his head and snapping out of the quiet moment. "Lemme show you around."

"I can *see* around, Anesh," James said in protest before sighing and following the retreating back of his partner. "Also, where's the other you? I would have figured the ability to move furniture would be the perfect use for a second human."

Anesh led him behind the counter, a curved bar of purple-painted wood that James assumed was another leftover from whatever had been here previously. It was set against the wall opposite the front door and half covered two doors that went through the wall it was against and one door to its right that went to what looked like a small office area. As Anesh took him through one of the back doors, James glimpsed old holes drilled in the desk, probably for cash register power cables, now being used as cupholders for the thirsty work of dragging desks off a truck.

"Other me isn't here," Anesh told James. "I'm out buying socks."

". . . Socks."

"Yeah, I'm still going down to California after this week's delve, and it turns out, when you dirty your pants at double the rate, you need to either commit to a life at the laundry or buy more socks." Anesh glanced over his shoulder through the doorframe as he rolled his eyes at James's question before turning back and pointing into the room. "Now, I got a contractor to take out this interior wall, because this room was just a small, unlit box otherwise, and now it's part of the large area that we can use as storage. I'm also having them stick most of the furniture here for now, too, and it'll be where we do planning and operations meetings."

"Wait, so, there's this giant-ass space—nice concrete floors, by the way—and then I'm guessing there's another one down that side hall past the bathrooms where Momo was talking about making a . . . well, a gym, basically. But what are we using the front room for?" James asked.

Anesh shrugged. "I mean, I didn't really think about it. We'll probably need the room eventually, and this place was still cheaper than most of the smaller places around town. And we *do* need to be around town; this is on a bus line, too." He scuffed his boot on the floor, frowning slightly at the hard surface. "We'll buy rugs."

James thought for a second as he watched Momo and Alex bring another table through the back entrance of the cavernous space. The room didn't have lighting in it for some reason; all the overhead fixtures had been removed by the previous tenant, so the back loading-bay door being open and letting in natural sunlight was all that illuminated it right now. He smiled to himself as he and Anesh stood there, acting like proper supervisors, listening to the two girls talk about how even *this* was better than being trapped in the dungeon.

"Oh. Oh!" James tried and fumbled a snap of his fingers, causing a brief pause where Anesh watched his friend attempt to get his fingers to work properly until he eventually got it. "Okay, there. Anyway! The support group! Sarah's been doing a great job keeping it up, but I still get this weird feeling about doing it at the public library, you know? So, why not just use that big front space?"

"Makes sense. We can get some nice chairs tomorrow. Oh, actually, talk to Sarah about it first, okay?"

James rolled his eyes. "Yes, yes. I'm not stupid; I would never be friends with someone who wanted unsolicited gifts."

"Was that sarcasm?" Anesh asked, genuinely curious.

"I'm not sure!" James replied cheerily. "Anyway. I brought these with me, and really it's the only reason that Alanna had a hope in hell of getting me out of bed before noon." He held up the small pouch he'd been carrying a cluster of green orbs in. "Do you want one? I'm totally willing to share. I'm magnanimous like that."

"I'll take one!" Momo yelled across the floor, young voice echoing over the empty rock and metal of the warehouse space.

James mostly ignored her, just tossing an orb her direction to be snatched out of the air while he focused on raising an eyebrow at Anesh. "No, thanks," his friend said. "I've got some at home, and you earned those, anyway." He cleared his throat and looked away before he could change his mind as James started pulling out orbs. "Anyway, I've been meaning to ask you something."

[Local Area Shift : Air Quality Improved, -32 PPM toxins]

[+2 Skill Ranks : Singing—Opera]

"What's up?" James asked Anesh over the wisps of dusty green smoke trickling through his fingers.

Anesh snorted out a sigh. "The skulljacks," he stated.

"What of them?" James asked as he pulled out another green orb, this one half the size of the first.

Anesh watched as James rolled the small ball around his fingers with a casual deftness. "We need outside help on them, and the world's leading cyberneticists just aren't taking our calls. Also, the amount of trouble they cause when it comes to getting on airlines is difficult for arranging meetings."

[Local Area Shift : Water Pressure—+/- 6 PSI toward 45 PSI]

[+1 Skill Rank : Interior Design—Feng Shui]

"Yeah, the security at the airport was really annoying." James nodded. "So, what's your thought?" He fished around in his bag, feeling for a good one.

"My *first* thought is that I hope you're writing those down. Especially in *my workspace*." Anesh affixed a stern expression on James, who froze sheepishly, ceased digging in the pouch, and pulled out his phone to start making notes. "Good. Now. I propose we find disillusioned, anarchistic engineering and comp-sci majors and hire them."

James held up a finger as he finished typing on his phone's difficult keyboard. "Water . . . pressure . . . okay. So, what? Just grab random people and bring them fully on board?"

"Well, the anarchist thing was Alanna's idea. She said they'd be the best people to design safeguards against abuse." Anesh shrugged. "And I agree? I mean, these things are literal magic that could redefine humanity. I can think of people who shouldn't get to be part of that process."

"I'm on board with that. My political leanings land somewhere to the left of fully automated luxury gay space communism, though. But hey, it's our project—we should run it how we think will be best for humanity." James pulled out another green orb and idly held it up to his eye, enjoying the slightly surreal tint of color. "Got any candidates?"

"For communism?"

"For the engineers, you goober." James broke the orb between his middle and ring finger, watching carefully as it vaporized itself.

[Local Area Shift : +1 Basement]

[+3 Skill Ranks : Athletics—Gymnastics—Cartwheels]

"Not yet, but I . . . what the fuck was that?" Anesh went from exasperated to alert in a split second.

James felt it, too. The floor literally rippled underfoot and left them feeling like they were standing on sand for a brief second. "Okay, good news! We have *more space* now!"

"James, what the bloody hell did you do?" Anesh demanded, eyes sharp.

"Excavated a basement?" James half asked. "We should go check that out."

Anesh just sighed and waved the two girls over, putting them to work searching the back half of the building for any sign of stairs while he and James took the front.

"Okay, well, barring any you-induced catastrophe, I want to talk to you and Alanna later about coming up with some kind of way to screen people for . . . I don't want to say loyalty, but the kind of people who we can integrate into this without too much worry."

"I'll think on it," James said as he checked the small manager's office for trapdoors and then cracked another green on the way back to where Anesh was looking in the janitor's closet.

[Local Area Shift : Fabrication Time—Clothing, -13 minutes]

[+2 Skill Ranks : Geography—New York—Hotels]

"Would you *stop that?*" Anesh asked, incredulous. "You're gonna give us another basement before we find the first one!"

"Okay, okay, just one more. *That* one, by the way, made it faster to make clothes here. We should see how that applies to armor." James dutifully recorded his results in his phone. In actuality, he was just composing a rather long email to Anesh, which he planned to send later. He did this with his head down, following behind Anesh without really watching where they were going.

"Just help me find the stairs first, please?" Anesh asked with a half-amused, half-frustrated tone.

James looked up, apologetic. "Right. Of course! Sorry, I'm not trying to be a dick—these things are just really fun. We haven't seen a lot of the greens, you know? Also, I'm pretty sure we can't get another basement."

The two of them combed over the building until eventually crossing paths with a grinning Momo and a concerned Alex.

"Found it!" Momo declared. "There are *spiders* in the basement!" She waggled her fingers in what she surely thought was a spooky fashion.

"Gross spiders or worth-experience spiders?" James asked, curious.

"Just regular spiders. Looks like no one's been in the basement for a long time," Momo answered. "Can I poke around the stuff down there?"

"Wait, *stuff*?" Anesh and James asked simultaneously.

"There's a lot of cardboard boxes and some furniture down there," Alex told them. "She wanted to open it, but I said we should ask first."

James gave a thumbs-up that got an awkwardly prideful smile in response. "Good instinct. The basement wasn't there until ten minutes ago, so . . ."

"So where'd the stuff come from?" Anesh finished for him. "I feel like this is punishment for something we did wrong."

"Or a reward! Okay, can I crack the last two now?" James asked, holding up his final orbs. Anesh nodded, ignoring the excited exclamation from Momo and the curious question Alex had. James didn't ignore them so much, though. "The greens change places," he explained. "We should really write a briefing book for this. Anyway, that's where the basement came from. 'Plus one basement.' Kind of a weird phrasing. Oh, wait! Maybe it's someone else's basement!"

"Please, no." Anesh sagged his shoulders. "This place is getting too weird already. Just crack the last two and let me start fixing whatever goes horribly right."

[Local Area Shift : +$46,050 Value—Bathrooms]

[+2 Skill Ranks : Manufacturing—Circuit Boards]

[Local Area Shift : +1 Basement]

[+2 Skill Ranks : Cooking—Food Production—Butter]

Beneath their feet, the ground rippled again. Before anyone could say anything, James turned to Anesh and said, "Okay, so, in my defense, you jinxed it, and this isn't my fault."

Then Momo and Alex spent a few minutes watching their boss try to put his boyfriend in an armbar.

Sarah ran into James in the parking lot when he got home. She was on her way out while he was just getting back from spending another half hour searching for a staircase while Anesh grumbled at him. He approached her as she was coming down the steps; two stairs up and only just over eye level with him, she greeted James in that way that he was coming to understand she liked conversations—totally devoid of small talk. "So I was doing tai chi in the living room, and . . ."

"How?" James interrupted.

Sarah's smile didn't even twitch. "How was I doing tai chi? It's not hard, James. I could teach you, actually! You'd probably like it."

"No, I know some already, thanks. I meant how . . ." James waved a hand at her.

This time, Sarah interrupted. "You know tai chi?"

James smiled back now, the banter feeling a lot more natural between them when they stopped worrying about memories and focused on just being themselves at each other. "Some. Focus! How did you do tai chi in the *living room?*"

"It's not that bad," Sarah defended herself.

"Sarah, the living room could best be described by the mental image of a crime scene investigation unit shaking their head as they report to their superior that 'there was definitely a struggle here.' How did you *fit?*"

Sarah thought of their living room, over three-quarters of the floor space taken up by a massive table, the rest of it occupied by the couch, the chairs, and the shelf housing the TV that was used for a lot fewer anime nights these days than she remembered, or preferred. There was barely a patch to stand comfortably. "Okay, yeeeeah, there was a struggle," Sarah admitted. "Now shut up and watch this."

She hopped off the steps, nudging James back a bit before glancing around them. Waiting patiently for the neighbor who was taking his trash out to get back around the corner and into his apartment, Sarah dug her hands into the pockets of her ancient denim jacket and rustled around until she came out with a small ball bearing.

"Ah, a silver orb!" James exclaimed, earning himself a light thwap on the arm with the sleeve of her coat.

"Hush, you interrupter! Now watch this." Sarah took a few steps back and stretched a bit before falling into a suddenly graceful sweep of her arms. She did a few basic motions before lunging forward slightly, her left arm extended forward, palm out, and her right arm pulled back near her breast. James noticed then that the ball bearing that she'd had in her hand was now hovering, suspended about an inch over the middle finger of her right hand.

And then it was *gone*. An instant later, there was the noise of tearing vegetation from the direction of the barrier of blackberry bushes that marked the boundary of their parking lot, the same direction that Sarah's other arm was pointed to like an arrow.

She stood up with a quick shake of her wrists and sighed a deep breath as she opened her eyes and looked at James.

"What the *fuck?*" he asked, perplexed.

"I've been trying to figure out how to use the purple orb that lets me control magnetic fields. It's super hard, 'cause it's not a muscle I've ever had, you know?" She gestured off toward the bushes where, presumably, the ball bearing had been launched. "I dunno how fast that can actually go, but . . . I think I probably should have checked there was no one on the other side, you know?"

"I'm suddenly very worried about our living room," James said with a grim frown.

Sarah winced. "That was actually what I wanted to tell you about?"

"Wait!" James held up a hand, and she looked at him, worried. He gave her his best serious frown and said, "Whatever it was, bring me back a barbecue sandwich and I promise not to be mad."

"What, blanket immunity?" she asked, looking at him expectantly before frowning.

James didn't miss that. "Ah. That was . . . that was something of ours, wasn't it?" He suddenly felt a lot sadder than he should for learning his old best friend was a living rail gun. With the smallest shake of his head, he tried to reaffix a smile to his face. "You'll have to tell me about it when you get back with my sandwich, and after I call the . . . glass repairman?" Sarah shook her head at him, his smile infecting her slightly. "Veterinarian? No, okay, good. Electrician? Wait! Wait, come back! Now I'm really worried!" he called after her as Sarah waved goodbye while climbing into her car. James just shook his head, now smiling for real as he saw she was as well. She had been his best friend for his whole life, memories or not, and she deserved better than to be forgotten.

James looked up the steps and sighed to himself. "All right, let's go do some damage control on today's newest crisis."

"We're funded," James stated.

"Mostly thanks to you," Anesh replied. "And only for a week or two."

"We've got an actual central location set up for meeting and planning and stuff," he continued.

"Yes," Anesh agreed.

"Neil dropped off those drones?"

"Yes, while I was in the basement."

James smirked. "Which one?"

"It doesn't matter, and it's not funny! They shouldn't work that way!" It was funny, and everyone in the room knew it. Including Anesh. *Especially* Anesh. Though the fact that different sets of stairs took you to different basements, despite going the same distance down, was a *little* worrying.

"We're still a well-kept secret?"

"Well enough," Secret told them from under the table, voice clear to them despite the barrier. "I can only really follow my own threads, but they appear to have not spread more than one jump."

JP had the next point. "Everyone is ready," he said, glancing up from his phone.

"Yes, yes," Anesh agreed.

"Everyone is *excited*," Alanna pointed out.

"We are, yeah." James nodded, and Rufus and Ganesh nodded along with him from their perch on the table.

"I am, too," Sarah said, softly. Everyone paused, and James reached over and touched her shoulder reassuringly.

"The list of things to test is ready," Anesh told them.

"The list of things to look for is ready," Alanna added.

"The list of surprises waiting is mysteriously obtuse." James couldn't help grinning as he reminded the group.

"I'm a walking rail gun!" Sarah cheerfully pointed out to James, who slowly nodded in acceptance that a lot of surprises probably folded against high-velocity metal balls.

"I remember the first time you invited me to this, there was a lot less of this part," Dave interjected.

The room laughed, and James eventually found the explanation he was groping for. "We've got more people now. And we're taking more risks, you know? We aren't worried about JP spraining an ankle again . . ."

"Hey!"

". . . we're worried about someone getting lost, or really hurt. We're going in deeper, and we're hunting for better rewards, and we need to be ready."

"But we are," Dave told him, in his oblivious way of approaching situations.

James was about to protest, but then he caught himself. Dave was, he realized, absolutely right. All this scrambling, all this running around and fishing for information and schedules and equipment— they were getting better at it. Hell, they were almost getting *good* at it. And this week, for the first time, what it added up to was this.

They *were* ready.

"Yeah," James said. "All right. Everyone grab some sleep or do whatever it is you do when I'm not looking. In twelve hours, we're gonna have some fun."

CHAPTER 10

"Wellll, fuck." James was the first one to speak after the group made its way through the door. Slightly different people than last week, but the composition was roughly the same.

Daniel wasn't here, but the other member of the security faction, Tyrone, was. And, apparently, Pathfinder had tagged along with him. He and Daniel were friends outside of work, or had *become* friends outside of work, or some permutation of friendship that made them close enough that they could pass complex infomorphs between them. Alanna had pointed out that it was mildly ironic that the people most interested in guarding the door were the people who had among their number a creature that fed on exploration, and James had felt kinda weird about it. Like, Path wasn't on the same level of sapience as Secret; they were kind of like a mental doggo.

James didn't really want to have to add "memetic animal rights enforcer" to his growing list of responsibilities. But then, Secret had also been kind of... small when he'd been created. And he'd grown, and learned, *very* quickly. Maybe Pathfinder was on a similar track.

Weirdly, *Theo* had come in with them. After last week, and her vehemence about this place being evil, James had been more or less convinced that she'd leave it alone forever. But apparently, she too felt like watching the door was something she should be doing. Or she was just free that evening and wanted something to do.

Sarah had joined them, feeling like she'd gotten her feet under her. Other James was absent for family reasons. One Anesh was out sleeping before he hit the road tomorrow. Deb, the nurse who had stuck with Karen, was around here somewhere, though James hadn't seen her yet. Alex had filled the gap, though it seemed more likely that she'd fit in with Momo's team than Karen's.

It wasn't too much of a shake-up, but it was enough to be noticed. James had still been excited to set foot in the dungeon again. As was becoming tradition, he, Alanna, and Anesh had taken point, striding through the doors together in a V formation, leading the charge into uncharted territory.

And then James had started swearing when they'd seen the office in front of them.

Near the door itself, there was that small open gap that there always was near structural walls in this place, about fifteen feet of hard carpeted floor space with almost nothing breaking up the monotony. Then the cubicles started, clusters of six or eight desks with low walls and their backs facing each other in geometric boredom. Beyond that, the walls got higher, the geometry warped, and trappings like paper vines and creeping cables provided the atmosphere of an ancient temple. All this entryway circled around the base of the non-Euclidean tower that raised its ten-floor hulking form overhead, occupying far more space than should be possible between them and the high ceiling above.

Except for one major variation this time.

"Fuck. Fuck!" James swore, sweeping an arm out to encompass the scene in front of them. "Fuck!" he reiterated.

"Okay, this is bad," Alanna agreed as the others started coming through the door behind them.

The nature of the bad was pretty obvious to the group that had spent the better part of an hour last week clearing a line of sight, building some basic barricades and fortifications, and making a nice little meeting area out of repurposed furniture. While previously, they'd always been comfortable leaving Fort Door to stand as their entryway to the dungeon, this time, it had apparently taken offense to their redecorating.

The whole space was exactly as they'd found it last week when they first walked in.

No braced walls, no choke points, no twenty feet of open lines of fire for oncoming tumblefeeds. Just cubicles, reset like the humans had never come through here.

"Shit, our gear," Alanna muttered. A spike of fear went through James's heart; they'd traveled light this time, mostly because all the stuff they needed was already *here*.

Karen had brought an old wood axe for dealing with plants, and Alex was wearing a turnout suit she'd inherited from an uncle who used to be a firefighter, but aside from that and a box of glow sticks that Anesh had bought on James's urging, and a swarm of surveillance drones, they were basically unarmed. All their stuff had been stored here.

The crowbars; the armor, both improvised sports padding and police body armor; the *guns*; all their emergency food; James's favorite hatchet, as beat up as it was; even the bikes they'd brought to move rapidly through the longer corridors of the Office. Was it all gone?

"We stored a lot of stuff in the tower. Let's check there," Anesh suggested.

James nodded and turned it into a directive for the group. "Everyone spread out! Be careful, don't wander off alone, but see if you can find anything that we left here. We're gonna go check the tower. If the buildings are back, the critters might be, too, so eyes open!"

James and Alanna took point while Anesh gave Ganesh an upward toss to launch off and carefully checked the drone's line of sight on his phone, scanning for anything moving near them. Around them, the different groups moved cautiously and in chunks of people that were probably a little too crowded. James made a note to talk to them about spreading out *more* at a later time; a teammate who could reach you and save you quickly was a lot more useful than a teammate that was in your way.

When they got to the base of the tower, James reached for the now-familiar flashlight attached to his armor's plate, only to remember with a wince that his armor was currently missing in action. "This," he said to Alanna slowly, "is probably the worst way the dungeon could hit us right now without killing anyone."

She nodded sourly at him. They had put a lot of time and effort into accumulating the collection of weapons, armor, survival gear, ammunition, food, and other assorted tools here. If the whole floor had reset, this was actually a massive financial hit that they would have real trouble fixing without the ability to find and open another briefcase. Not to mention that some of the things here had their own personal significance. The gun she'd inherited from her father had been here. So had a lot of the legacy gear from the first time James and Anesh had come into this place.

They wouldn't just lose stuff, they'd lose a chunk of their history.

So it got a massive sigh of relief when they ducked into the first floor of the tower and, through the few dim shafts of light in the darkness, saw the bikes that they'd brought in neatly leaned against the outside wall. A little more rooting around found a flashlight on a stack of boxes, which, when illuminated, turned out to be the food supplies that James had wheeled in here on the hand truck just before they'd left last week.

"Everything's the same . . ." Alanna said, cautiously optimistic.

Two minutes later, they came back out through the tight entrance, Alanna having to duck a bit more than James did to clear the low lip of the only door to the tower. As they exited, they were met by Karen and Dave.

"We—"

"It's not safe to do this if we aren't armed," Karen stated flatly, interrupting what Dave was about to say.

James gave her a cold look before turning deliberately to Dave. "Sorry, Dave, what were you saying?"

Karen clamped her mouth shut and ground her teeth as James ignored her, but Dave, blessed Dave, didn't even notice the anger in the air from the older woman.

"We've got the groups set up for tonight. Everyone agreed to not go too far in if we're out of gear again, but Anesh said we'd need the money to resupply, so I got them organized," Dave reported to James.

James glanced over his squire's shoulder to see groups of the other delvers, lined up like they were anticipating his words. He shuddered slightly—more responsibility.

"Okay." James shook his head before speaking to Karen. "Well, good news, most of our stuff is still here. The stuff around the tower resets, but not the tower itself, so it actually really does make a perfect base if that holds true. Hey, Alanna"—James turned to his partner, who was currently looking pointedly up at the ceiling and not snickering at how James had shut down Karen—"can you get everyone geared up? Make sure the kids are ready. We're still on."

The plan was, James felt, sheer elegance in its simplicity. They'd discussed it with everyone else and come to the conclusion that the way they were splitting loot was just . . . not great. So, he'd made an announcement to everyone, which was probably part of why Karen was so pissy today.

From now on, this operation was going to run like an actual operation. Not a bunch of disparate people coming in and vaguely working together. Everyone could have a voice and even a vote, but they were going to have a goddamn command structure. They were going to have objectives and assignments to those objectives, and they were going to get stuff done. Loot would be distributed via quartermaster, an unenviable job that James had immediately stuck JP with.

And if anyone didn't like it? Well, James wasn't the kind of monster to tell people they couldn't come into the dungeon. That would just be rude. But you wouldn't get to work with their group.

"All right, nerds!" Alanna called out, stepping past them and clapping her hands loudly. "Come get yer shit together!" She started directing people into the tower, barking out orders to grab more lights, open up holes in the walls, and get everyone ready to go.

James looked harshly back at Karen, who was still glaring at him. "Look," he said flatly, "you wanted to be part of this. And sometimes that means not being so goddamn rigid about risks."

"You're going to get yourself killed." Karen found her voice and spoke through a clenched jaw. "This is reckless. It is *stupid*. And it is *dangerous*. Both to you and to everyone who thinks you can lead them."

"Well, if I don't do reckless, stupid, dangerous things in the pursuit of wealth and magic, then how will I end up in Space Valhalla?" James asked before he could remember that this was supposed to be serious.

Karen scowled. "That's what you do. You treat all of this like it's a joke."

"No," James said flatly. "I treat this like exactly what it is. It's weird, unique, kind of magic, and just *life*. This is my daily life now, Karen. This is all I do. When I'm not here, I'm planning, or equipping, or dealing with interpersonal issues between delvers, or training. I am always here, even when the door is closed." He sighed and broke eye contact, looking off into the gray horizon. "And a lot of the time, my life is jokes." James turned back to the woman in front of him. "Look. We're going to run this like an actual organization from now on. When we started this, you said you wanted to make sure the victims were taken care of, and I told you you could have the job if you wanted it. Well, I'm telling you that again now. If you want to work with us, there's a role for you. But enough of this 'everyone's mom' thing you're doing."

"I'm trying to keep people alive," Karen said, almost sadly.

"I know," James told her. "That's why I'm not mad. But it's not helping. Now, we're burning time here, and I'm not interested in arguing today. If you want to participate, you can. If not, go home. If you're really interested in keeping people alive, I'll put you on the reserve team for when there's emergencies."

Karen was about to say something else, but James was done. Alanna had caught his eye; she'd found his hatchet and was waving him over, giving him the perfect excuse.

"You can take your time to decide," James said, cutting Karen off. "But before next week. And now I need to go. Time limits are no joke." And with that, he simply turned and left.

It took James a minute to recompose himself. Taking the weapon from Alanna and affixing it to his belt was a good, simple task that helped him refocus.

"You good?" she asked him, eyebrows raised in outwardly mild concern that James knew was secretly a pretty deep ocean of caring.

"I'm good," he said. "It's a weird part of being an adult that I sometimes find myself the equal of those older than me."

"Equal my ass." Alanna snorted.

James couldn't help a small snort of a laugh, even through the stress. "All right. Enough of that. Is everyone ready?"

Alanna nodded. "All set. You sure about bringing Other James and company along? It'll be confusing, *and* it's going to demystify us."

James stuck out his tongue at her and made a farting noise. "If I wanted to seem mysterious, I'd be a priest, not a tech support guy. Also, Other James isn't here tonight, so it'll just be the other two. Sarah said something about experiments, so she's staying back, I think."

"Touché." Alanna grinned.

James grinned back. "Okay, let's go. I'm still angry, and I want to hit something that's trying to eat me."

The strider made a wet, organic pop as James tore it in half. A second later, he dropped the corpse to the floor and snagged the manifested yellow orb out of the air before it could fall. He didn't even hesitate to pop it with his fingers before turning to check the state of the skirmish happening.

[+1 Skill Rank : Scrimshaw—Basket Weaving]

James watched as Momo and her magnetic distortion of a dog pinned down and systematically dismantled a nearby shellaxy, part of the swarm that had leaped to the defense of this particular little patch of cubicle ground. A quick check around showed that everyone had made short work of the handful of striders and pair of ambulatory PCs, with Alanna having battered the other shellaxy into submission and the rest of the team tearing into striders in ones and twos, avoiding getting swarmed and bitten.

The ground their opponents were defending wasn't exactly special, as far as James could see. A little patch of clear floor in a weird, offset square pattern, in the middle of a few rising walls. There wasn't much in the way of distortion to the walls here, just height. They rose up tall and proud, with the doors being equally tall columns of space cut out of them. The whole thing felt like being a child in a corn maze again, unable to see over the tops and uncertain about what was around the next corner. If it weren't for the upward curve of the dungeon, James wouldn't have been able to see the horizon at all, but at least this area wasn't "roofed over" and kept in the dark.

After Momo crowbarred in the front of the last shellaxy, the fight abruptly fell silent. There was a brief pause as everyone did a quick check around themselves for more enemies and then made sure they weren't hurt or secretly carrying a strider on their back. You only had to make that mistake once before it became habit to check one another's backs, literally.

"All right, good job. Let's clear this up and move on." James spoke in a low tone. They'd also learned, this deep in, that fights attracted more suicidally hostile dungeon life. The strider swarm James saw early on in his delving career hadn't been replicated again, but it was easy to see how it might have. A few minutes after the din of combat, they'd be having a few more striders show up to investigate, maybe some masks as well. Every now and then a maul cart, which actually was still a challenge to deal with. Speed and efficiency had become the game. If a fight did happen, they cleared the area, even if they still hadn't looted everything thoroughly.

"Good doggo! Who's a good doggo? It's you!" Momo praised her team's mascot, tossing the gauss hound a small yellow orb as a treat.

Today, James had decided to mix things up a bit and get their newest team experience deeper into the dungeon, so he'd trust them more on their own in the future. To that end, their party was made up of the original trio of James, Anesh, and Alanna, along with the new kids of Alex, Simon, and Momo.

James still wasn't sure how to feel about Alex. The girl felt kinda like she wasn't paying attention sometimes, but then she'd surprise them all by catching onto things weirdly fast, which felt pretty relatable.

She wasn't stupid, just easily distracted, but she made up for it with an almost instinctive aggression in combat. Alanna, unsurprisingly, had taken to Momo like the ready-made mentor she was, but Simon hadn't gotten close to anyone in their time together. He kept a polite emotional distance, and James was starting to suspect that it was because he still harbored some amount of hero worship over the rescue.

"All right, portion of the orbs bagged. Crack the rest," Alanna announced. That had been their operational plan so far, using the yellows and blues they found fairly openly, just in case. The rest, the ones they were hanging on to, they'd pay out to the others when they got back. "And good job, Momo. Nice teamwork with the dog."

"Magneto is a gooooood doooog," Momo reasserted, running her hands through the rainbow distortion in the air where the life-form's head probably was.

"Yeah, hey, Anesh?" James commented idly as he glanced down one of the corner hallways. "Remind me to ask Dave why we don't bring Pendragon in here. Having something stomp on our foes sounds pretty nice right now." He cracked his last yellow orb that hadn't been stored for later as he spoke.

[+1 Skill Rank : Etiquette—Cell Phone]

"Pendragon is the size of a bus and currently molting, so that's why. Don't you read our Slack?" Anesh replied as he tightened the straps on his armor, shouldering the backpack in preparation to move again.

"I could have sworn we weren't doing online communication." James grunted in frustration.

"There's a new encryption plug-in for it," Anesh said, like that explained anything. "I'll add you to it later."

"Will you explain how a whatever Pendragon is molts later, too?" James said with a small amount of sarcasm.

Anesh perked up, gave a small "Ah!" and raised his index finger. "She's being laminated!"

Both James and Momo stared at Anesh for a few seconds before collectively shaking their heads. "Nope, didn't help. I think the coffee is wearing off."

"All right, shut up, you goons." Alanna stole up behind them and gave James a light thwap on the back of his helmet. "We've gotta move before something shows up. Keep it down."

They obliged, letting the banter drop back to a sort of rustling quiet as six people moved in a tight line down the hallways. Every now and then, they'd leave a marker up to help themselves get back, and as a backup plan, James had brought along a GoPro, currently mounted to the shoulder of his armor. It was the kind of small thing that he'd wanted to do for a while but never really found the extra money for, or he had always gotten distracted by other things. If they did end up getting lost, the recording would let them retrace their steps fairly easily. Between that and their other trump card, they were safe from being trapped in here; James just had to make sure to leave the camera here before going out. No sense taking dungeon footage anywhere it might accidentally get uploaded to YouTube.

It had been JP's idea to stream a delve. No one had risen to the bait, no matter how many hits it was sure to get. Though James was seriously considering leveraging this place for internet fame.

On they soldiered, sometimes stopping to grab low-hanging fruit from cubicles. They found a briefcase, which got added to the small cart they pulled behind their group every time they moved up to an intersection, but no one could make sense of where it wanted them to deliver eighteen hundred number-two pencils, so that one went on the back burner. They really needed a full map of this place.

They passed, at some point, into the area where James and Anesh had first struggled to get through on their way to the spire that marked the Office's bathrooms. Here, walls warped to form overhanging arches, sometimes bridges between cubicles. Those little ramps were usually only suitable to striders or tapirs, or whatever other small dungeon life hung out around here, but every now and then they'd see one that was wider and bore dozens of small holes in it—telltale marks of passing tumblefeeds.

Here, the dungeon got darker as the lights were covered up by the warped pseudoceilings. Shafts of light caught on the bright white of vines of dot-matrix paper or the shimmer of strider carapace as the small creatures moved in the shadows. Staying quiet, Alanna and James pulled flares out of their stockpile of equipment and lit them, giving a harsh red glare to their procession as they moved on. They had a few run-ins with flashbulbs here, but after showing Simon how to dismantle them, the kid took to the dangerous task with an almost inhuman dexterity, and before they'd gotten past a hundred cubicles, they'd started to pile up red orbs. James even cracked one, on a dare from his partners. Well, a couple raised eyebrows; an implied dare.

He didn't want to seem unappreciative.

[+1 Emotional Resonance Rank : Satisfaction]

It was an almost explosive release of tension when someone finally got hurt. They'd been going for so long, everyone was a little on edge, waiting for the other shoe to drop. When one of the little computer mice rolled its way down the side of the wall on its adherent trackball and dropped onto Momo with a precision strike to the neck before she smashed it *through* the wall and into an orb, it was like things had finally started going wrong, *right*. At least now they knew that this wasn't just a dream or an episode of *The Twilight Zone* where things always went their way. Momo laughed it off, too, though she did spend more time rubbing the blackened skin patch than she wanted to.

They weren't empty-handed by this point, not by a long shot. The cart was filling up with stacks of bills and rolls of coins, a couple really nice coats, an actual functioning laptop, and a handful of candy. Of course, the candy. Get Choc'd was the flavor of the region, it seemed, though it contained no chocolate and was in fact a bar of caramel filled with strawberry jam.

And, best of all, a few magic items. A pen that wrote things that were easy to believe. A pair of headphones that were always, no matter what, plugged into the phone of whoever was wearing them. A hair tie that braided your hair and then put itself in your pocket. A binder that Anesh "had a good feeling about" but they couldn't find a function of. And then a big pile of blue orbs. James had snagged one for personal use, but they'd saved a good chunk of them. It was so hard to actually *find* magic items; not that there weren't any—there were a *ton*. But figuring out what even was magic was hard when they weren't glowing and didn't have obvious uses most of the time.

[+2 Skill Ranks : Engineering—Mechanical—Oscilloscope]

[Problem Solved : Room Cleaned]

"What room . . ." James had asked, mostly to himself, before they'd moved on to another cube and another exploding-lamp defusal.

When they came to a corner that was a little too sharp, the hallways arcing around back the way they came and the line of sight blocked off by a vending machine and a water cooler sitting at the end of the T-intersection, Anesh held up a hand to stop them. While Ganesh might have been back by the door with other Anesh, they still had one really, really cool option for scouting in situations like this, and James had been kind of excited to see them use it all night. Both Anesh and most of the other crew had been practicing this way more than he had because of his aversion to the tech, so it was Simon and Anesh that pulled wires up out of the back of their armor where they ran down to the drone controllers at their waists and plugged those wires into their skulljacks.

Two teammates closed their eyes while the others kept watch, and two quadcopters took off from the cart behind them. One wobbled, one didn't, and James and Alanna took quiet bets on which one of their pilots hadn't been putting in flight time. But both of the flying cameras took the corner roughly at the same time, each one going a different direction and feeding information back to the minds of the two people plugged into them.

"Left looks like a dead end," Anesh said softly. "Unless . . . no, wait. There's a gap here that leads to a break room. Yeah. We've got a break room. Coffee time?"

The left one had been the one that wobbled. "Pay up." James nudged Alanna.

"Bah. I should have known. He's been too busy lately, of course," she muttered, dropping one of her saved yellow orbs into James's hand.

[+1 Skill Rank : Rollerblading]

"Right seems fine. Just a long hall. Potted plant at the end of it, *absolutely* alive," Simon said a little too loudly. "Heading back," he announced.

A few seconds later, the two drones came around the corner. Anesh landed his almost flawlessly in his own hand; even though they'd learned that their shell upgrades didn't actually apply to drones they were flying, they still could attain a remarkable degree of finesse with the things.

When Simon's drone came back, though, it did so almost completely upside down, then rapidly lurched sideways and slammed into the vending machine before Simon opened his eyes with a *hurk* noise and pitched sharply to his left as well.

"Ow," he softly gasped from the floor.

"What the hell?! Are you okay?" Momo was instantly at his side, demanding, "What happened?" She spoke before James could ask the same question.

Simon rose to his feet, shaky. "Ugh. The direction changed when I turned around. I don't know what happened; it was like I was just suddenly upside down."

"Orange." Alanna and James spoke in unison, like they were old hands at this. Both of them looked at Anesh, who already knew the decision had been made. The two of them had been interested in trying to absorb an orange ever since Anesh had duplicated himself.

He rolled his eyes at them. "All right, all right. We'll get more coffee later."

"I'm not hauling a coffeemaker back again anyway," James said. "We have a perfectly good one at home and—oh god, I've become my mother."

"We also have a cart this time," Anesh pointed out. "And interns to do the hauling. That's an American tradition right there!"

James laughed. "Don't try to tell me England doesn't have interns. I *know* that's not true."

"It's different. We pay ours," Anesh asserted.

"You pay us?" Alex half asked, wringing her hands in front of her chest.

The two looked at her, feeling the wind go out of their banter. It wasn't as funny when someone was actually confused instead of just hamming it up. "Yeah, we do. Speaking of, let's go check out the hallway that flips people upside down. Sounds great."

Everyone followed.

It took three tries, a sprained wrist, and a half dozen bruises before they figured out that the hallway gradually changed the orientation of the horizon for those walking down it in one direction, but not the other. Hence why turning around kept throwing them into the floor. It didn't help that it was almost imperceptible to people who were watching from *outside* the hallway, so they had to form a kind of human chain to see how far up the walls or ceiling those in front of them were walking. From there, though, it wasn't too hard to figure out the limits of the effect and start scouring the nearby cubes until they found the hourglass-shaped totem holding the bright-orange orb in it.

Breaking it on the spot may have been a bit dumb, and James had taken a door panel with him as he'd fallen "down" about fifteen feet onto his back. The cubicle behind him had cushioned his fall, though the shellaxy he'd fallen on hadn't been happy.

And then they'd pushed on again. They had an hour left before they had to turn around and head back or risk getting trapped here. But they were almost there. James could *feel* it.

When they'd rounded the corner, after killing their way through a potted plant that refused polite negotiation, he'd felt so insufferably smug to see the blue-and-white tile spire reaching up a mile into the artificial sky overhead. As Simon's machete cut through the last of the paper vines obscuring their path forward, James felt the stirring in his chest that he lived for these days.

Here was somewhere new. Somewhere dangerous. Somewhere that was an *adventure*. Also somewhere that he and Anesh had never been able to find their way back to after the first time, until Secret offered to help cut through the mental fog in their heads. The bathrooms in this place were bizarre.

"Everyone ready?" he asked, looking at the faces around him.

Alex nodded, Momo gave him a thumbs-up, Simon silently tipped his head in assent, and Anesh cracked his knuckles with an intense glare forward. And Alanna was the only one who spoke up.

"Just who the hell do you think you're asking?" She smirked.

CHAPTER 11

"All right, before we go in there, does anyone new have any questions?" James asked the group. Naturally, Anesh raised a hand. "No, man, I mean the actual new people. Unless . . . are you the original Anesh or the copy Anesh?"

"That's kind of a rude question," Alanna inserted slyly. She was crouched on the ground, reshuffling her backpack after having pulled out a rolled bandage earlier for Momo's sprained wrist. "All Aneshes are equal in my eyes."

Both Anesh and James turned slightly amused glowers on her before turning back to each other. "If I say I'm the copy, can I ask my question?" Anesh asked.

"Well, you already asked something, so now that the entire conceit of this pause has broken down, go ahead." James made a magnanimous "at your leisure" kind of gesture with an open hand.

Anesh nodded in acknowledgment of James, fully ignoring the newer three members of their party staring at them like they'd gone mad, before saying, "Has anyone else noticed that all the doors in the dungeon are pretty normal?"

"Is now really the time for this?" James asked back, before then realizing that sometimes details like this *were* super important and turning to examine the bathroom door.

He started running through details in his head, trying his best to put aside real-world bias and look at things objectively. Alanna stepped up beside him and matched his gaze; she was really better at this kind of thinking, looking at things with clean eyes. They'd flipped a coin to decide which one they went through and ended up choosing the men's door. The dungeon was many things, but apparently it hadn't caught up to gender-neutral facilities. The door was a sort of paneled wood, with a pane of metal where people would want to push it open; James had always assumed that was there to be easily cleaned. Little blue plastic triangle on the front telling them it was the guys' restroom. Nothing weird there. It wasn't trying to mind-control him, assumedly; Secret would have manifested if that were the case. James started running his eyes around the doorframe, the floor, everything in the area around the door. Eventually, he and Alanna looked at each other, puzzled.

"Nope. It's a normal-ass door," James finally said. He turned and raised his eyebrows at the younger delvers following them. "Anyone else got anything before Anesh makes me look like an idiot?"

"It's a door," Momo said. "To the bathroom. Which is six miles tall and fits in a forty-foot ceiling space."

Waving a hand casually, James dismissed that. "You get used to that. Any other insights?"

It was Alex who tentatively started talking next. The girl had been nervous as all hell to come in here, and James had some reservations about bringing someone this far in on their first actual non-life-or-death run, but it should be fine with everyone here to give her pointers and keep her more or less safe. "Um . . . is it because it's a normal door?"

"No, that . . ." James started before Anesh cut him off with an excited "Exactly!" James looked at his boyfriend in exasperation before sighing and resigning himself to the upcoming explanation. "All right, fuck it. Hit me. Why is the normal door weird?"

"Okay, so, think of the cubicle doors in here. The dungeon clearly iterates on them; they start out as normal rectangle holes in the walls and then get progressively weirder shaped from there. But all the actual *door* doors we've seen have been just normal doors."

James rubbed the bridge of his nose with a gloved hand. The

phrase *door doors* was when he felt the headache start. "Okay, look, this is fascinating, but we're on a time budget. Can we . . . can we just field questions from the interns and then talk about the doors when we're eating pancakes at four a.m. later?"

Anesh flushed, the blush showing coppery on his darker skin. "Ah, right. Sorry, I forgot."

"No worries. Now, does anyone *else* have a question?" James asked with what he hoped was a welcoming smile.

Simon remained silent, which James had come to expect from the younger guy. His streak of nervousness was really starting to show around the other delvers, and James was concerned, but so far, he'd never faltered in a crisis, so he said nothing. Alex also shook her head; she really was more of the observe-and-think kind of person. If she had a question, she'd keep it to herself until she knew exactly what she wanted to ask.

The last party member, Momo, though. Well, she never hesitated to speak up. "I've got a question! Isn't this insane?"

"Correct!" James answered with a smile.

"But we're doing it anyway," she half stated, half asked.

"Well, here's the thing." It took James a second to find the words he wanted to use as he made a balancing gesture with his hands. "We could go home now, but we've never seen this place before. So it'll probably have some danger in it, but it'll also probably be really cool and might have something amazing for us. Like, remember the decision trees? We don't find stuff like that by not pushing out our map of this place."

Momo saluted him, almost unironically. "Got it, boss!" She stepped back, slapping Simon on the shoulder with a grin, as if to say, "Told you so." James shook his head with a smile at the little moment between them; this was clearly something they'd argued about when he'd not been paying attention.

"All right," James finally said. They'd tucked their loot cart along the wall, shucked their backpacks next to it, unsheathed weapons and tools, and were as ready as they were gonna be. "Alanna, hit it."

The door opened smoothly on silent hinges.

"Okay, now move in a bit."

Theo stopped as she heard the voice while passing by the main dungeon door. Sarah was standing there, Ganesh on her shoulder and with a clipboard in hand, as Secret obliged the request that she'd made of the snake . . . fish . . . thing. She wasn't doing anything in particular at the moment, so she stopped to try to puzzle out what the hell was happening.

"How's it feel?" Sarah asked, as Secret parked half his fang-and-eye-studded form outside the breach back to reality.

Theo shuddered slightly as the nightmarish infomorph replied. "I am . . . uncomfortable," he said. "Though I believe I may be the wrong person for these tests of yours. As I am not entirely on good terms with corporality, I do not believe that the differences in time zones is as pronounced."

"Yes," Sarah said, slowly drawing out the word while she made a note on the clipboard. "That's why we're starting with you, to make sure it's safe." She paused briefly before following up with, "Not that I'm trying to get you killed."

"I am aware," Secret said sagely.

"Okay, I've gotta know," Theo butted in. "What the hell is happening here?"

"Oh, hey, Theo," Sarah said, looking over. "We're testing the time dilation of the door. I always meant to, and Anesh did some looking into it, but now I've got a chance and I want to make sure before I go back in, ya know?"

"Why?" Theo bluntly shrugged. "We already know how long the door is open—why bother?"

Sarah tapped her pen to her lips. "Well, first of all . . . um." She paused, then rubbed her lips. "Cherry? Wait, what?" She casually snapped the pen in half with a gesture that seemed far too practiced to Theo, and a second later the whole thing collapsed to dust, leaving behind a glimmering blue orb. "Ganesh! New pen!" She rolled her shoulder and launched the drone onto his fetch quest.

"I never get used to how those look." Theo frowned at the orb.

"Ah, right. James mentioned you were color-blind, right?" Sarah tapped the orb in her hand. "Makes me wonder if we could sense these in other ways that humans don't normally have. Like, could we tell how hot they are without functioning nerves? It's cool. But also, I'm sorry you don't like it." She gave a sad look to Theo that made the other woman want to simultaneously reassure her and scowl.

Theo chose scowl, but not a very harsh one. "I don't need your pity; it's not a big deal. Tell me about the door."

"Oh! I just wanted to know where the line is, so we can work out if there's any danger to it. I don't want to be the one who discovers the hard way that it cuts people in it in half when the timer runs out or something."

Now *that* Theo could get behind. "Good point," she conceded. "Need any help?"

"Oh, I'm fine—thanks, though! Don't you have something else to do tonight? I know it's your first time back, too," Sarah queried, holding back her normally bubbling curiosity.

Theo just shrugged again, a gesture she used a lot in here. It felt awkward to her to go from being in charge to being out of place again. "I'm mostly just filling in for Daniel. He and Tyrone have been keeping an eye on the door in case anything tries to get out, and I can get behind that. I *could* do it from outside, but . . ."

"But this place is really cool and you wanted to see more of it?" Sarah asked hopefully.

The reply was a sarcastic sniff. "Ha. No. But if I'm going to fight the stuff in here, I'm gonna need to be ready for it. And since James has decided to throw support at us bouncers, it seemed like the best bet. Everyone wins. Except the fucking dungeon."

"Aw, it's not so bad," Sarah said quietly.

"How can you, of all people, say that?" Theo hissed angrily. "How many pounds did you have to put back on after we hauled you out of the prison? How many people *died?* It wasn't just those two that didn't make it past the first day, you know. Four people offed themselves, too." Theo swept her hand at the horizon, at the endless overlapping geometric patterns that grew like beige crystals out of the eternal floor. "This place looks pretty, but it's here to *kill humans*, and I'm not okay with that."

Sarah reeled back. "Wait, four people? James never said anything about..."

"James doesn't know," Theo snapped. "And he doesn't need to. I may be pissed at him, but at the end of the day, he's the best option I know of if there's more problems with this place. So don't tell him. I've seen him depressed, and I know I haven't seen the worst of it. We don't need that right now."

"But..."

"No. Don't." Theo's tone did not brook argument. She looked over her shoulder, casually sweeping her lingering glare across the scenery. "All right, I'm going back to patrol. You have fun with your tests." The words came out a bit more acidic than she may have meant. "Just remember that this place isn't a goddamn game," she shot as she stomped away.

It wasn't until Ganesh flew back with a fresh, nonmagic pen that Sarah wiped away the tear on her cheek. "Don't you think I know that?" she muttered. The drone, sensing her distress, leaned in and settled a clawed wing on Sarah's shaking hand.

Rising up to full height next to her and coming up to just over her waist, Secret spoke. "I do not like her," he said bluntly. "She speaks truths, but she misunderstands them. Also, she hurt you. And she keeps secrets."

Sarah laughed sadly. "Shouldn't you like that?" she asked the thing named Secret that fed on secrets.

"Do you remember James's attempts at cooking before he began to truly learn?" Secret asked.

"Of course. Wait, do *you* remember those?"

"I have heard stories." Secret nodded.

"He literally burned water once," Sarah said.

"So I am told." Secret rippled with amusement.

"But it's . . . oh. I get it! She's . . . bad food." Sarah looked after where Theo had gone. "Bad secrets."

Secret nodded in assent. "You do not need to tell my father," he said. "After all, you were told not to. Fortunately, that woman does not believe I am a person and forgets that I have ears." He noticed Sarah's raised eyebrows and small smile. "Of a sort, yes," he preemptively answered. "Now. If you are suitably cheered up, let us return to testing the skein of time."

It was enough, truly, to get Sarah moving again. She had been, and still was, apprehensive about being back in this place. After all, Theo wasn't *wrong*. The dungeon killed people. But then, so did *cars*, and Sarah still got in James's vehicle every time they went for two a.m. Taco Bell. Hell, Taco Bell probably also killed people, if you thought about it too much. But both cars and burritos when you were slightly drunk and had a sober friend to drive you around were worth it, overall. Worth the risk, worth the cost, and also worth paying attention to, just in case.

And for her, it was worth it to have Secret around. Sarah had been talking to him a lot lately. He'd actually stayed with her last week instead of coming in here physically. He was . . . a lot of things that James was, really. But something new. Someone new. He reminded Sarah why she liked James so much to begin with, almost like a remix of the original person. But without the still sadly upsetting problem of having no memory of their twenty years of life together.

And without the dungeon, Officium Mundi as she called it, Secret wouldn't exist at all. And James would never have . . . Wait a second.

Sarah paused briefly and looked over at Secret, where he was moving with her back toward the door. "Sorry," she asked, "tell your *what?*"

There was a sharp snapping noise as Momo fired off a ball bearing out of her wrist rocket. The rubber straps of the well-braced slingshot flailed wildly in the brief second after they delivered their payload.

Thirty feet away, the pellet tore through the intercepting form of a fist-size insect. The creature was made of white tile, with a multisegmented body and four triangular legs that tapered to needle points. Lines of hardened grout traced along its back and face, and on that face sat a single recessed black motion-sensor dot, occasionally flickering with a dim red light from within. A fluidly organic tail with a wide edge flicked back and forth behind it as it thrashed its death. Altogether, it gave off the impression of a silverfish, if someone had designed it from the ground up to be somehow worse.

There were approximately a hundred of these on this platform. And every second, more of them poured out of the scratched and graffitied bathroom mirror set stationary at head level hovering in the air only a few yards away from the group.

The first action taken was for Alanna to raise her shotgun, but the bugs were too close, and more than one of them leaped from the nearby wall to stab too-sharp legs through Alanna's wrist, as well as the gun's breach. When she pulled the trigger, the now-crushed bug had jammed the works, and nothing had happened.

Momo had noticed and raced for the cart and her stashed slingshot as soon as it had become clear that wading through the horde to get to the mirror was suicide. Anesh had done the same, for a different reason, the two of them leaving James and Simon—and a screaming, panicking Alex—to fend off the forerunners of the swarm. James had been initially both satisfied and then grossed out as his heavy boot had smashed the first one underfoot, a spray of foul-smelling sludge oozing out of the cracks in the shell. But then they'd started arriving in greater numbers, moving in fluid bursts along the ground and walls, and things had gotten bad.

By the time Anesh came sprinting back, James was bleeding from multiple puncture wounds down his left leg and one on his fucking elbow, of all places. As his boyfriend came running back in, working to trigger the magnesium igniter on the thermite lances that he was holding, Anesh had slipped on the slick wet tile underfoot. James's heart stopped for a brief second as Anesh fumbled the now-missing metal rod before, in a smooth split second, Anesh caught the thermite, caught himself, slid across the floor in a crouch, and flicked both of the four-foot-long thermite sticks out onto the tile to form a blazing barrier of heat and molten metal. The smell of burning sludge filled the air as two dozen of the little creatures died in an instant, but the rest of them didn't hesitate. More and more of them filtered around the wall and the small gap between the thermite, pouring in.

Then, hot on Anesh's heels, fumbling at the slingshot with shaking hands, Momo had stepped in and fired over their backs. Her first shot went wide, winging out into the open space that waited beyond the edge of the platform. Her second had come close to the mirror, but one of the bugs had lunged in front of it, taking the hit. After a few more tries, her aim getting better as her frustration increased, she'd slammed one of the pellets through the defending bug and into the scratched glass and shattered it.

Every single one of the porcelain fish dropped like puppets with their wires cut.

James frantically slapped at his arms and legs, shaking off the last stragglers and fragments still embedded in his armor. He winced as he hit one of the holes in his calf where the needle leg of the bug had gone straight through the softer cloth part of the armor.

"Sound off!" he called over the still-popping sparks of the thermite that was quickly working its way through the floor.

"I'm good!" Anesh called from the floor where he'd ended up.

"Fine," Simon said curtly.

"I'm covered in bug shit," Alanna called back, followed by, "And also bleeding. Oh, that's great. Oh . . ." James glanced over and saw her covering her neck as she turned and moved carefully back to the cart and their bandages.

"I . . . what the fuck was that?" Alex said, shaky. "I wasn't . . . what?!"

"Are you hurt?" James prompted.

"No, I . . ." she started to say before trailing off.

James nodded. "Good. Get out there and help Alanna. Double-check your legs while you're there. Momo?"

"I'm good. I'm okay," she gasped. "Whooo. That was fucking wild," the punk girl whistled out.

James spat on the floor, trying to clear the foul taste in the air from his mouth. His arm and leg burned from where they bled, sticking his skin to the inside of the armor he wore. As the thermite finally burned a hole through the floor and dropped down into nothingness, he started making his way toward the mirror, kicking aside clumps of dead or disabled porcelain silverfish, skin crawling as he did so. "Okay, so, I wanna start this with the phrase *I'm not mad*," he said to Momo, who instantly tensed up.

"Wait, what did I do wrong?" she asked, worried.

"Not much, which is the point. Good instinct, good tactical awareness. We should probably teach a class on that at some point. But . . ." He looked back at her. "I just gotta know—did you have to shift the bullpup to get to the slingshot?" James asked, worrying his lower lip.

"Yeah, I . . ." Momo trailed off. "Oh. Right, guns. Guns!" She punched a fist into her forehead, perhaps a little too hard. "I'm so sorry! I didn't even think about it!" she called over to James, who was now approaching the still-floating mirror shards.

"It's fine. I think you get seven years' bad luck for this anyway. And it's kinda my own fault for not thinking to bring my gun in with me. I figured Alanna could cover that." James stepped up to what remained of the mirror, still sitting in midair, and tapped at it. It was one of those untrusting bathroom mirrors that a lot of restaurants used, basically an unbreakable piece of shiny glass that still got worn down, scratched, and vandalized. One of the shards of it in the lower left had what looked like half a phone number on it, which James promptly pledged to never call.

In the middle of it, between all the broken glass, was a green orb. A very large one, too, with a smaller orange orbiting it in lazy loops.

James reached a gloved hand in, still being careful to avoid getting sliced open by surprise, and plucked them out. The rest of the mirror dropped to the ground with a series of chimes as it hit the tile floor. He started to sigh but coughed as the long breath he was sucking in brought the thick scent of decay with it.

Before he turned back to get his injuries bandaged and added to his growing list of scars, James stopped and looked, really looked without worrying about his impending death, at the area around them.

He stood on the edge of a slick platform. Underfoot was linoleum, slick with black sludge blood and a thin layer of what he hoped was water. To the left of the door, as they'd come in, was a blue tile wall with strangely rippling grout filling the spaces between the small panels. It rose up overhead, turning into an arched ceiling. But that ceiling only made it a few feet away from the wall before it ceased. It was like some massive creature had taken a bite out of a room; the ceiling, the right-hand and back walls, even parts of the floor, were all just missing. Carved away.

And beyond them, a scene from a fever dream.

Shapes that were vaguely recognizable as twisted versions of bathroom fixtures floated in the sky. There were outer walls, maybe five hundred feet away in all directions, that held within them an expanse of open air. Despite having entered at ground level, James peered over the lip of the edge he stood on to see that this place went down as well as up. Maybe thirty feet below, there was another platform just like this one, a small sliver of an office bathroom made manifest and stabilized to float gently within the open space. It was hard to make out in the gloom; oh, there *were* lights, but they were often tethered by cable threads to the islands in the air, and it left a lot of the area dark.

But through those occasional sources of blazing white light, James could see the air also held flowing rivers of water, some of them falling, or perhaps rising, in vertical columns. But others moved with serpentine casualness, wrapping in loops around or sometimes through islands. Sometimes moving alongside them, flocks of paper birds filled the air with flashes of white as their skins caught in the lights.

And there were other things out there, too. Over the noise of rushing water and fluttering paper, James could *feel* it in the air. Something lurking in the wet spaces. He just didn't know what it was yet.

When Anesh stepped up beside him, careful not to slide on the floor, he looked over at James after a minute. "Well, this is a hell of a thing," he commented as Alex and Momo also came to observe it.

"Yeah, fuck this place," James said, turning around. "I feel like I'm gonna be damp for a week."

James'd had his back turned for less than a second when Anesh slipped on a puddle and almost went over the edge. Alex had caught him by the wrist, while Momo lunged to wrap her arms under Anesh's shoulder and haul him back up. By the time James, startled by the yelling behind him, had turned around, they'd already yanked a panting Anesh back over the lip, and he was sprawled on his back on the floor.

"Okay," Anesh said. "I'm coming around to your way of thinking."

"We're buying kitchen crew shoes before we come in here again," James stated, hand against his chest as he calmed his breathing. He reached out a hand to help haul Anesh to his feet while Momo and Alex threw worried glances at the drop off the edge. "Also maybe some grappling hooks. Climbing gear in general. Anyway! Someone tell Alanna to come look at this if she wants to. I need to get some Band-Aids, and then I think it's time to turn back."

Turned out, being soggy was an almost universal sign that the fun for the day was over.

CHAPTER 12

"I am almost positive we took a wrong turn somewhere," Anesh commented, sounding a lot less worried than someone should be when they were potentially trapped in a dungeon. "James, do you have the map we were drawing?"

Drawing, in James opinion, was absolutely the wrong word for how they kept maps when they were first exploring. It wasn't anything so impressive as a sketch of hallway and room dimensions with marked points of interest. Instead, they kept a written list of turns taken, rough distances traveled between each direction change, and small notes about things to look for to orient around. He'd actually had an argument with Anesh about it and gotten perhaps a little too angry over the terminology.

There'd been an apology afterward, and they'd both blamed it on being slightly damp and covered in small cuts and bruises. But Anesh hadn't stopped calling the thing a map.

"Ah, I think I see it," James said, discussing with the others what path they'd taken. "We never took that turn that would take us back by the second break-room area on the way back. We just kept going straight. Thaaaat's probably my bad."

"What do we do *now*?" Alex asked. She'd been getting a lot better at reacting in danger situations, but when it came to strategic planning, she seemed almost terrified of the dungeon. It was behavior strangely at odds with James's initial impression of the young woman who'd tried to kick the head off a camraconda.

"We . . . make a small turn that way?" James said, pointing down past the vending machine that Momo and Alanna were eagerly using to turn nonstandard bills into weird sodas. "It's not a big deal. Space in here gets weird sometimes, but this isn't Hogwarts. The hallways are *mostly* a grid, and we know that if we go that direction long enough, we can hit the outside wall and find our way back from there."

As James got them rounded up and moving again, Anesh decided to take a moment to complain. "Okay, do you think the dungeon would consider it rude if I took my shoes off?" he asked curiously.

"Why . . ." James and Alanna said simultaneously, causing small grins on each other's faces.

Anesh rocked on one of his feet, producing an audible squelching sound over the low hum of the dungeon's air conditioners in the distance. "Because my socks feel like a swamp and I hate it," he said. "The bathrooms were a terrible idea, and I'm trying to figure out why we were ever excited to go there."

James laughed. "Okay, okay, I get it. I'm gonna tell you to keep your shoes on, though. We've still gotta head back, and if we have to run, I don't wanna lose you to a misplaced thumbtack."

"Aaaww, it's sweet that you think of that for him," Momo butted in.

"Don't read too far into it." James waved a finger at her. "This isn't a relationship thing; this is tactical. I'm gonna tell you to leave your shoes on, too."

"Fiiiine," Momo whined, getting a shared chuckle from James and Anesh.

"Okay, enough of this." James grabbed his bag off the floor, closing the booklet of directions and tossing it to Anesh, who shoved it back into a pocket. Throwing the backpack over his shoulder, James took a deep breath of recycled air as he slowly turned his eyes to look around them. "That way!" he declared authoritatively. "Alanna, radio in to the others, just to check in. We'll have them send up a flare when we get closer to the door."

Alanna saluted him, only mostly kidding. "Yes, sir!" she drawled out with a cheeky smile.

"Everyone else good? Wet socks don't count right now." James looked at the other members of the team and got a series of nervous nods or casual shrugs. "All right, let's hit the road."

"Aw, come on, react a *little*," Alanna groused. "You're not supposed to actually like getting saluted!" she reminded James. But while he shot her a knowing smirk, he also had a solid feeling in his chest at the thought. James *was* falling into a leadership role; only this time, it was more or less on purpose. He might have extra responsibility, but he also had the skills to rise to that challenge. So, for once in his life, he looked at the part of the mostly ironic salute that was genuine and realized that it felt good to be able to trust Alanna fully to do what was needed.

Saddled with damp clothes and armor, heavy backpacks, and dragging a cart now laden with a decent weight of loot, six delvers chose a direction. They tore down the curtain of printer paper obscuring the hallway, gave a few hostile eyes to the striders that perched on the edges of cubicles safely out of reach, and double-checked their weapons and armor straps. Then, in spread-out pairs, they began their trek.

They lacked the bold confidence that they'd had when they were on the way in, but they weren't afraid. They were armed, alert, and together. And they were ready for anything.

"I have a question," Dave said, breaking the long silence that he and JP had been sharing.

The two of them were perched on top of a desk that had been cleared of all random office debris, a statement that made JP realize how quickly he started thinking of pencils and documents as debris once he was exposed to this place. They were less human artifacts and more like . . . rocks. The wall in front of them was one of the lower cubicles, not so deep in that it was jagged or broken, but instead a smooth line parallel to the floor. "Lower," of course, meaning simply that they could peek over it from a half crouch when they were standing on a desk; the walls got tall in a hurry around here, without much of the normal office landscape that JP remembered from the first time his friends had dragged him into this madness.

They had been waiting here, in companionable quiet, for fifteen minutes now. Across the intersection, keeping watch over a different angle, Sarah and Tyrone had also been tasked into spontaneous sentry duty with them.

"No," JP replied to his friend, "I still don't know why Ganesh wanted us here, I don't speak drone." He thought for a second about the nature of the place they were in and remembered the trio of stored yellow orbs in his pocket. "Yet," he appended.

"It's not that," Dave reassured him, which was strangely not reassuring. JP had noticed that Dave had been more than a little transformed by the dungeon and by his own near-death experience. Not even six months ago, Dave had been JP's best friend. Still was, really. He was kinda whiny sometimes, he didn't really think too much about other people, and he had a bad tendency to assume that someone else was going to fix his problems for him. *This* version of Dave complained about things that were literally trying to eat him, which was always fair; he had a near-suicidal tendency to put others' safety over his own and trusted that James would fix not just his problems, but *every* problem. This, JP realized, was how cults started.

"All right, what's the question?" JP prompted.

"Do we have an etiquette?" Dave asked, earnestly.

JP tilted his head to the side curiously. "As Americans? Sort of, though it depends on exactly who you're dealing with. A lot of it is wearing the right suit, having a good handshake and first impression, that sorta thing. American etiquette emphasizes remembering how you're introduced to someone over, say, constant adherence to honorable behavior, like some—"

"No, I mean, us, as dungeon explorers. Though that's interesting," Dave cut him off.

"Oh. Then no. You've met James—he wouldn't know etiquette if it . . . or, you mean like our own set of traditions and stuff, yeah?" JP tapped a finger to his lips as he came to the realization, and Dave nodded at him. "Now that's a good question. Is this because of the whole 'loot shares or corporation' thing going on?"

"Mostly, yes," Dave answered while his eyes tracked the movements of a flock of paper in the sky overhead.

JP thought on it for a few minutes. This, more than anything, was what had made it so easy for him to make friends with Dave in the first place. Dave was really, really good at being quiet. Which didn't sound like a skill at all, and the dungeon probably didn't have an orb for it, but it was something that JP valued a lot. It gave him these quiet moments to actually think his answer through before he said anything, which was a contrast to the normal social circles he dabbled in.

"Okay," he started. "I think I've got some thoughts." Dave turned his eyes away from the paper birds to focus on JP. "So, the major one, especially with all the new people, is that we prioritize each other."

"Don't people normally do . . . okay, no, never mind." Dave could be oblivious to other humans sometimes, but he cut himself off here. He wasn't *stupid*.

"Right. If there was a choice between loot and playing it safe, or saving someone, I think our little growing subculture will always, *always* say ditch the loot." JP nodded. "And I like that. Also, kind of hand in hand with that point, we treat the loot mostly like a joke?"

Dave hummed in a low tone. "I like the loot," he said. "I miss my Game Boy."

"Sure. So. What else?" JP pondered for a second, taking a minute to peek over the edge again just in case. "Okay. Hero worship. That's a thing we sorta do, and I don't think it's a great one."

"You don't," Dave retorted.

"I've known you all for a long time. I know you're not . . . well, actually, no! You guys are literally heroes, to a lot of people. But I know that you aren't *mythical*. Have you seen how people like Simon or Harvey or especially fucking Ethan look at James? They treat him like he's a conquering king."

"I treat him like he's a paladin," Dave said with a shrug. "It doesn't seem like a bad thing, does it? We're basically creating a caste of knights, aren't we?" He paused as JP stared at him, head tilted and eyes questioning. "Oh. Oooooh."

"Yeah, caste systems probably aren't good, especially from our perspective." JP gave a considered nod. "Though, that said, even Karen respects James's authority here. But it's authority that's earned, from her perspective. The problem is that cultures like this one are almost doomed to lead to top-heavy power structures. That's not answering your question, though." JP cleared his throat, pushing away the awkward vibe he got. "What . . . what was the question again?"

Dave answered bluntly, neither annoyed nor amused, just providing information. "I just wanted to know if there was anything specifically I should be doing with the other delvers."

"For the culture we have? Answer questions, resolve disputes. Actually be the knight that they think you are," JP answered.

"I'm not—"

JP chopped a hand through the air. "Liar. But for the culture, we should maybe really be thinking about shaping, I don't know. I think… I think we should get into the habit of treating our teams like second families. We are, obviously, going to bring in more people in the future; we want to have a foundation down *now*. We'll just have to keep an eye on what language and behavior emerges and make sure to emphasize the stuff that's healthy."

"You thought about this a lot more than I thought you would," Dave commented offhandedly. It was the sort of blunt Dave-ism that annoyed a lot of people, but JP found it refreshing.

"Yes, well, I think this is why James keeps me around. I mean, I'm maybe two ranks above Helen Keller in the world of competitive dungeoneering." JP shrugged. "Hey, you keep watch. I need to go check in with the others. Don't eat all the candy while I'm gone," he said, hopping down off the desk and shaking the stiffness out of his legs.

He slipped out the door, heading over to double-check, again, that they were in the right place, mind now abuzz with ideas about artificial traditions.

"You know what I'm surprised about?" James said as he and Anesh stepped into a misshapen hexagonal cubicle while the others took a short break. The two of them had hit a second wind at some point, possibly because they weren't the ones in charge of hauling the cart. Anesh raised eyebrows at him as he casually grabbed the shirt still in the dry-cleaning wrapper and tossed it over the lamp currently in the process of exploding, prompting James to continue. "That you're here today. Not that I'm not super happy about it, but, like, I was certain you'd be spending all night trying to get the ritual that copies stuff to work."

Anesh fished through the drawer on his side of the desk, idly tossing a jewel case with an unknown band's logo on it and a roll of dimes onto the surface as he searched through the cluttered space. "It's good that you know me so well but bad that I think you weren't paying attention when I mentioned that I'd figured it out."

"What, really?" James looked surprised as he shook the beads of molten glass off the shirt before it could catch fire, the scent of melting plastic hot in the air.

"I mean, I'd thought so. All right, so, maybe I didn't. Look, there's a lot going on tonight." Anesh got defensive until James patted him on the shoulder and gave him a quiet smile that said a lot about how little he needed a justification from his friend. "Right. Right. Anyway, the bloody thing needs coffee to work."

"Who doesn't," James asked rhetorically as he shoved aside the rolling chair at the desk and started trying out passwords.

Anesh nodded in agreement. "Well, this sure sodding does. Those bags of coffee grounds have 'recipes' for the ritual on them—it's apparently very easy to make happen, but it takes a ton of coffee. And we haven't found *any* of it, except in the tower."

James hit upon the right password after a minute of typing—"hamlunch," written on a sticky note on the back of the monitor—and turned to face Anesh. "Okay, so, we need to find another tower."

"Yup. And as near as I can tell, we can use this to start doubling xenotech . . ." He broke under James's glare. "Er . . . magic items . . . without any trouble." Anesh cleared his throat as James nodded at the term correction and turned back to start sorting through the laptop's file system for anything fun. "Any suggestions if we can get enough to fire it up?"

"Honestly, unless it can just duplicate literal orbs, I feel like we might be better off using it to counterfeit a *lot* of cash." James shrugged. "Like, aside from the mapper, and maaaaybe the pen, what do we even have that has a lot of utility?"

"That seems *really* unethical," Anesh commented before thinking on what they routinely did. "Okay, so, the dungeon money isn't exactly ethical, either. You know what? I'm just gonna drop this and nod. Anything good on there?"

"Just a screen-saver file, which won't load anything but a preview, and I don't wanna wait five minutes for it to start normally." James hit the delete key and was mildly concerned when a red orb manifested in front of the screen. "Okay, that's new," he said, showing Anesh before pocketing the drop.

Anesh lightly clapped his gloved hands in a single muffled motion. "Oh, good! More things to worry about. Do you ever get the feeling this place is more trouble than it's worth?"

"Never." James didn't hesitate.

"Of course. Well, let's get moving. I hear Alanna being annoyed, so we should be good to start again. Only a half mile to home." Anesh patted James on the shoulder as he walked out, and James followed after throwing an alert eye around the room.

The group reassembled without too much comment. Simon and Momo were having a quiet conversation that quickly trailed off as James and Anesh reemerged into the wide hallway, and Alex was standing some distance ahead of them, leaning on a corner of a cubicle as she took a look at their upcoming path. Anesh silently dropped what they'd found into the cart; it was getting heavy but still had room for some more mass without going over the lip. Most of them had gotten into the habit of keeping relatively quiet, even when they were looting or taking a break and they had time and mental energy to devote to being snarky or to planning, they kept their voices low. It also helped that James had picked up a pack of earplugs from the local gun store, just in case, and most of them were keeping the things in—useful if they had to start shooting, but not great for low-pitched chats. Now, after hours spent together scouring wealth from this place, and more than a few legitimate fights, they had little to talk about.

Oh, James could always find something to talk about. Running his mouth wasn't the hard part. But right now, he just slung his rifle back onto his chest, checked the safety, and tapped Alex's shoulder as the two of them took their turn moving on point.

Two sets of feet moved forward, leading the way for the rest of them.

James let Alex sort of guide them. They already knew what direction they were going, and it wasn't a problem to keep their heading straight, unless the dungeon was oranging them. But the whole point of bringing the new kids on this run was to help them get acquainted with the dungeon personally. So he didn't prompt anything, didn't give orders. Just let Alex apply what she'd been seeing them do this whole time.

And she wasn't bad at it, either. She stopped James a couple of times to point out a mask overhead, waiting for the things to pass before moving on. Avoiding attracting attention from the floating creatures. When they reached a point with a potted plant and a water cooler, James had been surprised when she'd suggested they jump it, and quite happy with how that battle had gone. The plants were often the most flexible in terms of how strong they could be, and this one hadn't been a pushover, but the two of them had dispatched it without issue, and James had given her both the yellow orbs that dropped from it, much to her delight.

After refilling their canteens from the cooler, they moved on, the other four trailing behind them in their now-familiar caravan formation.

They didn't stop very often; the usual flow of taking the time to raid random cubicles was somewhat interrupted by their semilost nature and the desire to change into dry socks. So their course continued at a fairly steady pace for a quarter mile or so.

Along the way, they did get attacked on a couple of occasions. Once, by a single, very pissed-off shellaxy that burled out of the cubicle it was in upon hearing the sounds made by the passing adventurers. That one nearly got Alanna in the leg, and it was only quick reacting from Anesh that toppled the thing over and let them dismantle it. They saved the orb for later. The other time wasn't so much an attack as it was a natural disaster. In a place where the ceiling curved lower to the ground, a flock of paper passing overhead chose to skip flying through the hanging light platforms and instead flap its way across the tops of the cubicles they were passing through. James had known, on an intellectual level, that the paper was sharp; a piece of it had once sliced Alanna's skin, and however light that cut had been, it had still been to someone who could stop bullets. But it was another thing altogether to *feel* the burning sting as a few loose parts of the flock were pushed down into their hallway, and no one had expected it in time to get to cover.

It was a white storm. They hadn't known how *large* the flocks really were, thousands of loose sheets all flailing wildly through the artificial sky. The noise was thunderous, even through the ear protection, and even just the slim fraction that ended up in the hallway was enough to have the group constantly catching crumpled edges on their faces.

Afterward, when they'd salved cuts and duct taped the hole in the side of the cloth cart back together, after they'd restacked the overturned gear and loot and listened to Alanna swear an oath to bring a flamethrower in next time, James found a straggler.

It was a single sheet of white paper. Maybe a half dozen random creases in it, lines of gray that marked up its otherwise pristine surface. A slight tear marred one of the shorter edges, and perhaps that was why it had been dumped here on the ground, left behind by its brethren.

"I think it's young," Anesh said, curious, as James held up the still twitching page. "They flutter around all day; they should have a lot more folds and wrinkles. This one is new."

James had nodded and tried smoothing out the paper. And as he did, he realized his hands moved with a more practiced motion than he'd ever really learned. One of his first orbs—origami.

It was such a small thought, but it made him smile. Without really thinking about it, he'd pressed the folds flat, started shaping something new out of the barely resisting white sheet. A fold here, a bend there, a couple small turns of the page to cover up the rip. Press this, pull this, and then . . .

A frog. Just a little origami frog. Nothing worth writing home about. Except this one moved. Slowly at first, and then experimentally. It kicked the leg that hid the torn part of itself, and it turned a paper face that held a tiny spark of life up to James.

"Oh, this seems like a horrible idea," Alanna said cheerfully as James lowered his palm to slide the frog on top of the pile of stuff in their cart. It hopped away almost instantly, leaving the group behind, but paused at the corner of a cubicle to watch them leave. "But hey, good on you for making friends."

The laugh from that had carried them a long ways.

"All right, I think I recognize that." Momo had pointed out a weirdly shaped spire of wall maybe three blocks to their left as they walked. "Got no idea where we saw it, but I *know* I did."

"Good. Means we're getting close." James nodded. "We'll press on a bit more, and then find a place to sit and radio in. Get them to send up a flare for us to follow. I'd say do it here, but I'm suspicious of it."

"Is it the vending machines?" Alanna asked, playfully elbowing him. "It's the vending machines, isn't it?" They'd been encountering them at literally every intersection of hallways, far more frequently than normal. They still hadn't come to life and tried to eat anyone, but it was a deviation, which made James nervous.

He shot a look at the closest one as they passed, trying not to let his eyes linger too long on the four-mile-long list of buttons on its face. "Yeah, I'm suspicious." He wasn't really that suspicious of the machines themselves, just of what they represented. A dungeon that was now changing on them, day to day. It wasn't a comforting thought, even if it *was* an exciting one.

They kept moving in silence for another five minutes, making steady progress and adamantly refusing to do any bonus looting or engage the sleeping shellaxies and striders they spotted in the cubes around them. Until, eventually, they reached something that really was different.

Alex and Simon, who had been put on point together, stepped out into the open area first, and James made a mental note to remind them to always scan for danger first before being awestruck. Still, they recovered quickly and stepped to either side of the mouth of the hall, taking a few seconds to look for anything hostile before waving the others forward with thrilled looks on their faces.

Anesh and the others dragged the cart forward while James followed their pathfinders out of the slightly too-narrow hallway.

When he stepped out of it, it reminded him a lot of the first time he'd encountered a break room or a decision tree. Suddenly, the enclosing walls fell away, the tall structures of cubicles no longer looming overhead, just forming a wide, enclosing ring. There was nothing to obstruct the overhead lights from shining down here, making it seem brighter than the rest of the dungeon atmosphere and the mild gloom they'd been going through.

There was a chest-high wall running in a line through the middle of it, slightly off center, presumably to annoy James's sense of symmetry. There were a couple of desks with low fabric walls around them, though the walls seemed more for show than real cubicles. A couple of whiteboards stood mounted on rolling frames, though those were mercifully blank. The whole place had this kind of vibe to it that this was where higher-level people did their work, where HR reps and building managers stopped in during windows in their busy schedules to have power lunches and check emails. There was a water cooler here, of a different style than they normally saw, all smooth lines and shiny black plastic. And a lone copier sat against that low wall, next to a counter with a minifridge underneath and a diner-style coffeepot with a thick black brew percolating in it on top.

The copier caught James's attention almost right away, even if it did look different than the one that he and Anesh had had so much trouble with early on. But what got his attention even more, especially since the mechanical horror seemed either asleep or not alive, was the small black cat curled up on the glass of the open device.

Momo turned to James with a look on her face that silently screamed, "Look at it! Look at how cute that thing is! How can you not be excited?" And as the others stepped up, he heard a joint noise from Anesh and Alex that basically mimicked that sentiment. But James wasn't fooled.

"Shh." He hushed everyone except Alanna, who wasn't a cat person anyway, and had her shotgun loosely pointed downrange toward the new potential threat from the start. "I know it looks cute, but . . ."

He trailed off as the cat—kitten, really—stirred. Raising its head and letting out a ferocious yawn, it eyed their group with that kind of arrogance that only cats can have. Of *course* it wasn't surprised to see them; that would be undignified. Uncatlike.

It casually arced its back before it did that cat thing where it sort of oozed down to the floor with a loud thunk as it hit and started slowly moving toward them with slinking movements.

"It seems friendly enough," Simon half whispered, flicking his eyes over to James, as if looking for approval. "We don't just shoot it, do we?"

James let out a low hum as Momo stepped forward and knelt down to reach out a welcoming hand to the cat as it approached and stopped a yard or two away. "It seems okay," he said, still suspicious as all hell. "But we should maybe not . . ." He trailed off as the cat sat itself down, still a couple feet away, and casually raised a paw to its mouth to run its tongue through its fur. James winced at the noise of it. "Is this cat too loud to anyone else . . . ?" he started to ask.

Then, the cat made a fast, swatting motion with its paw, swishing its limb through the empty air in front of itself. And Momo, kneeling on the floor a yard away, buckled as something heavy and forceful slammed into her shoulder, sending her head smashing into the floor before she tumbled across the open space and into the cube wall to the group's right with a shocked grunt.

"Fuck! Everyone down!" James yelled as he and Alanna brought their guns up.

Explosive noise filled the air as the *ptang* of James's rifle joined the thunderous blasts of Alanna's Mossberg. Two shots from her and seven from him launched downrange at the cat that was now casually bathing itself again, lead in the air over the crouching heads of Simon and Alex as the two of them crawled over to pull Momo back. Behind them, Anesh clapped his hands over his ears, covering against noise that was still powerful even through the plugs they were wearing.

They stopped firing and looked down their sights at their handiwork. To where the sleek, black form of the cat was . . . still sitting there. Unperturbed by the sudden violence against it. Then it turned toward James, ears flattening against its head, raised its hackles, and *hissed*.

"Uh-oh," James said, barrel of his gun dipping slightly. Next to him, Alanna swore a lot more vigorously than him as the cat rose to its feet and bolted toward them.

The little black furball launched itself through the air toward James's chest, and he reflexively ducked under it. But even though the cat itself didn't touch him, a massive weight still landed on his back, slamming him face first into the floor. The hard plastic shell of his armor kept the impact from hurting too badly, and if his head hadn't been spinning from the hit, he'd count himself wise for wearing the rifle strap and keeping his gun from skidding across the floor as he lost his grip.

Alanna took a swing at the cat as it passed by, her fist shooting out in a jab that contained a ferocious amount of power behind it. But just like the bullets, her punch passed right through the body of the feline assailant, leaving just a few shimmering ripples where she should have impacted its ribs.

Then it landed, tail lashing, and Alanna felt something heavy and thick smash into her torso, driving her back a few steps. And without a sound aside from a satisfied *meow* that echoed loudly even in the aftermath of gunfire, the cat started pacing a lazy half circle around their group.

Four seconds and half of them were hit without knowing what the hell was going on.

James dragged himself up to his elbows and struggled to stand. "Get Momo on the cart!" he shouted to their two interns. "Dave!" James clicked the radio on his belt active, holding down the button as hard as he could. "Dave, now is a good time for that flare!" He looked over to where the cat had reached the side wall and turned to start pacing back as it kept cunning and hateful eyes on them. The wall rattled with its passing, even without it so much as brushing it. Then Anesh was hauling him to his feet, pulling James away from the cat's path with one arm while in the other he held an unlit thermite lance.

"What's the plan?" his boyfriend calmly asked him.

"You're cute when you're calm in fights," James told him with slurred words.

Anesh narrowed his eyes. "You have a concussion," he stated, pushing James behind him, next to their cart, where an unconscious Momo had been lain heavily on top of their collective loot and gear. "We need to get out of here; we can't fight something like this." Anesh needlessly spoke to anyone listening.

"There." James pointed a shaking hand overhead. In the distance, but not *too far* distant, the red streamer of a survival flare blazed overhead. "Dave's there."

"Got it," Anesh said. "Alanna! Keep shooting! We're heading toward the others!"

Alanna didn't respond except to fire off another two shells at the cat, neither of them bothering it at all. But it did catch the thing's attention, and as it prowled over her direction, letting out another sharp-toothed yawn, it gave a window for Anesh to slap Simon on the shoulder, give a curt order, and send him and Alex with the overweight cart on their way to the far exit of this space, and hopefully closer to safety.

As the cat neared Alanna, she backpedaled, keeping distance between herself and the monster. Her gun was certainly *working*; it was tearing holes out of cube walls, splintering wooden desks, shattering coffee mugs. It just wasn't doing a damn thing to the fuzzy form that was now encroaching on her rapidly. That left two options. Either the cat wasn't *real*, and this was just an elaborate trap, or the cat wasn't *correct*, and this was something more difficult.

She didn't have time to mull it over as she felt her back hit the wall, and the cat in front of her shifted to its rear legs, showing off a white furred belly and batting at the air in front of itself with its front two paws.

Alanna brought her arms up, instinct pushing her into a blocking stance even though she had no idea what she was blocking. But then her crossed forearms caught something thick, coming down toward her head with the force of a bus. She could feel something like hair, or perhaps long fur, brush against the exposed parts of her skin for just a second before a second strike clipped her shoulder and sent her wavering to the side.

There was a gash in her armor, and long marks on the wall next to her where a third hit had apparently missed, but she wasn't seriously hurt. And now, rolling along the wall and out of the cat's range, she eyed it with a grin.

She had its number now. The thing wasn't a cat at all; it was just the light on the end of an angler fish.

Alanna shifted her gaze upward, locking eyes with a random

patch of air just over the cat. No, that didn't feel right. She tilted her eyes up a bit and more to the left. Yeah, that was right. Something stirred there, something that wasn't used to being looked at.

"Alanna!" Anesh's voice reached her from the hallway entrance that they were heading down. "Come on!" He'd lit off that piece of thermite, holding it in front of himself like a knight, and he and James stood ready to provide covering fire for her while the other three bought distance on this thing.

The distraction almost cost her an arm as the cat thing lunged in, and she threw up a block to catch scything claws on her bracer. But then she flung it to the side, and it clearly wasn't expecting prey as muscled as she was, because she could *feel* the space open up. Ducking through the opening, Alanna ignored the illusory cat as she stepped through it and booked it for her partners.

"Aim high!" she yelled at them as she slid between the two of them, clearing the space for James to start shooting.

Anesh flung the thermite brand in a spinning arc as James unloaded the rest of his ammo. James's head was still spinning, and his aim was off, but they could all see the brand clip *something*, and a small puff of flames that rippled in midair before vanishing. Similarly, some of James's bullets hit that same something, leaving splatters of blood that painted the floor and walls, even as the dripping sources became invisible to them. The splats of blood and the sprays of sparks briefly outlined a shape before them before they seemed to slough to the ground.

The visible form of a cat twitched a few times and then yowled, a cry that was ten times louder than it should have been, as it took damage. Then, it composed itself, opened its mouth, and *roared*.

"Run," James suggested, the first word oddly calm. The follow-up words weren't. "Fucking *run!*"

Everyone listened.

"Hey, guys." JP ducked his head into the other cubicle, getting a slight jump out of Tyrone and a smooth wave from Sarah that indicated that nothing in either world was ever going to surprise her again. "Just checking in. How's it going?"

"Dude!" Tyrone stretched the word out to its limits. "You scared the shit outta me!"

"We're fine," Sarah said. "Still don't know why we're here, though."

JP nodded at her. He'd always liked Sarah, in the way that he liked anyone who was honest enough that he didn't need to put effort into understanding them. "Yeah, about that. Are we sure this is the right place at all?"

"Ganesh seemed pretty clear about it, though I wish he could have explained why in the first place. We need Pokémon that can actually talk." Sarah got the closest she ever did to complaining about things. "Oh, and he actually left a few minutes ago—deeper in, too."

"Yeah, dude. Also this is where Path said we were supposed to be," Tyrone chimed in.

JP sighed in a deep breath before asking the question he'd been meaning to voice since about five minutes into their stakeout. "Okay, so, I get that Daniel is probably the best person to ask about this, but what exactly can Path *do*?"

The kind of person JP was in the dungeon was, in his own opinion, kind of just an unpracticed reflection of how he behaved in the tabletop RPGs their group played. He was a plotter by nature. He gathered information, processed it, and alloyed it into a *plan* that maximized their profit and also usually Anesh's frustration. And here, in this place, that was exactly the sort of thing he felt like he could bring to the table, when he wasn't being pushed into the position of group diplomat. But that sort of operational masterminding wasn't easy when he didn't know what everyone could actually do. Hell, he barely knew what he could do; JP wasn't a slouch—he jogged daily and he'd been on the track team when he was in high school. But that didn't translate at *all* to combat capability. Even Dave did better than that, much to his frustration.

So he'd been asking. Sometimes about orb powers, sometimes about general skill sets, and sometimes about what infomorphs were capable of. It was how he knew that no one could tell him what Secret could do, because the nature of Secret kind of forbade that.

"Path? Oh, dude, it's pretty cool—lots of stuff! Like a chill dude who's also a map," Tyrone answered. The guy kind of annoyed JP sometimes; he was always upbeat, which didn't seem quite right for someone who had almost died here.

"I'm looking for specifics, dude," JP replied, accidentally slipping into similar mannerisms. "Like, how'd we get here, if Ganesh was the one that told us where to go?"

"Oh! Path can pull maps freely given from the minds of those he's near. Dude's cool like that. Also, he's growing some kind of metaphysical compass that sheers toward stated desires instead of magnetic north," Tyrone said, in exactly the same tone, with no hint of irony.

There was a pause as JP absorbed the words, ignoring the smirk Sarah was trying to hide. ". . . Okay," he said, pinching the bridge of his nose. "I'm gonna have more questions later."

"No worries, dude." The younger man threw him a thumbs-up.

As JP dealt with the whiplash between the open book that was Sarah and the apparently labyrinthian mess that Tyrone was apparently hiding, he shelved his confusion and opened his mouth again. He had a lot of questions he wanted to ask both of them now. Not just about the living meme that Tyrone was hosting in his head, either, though *yes*, that was a curiosity, but also about how they felt about the dungeon.

Dave had done something really annoying and gotten JP thinking. James had kick-started building a society here and then left it unattended. And JP, for all that he might not actually want to be an adventurer in real life, really did trust his friend. And if James couldn't do it, then maybe he could shape something useful and good here.

Before he could say anything, though, the two-way radios he and Sarah were wearing on their belts crackled to life.

"Dave!" Static laced James's voice on the other end of the device, but they could clearly tell he was yelling. "Dave, now would be a good time for that flare!" The words came through. Then a thud. Then nothing else.

"What . . ." Behind him, JP heard the fiery hiss and thump of the flare gun igniting. Dave hadn't even hesitated for a second before following orders. "Guys, what's that noise?" JP asked, his ears just barely picking up a cracking on the edge of his hearing.

Around them, noises stirred in the dead air of the Office. Clinks and scratches leaping to life, rippling down the hallway they were watching in a restless wave toward them. JP turned and stepped out of the cube, one hand on the wall holding himself up as he watched down the corridor. Behind him, Sarah hopped off her perch on the desk and joined him, and the two of them stood and watched as clusters of striders and shellaxies emerged from the cubicles.

In the distance, another series of explosive cracks sounded, accompanied by a flare of white as a flock of paper took to the air.

"Gunshots," Sarah said. Her voice was calm, but when JP threw a glance at her, he saw her fingers twitching against her thigh. "That's them."

As if to accentuate that point, the vaguely bat-shaped green form of Ganesh buzzed into view. He took the corner almost totally sideways, spinning through the air to stabilize himself before launching forward at full speed toward where they were standing. Out of the other cubicle, a small projectile whipped out of Dave's hand and down the hallway, clipping a strider off the wall of a cubicle just as Ganesh flew underneath and cut short the strider's planned ambush.

In a flurry of buzzing wings, Ganesh alighted on Sarah's shoulder, gesturing frantically down the hallway. "I don't understand!" she told him, frenzied, a thin layer of panic in her voice as she tried to interpret the claw movements of the tiny drone.

"Tyrone! See if Path can translate!" JP commanded, bringing the other guy out of the cubicle.

It didn't take him long to go from confused by the sentence to a look of understanding. He reached out and tapped Ganesh, the drone reciprocating the gesture with one of his wing arms. A second later, there was the feeling in the air of an old map unrolling, which on any other day would have been fascinating to JP but right now was just a distraction he ignored. While that was going on, he stole the chance to duck back into the other cube he and Dave had set up in and grab the sledgehammer he had been hauling around all night.

JP had, on his first night here, shown up with a sword. That had proven to be utterly useless, but he still insisted on wearing what he saw as the symbol of a real adventurer on his belt, and it wasn't heavy or in the way or anything, so no one told him to stop. But Alanna had passed off the hammer to him and told him that actually being armed was important. That, and two blue orbs he couldn't figure out how to absorb, were the weapons he had to work with to deal with this whole crowd of enemies.

By the time he got back, Tyrone was speaking to Sarah. "...about a minute and forty seconds. Dudes are running from something."

"What is it?" she asked, a stern look on her face that JP hadn't seen there before.

"Map doesn't say. Just vectors. Sorry, dude." Tyrone shrugged sadly. "What do we do?"

Sarah looked down the hall, and everyone looked to her. Even JP. He wasn't a leader, not in the way that James was. Or, apparently, Sarah was. No one asked him how to win a fight, and that was just fine with him. Now was the time to book it, in his opinion, to get clear and not be in the way when the actual fighter types came through.

"We clear the way," Sarah said. "There's a swarm waking up. If they're running, we make sure they don't get stopped here. Why are there so many hermit comps here?" She mused the last bit to herself, concerned.

"How are we supposed to do that?" JP asked, sweaty hands wringing the haft of the hammer he held. He tried to remember one of the lessons Alanna attempted to drill into him. How did you kill a shellaxy? Don't aim for the faceplate, he muttered under his breath, it doesn't hurt them; go for the corners. He repeated it a couple times, like it was a mantra.

Sarah looked back, worrying her lip. "We've got a minute left. Let's get to work," she stated. And it was almost with enough conviction that JP felt reassured.

Momo was still down for the count, and James was starting to get worried about it. Well, *worried* was a strong term; worry implied that he had time to really think about it, get a good concern going, and then turn that into a weeklong fret. That wasn't happening.

What *was* happening was that he had run out of bullets, Alanna had run out of bullets, the cat was starting to suspect it didn't have to waste time sneaking after them, and they'd caught up to Alex and Simon trying to haul the heavy cart along, so they were now really losing ground.

Anesh, trying his best, lit the magnesium strip on another one of the thermite bars and hurled it down the corridor behind them as they kept running, but James knew that wouldn't stall the creature for long. It was tenacious, and also kind of stupid, which was just the worst combination.

In panted words during their sprint, Alanna had told James what she suspected about it—that the creature had a body tethered to the illusion of a cat and that they could kill it if only they could pin it down. But that was a big if right now. Still, it was nice to see their mornings of jogging together paying off. That would be a happy thought to hold on to while being mauled by an invisible monster.

His leg hurt. Those holes from the weird silverfish things burned, not from poison or anything, just because they were holes in his flesh and he'd been sprinting for five minutes straight. His arm hurt. His lungs hurt. His head was throbbing. Death snapped at his heels, and safety was an eternity away.

James almost laughed, he was so excited.

And then they rounded one more corner, the kids ahead of him shouldering the wheels of the cart onto the right track before shoving it with all their might to get their unconscious friend moving. And James turned, and saw . . .

A lot of dead striders. And more than a few gutted shellaxies. And only a few feet away from him, JP, eyes wide, plucking the orb out of the side of the tipped-over shellaxy with a sledgehammer buried through it like Thor had been in town recently.

James tried to gasp out that they needed to run, but JP got the message right away and had already dropped the hammer back into the computer case when the cat rounded the corner after them.

It paused when it saw the wreckage the other group had made of the hallway here. Dave and JP, standing this close to it, both noticed the cubicle walls rattle as the tiny black cat came bounding into view, but neither of them understood why.

"Oh, hey, a cat!" Dave said, perking up, as Alex and Simon and Anesh, all totally out of breath and unable to say anything, tried to pull him along with them.

JP wasn't fooled for a second. But he didn't make any hostile moves. And the cat, assessing the new situation, paused for a second and let out a thin meow.

Then it ran forward, under Dave's legs, and something JP couldn't see crashed into Dave hard enough to fling him into the air and over the wall of one of the cubes. There was a rough crunch as he landed on the desk on the other side, and JP yelled something that even he didn't really catch.

The cat was going straight for Alanna, JP realized, and he assumed that she'd pissed it off somehow. As he started to react, and with horror realized that his legs had decided to take him toward the monster, he saw Tyrone step out to swing a crowbar at a low level through the small black form, only to overcommit to a blow that never landed and get slapped into the ground by an unseen force as the cat raced by.

Then Sarah stepped out of a cubicle, rolling her arm in a smooth upward arc. Around her, chunks of material from shattered shellaxies and even a few bits from the dead striders made whistling sounds as they catapulted through the air. JP was terrified that she'd just mowed down the rest of his friends when he saw her aim upward—until he saw the splotches of blood pooling out of wounds in thin air. Even as the injuries vanished and the cat turned, roaring far louder than it should have been able to, Sarah was moving to another patch of floor to reload and fire a second barrage at it.

Until something yanked her arm forward, blood now showing on her pale skin, and smashed her twice against the nearest wall with ruthless efficiency.

As her suspended arm dropped from its position in the air, and the cat on the floor in front of Sarah's prone form licked at a paw, JP's brain made all the connections it needed to.

The fake cat turned, just in time to see an angry, terrified human rip a sword off his belt. And then, with almost pinpoint accuracy, jam it straight into the cat's eye. The real one.

JP felt something gooey and sticky part under his two-handed thrust, and he put all his weight behind the strike before planting his feet and screaming wordlessly as he yanked the blade upward. He could feel the rough vibration as it ground against the bone of an eye socket, hear from close up the tearing of flesh and the sloshing of aqueous humor as he tore the invisible cat's eye in half. And then he could see, as the illusion failed with a yowling scream, the ruined mess that he'd made of the beast's face.

Then Alanna was there next to him, catching a paw in an open palm and uppercutting the cat that was slowly losing its invisibility. Her fist staggered it, for all that it was the size of a car, and she didn't let up. When it tried to stand, James and Dave smashed its rear legs out from under it. And then Tyrone and a wobbling Momo piled on as well, using knife and crowbar to lay wounds down its back as they pinned it to the floor.

The thing died, screaming in pain and soaking the floor red.

And afterward, as they stood there, many of them hurt pretty badly, most of them painted with blood, and all of them in some way disgusted by the ragged pile of meat they'd turned the creature into, it was James who spoke.

"Teach you to play with your food, you fucker," he said, turning on his heel to stalk away from the corpse.

Then he ruined it by tripping over a shellaxy husk and swearing profusely. Which was, JP realized as he joined in the group's nervous laughter, exactly what they'd all needed.

Anesh rolled over in the empty king-size bed he normally shared with two other partners and one other himself. He shuffled through the blankets he'd shaped into a shell around him and pulled the stuffed bear that he'd acquired from James close to his chest. He was, mostly, asleep.

But not quite asleep enough to miss the ding from his phone that alerted him to a text. It was a special ding, because it was the one that he used for himself.

Nine injuries. Momo and Sarah going to ER to get checked out. No deaths. New cat thing. Bathrooms dangerous. Expense covered. 258y 16b 5g 5o 18r.

He looked at it for a few minutes before his brain processed the "no deaths" part, and he felt a bit of himself that he hadn't realized was tense relax. Then his phone dinged again.

Getting pancakes. Go back to sleep. Sync when home.

It was exactly how he liked messages to himself. Anesh thought about how he felt about pancakes right now and realized he wasn't that hungry. But his other self was, and the experience of food and friends and the diner atmosphere sounded nice right now.

He rolled over and went back to sleep. It would be nice when he got to remember that.

CHAPTER 13

It was a cold night—no stars overhead; the layer of dark clouds saw to that. Not much wind, but the low temperature and the smattering of rain made sure that everyone knew that winter had arrived. There hadn't been much warning of it this year; to James it felt like they'd gone straight from a late summer to the middle of winter almost overnight, and he'd been caught off guard stepping outside without a coat to find that he was actually chilled.

"We should consider storing changes of clothing in the dungeon," James said as he held the door to the diner open for Alanna. The two of them were catching up to the rest of the group who'd either not soaked their pants in their own blood or who had already had the same thought James did and brought backup outfits.

Alanna nodded and clicked her tongue in agreement. "I'll make Anesh add it to the list," she said as they stepped out of the cold and dark and into the warm lighting of the diner. The smells of grilling meat and sugary deserts drifted through the air under the orange-tinted hanging lamps, and the whole place was filled with the sounds of raucous conversation. Not from their group, though; no, it was what looked like a collection of high school students, inexplicably out at four in the morning, that occupied half the diner.

"Oh good," James deadpanned. "Teenagers."

"I don't see everyone else. Did they get run out of the building by yelling children?" Alanna looked around, taking a step past the people who were waiting for a table in front of them to check around the corner. "Also, why are there so many kids here? Is it prom night?"

"It's *Wednesday*," James said in disbelief, as if the concept of a prom in the middle of the week was totally alien to him.

"Excuse me." A server behind the cash register and pie display motioned them forward, giving a polite smile to the other couple as he told them that he'd be right back. "Your group is this way," the waiter said, leading James and Alanna around to the half the restaurant normally closed off this late at night.

James and Alanna raised eyebrows at each other as they walked back to the cluster of tables and chairs that had been arranged for their group. "Hey, you made it!" JP called them over as they walked in. He was seated next to Dave and the only representative from Karen's team that anyone had invited, Deb. Actually, he was seated quite close to Deb, and James arched an eyebrow at his friend that no one noticed in the seconds before they were seated.

Also occupying the table were a singular Anesh, Sarah, and Alex. Upon asking, James was told that Momo was still in the hospital being looked at for a concussion. "Like *you should be, too*," Sarah chastised him, which James promptly ignored. Simon was also absent, which didn't surprise James at all; that kid was skittish. He was mildly bummed that Tyrone had chosen to resume his actual work shift after the whole ordeal of the night. The dude seemed cool, which was a real commodity that James wanted in his delvers.

As their small exchange died down and James and Alanna found seats, the waiter politely handed them menus. "Is there anything I can get for you?" he asked, and James found himself suddenly realizing that this was the same person that Anesh had tipped a rent check to all those months ago, when the dungeon had been fresh in their lives.

"Can I get an absurdly large amount of onion rings and a milkshake?" Alanna asked.

"Of course. What kind?"

Alanna grinned, the kind of toothy smile that meant she was testing someone. "Surprise me," she told him.

"Yeah, that sounds good. One surprise milkshake for me," James agreed. The waiter neither hesitated nor wrote anything down; he simply nodded at them and swiftly vanished. "Is this what preferential treatment feels like?" James asked. "I like it."

"This is mostly JP's fault," Anesh said, shrugging and then wincing as the motion pulled at the bandage on his shoulder. "I'm not quite sure how it happened. Anyway, good to see you again. Have some fries."

"Technically, you just saw us," James informed his friend.

Anesh frowned. "Did you wake me up? That's really rude—that me is leaving in the morning."

"Your conversations are so screwed up," Deb interjected, leaning over JP in a way that was absolutely intentional to grab a fry out of the basket in the middle of the table. "How do you even keep track of all this weirdness?" the other girl asked Alanna, coy.

"We don't," Alanna mentioned. "We forget stuff all the time. James once forgot that Secret existed for a day."

"That was a tactical forgetting," James pointed out. "Have you guys ordered yet?" he asked the rest of the table, looking over the menu and getting a negative from his friends. "I think I want fish. Does anyone wanna get this giant-ass fish platter to split with me?"

There was, within their group, and now spreading to the new people, an interesting window of time when it came to sitting here in their diner at this hour. They had, all of them, just defied death. Some of them more than once. They'd kicked in the door, fought the monsters, and walked out both injured and empowered. And now, after cleaning up, checking their stitches, and actually scoring a really nice side-room seat at the restaurant, they were *exhausted*. So after that opening salvo of banter, most of them were content to simply sit, read stuff on their phones, and not really put any more stress on themselves until they could have hot food in front of them.

And even though James had to restore a backup on a rather outdated smartphone he'd had in the bottom of his desk drawers after he'd gotten his actual one smashed in the dungeon, it was still a comfortable tradition to him.

They were tired. Conquering, yes, but still more or less human. They all needed downtime eventually.

So James leaned back in his chair, coat draped over the back of it while Anesh leaned against his arm and everyone just kind of got quietly comfortable with each other without having to speak.

When their food did arrive, somehow showing up earlier than the orders from the groups in the main dining area, it was like a signal for everyone to take a deep breath and jump back into socialization.

"So!" James said around a mouthful of salmon. "Anyone . . . I'm sorry, hang on. What the hell is happening over there?"

JP looked up from where he'd precariously balanced on the end of his fork a single yellow orb drenched in maple syrup. "What? No idea."

"You can't eat the orbs," James informed his friend, angling a fork in JP's direction.

Responding in the most mature way possible, JP gave a toothy smile and clamped his mouth around the fork, making a show of chewing dramatically before swallowing and letting out a small puff of yellow dust. "Delicious." He nodded to himself. "Tastes exactly like how I imagined fungal classifications to taste."

"How . . . and I hesitate to ask . . . did . . ."

"Not great," JP answered preemptively. "That's why I slathered it in syrup."

"They taste better with soy sauce," Sarah informed him adroitly.

Alanna snickered, and most of the table joined in. Rolling his eyes, James conceded the point. "All right, I guess there's no wrong way to eat your orbs. Except for everything both of you just said. But whatevs. So! How'd everyone feel about tonight?"

Six people tried to answer James at once, all of them chorusing off positive or negative things. All of them also talking over the waiter who silently ghosted past their table, refilling water glasses. Eventually, voices evened out until one person took the spotlight.

"We need better armor," Alanna loudly insisted. "And not just because mine has holes in it now, though that is very much a reason." She spread her arm on the table between the plates of food and rolled back the long sleeve of her sweatshirt to reveal a series of bandages, many dyed red already. "I have been stabbed *so many* times tonight. We need something more resilient than molded plastic."

Anesh nodded at her as he drove a fork into his salad. "We should take advantage of the one green that James used at our real-world base space to try to bang something together that suits our needs." He looked around at the blank looks from a few of the others at the table. "You know, the one that makes it faster to construct . . ." —he checked his phone— ". . . clothing? Yeah. Clothing. We can test out if that works on armor as well."

"Sorry, hang on," JP cut in. "We've been using green orbs at *our* office?"

"We're not calling it an office," Sarah, Alex, Deb, and Alanna chorused in unison. Even JP joined in for the last few words, rolling his eyes.

Anesh waved them into silence. "Yes, well, James did, anyway. There's a list on our server."

"Sorry, I would also like you to hang on," James interrupted. "Do we, or do we not, have a chat group? I feel like we change our minds constantly on whether or not the government is listening in." He gave an exaggerated frown around the table as three people pulled out their phones to look up the list Anesh had posted.

It was Alanna who got there first. "Okay, first off, you two fuckers should be actually telling me this stuff. Second off, why does this say plus one basement *twice?*"

"We have two basements," James told her, laughing and flailing defensively as she punched him in the arm for insolence. "Okay, okay! So, I got the extra basement prompt twice, but it's not what you think. We don't have two *levels* of basement; we have two separate sets of access points to two different basements, which are both the same distance under the building and should in theory occupy the same space. But they don't."

"More ibuprofen?" Deb asked JP quietly, holding out the bottle she'd just pulled from her pocket. "'Cause this is giving me a headache."

"Okay, this is funny and all, but none of it answers my question," James said. "Any other thoughts on the delve itself?"

This time, Dave spoke up. "We really need better organization and coordination. Like, actual assigned teams and objectives."

JP nodded next to his friend. "I don't know if we really have enough actual objectives to make that second part work, but tonight was a bit of a mess. I would really, really like it if we could set it up so that someone else could be assigned to pull your ass out of the fire"— he pointed over at James, giving a relaxed smile to show he wasn't actually too angry— "especially when it means I'll have to stab a weird invisible cat thing." JP adjusted the collar of his buttoned shirt. "All that ichor ruined my jacket."

"Okay, so, that's *your* fault for wearing actual nice clothes into the dungeon," James chastised him.

Patting JP on the arm, Deb stage-whispered to him, "Also, it's aqueous humor, not ichor, since you stabbed it in the eye."

"Euuugh." James bit his tongue and winced as the words reminded him of the scene. "Anyway, all humor aside, how do you figure we set up teams then?"

"I dunno. That's kinda your job." Dave shrugged. "But maybe go back to the three-person groups that work best for exploration, and then pair them together for longer or more dangerous parts of the dungeon? Then we—and by we I mean James—can decide when we get in there where we'll be scouting, or how we divide up hunting grounds."

Anesh cleared his throat. "I take mild offense to that," he said.

"Dividing up hunting grounds?" Dave asked.

"Yup," Anesh responded, instantly.

James nodded. "Personally I'm against it, because I feel like it turns this into a game or something. Also, it does that thing I hate where it diminishes the value of life in the Office."

JP rolled his knuckles on the table "The value of stapler-spider-crab life?" he asked, coy.

"The value of any life," James replied, without sarcasm.

"I feel like I should also point out that I am called by my blood to resist any attempt to divide up conquered territory with lines on a map." The group at the table turned as one to look at Anesh.

There was a long pause before Dave raised a hand. "I know I don't get a lot of social things, so this might be stupid, but why?"

James raised an eyebrow at Dave before theatrically turning to Anesh and looking up and down at his boyfriend. "Okay," he said, poking at Anesh's face and getting smacked away repeatedly. "Really pronounced jawline, expressive nose, kind of a shorter face, black hair, fairly dark bronze skin . . . yeah. Yeah. The prognosis is Indian," James concluded, nodding to himself with a lopsided grin.

JP snorted a laugh, but Dave just opened his mouth in confusion. "No, I don't actually get it."

"Did you miss every world history class in high school?" Alanna asked, maybe a little more meanly than she meant to.

"I actually never got any," Dave said. "Is this a history thing? Wait, wait. Hang on. Is this about how Britain did basically everything for a few hundred years?"

"Yes, Dave," Anesh informed him with a frown. "This is a colonialism thing."

Dave nodded. "Okay. I'll just believe you. If we don't want to farm the dungeon, that's okay." It was weird, sometimes, to other people, how quickly Dave could just abandon his own ideas. He had an ability unique in their group to simply drop something that he saw as not quite working out and pivot seamlessly into something else. "What about the rest of it?" he asked.

"Anesh and I will work out a team roster once he finishes being furious at the concept of an empire," James agreed, rubbing Anesh's head. "Shouldn't be too hard. Anyone who wants to join up with us kind of already has a team, you know? We may need to mix it up to fill experience gaps, though. Ah, I'll sort it out," he concluded, noticing everyone looking at him like he was some kind of leader and instantly self-conscious. "Let's go back to talking about how JP now gets to rub it in my face that his dumb sword finally came in handy."

JP groaned as everyone laughed. "Please, no! God, the sound that made was just the *worst*! Also, at this point, it's not like you haven't been bringing spears in anyway, right?"

"The spears actually vanished," James told him with a shake of his head. "Turns out, the dungeon cleaning up when we're not there is actually a huge pain in the ass. And the spears were one of the things we left by the door as fallback weapons, so they got poofed away."

They cut their conversation as their server came by again with a pair of drinks on a tray. "Sorry about the wait," he told them with what seemed like weirdly sincere concern. "Here's the milkshakes you ordered."

"You don't need to . . ." James started, but the server was already gone, having deposited the tall glasses on the table. "Okay, what the heck is this?" He looked down at the dessert in front of him. It looked like an actual masterpiece of a beverage; the whole thing was layered like a parfait into colored sections. On top, a spire rosette of whipped cream held a pair of cherries pinned together with a plastic umbrella, and a slice of strawberry and lemon was wedged over the side. "This looks like something absurdly alcoholic that I'd get on vacation in the tropics." Next to him, Alanna had a similar concoction, though with far more chocolate than fruit, which she'd already started devouring with aplomb. "I think they might be trying to bribe us," James said.

"Nooooo." Sarah let out a surprised gasp. "But yoiks, how much have you been tipping them?"

"Some." Anesh guiltily looked out the window.

They turned then, after a bit of friendly ribbing directed at James and Anesh for their habit of financial uplifting, to stories from the evening. Most of them here had been with James as they'd aimed for the bathrooms, but that didn't account for the whole table, for the whole dungeon experience.

Sarah talked about testing the limits of the time dilation and was hopeful that she could get some more exact numbers for them next week. Anesh, drawn to the scent of math, was instantly interested in her experiments with Secret and the prospect of getting to find more reliable ways to exploit the time zone shift.

From JP and Dave, there was the brief explanation of their own side of that fight with the cat. Initially, there had been some confusion as to why Ganesh hadn't just alerted Anesh in the first place to the line of backup waiting for them, and it was with a sheepish look that Anesh explained that his partner in the sky was actually tethered to a specific phone. His phone, technically. But Anesh was a creature of habit, and so when there were suddenly two of him, and they needed another phone, well . . . he'd bought the same one. So the interface with Ganesh, by complete accident, ended up with the Anesh, who was currently sleeping cozy in bed, and not the one who actually needed it.

"We're putting stickers on your personal electronics from now on," James had threatened him.

Aside from that brief diversion, JP talked about their experience skirting the outsides of the office in the time between major events. He and Dave hadn't really gotten any huge hits, but he was just overall very proud of himself for getting through a whole day of this without spraining anything.

The duo had also noticed a tower, only a few miles away along the wall, which instantly interested Anesh.

"That's only a couple minutes by bike. And I'll bet you it'll have coffee," Anesh pointed out. Then there was another round of catching people up as to why coffee was suddenly a commodity.

"Hey, I only just thought of this . . ."—Alanna started cautiously, but she picked up a smug energy as she saw the same realization hit Sarah's face— ". . . but couldn't we just bring in our own coffee? Like, I'm not the mathamagician here, but thirty bucks at the grocery store seems like a fine investment if it lets us duplicate, like, another thousand dollars."

"Oh, on that note, we were talking earlier." James addressed the group. "Does anyone have any magic items or other suggestions that would make good candidates for duplication?" Sarah and Anesh both raised their hands.

"Anesh, you're already duplicated; we aren't copying you when you can do it yourself," JP shot across the table, casually chewing on his straw while he listened to the discussion of broader group strategies.

"Anesh, go ahead, then Sarah," James said with a tired tone. It had been a long day; snark was his lifeblood, but he was kinda running on empty at this point.

Clearing his throat with a sip of water, Anesh reached into his pocket and dropped a balled-up set of earbud headphones on the table.

"Are these the ones that can't tangle?" Deb asked, having heard rumors. "Because I would trade you something for that."

"No, and those probably wouldn't be worth copying," Anesh told her. "I don't know if these are magic—sorry, I'm actually clearing my pockets looking for *this*." The this in question was a yellow legal pad, fairly thin. It only had maybe five or ten sheets left. "This one is actually really dangerous, and I got lucky testing it. And this is why we should be copying it," Anesh said, writing something on the top sheet.

James looked over to see the phrase *behind JP's chair, Parlor Street diner, Oregon* written down, before the page was gone. Just gone, not ripped away or anything, but like it never was. Anesh, too, was gone, which was slightly more concerning. It was especially concerning for JP, who just had Anesh lean in behind him and whisper something creepy.

"There's only seven pages here and you wasted an actual teleport on a cheap joke?" Alanna demanded.

James intercepted her frustration. "No, no. It's important to make the point. And also show us all how it works firsthand. And also that was hilarious." He smirked while Anesh sat back down and JP panted, grabbing at his own chest. "Okay, that's on the short list. Sarah, what about your thing?"

"Oh, I was just going to suggest we duplicate the red formations. You know, figure out some that project exploitable information, like stock market tips!"

"It cannot be that easy to farm the stock market," James protested. "Besides, aside from Lily, no one can make the red totems, and she makes really weird ones, anyway. Also, having more doesn't help, unless it's . . . another corner case." He sighed. "Why is everything so specific? It frustrates me," James declared, stabbing his fork into a helpless shrimp as if doing so would right some cosmic wrong.

"I've actually been trying to make some myself," Sarah said. "If anyone has some free time this week, and wants to help . . . ?" She angled the question mostly toward Alanna, who instantly became occupied staring out the window. "All right, fine. Deb?"

"I've got some time before classes start up again, sure," the nursing student replied with a shrug.

"Yay!" Sarah clapped. "New friend!"

"Okay, so, the notepad seems like the obvious test run for the duper, yeah?" James asked the table.

Dave shrugged and pointed out what everyone was thinking. "You're the one in charge now," he told James.

"Ow, my organ that's in charge of personal responsibility." James mimed being shot.

While everyone rolled their eyes, JP took them back a couple steps. "Okay, quick tangent—that's actually something we were just talking about. We're talking about things to copy, right?" Nods from the table. "So, I'm curious, why aren't you making more Aneshes?" he asked the singular Anesh eating with them. "It just seems like it could be so useful. If nothing else, it would be a way to test dangerous items without risk."

"Okay, no." Anesh's voice was hard as he answered. "Every me is still me. I don't even know if I'm the original or not, but I still fear death and pain. I'm not expendable."

"That's literally the opposite . . ." James started before Anesh set a hand over his mouth to stop him.

Carrying on like James's muffled words were normal, Anesh continued. "It's also mostly a logistical problem. I need to eat food, have something to do during the day, sleep somewhere, that sort of thing. Each me consumes resources and still needs to have a purpose. Also, James's bed is only so big, and it's already kind of cramped."

Alex raised her hand timidly. "I'm sorry if this is rude, but what are you guys, anyway?"

"Partners," James, Anesh, and Alanna all said at once before grinning at each other.

"More specifically, we're one single romantic relationship. We also live together, since Alanna apparently has occupied our extra closet space now," James clarified.

"Doesn't that get confusing?" Alex asked. "Or, like, weird?"

"They said that was rude when I asked," Dave told her, but James waved him off.

Honest questions never bothered him. And actually defining this to someone who wasn't just Anesh or Alanna was kind of refreshing. "I admit, it can be awkward sometimes. Especially when I have to not tell my parents who or how many I'm dating." Anesh patted him on the shoulder reassuringly as James said that. "But weird? I mean . . ." He waved his hands to indicate the table in general. "Eh? Like, we just came out of a hole in reality that has mobile and hostile staplers in it." James reached into his pocket and pulled out a midsize yellow orb, which he thunked onto the table. "I got this for murdering a potted plant that was trying to murder me. It's probably going to teach someone how to swim or something, and I'm seriously considering leaving it as a tip. We are so far beyond weird these days."

Alex nodded. "That's fair. I guess as long as everything else is weirder, it's not a big problem then, huh?"

"Okay, now *that's* rude," Dave said. "Am I right this time? Is that rude? Someone help me." Dave cast his gaze around the table to everyone who was now quietly staring at him, seeing how long this would go. "All right, never mind," he said, breaking the stalemate.

"So anyway!" JP picked up the conversation as if that had never happened. "I kind of wanted to . . ." He cut himself off with a massive yawn. ". . . augh. Okay, well, I had wanted to talk about dungeon etiquette, jumping back to what Dave was saying earlier. But I think I might actually be a bit too tired."

"You gonna head out? I could use a ride," Dave asked.

"Yeah. How are we splitting the check?" JP asked them.

Before anyone could answer, Alanna half threw a handful of yellow orbs onto the table. "Best skill pays the whole thing!" she announced, dramatically.

"How long have you been waiting with those?" James asked her, playing up his mild concern.

"Also, why best skill? Why not worst?" Sarah asked, raising eyebrows at Alanna.

Alanna shrugged. "It's just what I had in mind. Are you guys in?" she asked, cracking one of the small orbs without waiting for the answer.

[+1 Skill Rank : Cleaning—Sweeping]

"Bah," Alanna said as she relayed the skill. "But at least I'm not paying for my food."

"This seems like a way more fun way to use these, sure," Sarah commented as she rolled one onto her finger before snapping and making it disappear like a stage magician.

[+1 Skill Rank : Geography—United States—Eastern]

"Five out of ten!" Sarah exclaimed, ranking her own skill before telling anyone what it actually was. Not even exhaustion, it seemed, could fully suppress her bubbly nature. "I'll probably never be in Boston, but if I ever am, watch out! Still, puts me in the lead—probably pretty hard to beat."

"Oh, well, in that case, I'm totally in," JP said, smushing the orb that had rolled closest to him between two fingers.

[+1 Skill Rank : Driving—Rally Racing]

"I give that a six out of ten," James said as JP described the skill. "Which puts you in the lead! Congratulations!" He and JP traded grins, both knowing full well that the money they'd gotten from the dungeon just tonight would more than cover their tab either way. "My turn." James selected carefully, to a chorus of jeers as he took his sweet time selecting the perfect orb. "This," he said, "this shall be my magnum opus."

"Not what that means," Alanna chided him.

[+1 Skill Rank : Fabrication—Costumes—Pirate]

"Yarr." James flatly frowned at the remaining dust of the orb. "Welp. That's me safe, I guess. Alex?"

The teenager looked at him curiously. "Am I allowed to? I mean, I don't know the rules on these things."

"You don't . . . what?" James was perplexed, and from the expression on Anesh's face and the quiet words Alanna was mouthing next to him, it seemed he wasn't the only one. "Of course you're allowed to. You've been cracking them anyway, right?" The sheepish look on her face was almost, *almost* worth the exasperation James suddenly felt. "Fuck's sake, of course you're allowed to," he repeated. "Just pick one. They're harmless and sometimes useful, and I am now giving you explicit permission to use any orb you find, in any way you can manage, and Alanna's glaring at me—oh god, what did I forget?" James stuttered out the end.

"Not the greens," Alanna reminded him.

"Right. Right! Any *nongreen* orb." He looked back at Alex, who seemed torn between embarrassment, amusement, and horror. "Just try one," James said, trying not to think of how much he sounded like a peer pressure PSA gone awry.

[+1 Skill Rank : Music—Flute]

"Damn, now I feel bad," Anesh said as Alex told them what it was with a growing smile. "You might have to pay for our dinner." He selected his own orb.

[+1 Skill Rank : Animals—Birds—Hawks—Northern Goshawk]

James blinked slowly at his boyfriend as the information was revealed. "I think that is singularly the least useful skill we've ever gotten, and also the first four-tier skill. Neat! Congratulations!" He cheered Anesh on with a pat on the back. "All right, Deb or Dave?"

"Oh, I'm out of this." Deb held up a flat hand, deflecting responsibility. "I only got a drink, and JP said he'd pay for it anyway."

"You ate half my fries!" JP protested.

Deb nodded. "*Your* fries." She pointed over at Dave. "You go. I believe in you!" she told him.

"I like her," Sarah muttered out of the corner of her mouth to James, leaning across the table to talk to him. "They're cute."

"You always say that about people," he replied.

"Only cute people," Sarah corrected him. "Also how could you possibly know that?"

James winked at her. "Instinct?" he tested, and was rewarded by Sarah grudgingly nodding.

Meanwhile, Dave had broken down under the constant barrage of encouragement and picked up an orb to use.

[+1 Skill Rank : Medical—Surgery—Lung]

"Really?" Deb demanded when she heard the skill. "Really. Just a flagrant disregard for how hard medical school is, huh?"

"Hey," JP reminded her with a reassuring voice. "At least he's paying for dinner."

The night wound down after that. JP headed out, taking Dave and Deb with him. Anesh gave Alex a ride home when she brought up taking the bus and promised to meet the rest of them at their place later. Collectively, they left a tip that totaled somewhere in the realm of two thousand dollars, with a good chunk of it in two-dollar bills. And before leaving, Dave cracked a green orb he'd picked up at some point, in what he called a "bonus tip" and what James called "probably unethical."

[+2 Skill Ranks : Forgery—Signatures]

[Local Area Shift : Food nutritional quality, +820 mg trace vitamins/serving]

And then there were just the three of them.

James picked idly at cold fries on an abandoned plate, watching Alanna as she threw her coat on. "You coming?" she asked him. "It's time to go."

"Yeah. Yeah, I'm just a bit tired," he said, voice flat. Almost angry, even.

Sarah and Alanna glanced at each other, then back at him. "Are you doing all right?" Sarah asked him. "I mean, aside from all the holes in your human bits," she clarified.

"Fine," James said shortly, ignoring the joke. He stood abruptly and looked around for his coat before realizing that he'd lost yet another thing to sharp parts of the dungeon. Without any indication of this thought process, he palmed his keys out of his pocket and strode toward the front door of the diner.

"He's not all right, is he?" Alanna asked Sarah, in a way that made it clear she already knew the answer.

Sarah grimaced. "He's tired. You've known him more or less for a while now. Heck, you're dating him. Have you seen James when he's tired?"

"Not really?" Alanna half questioned herself.

"I think it's something about how he holds himself together. When he gets tired, he stops focusing, and everything that's bothering him comes to the surface. But then he's too tired to talk about it." Sarah ran a hand through her hair, fiddling nervously with her braid. "Ask him about it when you're in bed—and isn't that just an awkward sentence? If it's actually important, he'll probably tell you. Otherwise he'll fall asleep and forget that he was kind of an ass right now."

"He *has* been up since seven a.m.," Alanna told the other woman as they followed James out to the car, at a safe speaking distance for privacy.

"Why the floop was he up that early?" Sarah asked, incredulous. "Wait, we were also in the dungeon for seven extra hours. He's been awake for thirtysomething hours straight?!"

"Ah. My fault there, I think." Alanna's turn now to look sheepish. "We went on a morning jog."

"Is that a euphemism?"

Alanna just rolled her eyes as the two of them got into the car and drove home with only the radio for company. They were either too tired or a little too concerned to talk now, so the only noises in the car were the music and the occasional hum from Ganesh's rotors.

When they made it home—and they did make it alive despite all of them practically dozing off, including their driver—the postdungeon ritual felt almost abrupt. At least to Sarah. They stumbled in, let loose their two small companions, unceremoniously dumped a sleeping Secret onto the couch to be harassed by a very excited Aberdeen, and just sort of plodded to bed. Even the least tired among them was eager to just lie down and untense from the trials of the day.

"Oh, hey, Anesh is already back," Alanna noted in a whisper as she and James stepped into their shared room and quietly began peeling clothes off before dropping onto the blankets.

"We're both awake, kinda," an Anesh on the bed muttered. He rolled over as James climbed under his comforter and wrapped an arm around his partner.

Alanna joined them shortly, and there was a moment of just warm comfort before she rubbed a hand down James's back and asked him what had been on her mind for the car ride home. "Hey, are you okay? You seemed really upset back there."

"It's . . . nothing," James blatantly lied.

"Woah, even I caught that." Anesh pulled back a bit. "Hey." He looked James in the eye as his double stacked up on top of him and did the same. "Talk to us. What's up?"

"It's stupid," James lied to himself this time.

"No, it isn't. Stop it. What's going on?" Alanna said, more forcefully.

There was a moment where James considered just saying nothing until they left him alone. Or where he tried to come up with some kind of witty remark to ease their worries. But then, something in him just crumbled apart. Maybe he was too tired to form a mental defense, or maybe he really did just trust them enough, but either way, he started talking.

"So I was at Subway the other day—don't look at me like that, it's cheap and adequate—and I'm standing there in line, and the guy in front of me is just going *off* at the artisan sandwich master about how he doesn't like the quality of the meatballs. Like, he was swearing his fucking ass off over this. And I'm standing there, waiting for my turn to complicate the employee's life with my weird order, watching this grown man throw a tantrum, and that was sort of when it hit me, you know? That I almost died."

Alanna opened her mouth to say something, but one of the Aneshes caught her eye and gave a slight shake of his head. James didn't notice any of this; he'd pressed his face down into the pillow and was staring off at the wall, so he kept talking.

"When we were at the door, when the dungeon woke up pissed from whatever Monster Karen did to keep it down, and it threw everything it had at us, remember . . . yeah, of course you remember." They did. Alanna especially. "But, like, I made the choice to buy time for everyone to get out. And at the time, I was terrified and my heart felt like it was on fire and I don't even remember half of it. I think Secret bit a guy in half?" James felt like he was rambling, his words becoming more frantic, tumbling over each other in a cascade. "Like, I *feel* like that happened, but I can't get at the memory. But what I do remember is, by the time everyone was out, we got overwhelmed. And I went from fighting to pinned to dead in less than a second. I was on the ground, and I was inches away from death. But all I remember is seeing Alanna go down, too, and being afraid for her."

Her hand traced small motions across his back as he spoke, and Alanna felt a surge of something in her chest as James talked about this. But still, she didn't interrupt.

"I didn't get that thing where my life flashed before my eyes, or I had some kind of moment of revelation or inner calm, or where I saw God or whatever. I didn't have time to be anything other than ready to fight, and angry. And then I was down, and then I was going to die, and then, all of a sudden, *you* were there, and I wasn't anymore. I was dead, and then alive, all before I got to think about either of those things or what it meant or if I *cared*."

James turned to look at Alanna, and she saw his eyes were wet even in the dark of their room.

"I think so *much*. I don't know if I ever say it, or express it, but it doesn't *stop*. I can't make it stop. Every day in my head, I do this long-form analysis of conversations, of books or games, of ideas and tactics. And every single night, I go to bed afraid to die. And then, instead of having time to think about how I felt, this thing just *happens*, and then you stop it, and that's just it?

"And then we got up, got out, and the day was saved.

"And apparently, I've been walking around having a near-death experience for the last four months, because it was only right *then*, while Meatball McYellsman was screaming about red sauce, that it occurred to me that I would have been *gone*. Wiped away, into oblivion, forever, no take backs. Probably. Things are weird now."

James didn't find what he was saying funny, but he still got a snort of surprised laughter from Anesh.

"Part of me felt like taking it out on yelling dude, you know? It would have been so easy—it's not like he was a stuffed shirt in the nonmetaphorical way. Throat strike, grab the neck and one wrist, slam his face into the glass, done. And I had a lot of those thoughts, too. Different things I could break, how fragile the world seemed around me, how many ways I could hit something with my car . . .

"But I thought that, and I felt just disgusted with myself, on top of the existential dread of almost death. And then I just thought about if I should, you know . . . die. Like, maybe if I just slump down on the floor, everyone will forget about me and I can disappear and not feel this way anymore. Or maybe a mix of the two, also involving hitting things with my car, but at higher speeds.

"I don't know how someone is supposed to feel when they dodge death. It's not a thing they ever taught us in school. Anesh, I dunno how schools are in London, but for reference, *feelings* aren't something anyone explains here in the States. But I don't like this. I just keep . . . jumping around. I'm furious, or I'm hollow, and there's no in-between, except for right now, where I can't stop talking and I feel like I'm going to start crying any second now. I don't know what I'm supposed to feel, but this *can't* be right.

"And I wish all of this was just a roundabout way of telling you that I had to pay for some angry asshole's sandwich after I pitched it at high speed into the parking lot. But the truth is, I'm scared, and cold, and I don't know what to do."

Anesh and Alanna both moved in and wrapped their arms around James in a silent show of love, burying him in their embrace. He let out a short series of sobs before composing himself a bit and gasping in breath, letting the last of his thoughts trail out in his words.

"There's this part of my brain, the part that wants to be a hero all the time, that tells me that trading my life for fifty others' was the right call. That it was a steal at half the cost. That even one life is worth the trade. And that's great and all. But there's the rest of me that screams that no matter how dearly I sell my life, some things simply do not have a price. Ever.

"And I want to be heroic, but I don't know if I can ever do something like that again now. I'm not even really sure I want to go back into the dungeon at all. But we are going back. We just did it, and it was great, and I'm still having fun, and it's great. Really, really great. New friends, new adventures. It's everything I wanted, I thought. It's just that afterward, now, all I think about in the quiet while I wait to fall asleep is how close to the edge I feel all the time."

He opened his eyes as he sat up, rotating to look at the two of them as they lay in their shared bed. "And now I feel even worse about this, because I know that you must have gone through the same thing, Alanna. And Anesh, you literally saved my life. And I'm just falling apart over it for some reason."

"Hey," Alanna said, reaching out to him.

"What?" James didn't move, sitting there and starting to feel his hands shaking.

"Hey," Anesh echoed her, each of him reaching one hand out to James.

"I don't..." James started to say. But then they reached him, and he felt their hands on his shoulders and arms, comforting and warm and loving. And together, they pulled him back to his pillow.

"We're here for you," Anesh said. "That's the point," the other one picked up.

"I know this is going to sound cliché," Alanna told him, holding him as tightly as she could without reopening either of their injuries. "But everything is going to be okay."

Anesh nodded, unseen but still there. "Now," he said. "Go to sleep before the birds start screaming. Some of me needs to be up in two hours."

And just like that, the tension broke. And James laughed, and things were back to normal. But even though the hurt was still there, some of the poison was missing from it, the fear in his heart withering when it was out in the open and dying wholesale in front of his partners' love. And tonight, exhausted and drained both emotionally and physically, when his head finally hit the pillow, he was asleep in an instant.

No fear or dread, only dreams.

CHAPTER 14

Eleanor sat in a booth at a fast food joint that hadn't been cleaned in a week. She looked down at the burger in her hands and tried to find the words to describe it. As a whole, El thought, she was an artist; she didn't deal with words that often. When she spoke, she liked to use dumb slang, rambling and uncouth sentences, and not a whole lot of words like *rambling* or *uncouth*. Which made the task of describing the uniquely awful burger quite a challenge.

The thing of it was, it wasn't *inedible*. It was just the worst burger she'd ever had that was still clearly food. The lowest-quality meat, the most overmicrowaved bread, soggy, warm lettuce and inexplicably frozen tomato slices. It had some kind of yellowish substance melted on top, which the image on the menu insisted was cheese, but Eleanor knew must certainly be something from a place like the endless road, what she called Outside Influence.

It was so bad. She took another bite.

She felt like she needed to make friends with a poet or something, just to have them craft a sonnet about how little she was enjoying this meal.

All of this was a distraction, and she knew it. El sighed and half tossed the barely food object back onto her tray as she leaned back and looked out the window at the overcast day and the litter-filled drive-through. It wasn't, she mused, like she had anywhere in particular to be. But still, somehow, against all reason, she felt like she was wasting time here.

She didn't actually *want* to leave. This small California town was basically perfect for her at the moment. She had an old clunker of a car to work on and sleep in, she had a few hundred bucks from a few odd jobs she'd done on the road, and she had constantly eighty-degree heat, even on days like this where a thin drizzle threatened everyone. She even had a bag of spray paint cans "liberated" from a bunch of high schoolers and some cool panels of old ceiling tiles to make some rad art on. She'd only sold one of them, to a random elderly couple who were probably higher than she'd ever been at the time, but profit wasn't really why she was doing it anyway.

And yet.

And yet and yet and yet.

Eleanor wanted to leave. Partly because a month of nomadic lifestyle had grown on her, but also because she *knew* this wasn't where she was supposed to be. In a way that was totally internalized and absolutely not her own thought, El was certain that she had to go. She had somewhere to be, somewhere in the direction she'd eventually learned was north.

It annoyed her. She crushed the feeling down by jamming some onion rings into her mouth. They were paradoxically fine, compared to the burger, and did nothing to alleviate her need to leave.

It didn't really help that her magic didn't refill just sitting around here. Her personal arcane secret, the chunk of Velocity that had been implanted just behind her heart, needed her to get off her ass if she wanted to do anything with it.

Most of the time, she refilled it steadily while on the highway. Eleanor had only three spells, and each of them cost her a decent chunk of time to really build to. And each of them was precious to her in a different way, each one representing a different adventure survived and triumph won. On top of being literal magic, of course.

El missed the adventures. She missed the open road, danger and the monsters and all. Especially, she missed her own car. Also her phone. Her mom probably thought she was dead by now and would take that super hard. But El couldn't contact her, couldn't turn back until she got to the end of this road.

A month ago, two people and one *thing* had walked into her workplace and made El realize how insanely narrow-minded she'd been. Of course there were Wizard Police and their pet monsters out in the world—of *course*. But it had kicked off this journey for her, and now, at least, she could find some measure of truth before either her return home, or her death. Whichever seemed most appropriate.

Ugh. The terrible burger was making her maudlin. *That* was a word she'd stolen from a writer friend back in college, one that she knew how to use.

El shoved herself up and tossed her trash. A few more days, she decided. She had this image she was trying to get just right with the spray paint, a highway that went on forever into a sunset. But spray paint was a fickle mistress, and also El owed the guy who'd given her the car some help around his place. Also she owed that car an oil change.

Yeah. Just a few more days, and then she'd hit the road. North, and the end of the road it offered.

"Okay, you know what I hate?" James said as he held the back end of the piece of machinery, applying leverage to try to help Alanna roll the wheeled cart they'd set it on over the lip of their building's loading dock. Alanna grunted wordlessly as she pulled the cart up and over the small bump. She didn't answer James, instead focusing on balancing the hundred-pound and thousand-dollar equipment on the wheeled frame they were using to move it. He kept going anyway. "The absolute lack of bags of holding," James told her.

Alanna didn't answer him until after they'd pulled the thing off the cart, recklessly kicked the cart away and into a desk, and then much less recklessly set it down in the space Anesh had taped off on the floor. "Okay," she said, "now that we're done trying to not break our investment, go ahead."

"The lack of—"

"You know," Alanna cut him off, "I'm actually really annoyed that I know exactly what you mean."

James paused briefly before recomposing his point. "Yeah, I just feel like it's a bit unfair that we haven't—"

"No infinite bags, no storage rings, no ability to warp space. We're being cheated!" Alanna kept rolling over James. He stared at her for a second, waiting briefly before opening his mouth to say something. "At least a magic lunch box!" Alanna instantly interjected.

"Am I being punished for something?" James glanced around the warehouse space with a puzzled look on his face. "Sarah. Sarah!" he called over to his friend as she brought in a box of plastic sheets and dropped them on a nearby table. "Am I being punished for something?! Cosmically or otherwise?"

"Probably!" the other girl called back, smile and cheer infectiously upbeat, even through the bad news. Without sticking around to figure out what was going on, she was already back out to unload another box from the truck they'd rented.

"Okay." James addressed Alanna. "Clearly you've got opinions on this. Is there . . ."

Alanna swatted her hand onto the top of the table. "An extradimensional mail cart!" she exclaimed. Then, in a more normal tone, "Okay, that's the last one I've got. I'm just messing with you, but really, I'm on your side. It's kinda weird that we haven't found anything like that. I mean, we've got a lot of literal magic kicking for us now, right? Skill levels and things akin to spells, so why not the classic inventory?"

Nodding along, James agreed. "It is weird," he said. "But then, we're also in here on my day off to try to turn polyethylene and sheet metal into workable armor, so what the fuck do I know about weirdness anyway."

"Also so I can show you a thing!" Momo's appearance wasn't surprising; they'd both seen her wandering in from the front of the building where Sarah was currently setting up for the support group meeting today. "Hey, guys. How's it going?"

"Not bad," Alanna answered. "There's a lack of *bags*," she intoned sagely.

"Right." Momo nodded like she understood. "So . . . actually, what's the machine?" She said the word like it was a sacred idol and not just a table-size tool still in its shrink wrap.

James patted it affectionately. "A compromise. Anesh wouldn't let me spend thirty grand on an injection molding station, so we have this thermal one instead. Basically, it shapes plastic to our specifications."

"Why? Like, fuckin' rad, but why?" Momo bounced on the balls of her feet as she peered at the case on top of the contraption.

"Because we're taking too many injuries, football armor isn't cutting it anymore, and we can't afford to keep replacing the riot armor that we use," Alanna explained. "So, we got this thing to do part replacements and eventually work up to being able to make our own whole suits."

"With any luck, we'll be able to put together the money to start getting into really bonkers material science stuff, like the injected polycarbonates and such," James said. "Until then, we're going with making molds for arm, leg, and chest pieces that have mounting points for steel plate and the Kevlar underlayer. That *should* be *incredibly excessive* for the dungeon, but then, I've been shot by at least two things that would disagree." He rubbed at the point on his side where a rogue pencil had once threatened to end, if not his life then at least that of his kidney.

"Also we want to see if the green orb that makes it easier to make clothing works on armor plate," Alanna added.

James wavered a hand in front of him. "Faster, not easier," he said. "But if we need to mass-produce, that'll be huge. And we need to use more greens. Find those little exploits."

Momo shot them a double thumbs-up. "Yeah, that'll be cool. Though it didn't do much against the cat," she said.

"Yeah, how's your head?" James asked, concerned.

"I'm fine, just sore," she replied.

Alanna and James shared raised eyebrows. "Really?" James asked. "Because you had a pretty bad concussion. I feel like you shouldn't even be here—you should be resting."

"Oh! No worries on that. I've got a nest set up in one of the basements. Anyway, I've been getting a lot of work done, and by 'work,' I mean 'fucking with the red orbs until something clicks,' and I got something to click." Momo rattled off the words in a blur before turning on her heel and walking toward the door that led out of the back workspace and planning zone they'd set up.

Alanna leaned down to James and muttered in his ear, "Did we move the coffee machine here? Or is this normal?"

"Did she imply that she's been sleeping here?" James hummed back at the same tone. "I'm worried about that girl."

"We should go see what she has for us before she combusts. And also before the support group tonight." Alanna sighed.

"Is this what being parents is like? Also, give me an excuse to skip the meeting. Sarah keeps asking me to show up and test out the skulljack, but I . . . can't."

"Tell her that."

"It's not that simple. I feel like I'm letting her down, and that I'm making her feel like she's ignored because I'm not using the tool that could instantly repair our friendship. It feels selfish, even though I'm legitimately afraid of it."

"Tell *her* that."

"But I don't want her to be mad at me. And I'm not sure I'm ready to connect to another human yet, especially one that I 'don't know,' you know? I'm still getting used to using it for drone practice. Which is rad, yes, but absolutely not the same."

"OH MY GOD," Alanna bellowed as they reached the door and she threw it open to reveal the front half of the building. Among the comfortable chairs and the table of snacks, near where someone had showed up one day and left a pool table, Sarah stood setting up a router in the middle of a ring of chairs. Alanna thrust out a hand toward the other girl, grabbed James by the back of the neck with the other, and ordered him, "TELL HER THAT."

Then she stomped over to where Momo was holding open the elevator doors, stepped inside, and hit the button for the basement.

The last thing she saw was James giving a sheepish, "So . . . uh . . ." before the doors closed.

Alanna took a deep breath as she stared at the doors, hands clasped behind her back.

"Um . . ." From the corner of her eye, Momo looked bizarrely out of place. Alanna quirked a bit of a smile at the juxtaposition of the short girl with a neon-green mohawk, too many piercings, and a T-shirt with a skull on it, standing next to her towering form. "So, what was all that about?" Momo asked.

"Ah, don't worry about it." Alanna let out a tense breath she'd been holding. "I feel like I might be . . . well, never mind. It's a personal problem, nothing to worry about. Hey, so, what are we going to see?"

"Well, we'll need to go back up first," Momo said sheepishly. "You, um, hit the wrong button."

"For the basement?"

"Yeah, we need to go to the left basement, not the right basement."

The doors opened, and in front of them was a pitch-black square of nothing. There were no lights on in this basement.

"Fuck's sake, this is the kind of problem that only James could manifest. And that *cannot* be OSHA compliant." Alanna rubbed at her face with one hand while she sent the elevator back up with the other. "Anyway. What've you got?"

"Well, I've been messing with the red orbs ever since you brought that one here that Lily made. The thing that tells you the temperature?" Momo fiddled with the studs on the front of her belt, looking like she was under review more than just having a conversation.

It wasn't lost on Alanna. "Hey, calm down," she said, before acknowledging, "I know that literally never works, but I'm not gonna fire you if you don't get results, okay? We literally didn't ask you to do this, so it's just a cool extra thing, okay?" she reassured the younger woman. "I also don't think I can fire you. I don't think we *hired* you."

"Right. Sure." Momo nodded as the doors to the elevator opened again, this time showing a totally different basement space. Albeit one with lights on, unlike the dark zone that was the other basement. The basement that occupied this same space. Alanna felt a headache coming on again. If Momo noticed, though, she didn't let it bother her as she led them out and over to one of the three walled-off rooms that covered the far side of the basement opposite the stairs. "So, I've been trying to figure out how to make one."

"Did it work?" Alanna asked, mildly surprised.

"Yup! Well, I mean, I can replicate the one Lily made, and it does the same thing. So it's not magic to *make* them." She opened the door to one of the rooms, and Alanna instantly knew that outside it was a chilly sixty-two degrees, while just inside the door of the office it was a balmy seventy-four. It was also drizzling. "Mine stops at doors, though?" Momo explained, as if that explained anything. "I don't know why. Lily's didn't, but that one got . . . um . . . broken?"

"Don't worry about it," Alanna said as she followed Momo inside, looking around the room. The space contained a couple folded card tables, one of which had the red orb totem sitting on it, next to another totem-esque object that lacked a red orb in the middle and seemed to be made out of pipe cleaners and tape. There were also dozens of pages of paper taped to the walls, with different patterns drawn on them and scrawled notes next to them. A Jolly Roger flag, black and white skull grinning down at them, sat above the van-size pile of blankets and pillows that dominated the corner of the room. Scattered on the floor were shirts, socks, and a pair of bright-orange panties that Alanna discreetly nudged out of the way with her foot. "Okay, so, I hate to ask, but have you been living here?"

Momo laughed, nervously. "Um . . . yeah. Kind of. I sleep here a lot. The dungeon money means I can eat out all the time, so I don't worry about food. I didn't really ask, but I figured we weren't using the basement, and . . ." She looked away, and Alanna heard her sniff quietly in the otherwise silent air of the place. "Ah, it's nothing."

"No, it isn't," Alanna said firmly. "Your welfare matters to me. And if you need a place to stay, we're getting you some furniture. Like a dresser."

And just like that, Alanna crushed all the worries Momo had. No discussion of *why* she was here, no more panic that she'd get kicked out. No more feeling like she was wasting Alanna's time. Just an unquestioning offer of help, and a quiet assurance that everything was fine.

Momo liked Alanna. A lot.

"Ah. Well." The goth wiped her eyes on the sleeves of her shirt, absolutely not crying in the slightest. "We can talk about that later. I wanted to show you this!" Her energy spiked back up as she turned to show Alanna the totem. "This is attempt number . . . oh, fuck, I dunno, three hundred? The lines don't actually seem to correspond to anything, as far as I can tell, *yet*." Momo plucked the red orb out of the other totem, and the knowledge of the local weather patterns was gone instantly. "But check this out." She inserted it into the bizarre dream catcher shape she'd built, and all of a sudden, Alanna knew.

There was a hospital thirteen miles away. The wait time for emergency care was sixteen minutes. There was a veterinary clinic eight miles away. The wait time for emergency care was eight minutes, but the chance for survival for major trauma was reduced by sixty-eight percent. There was a private physician two miles away. The wait time for emergency care was under a minute.

Momo popped the orb out as Alanna's head started to hurt.

"Fucking *ow*," Alanna muttered, dabbing at something wet under her nose and finding that she was bleeding. "What the hell was that?"

Momo tossed her a roll of paper towels, which she caught and started using to mop up the bloody nose; Momo herself seemed unaffected. "It lists sites for emergency trauma care by distance," she explained. "But I can't figure out how to get the limiter on it, so it just keeps going if you let it." She suddenly looked so sad. "I know it's not that useful, I just wanted to show . . ."

"Are you insane?" Alanna cut Momo off midsorrow. "This is an actual *tool*. Can you make more of these?"

"I mean . . . yeah?" Momo said, confused. "But why?"

"Well, if you can figure out the limiter, keep it from hurting people"—Alanna tapped a finger on the table as she thought—"let's list uses here. Us, for one thing. Where's the most efficient treatment for dungeon injuries? That could save lives. But more than that, these things should come standard in every ambulance in the world. This bypasses radio, skips over bureaucracy. Sure, it ignores some context; I bet that private physician would charge through the nose. But this? This could help so many people on a daily basis. This is amazing." Alanna wiped away the last of her blood and looked down at the dyed-red towel. "Okay, so, it needs some work," she admitted. "But damn, girl."

Momo flushed bright red with pride. "I didn't think . . ." she started, before trying to find the words. "It's just a trick, though. It's not like I'm making armor or giving anyone superpowers." Her words tried to deflect how much weight Alanna was putting on her little project.

"Pff." Alanna's snort and waved hand dismissed that deflection without a single word. "We have a stockpile of reds. It's yours now. Pull anyone you want from the noncombat team. And I'll get JP to issue you a budget for this." Alanna looked at her seriously. "This isn't responsibility, to be clear. Don't think I don't see that look in your eye; James gets that way whenever he thinks he owes someone something. This is your reward for making something *useful*." Alanna ran her hand over the top of the unassuming totem, feeling the fuzz of the pipe cleaners against her skin. "Now. Make more."

Daniel groaned to himself, tapping his pen against the desk in a staccato rhythm that matched only the music in his head. He'd gotten a skill point in drumming, and while he was nowhere near the level of the guy from Def Leppard, he was having fun being able to keep a beat as a time-wasting distraction while alone at the front desk at work.

His job was security. His calling was also a kind of security. Those two things did not correlate as much as the average person might assume.

He and Tyrone, the other survivor who was still his coworker, had taken to it with shared grins and fist bumps. Theo hadn't, but whatever. Theo was kind of a jackass, anyway, and Daniel didn't answer to her.

Technically, Daniel answered to Frank. But Frank, as far as he knew, was in prison. And he *did* know, because he made regular Freedom of Information requests about exactly that fact.

With Frank gone, there wasn't actually anyone in charge of the mundane corporate security department. So Daniel had taken to scheduling shifts, filing the reports, that sort of thing. But a couple people had quit, and he needed more bodies, so he was trying to figure out how to actually hire someone without losing his own job. Oh, he'd also made sure they'd actually quit and not been eaten. He took his calling seriously, even if he treated his job more like a distraction these days.

Currently, his best friend was the voice in his head. Pathfinder—Path for short, which was a joke Daniel always grinned at—was pretty new to the idea of being alive. He was supposed to have withered and died after they left the dungeon, but Daniel wasn't the kind of person to just let that happen. He fed stray cats near his place, and he bought the good seed for his bird feeder; he'd be damned if he let some critter inside his own head starve. Also, it wasn't like he had many close friends anyway. None, to be precise, and his short time in Officium Mundi had wiped him from the minds of his casual acquaintances. No loss there, really.

So Pathfinder had become his pet. And then his friend. They went on walks a lot and talked while he explored new parts of the city, new food carts and parks. It was *like* being in a relationship, only . . .

well, he didn't really know what came after the only. But they agreed they liked it.

And the more he got to know Path, the more he felt like maybe the dungeon couldn't be that bad. It felt more *wild* than hostile. And when they were sitting here, she itched in his eyes and his feet to be back in *there*, seeing what it had to offer, finding the strange and curious. So even though he served his time keeping watch around the door, making sure nothing left, he still made sure to make time to poke around a bit. For her sake, of course.

If the door was secured, there was less chance the dungeon or its residents could hire someone like Frank again. That was important. Also less chance someone might fall in and vanish. Equally important.

Daniel also made regular checkups of the vent over James's desk. There was a strider nest there, though they were those cute little mini-staplers, and he didn't want to disturb them. Still, didn't hurt to be safe. He had a webcam there, too, wired into the monitors with the rest of the security system. He *knew* there was at least one more dungeon door but couldn't find it so far. But between himself and Path, it was only a matter of time before any secret way was opened to them.

Right now, though, he was bored. He groaned again and stretched his legs under the seat, wishing that someone else were here so he could go patrol the building or something. He idly flicked through the camera feeds, watching nothing in particular.

"Dammit, I can't believe I'm actually wishing it were dungeon night," he muttered. In his head, Pathfinder sang derisively at his hesitation. She could believe it; she knew his heart.

He was about to reply with a bad joke when he froze, eyes on the screen. He flicked back to the previous camera feed, and his eyes went wide.

They were wearing masks, which gave them the appearance of human faces. They were dressed in suit coats and slacks, so no one gave them a second glance. Maybe the employees they passed were just oblivious, or not looking up to avoid sparking work conversations, or just being affected by something like Pathfinder. But Daniel recognized the inhumanity of the two things on his screen instantly.

As he watched the pair of paper pushers make their way down the back stairwell, he fumbled his phone out of his pocket. He didn't care if the cameras saw him on his phone at work; he was basically in charge anyway. Watching for a minute, heart hammering, he tried to figure out what they were doing so he knew whom to call right now.

His finger hovered over Theo's name, but as the two of them turned and opened the back door, striding with confident, almost human motions out into the parking lot, he flicked the screen down and settled on James instead.

As he watched the two of them get into a car that he would have sworn he'd never seen in the lot, James picked up.

"I think I've got a new problem for us," Daniel told him.

CHAPTER 15

"Got it." James slipped his phone back into his pocket, thumbing the button to end the call. He looked up at Sarah, who was staring at him with raised eyebrows. "I've gotta go," he told her, confidently. And then, repeating it as if to convince himself, in a much shakier voice, "Oh shit, I've gotta *go*."

She arched eyebrows at him. "What's up? Family thing?" Sarah asked him with concern. The two of them had been talking about some fairly personal stuff before the members of her support group were due to show up, but Sarah well understood that the nature of their new lives made them . . . mildly prone to chaos, shall we say.

James gave a single shake of his head. "No, it was Daniel." He made eye contact, determination and worry warring in his gaze. "Two suits just left the dungeon. And the building. I've gotta write down their license plate before I forget." He stole around for a piece of scrap paper.

"Wait, what?" Sarah was shocked. She had more experience with the dungeon than James, in theory, but almost everything that happened these days seemed totally fresh to her. "They can do that?"

"Apparently!" He threw his arms up in a frustrated shrug. "Alanna. Where's Alanna?" James demanded of no one in particular.

As if on cue, the elevator doors dinged open, and Alanna and a grinning Momo stepped out into the lobby. "Sup nerds!" Momo called over to them. "Boy, have I got something . . ."

"I'm gonna stop you there," James said, his serious face faltering Momo's energy midword. "Gear up," he told the two women. "Meet me at my car as soon as you can. We've got a problem." He filled them in on the suits in as few words as he could while striding toward the back area. "Sarah, can you see if anyone's in the gym that we can pull in? And are you coming, or . . . No, you should stay here for the group. Okay, it'll be fine," James reassured himself without waiting for input.

"Now, hang on!" Sarah started to object before James was through the door and grabbing a long knife from their armory. "All right, you boob, fine," she muttered to herself more than anything else as Alanna and Momo were already rushing to grab anything useful.

A quick check showed there was no one in the back; the place tended to be more or less empty during the afternoons. They'd set up their space well for practicing the kind of brutal melees that ended up happening in the dungeon, but also just generally had a solid little workout area here with plenty of natural light, and no one who would look at you funny for having weird scars or the occasional emotional breakdown. Sarah didn't bother peeking into the kitchen; this place used to be some kind of restaurant that got used for a lot of kids' birthdays, and it *had* a commercial kitchen. Operative word being *had*. Those things, it turned out, cost way more than a single delve was gonna make them, and refurbishing it wasn't high on their priority list compared to more useful tools like armor, wireless cameras, and medical supplies.

Sarah got back to the main room just in time to see Momo jogging out to James's car in their little parking lot, carrying a cardboard box with a fire extinguisher poking out of it. James and Alanna followed shortly thereafter, and Sarah was treated to a view of Alanna's perfect midriff as the other girl buckled on the one Kevlar vest that one of their new delvers had picked up but not gotten into the Office yet. "All right, you two have fun. Be safe, okay?" Sarah told them with her trademark smile. Of course, she was worried. Of course, it wouldn't be safe. But they were, memories or not, her *friends*, and she would literally always find the energy to be happy for her friends.

"Thanks," James said with an appreciative exhale. "Okay. We know what direction they went, Daniel got us the license plate, and he says Path thinks they're going south. We're technically ahead of where they should be, so we're gonna see if we can spot their car and then aggressively stalk them if that works."

"Big if," Alanna pointed out. "There's a few roads, I'm told."

"I'll call Anesh, get him to wake Secret up," Sarah volunteered. "If the car's blanked, then Secret might be able to help you spot it."

"Good plan," James said. "All right, we're in a rush. Let's . . ." He broke off, his sentence stopping abruptly as a car pulled into their parking lot. "Okay, looks like your group is getting here. Have fun. See you later."

"Oh, that's not one of mine," Sarah mused as she peered out the window. "Maybe they're lost? Looks like an older guy. Dad old, not grandpa old." Indeed, as she watched, the driver's side door popped open, and a nervous-looking gentleman stepped out. He checked something in his hands multiple times against the front of the building. Eventually, he seemed to work up the courage to make his way to one of the two front doors and push his way inside.

Mousy, was how James would describe him. He was five-four at the most, and balding fast. But not so bald he'd given up on hair altogether. He didn't wear anything as foolish as a bowl cut, but the hair he did have was kept clean and combed—the sign of a man who knew what he was working with. He had wide eyes, decorated with dark circles under them, the kind James knew from experience came from a life of too little sleep and too much time at a computer monitor. Around those eyes were glasses. Spectacles, really. Wide rings of glass to match the dark rings behind them, taking up half his face. Ears like satellite dishes. He wore a tan coat reminiscent of what James would have worn in high school to look cool.

It was the kind of coat James would wear *now* to look cool, if he was dressing like a private eye.

If JP reminded James of nothing more than a weasel, with his mischievous face and smooth voice, and Alanna was reminiscent of a falcon with her sharp nose and keen eyes, and Dave, maybe just a little, was the derpiest golden retriever ever made, then *this man* looked for all the world like someone had taken a lab rat and stuck it in a trench coat.

"Ah, um . . . excuse me," the man said, his voice a nervous squeak. "I . . . ah . . . I, ah, was looking for some . . . um . . . help with something?" His tentative tone made it clear he wasn't sure this was allowed.

"Well," James told him, "we are kind of in a hurry and are leaving. We also, you know, aren't open to the public. Sorry, what are you looking for?" He looked over the man's shoulder and through the plate-glass window at Momo standing by his car, waving frantically at him.

"Well, I . . . well, you see." The stranger let out a nervous chuckle. "I was, I was, ah, I was talking to a friend of mine. Well, an old friend. Well, someone I knew from college. He contacted me, you see, said he was trying to get in touch, in touch with old friends. I, ah . . . I assumed it was an Alcoholics Anonymous thing, you know? Of course you know. But then he said he wanted to get a beer . . ." The man didn't notice everyone's frustrated looks as he rambled on. "Harvey, that was his name, Harvey. Yes. Well, Harvey asked me how my life had been going, and I said . . . I said . . ." His voice broke a bit, and he cleared his throat before recovering. He scratched at his nose with small hands cupped into claws.

"You said?" James prompted, curious, even as he was inching toward the door.

"Ah, yes. Yes . . ." The other man started speaking again, not noticing the raised eyebrows. "I told him, you see, I told him that I had the strangest problem. The strangest problem. And I told him, I told him, oh, yes. And he said to me, 'That's very weird!' and I said, 'I know it's weird, and no one believes me, and you don't believe me, either.' And he said, 'No.' He said, 'It's weird because I *do* believe you.'"

The man ran out of breath, gasping from the exertion of his rapid-fire words. "And then, he . . . he . . . he told me that maybe he knew some people that could help me." He looked around the room. "But you seem busy. So I'll . . . just go?"

At this point, mercifully, Sarah stepped in. "Hey!" she said with that special bubbly grin of hers. "They're going, but I'm still here. Come on, let's get you a cup of coffee and you can tell me what's up." At a glance from James, she rolled her eyes and reassured him, "Regular coffee, not the weird stuff."

"What, ah, if you don't mind my asking, what is the weird coffee?" The man wrung his hands in front of his chest.

Sarah paused briefly before snapping her fingers and shooting him a smile. "I'm not gonna answer that!" Her voice held laughter. "Come on, let's get you coffee. *Decaf* coffee. James, go, I'll see you later."

It took James maybe four seconds to come to the conclusion that Sarah probably had this handled. "Got it." He gave a sharp nod. "Alanna. Let's roll."

Three car doors slammed, three seat belts clicked into place, and one late-nineties Subaru rolled out into the light traffic, intent on intercepting incredibly dangerous prey.

"This is," Momo told them as James followed directions from Alanna to the intersection she wanted to be dropped off at, "the coolest thing we've done. I mean, sure, the dungeon is cool. But we get to be on a stakeout!" She said it like she'd spent her whole life watching spy movies, and this was the pinnacle of her childhood dream. "Can we buy doughnuts?" she asked from the back seat as James took a corner at a speed he normally wouldn't dare.

James filled her in. "This isn't a stakeout. I'm gonna drop each of you at a different intersection, and we're gonna try to cast a net to spot this one single car."

"What kinda car?" Alanna asked, all calm business.

"White Toyota Prius, older model, license plate—" James started replying in the same tone as he stopped them at a red light.

Momo cut him off abruptly. "Like that one?" she said, leaning through the gap between the two front seats to point across the intersection.

"Yes, like that one, now sit down and buckle up. The license plate is—"

This time Alanna interrupted him. "No, James," she said, stabbing a finger toward the other car. "Like *that one*," she insisted as the light for oncoming traffic changed and the car rolled past them.

James looked out his driver's side window and caught a flash of a face that was far too unreal to be human in the other car. "Fuck," he said. Then, a second later, he exploded into motion as his brain caught up. "Oh, fuck!" He yanked the wheel to the left in a move that looked haphazard to his passengers but was secretly a precise act, his skill points in driving firing on all cylinders as he slammed the gas down and slotted them into the oncoming lane of traffic with a laser-guided U-turn.

The two girls shouted conflicting instructions at him to either take it easy or floor it, but James wasn't listening. His world tunneled down into the road, the wheel, the obstacles around him, and his target.

The car ahead of him took a left, leaving James with a red light looming in his way. They were too far behind; any farther and he'd lose the target. So, he flicked his turn signal just long enough that it wasn't technically illegal for him to skip the car through a barely large enough gap in oncoming traffic and into a corner gas station. Then, before the attendant could even get up to come help them, James was out the other end, taking another perfectly timed left turn. Back on the tail of their opposition, without the precious seconds of delay.

"James! What the fuck!" Alanna was shouting at him, while Momo cheered raucously and threw one hand up as horns in the back seat. He noticed all of this, but it wasn't important right now.

James felt the wheel, felt the pedals, felt the tension of the engine and tires and road. And everything else wasn't important right now. He let his mind fall back into the comfortable embrace of those three points in car.

He kept the car on their tail, employing every ounce of control he had to make his driving seem as normal as possible. It wasn't as if the skill flooded his brain with facts; there were just a few things that he was now much more consciously aware of. Like how he didn't need to be right on their tail; eventually there'd be only one or two vehicles between himself and the target, and at that point, you were kind of the perfect distance from them. Other drivers would turn off, peel away, while you kept yourself to your quarry; you'd catch up sooner or later. No need to rush. Play it cool, his brain told him, just relax and let the reflex take over. Drive natural.

So he did. The tension left his hands as he settled back into his seat. As casually as possible, James turned his head slightly toward Alanna, who still had a white-knuckled grip on the passenger handhold. "Sorry, what were you saying? I missed it."

In the back seat, Momo exploded into laughter.

"Are you *sure* they don't know we're following them?" Momo asked for the fourth time. It had only been ten minutes, but the stuffed shirts were taking a path that sometimes crossed over itself, winding through much less populated roads.

"Can't be sure at this point," James said. "But they aren't directly reacting to us, and we've been out of sight a few times, so I don't think they're making an effort to lose us." He frowned. "Not much we can do except keep driving. If they do notice us, we'll probably just have to have a fight and hope the dungeon doesn't mind losing a couple agents."

"We don't have coffee and they're full strength; you think we can take them?" Alanna asked. She clad her voice in professional analysis, but inside, she was nervous. Every time they'd killed one of those things, it had been with bullshit. They'd caught them off guard, or starving, or with bullets. They'd had magic coffee, or Secret, or a *plasma gun*. Now? Now they had a car, a knife, a crowbar, and . . .

"Momo, what did you bring?"

"That fire extinguisher that restarts and/or amplifies fires and a bag full of used matches," the other girl answered. "Also a sword!"

James winced. "Why . . . why the sword," he whispered to himself. "I'm gonna kill JP. Now everyone's gonna want swords."

"Swords are cool," Momo said, having overheard him.

"We'll call the sword 'plan D,' for Damocles," Alanna told her. "The fire is a weird call. James, how're we looking?"

They were currently two cars back from their pursuit quarry, on a somewhat winding road surrounded by thick evergreen trees. The winter light cast everything around them in the same shade of bluish gray, no pleasant yellow beams filtering through the branches at *this* time of year. Alanna checked their position against her mental map, making use of one of her few legitimately powerful skills, and tagged them as being somewhere about six miles from where they'd started.

"We're doing good," James said. "I wanna back off a bit here, maybe pull over for a turn so they don't think we're the same car the whole way," he told them. "Anyone have any distractions while we wait? Help keep me from freaking the hell out about this?" James asked while he turned the wheel and pivoted the car into an open spot on the side of the street.

"I've got one," Alanna said. "But it's gonna take you longer than thirty seconds to answer."

"Okay, Momo?" James tried catching her eyes in the rearview mirror, but she was watching the other vehicle as it took a right at the stop sign ahead of them.

"I figured out what that aux cable I got last week did," she said aimlessly as she tried to turn her head as if it would help her see around the corner ahead of them, past the brick facade that announced the name of the neighborhood as Summerlake Ridge.

"Cool, cool," James agreed, suppressing the panicked desire to start the car again and get right back on the ass of their targets. "I hate how hard IDing magic items is. What's it do?"

"Turns audio files piped through it into metal. My James says it's nineties power metal and offered me a hundred bucks for it."

"Your James is wise beyond his years," James agreed. "I'll give you two hundred."

"What," Alanna barked from the front seat. "No. Momo, I'll give you three if you don't give that to James."

"Four," James countered. "And I promise to use it only on weird podcasts."

"Um . . . shouldn't we go?" Momo asked, nervously.

James nodded, the short bit of banter enough to clear his mild panic. "Yeah. Let's get back to it." He took the same turn as the other car, and they were just in time to see it taking a right two intersections down. Now properly far enough away, James followed at distance as the masked dungeon entities drove through the residential streets.

There were people here. Not that many; it was getting colder these days, after all. But they passed people—normal humans!—out walking dogs or unloading groceries from cars. At one point, they crossed an intersection near a park with a children's playground over a carpet of bark chips, and James silently went a little insane at the thought of having kids in the line of fire if it did come to a fight.

But the car in front of them didn't deviate, didn't start shooting at them. Just kept rolling, until, after going down a huge hill where the sidewalks were a grassy slope with a walking trail, and around a bend that had another one of those brick signs announcing the name of the neighborhood, it stopped.

More specifically, it pulled up into the driveway of a house. A normal, almost stereotypically normal white picket-fenced home in a suburban expanse.

"Why," James asked, quietly. Alanna just shrugged, watching through a pocket scope she'd brought along, as James drove past, and then turned when out of sight and parked the car curbside a couple blocks away.

"What a weird place," Momo said, looking around at all the three-story homes in the area, manicured gardens and new-model cars.

James snorted a laugh. "Don't try to tell me that you're confused by suburbia. I know you stayed with Karen's family for a while."

"Yeah, yeah." Momo made a farting noise with her lips. "And this place still weirds me out. How fucked is that?"

Shrugging a little as he adjusted his coat on his shoulders, James replied with, "I mean, it weirds me out, too, and I grew up somewhere like this. I think it's because I'll never be able to afford living here."

Both Momo and Alanna gave him incredulous looks. "Are you fucking kidding me?" Alanna asked him. "Did you forget what it is we're doing?"

"I . . . yes," James confirmed. "Yes, I did. Shut up. Oh look, activity. Please ignore me and watch them."

In the driveway of the home, the two suits had gotten out of the car. One of them carried a briefcase, the other was unarmed, but both of them calmly walked around the house to the gate to the backyard. As if they owned the place, James thought.

"Do we follow them? What if they attack the people in the house?" Momo asked, starting to open her door.

With an outstretched hand, Alanna stopped her. "No," she said, and James shook his head likewise. "Look how they're moving. They're here on purpose, like they belong. The one that came after us didn't move like that—it was hostile. These guys don't . . . they don't . . ."

She didn't want to say it, so James did. "They don't feel like they're here for a fight," he said. "Dumb as that sounds."

So they watched the house. A few minutes passed in silence, then a few more. At one point, Momo stepped out for a smoke, while Alanna chastised her for it and James silently did the same in his head. They waited, and waited a bit more.

"You shoulda let me buy those doughnuts," Momo told James. "I knew this would be a stakeout."

He huffed at her. "If I'd done that, we'd have missed them entirely. And then . . . wait." James trailed off as the two suits came out of the house. They looked exactly like they had going in—no signs of a fight, not even a ruffled haircut. The briefcase was missing, though.

Without a word, they got in their car and started driving away.

"Do we follow them?" Momo asked. "Or try to take 'em out?" She put on a mobster voice for that last part, or at least what she thought of as one.

"No," Alanna and James said in unison, as they popped their doors open and stood up. James finished the thought. "Let's go check out the house. Fuck, we shoulda brought more cars. And where the hell is Secret? He should be here by now."

"How?" Alanna asked. "I thought he needed an open secret to teleport and manifest at."

"Maybe?" James said. "Sometimes. I honestly don't know how he works, and I think he does that on purpose. We could try the open-secret thing, though. But I can't . . . think of any of those right now."

They crossed the street, weapons tucked into waistbands behind their backs and under their coats. Except Momo, who couldn't fit the sword on her five-foot frame and who certainly couldn't conceal a fire extinguisher. She got an *I told you so* for that one.

The cold air was only getting chillier as the sun started to set, and so it was with half-frozen fingers that James undid the latch on the back gate and led them through to the backyard.

It was normal. Mowed lawn, stone birdbath, neat rows of flowers, and what looked like a few tomato plants that refused to die in the cold like everything else. A raised wooden deck led to a sliding glass patio door, behind which closed curtains concealed the interior. The house had no lights on behind its windows, only curtains, but the yard looked cared for.

"Maybe we should knock on the front?" Alanna asked, questioningly.

James casually tried the back door. "Locked," he said. "But no key. It's a latch; this opens from the inside only."

"How'd they get in? Window?" Momo asked, glancing around. "You know, I got a skill point in hide-and-seek last week, and I really feel like this should be a situation for it," she told them.

"Skills are finicky. No bleedover, usually," Alanna told the younger woman with a sigh. "It sucks. It's why I can't fly any helicopter I want."

James looked around the yard, ignoring their banter. "Something is wrong here," he muttered.

He looked again. Tried to see with eyes unclouded. What was *here*, he wondered? His brain told him there was something out of place, but he couldn't figure it out.

The deck. A glass table and three patio chairs sitting on it, next to a box that contained a garden hose. James checked that box—yes, hose. Under the porch, maybe? He walked down the three steps and checked beneath the wood slats; nothing at all. That itself was suspicious, but it did confirm in part that no one lived here. It was literally impossible to not put *something* under a deck if you lived in a house like this.

He looked around the garden as Momo and Alanna continued their own search and conversation. A row of trees separated the yard from the wild forested area behind this row of houses. A shovel and rake leaned against the fence to the side. Rows of planted shrubbery sat in trimmed lines. A garden waste collection bin sat around the corner. There were a few knotholes in the fence. There was . . .

James looked again and smiled a vicious grin. "Got it," he said.

Fresh soil. Now, normally, a garden should have fresh soil. That was part of how you grew plants. James had both common sense and a skill point letting him know that was true. But he also had a skill point letting him know that the soil around the one tenacious tomato plant was basically a waste of dirt this late in the fall.

He walked over and prodded at the mound of dirt with his foot. After a minute of considering the shovel, he remembered the suits walking out essentially spotless, so instead he decided to try something else first. Reaching out, he yanked the tomato stalk up and was rewarded with the creaking of hinges and a scattering of dirt around his shoes.

"Got ya," he said again, trying and failing to think of a good *Scooby-Doo* reference. "Hey!" he called over to the women. "Got something here!" James knelt down and out of the hole pulled up a briefcase with a manila envelope taped to the outside.

The three of them used the glass table as a space to spread out the contents of the envelope, and as they did so, the mood went from excited to furious to grim, all in a big hurry.

Three photographs of a young man. A teenager, more likely. One of the photos was from a middle school graduation yearbook; the other two were almost surveillance photographs. Six pages of neatly typed text, two of them describing the kid's routines, one of common hangout spots, two of known family and friends, and one that was . . . well, for lack of a better term, an invoice. Though James recognized it more as a quest notice, something familiar to him from the one briefcase they'd managed to open in the dungeon, mostly by accident.

"This briefcase," Alanna said, in a softy furious tone, after they'd looked over the material provided, "contains six hundred thousand dollars." She quietly clenched a hand into a fist so hard her knuckles cracked. "On the provision that Javier Lopez is dead before the fourteenth of November."

"It's November eight," James informed Momo, who was starting to pull out her phone.

"I knew that," she said, but there wasn't much comedy in her voice.

"Okay," James said. "Pack it up. We're taking this with us."

Alanna frowned like a thundercloud. "We can use this to trap whoever is supposed to do the job. This is obviously a dead drop, and the dungeon has otherwise perfect payment security with the quests. We can stop an assassination with this."

"No, we could stop one or two hit men with this," James said. "To stop the dungeon, we need to form an actual response force so it can never hire hit men again. Right now, we cannot, and I *will not*, play games with this kid's life. I don't care why he's a target; pack it up." He did not, in any way, phrase that like a question.

Momo shrank down a little. "Is this gonna be a fight?" she asked, more timid than either of them had ever seen her. "I . . . don't wanna . . . be around if it is."

Alanna and James glared at each other for a few hard seconds before Alanna sighed and tilted her head sideways. "No, no," she said, voice warm again. "James is right this time."

"I won't let it go to my head," James informed her.

"Pack up the briefcase," Alanna said. "Momo, burn the house down."

"What!" Momo looked shocked.

"No, yeah, okay, I get it." James nodded. "It's a dead drop; no one lives here. But if we torch it, it covers for why the job isn't done. It also disrupts the now apparently existent *local assassin culture*. What the *fuck*, you guys, this is a thing now!" He threw his arms up in the air. "Anyway, Momo, burn the building down."

Ten minutes and one briefcase thrown in the back seat later, and Momo was on the phone with emergency dispatch.

"Yeah, hi? I just wanted to say I see a lot of smoke coming up near me, and I was wondering if you guys should send the, like, fire department?" She played up a sort of clueless-sounding voice. "Yeah, I was just driving past, and, like, it's *really* smoky. I wanted to, you know, like, be a good ameritan."

"Samaritan," James automatically corrected from the front seat, earning a grinning slap on the arm from Alanna as Momo made up an excuse about why she was currently headed away from the fire.

"Okay," James said to Alanna while Momo carried on answering dispatch questions in the back seat. "Let's get back to the compound and figure out a plan to meet this kid. I wanna know why the dungeon targeted him."

"Also that one guy Harvey sent our way," Alanna reminded him.

"Fuck, of course. I wonder how Sarah's doing with him?" James mused. "I feel bad leaving her. Do you think the support group is going well?"

Alanna clicked her tongue in disbelief. "We dumped a random stranger on her, you were in the middle of telling her about your personal emotional turmoil, and she's running a support group for people who are coping better with her own trauma than she is. No,

James, she's not okay." Alanna sighed. "But fuck, I get why I used to be friends with her, you know? She reminds me of you, a *lot*. I don't think she's okay, but I think she's exactly as strong as she needs to be to get through. Especially if we're here for her."

They drove on in quiet for a while, until James passed by two screaming fire trucks going the opposite direction.

"Hey, do you ever wonder if we create more problems than we solve with the dungeon thing?" James asked.

Alanna nodded. "It's an investment in the future."

From the back seat, stifling a laugh, Momo asked, "Hey, do you guys know where you're going?"

"No." "Yes." James and Alanna glanced at each other. "Okay, yes," James conceded. "Please tell me where to turn. I wasn't paying attention the first time."

CHAPTER 16

"All right." James announced his presence as he strode through the loading dock door to the building they were leasing as a glorified clubhouse. "We're back. Let's solve problems."

"You can't just say that every time you walk into a room." Alanna's chiding was done with a smile, but she still rolled her eyes. "Besides, we're not exactly qualified to solve this particular problem."

James snorted as Momo laughed at him, letting the younger girl pass through the door he held open with the cardboard box of equipment to return and documents to worry about. "Nonsense. We're perhaps the only people qualified for it. Or is this the point where we tell the police or the government? I've been thinking about it lately, being honest." His voice lost some of its humor and cheer. "Like, really, at what point do we decide that what we're doing is just a little too selfish? A little too not worth it?"

"We're not killing the Office," Alanna reminded him firmly.

"Nah, I know," James said. "We've had that conversation too many times. I get the reasons. But this is . . . this just feels beyond us, a bit. I fight monsters, not people."

The two of them walked into the strangely well-furnished warehouse area, closing the back door behind them and finding a pair of seats at one of the desks. As Alanna replied, she pulled off one of her shoes and started shaking bark dust out of it. "So, I know I catch flak for being a bit too opinionated sometimes . . ."

"It's part of why I love you," James reminded her.

She flashed a smile but didn't miss a beat in her sentence. "... but I'm just gonna tell you now, if there's anything I'd call a monster, it's a human murderer over a sentient pile of desk fans."

"We really need to stop thinking too hard about desk fans," James said. Alanna just glared at him until he relented and took her seriously. "Okay, okay, yes. I . . . I see where you're coming from. But what the hell are we supposed to do about it?"

Her answer was simple. "We either gather enough information that we can pass it off to the authorities—anonymously, of course, I'm sure Secret can help with that—or we kill them."

"Jesus, that escalated."

"Well, we don't specifically need to kill them," Alanna conceded. "Just render them unable to continue assassin-ing," she said with a shrug. "I dunno, take their arms off? We'll figure it out. In some way remove their ability to do harm."

"Fucking hell, that's really vicious!" James exclaimed. "Where was this when we had the option to shoot Frank?" he asked her, morbidly curious.

Alanna finished getting her shoe back on and swung her legs up to the desk while she leaned back in the chair. "I'unno." She shrugged. "Maybe I was just feeling charitable at the time. Maybe I didn't really get just how many people Frank probably killed. I think . . ." She sighed, not meeting James's eyes. "I think if we had the choice again, I'd probably just shoot him?"

James opened his mouth to argue, then stopped. Honestly? If he really thought about it? Well . . . "I think I might do the same," he confided in her, quietly mourning for the loss of his own ethics.

"Hey!" Momo's voice cut in between them, happy even though it was a bit overexcited. "What're you guys up to now? Do you wanna go get food? I feel like food."

James and Alanna shared a look between the two of them. A look that communicated a lot of different ideas but basically boiled down to "Can you tell what's going on with this girl? Because I cannot tell what's going on with this girl. I think we're her dads now? Help."

They didn't say that out loud, though.

Instead, James shook his head. "Nah, we've gotta meet with Benny first."

"Who?"

"Benny. The guy that came in before we left. I don't know his actual name, but I think Sarah's talking to him now. He's got something weird going on and wanted our help, and I feel up to playing the role of ghostbusters for a while, you know?"

"He's not talking to Sarah," Momo commented idly with raised eyebrows. "Sarah's doing her group."

"Oh. Maybe he's in the bathroom?" James shrugged. "It's fine, we can wait."

Momo let out a low note of confusion. "Uh . . . do you mean that guy?" she asked, pointing at one of the desks on the other side of the concrete floor.

There, sitting alone, almost perfectly still, was the man from earlier. His coat and hat sat neatly piled on the desk next to him, and his eyes seemed locked on one of the standing corkboards with a growing map tacked up in segments. He hadn't caught their attention when they'd walked in, and James was sort of suspicious of that on its own. If not for the fact that the guy looked like he was absolutely paralyzed with fear and indecision, James might have been mad about it.

"Well, shit," Alanna said. "What's he even doing back here?"

"I guess Sarah told him to wait here for us?" James guessed, unsure of his own words.

"That," Alanna pointed out with a drawl and a waved finger, "is not operationally secure. We shouldn't be letting people back here. Or really into the building."

"I'm further guessing she just didn't think about it," James told his girlfriend. "Honestly, consider how hard it is for us to keep track of dungeony things. We basically keep JP around just to do our accounting now, because it's actually work to track all this shit," he said. By way of example, he pulled a blue orb out of his pocket. "Like, watch this."

[+1 Skill Rank : Cooking—Food Preparation—Coffee—Dark Roast]
[Problem Solved : Laundry]

"What am I watching for?" Alanna asked, eyes narrowed in suspicion.

James tapped the table. "Nothing in particular, I just found that in my pocket and wanted an excuse. But thinking about it, I just made more work for Anesh and his skills spreadsheet, and for whoever is distributing orbs to know that I need a replacement blue for when I eventually burn through all those meetings I can schedule." He leaned in toward Alanna, who smiled at him as his rambling got more heated and passionate. "And while, yes, I just realized that *we* are the ones who distribute orbs, my *point* is that almost every action we do creates more work to track and remember. That's a hell of a mental load! We should, honestly, be giving someone specifically the job of operational security. Someone who is entirely there to remind us that we can't, like, let random people into our secret base, or, or . . ."

"Or burn a building down in broad daylight?" Momo interjected with a far-too-wide grin.

"Yes, that! We should have probably considered coming back at night for that!" James knocked on the desk vigorously. "And now it's a bit late for that, but whatever. I'm just saying, we should at the very least have more conversations about how *open* we want to be with our bizarre powers."

Alanna cleared her throat. "On that note," she said, pointing over at their guest. "Should we maybe talk to him before having this conversation?"

"Shhhhhhit. Yes." James drew the word out with a bit lip. "Okay, yeah. Let's go see what's on our plate now. Actually, while we do that, Momo? Can you go see if you can find anything on our hit-list target? I don't wanna overwhelm this guy with too many people, and . . . actually, do you have time? Were you gonna get food?"

"Eh, I'll eat later" was Momo's response. Alanna held back a comment about how Momo could probably stand to eat a little more often as it was; the thousand extra pockets and buckles and leather coat that made up Momo's goth outfit hid it a bit, but there was no denying that the girl was still a little too thin from her time as a prisoner. "Gimme the folder thing. I'll go google the guy."

"This is an *envelope*, thank you very much," James said as he stood from his chair and handed the files over. "Your generation may not recognize it."

"No, I get it! It's the thing from email." Momo bit back with a wicked grin. She stretched out languidly, and her grin only got a bit wider as both James and Alanna sighed at her. "All right, have fun with your interrogation. I'm gonna go check up on this and say hi to Sarah. Might be a while if James or Simon are here; we're doing connection therapy today, and I don't wanna miss all of it."

With that, she strolled out of the makeshift operations center, leaving behind the desks and maps and heavily encrypted unnetworked computers to step out to the open front room, a welcoming group of other survivors, and snacks.

Sarah had brought fudge cookies this week. It wasn't a challenge to choose what side of the building she wanted to be on.

"Can you tell what's going on with that girl?" James said, leaning conspiratorially toward Alanna as he muttered. "Because I cannot."

"I think she's got the opposite of PTSD. Or she's just covering for normal PTSD," Alanna said. She let out a heavy breath as she stood herself, tapping her shoe fully back into place. Rolling a shoulder, she gestured toward their guest. "Come on, let's go ask some questions and worry about our resident goth later."

"Everyone have a safe trip!" Sarah stood in the door to their secret base, which she was still trying to think of a good name for, and waved enthusiastically at the cars pulling out one by one. Sarah was almost always enthusiastic, really; she kind of couldn't help it. It was just what she was. Though it did mean that when she did get overwhelmed, it was . . . well, overwhelming.

Now wasn't overwhelming, though.

Twenty-six people had shown up to survivors' therapy. That wasn't a record, but it was a lot, and she was now out of cookies. Such was the life of an impromptu counselor.

Of the survivors, about half of them had cut all ties with the group as soon as they were out. Many of them had managed to stabilize, reclaim their lives. But a few—more than a few, sadly—had been too broken by it. Suicides weren't unheard-of, and that was just within the people that Sarah and Karen had kept track of. This support group was, in large part, a way to try to provide a foundation for those who were somewhere between—the survivors who were now fully aware that reality was weirder than expected, that they couldn't just go back to their lives and pretend it was a dream, but who also were kind of okay with that and wanted to see what they could do with their new knowledge and power.

And it was a power, Sarah was becoming increasingly aware. The skulljacks, specifically, were an incredible asset. Many of the survivors had worked in IT alongside herself and James at one point, and that knowledge, paired with the technology they now had, gave them a much wider range of ability than expected. Untrained humans were clearly worse at it than whatever Monster Karen had been, but still.

Mind links. Drone control. Instinctive programming. Biological drivers for hardware. Networking and indexing with subconscious thought. Bandwidth that was, apparently, unlimited? Or perhaps simply more powerful than a mundane device could ever manage, due to the magic that powered the jacks.

The support group was partly there to keep people sane. To give them a place to meet, talk, understand, and be understood. But it was also there to give the first batch of transhuman wonders a place to learn and grow.

It almost made Sarah embarrassed by how afraid she was to use her own skulljack. A sentiment, it seemed, that she shared with

James. It didn't make sense that the most outspoken transhumanist in their group would be the one afraid of his own upgrade, but then, it had come at the cost of a total violation of self.

James didn't come to the support groups. He always said he was too busy. But really, Sarah was pretty sure, he was just afraid. It made sense; she was, too, after all.

The remainder of the group of survivors, the ones that stuck around after the group session ended, were the guild's newly acquired support staff. People who didn't want to go delving but were already in on the secret and so were capable of providing a range of skills to the team as a whole.

There was one guy who was actually a gym instructor before his capture who ran their back training area. It wasn't like they were turning into superheroes, but the difference between no muscle and *some* muscle was critical when it came to delving. And having someone there to keep you on the right track was useful. There were a couple people, whom Sarah suspected were dating, who were constantly looking into how the orbs worked. That was useful just because Anesh was so busy with *everything else* these days, so offloading the skills recordkeeping was handy, if nothing else. They had been the ones to suss out the limits of the blue absorbs, too, which was cool. They also liked testing the things in microwaves, which Sarah saw as an eccentricity but James assured her was probably close enough to real science. Then there were a handful of others who ran errands, helped with cleanup or getting the building into working order, or just lent a hand moving tables around when needed.

And then there was Harvey. Harvey was a good guy. Sarah had been relying on his help with the other survivors, in terms of taking care of them, and by this point he was basically a full-time employee of Dungeon Problems Incorporated, or whatever they ended up calling themselves.

Harvey had dark skin and a darker beard. He'd trimmed it back after they'd escaped, going from mountain man down to immaculately curly. His hair, likewise, mimicked his goatee, a wiry mop of curly strands kept in a perfect little cap on his head. He smiled, a lot. Big, toothy smiles, emotions worn on his sleeve. And he didn't let being a decade older than most of them get in the way of being polite.

While Karen was focused on keeping everyone fed and housed and was constantly pressuring them for more resources, more *money*, Harvey was busy trying to make the survivors into a family. He brought people food, checked up on anyone who was out of touch for too long. He always had time for you, no matter what. Essentially, he was their ombudsman, hearing grievances and passing them up the chain to the people he still saw as the heroes of their lives.

There weren't many grievances, really. But if there ever were, Sarah trusted that Harvey would be there to help. It didn't hurt that James got along with him, too. Not that that was a surprise; James was getting better about getting along with just about anyone these days, and Harvey made it easy.

"Everything's put away," Harvey said from Sarah's side as he stepped up to the doorway. "How're you doing? You didn't talk much tonight."

"Oh, I'm fine," Sarah said, shooting him a smile. "Just kinda worried. Your friend came by before group and I didn't really have time to figure out what his deal was. Then there was the whole thing with the suits and James and Alanna running off, and then James just being *James* all over the place."

Harvey laughed, a deep rumble that built up from his chest and poured out into the world. "Ha! Yeah, that kid's something else, huh?" He kept smiling, but his voice took on a more serious undertone. "Hope it was all right to send my old brother this way. I thought, what with how things went down in the Office, maybe James could do something for him."

It wasn't lost on Sarah that Harvey treated James like he was *the* hero in the group, but she still nodded. "He'll probably be up for it. What exactly *was* going on, though? He didn't say much except that his house was weird?"

"Yeah, he was quiet with me, too. Well, quiet in the way he is, where he makes lots of noise but doesn't say much. But from what I get, his attic is cursed. Not like the cube farm. Just an attic that's not . . . completely . . . attic." He trailed off with a shrug.

"That sentence got away from you." Sarah giggled as she ribbed Harvey. "But yeah, okay. That's borked up. We knew there were other dungeons out there, and now I'm wondering if this is one of them." She hummed, toying with the edges of the sleeves of her hoodie. "Well, Alanna said to let them talk to your friend . . . what's his name, anyway?"

"Fredrick. He goes by Fredrick, too," Harvey answered.

Sarah clicked her tongue. "Not Fred?" Harvey shook his head at her. "All right, so, Alanna said to let them talk to Fredrick for a bit; they don't wanna surround him with people." She sighed deeply as she walked back inside, shutting the door to keep the harsh November air out. "Did you know that I completely forgot about Halloween this year?" she asked Harvey.

"I didn't know you were . . . no, hang on. I should have of course assumed that Halloween was your thing." He nodded to himself as he imagined Sarah's perfect holiday. "Yeah. What happened?"

"Just busy, I guess. But imagine the costume I could have had! I could have just worn Secret and won every costume contest ever!" She bemoaned her forgetfulness.

"Okay, so, why bring this up?" Harvey asked. He wasn't annoyed, but it was kind of a non sequitur, and he was waiting for the other shoe to drop.

"Oh, I just noticed Momo dyed her hair and it reminded me," Sarah said, tilting her head at the younger goth girl as she came running up to the two of them, carrying the manila envelope that she'd been fidgeting with during the support group meeting. "Hey, Momers. What's up? They done back there?"

The girl blinked at Sarah for a second before catching what she'd been asked. "What? No. Maybe? I wasn't really paying attention. I think they left when Anesh showed up? Look, check this out, I found this guy." She gave a light thwap to the documents she had in hand and held out her phone to Sarah to see what she'd dug up.

But Sarah wasn't really interested in that. "Hang on, Anesh showed up, and they just *left*? Why didn't they tell me?"

"Well, you were still talking to people, I guess." Momo faltered a bit. "I don't think they were trying to ditch you; they were just going to check out Melvin's house."

"Fredrick," Harvey interjected. "Though he does look like a Melvin, doesn't he?" he mused to himself as he started clearing up the support group's area, an armful of folding chairs carried off to their proper waiting place.

Here was the problem: it was personal. Despite Momo's assurances, and the casual mood in the room, it *was* personal to Sarah, because it didn't feel personal at all. If, five years ago, James had discovered a literal haunted building, then Sarah could say with absolute confidence that she would have gotten a call about it as the highest priority. Before the local news, before any of their other friends, and before the police when James realized that he'd actually just disturbed a nest of very angry raccoons and not ghosts. But today . . . today James had, over the span of two hours, learned about a local cabal of assassins, been apprised of the location of a ghost-infested attic, and *also* used at least one of those events to skip out on actually talking to her about his feelings. And the worst part was, well, exactly what Momo said.

It wasn't personal.

"Okay, before I get angry about this," Sarah started, a hand cupped over her mouth in frustration, "how exactly did Anesh get here so fast? He was tutoring downtown when I called him."

Momo had the look of someone who knew they'd just stepped into a social minefield but replied anyway. "Oh, James used his blue power to create a meeting, which Anesh was then on time to. He tried calling but couldn't remember which Anesh in his contact list was the Anesh that was in town, so he felt awkward." Sarah nodded along with Momo's explanation, totally understanding what she meant by James feeling awkward, until her brain clicked on something.

"Wait. The blue. It . . . can do that?" Sarah was shocked. "That kinda flubs up our estimation for how powerful that ability was—does he get that? Does that dork even *care* that he's running around breaking causality?" She threw her arms wide, turning as if to address an audience that wasn't there; only Harvey was left in the room, and he was only back for more chairs. Everyone else had either gone home or was helping out with sorting through one of the basements. Disgruntled, Sarah turned back to an uncomfortable-looking Momo. "Sure, whatever. Fine!"

"You don't sound fine," Momo ventured timidly. "Are you okay?"

Sarah closed her eyes for a second. Was she okay?

She was tired. She wasn't even really mad at James; he'd at least made an effort today to try to talk to her, and things going sideways wasn't really his fault. She was so tired. But the support group had been good, everyone was doing okay, and she had *almost* gotten herself past her phobia of using the skulljack to plug into another person. Was she okay?

"Yeah," Sarah said, letting out a breath. "I'm doing fine!" She felt her voice pitch back toward her preferred chipper self, felt the tension drain as she relaxed her shoulders and stuck a smile back on her face. It wasn't fake, not really; she didn't just act happy all the time, she really did tend toward it. She just got tired easier, these days. "Hey, so, here's an idea," Sarah said to Momo, "Simon and your James are in the back. How about you go grab them while I look at what you found and we can go check this kid out. This is the kid, right?" she asked as she finally took the offered phone from Momo and started flicking through the screen.

Momo nodded, grateful to be back on track, but still worried about Sarah. "Yeah, okay!" she said, thumping her fists into the palms of her own hands in excitement. "You sure you're okay?" Momo asked as she started backpedaling toward the hallway that led back to their little gym.

"I'm *fine*," Sarah insisted with a grin. "Though thank you for asking, you dingus." She waved Momo off, sending her to fetch her friends. Sarah peered down at Momo's smartphone in her hands, currently pulled up to a page for a local high school football team. Momo had, helpfully, zoomed in on one of the faces. "Javier, eh? Football player, seems," Sarah muttered to herself. Looking up as someone entered the room, she called over to the man, "Hey, Harvey! Wanna go help us scout out a kid targeted for assassination by an entire living office complex?"

"Oh, *hell* no!" Harvey drawled back, carrying the last of the chairs. "I got enough of your weird shit three months ago! I'm just here to help out."

Sarah let out a chiming laugh. "Yeah, okay!" she called back, shaking her head. She forgot, sometimes, that not everyone was as *into* the weird stuff that she and James and the others thrived on. "All right." She nodded to herself. "Well, floop it. If they went off to explore a ghost attic on their own, I can go have a chat with one kid, right? Time for an adventure."

"Hey, Rufus," Dave said as he entered the apartment, the spare key James had given him so long ago letting him in. That was weird on its own—normally the door was never locked. "Where is everyone?" he asked as he set the box he was carrying down on the table.

The stapler-spider-crab-friend-thing gave him a *look*. Dave stared back at it, keeping his face blank, while he privately admitted to himself that it was actually pretty impressive that Rufus could do a *look* with just one eye and without really moving his legs at all. It was something to do with how he tilted his body, just a little bit to the side, just a fraction, to indicate disdain.

"Okay, so, you can't talk, right." Dave nodded. "Is Secret here? Secret can talk." He walked past Rufus, who was now affecting the *very* human gesture of rolling his eye behind Dave's back, and headed down the hall to the bedrooms.

The place looked a lot nicer, Dave thought. All the extra furniture and whiteboards and stuff really took up a lot of space. Maybe they could start doing anime nights here again. Though, of course, they'd need to reschedule it to be on a night when they weren't dungeoning. Also a night when Dave didn't work, but that would be harder. He'd gotten weird looks from both Alanna and James when he'd told them he was still working at the kennel, like they expected him to quit just because he had another source of income.

The kennel was also the reason Dave had gotten out of helping move all that furniture in the first place. He thought it was great that they had an essentially endless warehouse of desks and things they could use to furnish their new secret clubhouse, but the act of having to carry them out into reality, into the elevator, out of the building's door, into a truck, *out* of the truck, into a *different* building, and then to where they wanted them? That wasn't a thing Dave was super interested in doing.

Especially not when there were dogs as a second option.

"Hey, Secret? You awake?" He rapped his knuckles on the bedroom door. No response. Dave let out a defeated sigh.

He looked around the place as he walked out into the living room. Rufus looked like he was trying to teach Lily how to use the TV remote, or maybe just get her off it. Her app was currently on, the one that gave meaningless statistics for things she caught on her camera, informing Dave that the remote had 1,406 button presses left on its battery life. The kitchen looked like it was a bit of a mess, which was to be expected with how busy everyone had been. But overall, the whole apartment radiated a sort of quiet that left him feeling mildly alone.

"I thought Anesh would be here, at least," he said to Rufus. "He's the one that asked me to bring all this coffee." Dave idly picked up one of the grocery store bags of coffee grounds out of the box. "No one was over at the clubhouse, either," he said, sitting down on the couch and trying to make conversation with the uninterested strider.

Dave sighed deeply to himself. No one appreciated all the trouble he went through! They just assumed he always had time for this stuff, even when he was at work or something. He'd spent two weeks laminating all the paper on Pendragon's frame, and no one had even offered to help, but as soon as Anesh needed *coffee*, it was down to Dave.

"Oh. I guess the coffee is for the ritual thing," he realized as he thought about it. "I probably shouldn't be as annoyed, right?" he asked Rufus, who just shot him a tired expression as the strider tried to muscle the iLipede off the household electronics. "Right." Dave nodded.

He looked around again, as if waiting for someone to show up. But no one did. The apartment that usually held all his friends was quiet and empty.

"Well," he said as he stood to leave, "I guess it's good that everyone has a quiet day every now and then."

Anesh had a lot of time to think on this road trip. He'd left a couple days ago and was more or less making good time, but he was also making plenty of stops. For food, for gas, just to stretch his legs, whatever.

America was *huge*. People in this country, James included, didn't seem to *get* that. Anesh had been driving for four *hundred* miles and still had a third of his trip left to go. When Alanna had helped him plan the trip—and surreptitiously handed Anesh a shotgun for it—she'd told him that he could probably make it in about two days. Two days? Not bloody likely.

It was also beautiful, especially a lot of the parts of southern Oregon he'd driven through. And even some of California, when it wasn't busy ruining it with cities or sales tax. God, but he'd gotten used to not having to pay sales tax. That was the last reminder of home he needed. His old home, the one overseas, that is. These days, his home was, as the saying so often went, where his heart was. The reminder of *that* home was the eighteen-foot-long blue serpent with too many eyes and teeth curled up in the back seat.

When he wasn't admiring the scenery, though, he let his mind wander. And it wandered, as it so often did, to the dungeon.

More specifically, it went to some of the things that he and his partners had talked about, in terms of using the dungeon for the gain of humanity. Anesh was, at his core, a mathematician, but he also *loved* deep dives into logistics and planning and how large-scale projects worked. He had at least three YouTube channels he watched just to learn about how people built anything larger than a barn. And some of their long-term plans presented fascinating challenges.

Skulljacks. That was first on the list. They could, as had been proven, just give them to anyone. But *should* they? Well, yes. That question they'd answered early and then reinforced over the months. Yes, this was certainly a good idea. Not perfect, no, but it would absolutely cause more good than bad. So how did they *do* it? That was the question Anesh rolled around in his head.

It all hinged on their willingness to breach the veil. To just throw off the masquerade and tell everyone that magic *was* real and that they *were* wizards. Of a sort, anyway. Improvised wizards.

Anesh wasn't ready for that. He felt like there were still too many unknowns, and Alanna agreed with him. James, on the other hand, was of the opinion that they shouldn't industrialize it right off the bat but should instead just start handing the things out. That was, honestly, maybe not the worst idea. But it would eventually lead to the breach of secrecy anyway, unless the infection effect only went so far down the chain. Still, it would be a way to test in the small scale whether humanity as a whole was ready for this.

He'd been worrying over that one for a long time. It would have been a lot easier if any of the world's leading researchers into mind-machine interfaces had taken their calls. Turns out, there was a limit to James's power to get a meeting, and it also relied on the other person actually being the kind of person who would *go* to meetings. Most mad scientists, and that *was* what Anesh was filing them under, did not.

That was the big one that was within reach, right now, but there were so, so many others. The magic items they found tended to have either no useful effect or *the* useful effect, and it really only was a matter of time before they hit on something that could cure crippling diseases, regrow limbs, roll back climate shift, destroy nuclear weapon stockpiles, end aging, or solve any *number* of other problems the world faced.

Anesh had a list, of course. Anesh liked lists, and it helped to have guidelines for what they were looking for. Make it easier to recognize a treasure when it fell into their hands.

The other one that he was currently seriously considering was a suggestion Alanna had made, which was that they could effectively combat homelessness, locally at least, by colonizing the dungeon.

Now, Anesh had issues with the word *colonize*. He'd brought this up before, but basically anyone of Indian descent was going to be more than a little suspicious of plans that started with "what if we just take the land we want?"

But in this case, it really did seem, if not purely good, then at least not *too* evil. The denizens of the Office were almost always instantly hostile to an alarming degree, and those that weren't had so far tended to end up becoming long-term friends. Introducing more humans probably wouldn't be the worst thing ever, considering it didn't hurt when they started bringing in the larger guild.

The holes in the plan came down to the same two holes in almost every one of their plans. In every human plan ever. Security and logistics.

Anesh tried to imagine the best-case hypothetical, where secrecy was maintained out of goodwill and human decency. They still had to approach, individually, anyone who was currently homeless, then offer them a place to stay, then *explain* it, then, assuming the idiot said yes, they'd need to craft at least a small personal space for them in the dungeon itself that would be livable. Food would not be too much of an issue, now that the dungeon was seemingly "awake" again and respawning things sometimes, but other human needs were problematic. For one thing, the bathrooms outside were only accessible once a week, and the bathrooms *inside* would try to stab you with bugs and erase themselves from your memory. Add to that the risk of attack from dungeon life-forms, and it was a pretty hostile proposition to begin with.

But, assuming they could entice people, make them homes, take care of plumbing, shelter, food, safety, and the dozens of other little problems that would pop up . . . then what? How many people could they support? The dungeon had seemingly infinite space, dozens of kilometers at least, so it really came down to if they could support the secondary needs. And then how many people they brought in or out each week.

"Bah," Anesh grumbled to himself. He didn't need advanced calculus to know the numbers just didn't line up.

As with so many of their plans, he was going to have to table this one.

"Hey, Secret," Anesh called into the back seat, breaking the rumbling silence of the road. "All this thinking is making me hungry. I'm gonna stop at the next diner I see; you want anything?"

Secret sleepily raised his head, uncoiling a bit as he slithered up to poke his head over the passenger seat and stare at Anesh. "I desire a burger."

"I feel it's only right to tell you," Anesh said as he turned the wheel to pull the car off the highway off-ramp, craning his neck to check oncoming traffic, "that it is right disturbing that you are so into burgers."

"They hold the secrets of generations," Secret told him solemnly. "Each one crafted by hands that have stolen their own knowledge from echoes that came before them, each one special, each one a personal touch that itself creates more echoes for those who follow. The burger is the perfect expression of this world's knowledge."

Anesh sat in silent contemplation of the infomorph's words as he scanned the signs around them for any hint of somewhere to eat that wasn't fast food. After passing through a particularly long traffic light, he asked the question that Secret had put in his mind. "Is literally anything you just told me true?"

"Perhaps," Secret hissed back at him, joy bubbling beneath his surface.

"Okay, new question for you that's not food related. Mostly." Anesh sighed as he hit another red light; every single stop he'd made in California had been like this so far. It was like the state hated him. At least it was better than when he'd first moved here and forgot at least once that he had to drive on the wrong side of the road. "Let's say we're willing to make use of the dungeon space. How would you use that to help with the problem of homelessness?"

Secret gave him a look like he didn't understand. "I have not had a home long enough to grasp your meaning. Homelessness? You have a home."

"Oh, bugger me," Anesh breathed out. "This is gonna be a hell of an awkward conversation." He sighed and started explaining one of the worst parts of modern civilization as he pulled into the parking lot for Penny's Diner, slotting his car neatly into a parking space between some old clunker and a moving van. Anesh stepped out into the evening air, weirdly warm compared to back home, leaving a confused and angry Secret in the back seat to think about what he'd been told. He gave an appreciable nod to the spray art someone had done on the hood of the beat-up old sedan next to him, of a highway stretching into the sunset.

As he placed a to-go order, making sure to ask for Secret's burger with whatever special house sauce they had, he considered calling James and telling him to have a long talk with his meme-son about the harsher realities of the world. But then shook it off. He needed to get into the habit of accepting that there were two of him now, that sometimes he wouldn't *feel* like he was spending enough time with people until a day or two afterward, when he could recombine his thoughts and memories with his other half. It sucked, now, sure, but . . . well, he didn't want to be double the relationship burden. Calling to check in would just be a hassle, especially when he'd get home in a week or so and have it all to himself again *anyway*.

It was times like this Anesh lamented that no therapist on the planet would actually believe him if he tried to talk about his personal problems.

At least everyone back home would be able to have a quiet night, though. Sometimes, that thought was enough to keep him going.

CHAPTER 17

"I bet you ten bucks it's just a raccoon," Alanna said as James followed behind Fredrick's car. She hadn't really paid attention to this before their mild chase scene earlier today, but now that she knew, she couldn't help but notice that almost every move he made on the wheel was precise. No wobble in the car, no sudden starts or stops—it was just kind of casually expert. The value of skill orbs, it would seem.

From the back seat, Anesh barked out a laugh. "Okay, I know he's an almost stereotypical coward, but who jumps from a raccoon to trying to hire . . . James, what did you call us?"

"Ghostbusters," the driving boyfriend replied. "Like from the movie *Ghostbusters*."

"Thanks for clarifying," Alanna said in a dry tone. "Anyway. Wanna bet on the raccoon thing, Anesh? No? How 'bout you, James?"

James shook his head. He was staying out of this one. No matter how much of a wuss Fredrick seemed like, it would take at minimum a whole family of trash pandas to cause the amount of distress he'd seemed to be in.

"No bet," Anesh said from the back seat. "But it does make me curious what you both think we're walking into." He glanced down and eyed the duffel bag carrying their extra set of armor and a bushel of crowbars. "You guys think this is something like the Office?"

"How could it not be?" Alanna asked, vaguely annoyed at the question.

James interjected mildly, "Well, hang on now. We had this talk a while back, right before we found out about Sarah. Just because all *we've* encountered is a dungeon doesn't mean that the world *doesn't* have, like, wizards and dragons and things."

"Wait, don't you have a business card that lists your job title as 'sorcerer'? Are you projecting here?" Anesh asked with a smile.

"Shaddup," James threw back at him.

Alanna sighed. "It's a good point, I guess. I mean, we know magic is a thing, to an extent. Maybe his attic literally is haunted by an actual ghost."

"That'd be problematic," James said with a wince.

"Because of what it would mean for a world to suddenly have verifiable proof of an afterlife and a mystical reality beyond what we've so far discovered?" The words fountained out of Alanna like she'd rehearsed it.

"No," James told her, "because we don't know how to fight a ghost."

There was a moment of quiet, but for the radio lightly playing classic rock, before James rolled them up to a red light and Anesh picked up the conversation. "Okay, so, I like to think I've been pretty good about rolling with the punches for the last several months." Nods of acknowledgment from his partners. "But is it maybe about time we questioned what the dungeon *is*?"

"Aw, no. Not now," James grumbled, thumping his forehead on the steering wheel. "Ask me something easy, like how the hell I shower with the skulljack in my head."

Alanna raised her eyebrows over at James. "I'd never thought of that. How *do* you guys do it? Are they waterproof?"

James gave a nod back in response, ignoring Anesh trying to get their attention again. "Yeah, it's weirdly organic. Kinda feels like a belly button, if you know what I mean? Like, it's not perfect, but I can wash it out and it doesn't short-circuit my brainmeats. That's a plus. Also I think the little clip that holds the cable in is some kind of keratin, because it grew back when I accidentally . . . never mind." He dropped the sentence and poured his focus into the road, avoiding eye contact with the incredulous look that Alanna was giving him.

"Wait, wait, hear me out." Anesh leaned through the gap between the front two seats slightly. "So, we're thinking of the Office as a set place, but maybe that's not what these things always have to be. We don't have any good data on it! It's possible that all the weird stuff throughout human history has just been . . . one of these things."

"Doesn't hold up." Alanna shook her head. "No records of them. Closest thing we get is the labyrinth of the Minotaur, and that . . . I mean, sure, yeah. But that's kinda it. I've checked."

"Also—" James started.

But Anesh cut him off. "Now hang the bloody hell on!" He threw an accusatory finger at Alanna. "You can't just discount literally every other human myth on the planet! Everything from gods to monsters is explainable if there was a dungeon in the background, regardless of the fact that it *could* have been an outside effect!"

"Also—" James tried again. It didn't work.

"Maybe I just don't like the idea of explaining Jesus away as 'some guy who had a few blue orbs,' Anesh!" Alanna retorted. "Besides that, it still doesn't tell us where the powers came from, so it's useless for the purpose of this conversation, *and* it's more likely that any dungeons present throughout history just wiped records of themselves from human minds and documents. Have you *seen* our Slack lately? About a fourth of the old messages that directly talk about the dungeon are gone. I assume. I can't do the math without the record."

"That's scary." Anesh raised his eyebrows. "And also a good point. Though the myths may just be knock-on effects of the dungeons themselves." His voice stilled back to intellectually interested, but not upset. Anesh's ability to toggle between mild curiosity and passionate defense of a thought at will was his trump card for keeping conversations civil.

"Also," James said, "you just said we can't know. I totally want to learn more of the dungeon's secrets, but holy shit is it hard. So while

I know it would be cool for us to derive the nature of the dungeon on this car ride, I also am not holding out hope that we'll suddenly come to the realization that it's some ancient alien power core machine intelligence gone mad. And then be right."

Alanna stuck her tongue out in derision. "Can it please not be aliens? Just once?"

"*Just once?*" Anesh exclaimed, voice rebounding through the car. "How often are aliens a problem for you?"

"On reflection, never," Alanna said, tapping her chin and pretending to be deep in thought. "I'm more or less in favor of immigration, as long as the immigrants aren't building elaborate deathtraps."

"Is that a blanket statement?" James asked her, trying not to laugh.

She nodded sagely. "It would have to be. Otherwise it's not fair."

"Are you posing that the dungeon should be a citizen, then?" he asked.

Alanna shrugged. "Why not? The law already says that corporations are people, for some idiot reason."

James cleared his throat and quickly rattled out, "I would like to point out that the dungeon has done a monumental number of crimes, including a truly staggering amount of counterfeiting, so maybe giving it legal status as a citizen wouldn't actually help us at all."

From the back seat, Anesh sighed deeply. "We're getting off track, and I am intensely interested in what we all think the dungeon is now! I didn't realize it before, but we basically never talk about the metaphysics of it." He leaned his elbows on his knees and set his chin in his hands and watched the scenery through the front windshield. "Is it a living thing? A natural process? Is it a god, or what people used to call gods? Have things like this always been around? Can we *kill it*? Why does it work the way it does? Is it feeding off us being in it, or trying to kill us, or what? Why the monsters, why the *orbs*, and why do we never talk about this!"

"We talk about this *all the time!*" James reminded him loudly. "We stopped doing it because we never get anywhere! It's always just guesses and talking in circles."

Alanna nodded and shot an acknowledging gesture at James. "Yeah, what he said. Remember how for a while it seemed like the skill orbs were all made up of dead people, but then we found the guy that the one orb was supposedly from?" She shrugged. "Every time we start to build a foundation for answers, it turns out it's wrong. Or . . . or . . ." She trailed off, now thinking for real.

"Or a smokescreen?" James picked up. "You think the dungeon is intentionally screwing with us?"

"Why not?" Alanna asked. "Like, why not? Everything we've seen feels like layers of defense, right? Monsters get harder as we go in, environments get more hazardous. Standard fortification stuff, right?"

Anesh snorted. "You know we have no frame of reference for military fortifications." Unless, his brain filled in suddenly, they had an orb for that. That was a possibility that had to be accounted for these days.

"But what would be an even better defense is if we don't even know what's being defended!" Alanna finished. "If we can't identify the target, we sure as shit can't hit it. For all we know, the entity in charge is up in the ceiling, with all those armor-plated air-con spiders. Somewhere we'd literally never see if we go through 'normally,' right?"

"Well, that hardly seems fair," James said, dejected.

"Who said it has to play fair?" Alanna shrugged. "And that's sorta the point. It should have tried to murder us, full power, from day one. But it didn't. It doesn't even have full control over its own monsters, unless Rufus is also part of the elaborate lie."

James shot her a look, pleading and worried, before turning his eyes quickly back to the road. "Please don't make me mistrust Secret."

"Sorry, buddy, but we literally *cannot know*. Secret's whole thing is keeping secrets, after all."

"Okay, okay," Anesh piped up again. "So, Alanna raises good points, and they're all bollocks. You're saying it's using us?"

"Using, toying with, maybe just feeding off. Some kind of symbiosis without trust. I dunno, but I think we should acknowledge that the Office isn't playing fair because it has to. And so"—she got to her original point—"if Freddy's attic is another dungeon, we can't trust *it* to play fair, either."

They mulled that over as the roads around them changed from commercial to residential, and they found themselves in a suburb near downtown. Cramped roads with lines of cars parked on both sides so tight that James assumed they'd parked there decades ago and never moved, for fear of losing their spots. Yes, even the 2019 models.

He followed Fredrick's car closely through the leaf-strewn streets; the other man had insisted that he could guide them and didn't give up an address. This would have been suspicious in the extreme, but a word from Harvey assured them that Fred was just prideful and eccentric.

"I hope it's not a dungeon," James said quietly as he pulled them up in front of the curb at the house where Fredrick parked in the driveway.

"What?" Anesh asked, not having heard.

It had been hard for James to find his voice for this part, but now, having said it once, it was easier the second time. "I said, I hope it's not a dungeon." He met their eyes as he parked the car. "The Office is special to me. To us. It . . . I don't think you guys really appreciate how much it changed my life. If nothing else, it really brought us together, and you two are *so* important." He took a slow breath. "I just don't want to lose that sense of it being something special. Something personal."

They sat in the car for a few minutes, looking down the driveway toward the house, as Fredrick peered at them curiously from his front doorstep, waiting for them to come out of the vehicle. It was quiet, and warm, and they were together and happy and loved.

"Everything has to change," Alanna said, sadly. "But hey. If it is a dungeon, maybe it'll give us actual superpowers."

"Bagsy on heat vision," Anesh exclaimed.

"What?" both of the others said at once.

"Heat vision. Like, shooting lasers out of my eyes. You've read the comics."

"No, the . . . you know what, screw it. I'm assuming this is you being British all over us." James sighed and popped his door open. "Also I feel like you always have more slang words I've never heard. Do you ever just make them up to confuse me?" The group stepped out into the darkening November night, which was no longer warm or quiet. But they were still feeling confident and companionable as they stalked up the walkway to the house.

"I don't get how you can just . . . talk to them," Simon told Momo as he and Other James pulled on their street clothing at her request. "They aren't . . . approachable?" He looked to James for guidance, who nodded.

Momo rolled her eyes and flipped her teammate off, making a rude noise all the while. "It's not hard; you just have a giant stick up your ass about it because Alanna saved your life, like, three times."

"Twice for him, counting the thing on the bridge. Once for me, though their James did also probably keep me alive at least one extra time," James said. He was still winded, catching his breath from his workout with Simon.

Workout was a mild term. Each of them had at least one martial art skill orb, gained through the chaff of two dozen mildly useless yellow orbs, and Alanna's idea of a training regimen for delvers included learning to fight under the effects of speed coffee. So when the two of them tore into each other, it was with blurring blows that would have been right at home in wushu movie special effects. It was also exhausting.

So when Momo had run back and told them to put coats on and come with her, they were simultaneously energized and drained.

"They're just people, guys," Momo told them as the trio walked down the short hall past the bathrooms to the front area, where Sarah was waiting for them. She tossed the shorter girl's phone back to her. "Sarah, they're idolizing the boss! Tell them they're wrong! Alanna and James are just people!" Momo tattled to the woman she idolized.

Sarah shook her head, that big, goofy grin on her face. "Sorry, no can do, kids! I'm pretty sure at this point that James and Alanna are treading the path to divinity. Also Dave is, like, turning into *the* silent hero type. It's kinda hot, and if you tell anyone I said that, no one will ever believe you."

"Wat," Momo gasped out.

"Sorry, what? Oh, I spaced out for a second." Sarah's grin was brilliantly mischievous. "Yeah, of course they're just people! Alanna's a cool lady, and James is . . ." Her voice faltered for such a small moment that no one noticed. "James is my best friend. You guys can relax around them a little bit."

Simon and James shared a look. "You'll forgive us if we take some time to do that," Simon said diplomatically.

A shrug was Sarah's response. "S'your call. Anyway, you three ready? Did Momo tell you what we're doing?" Sarah threw open the front door, letting cold wind rustle her skirt.

"Something about high school football?" Simon asked tenuously.

"Something like that. I'll explain in the car."

The wooden stepladder creaked under James's boot as he tested his weight on it.

It was narrow, just barely enough for one of them wearing the makeshift armor that they'd come to call their own, with steps that were far too thin for anyone to be comfortable with. Not for the first time, James wondered how often Freddy was going up into his attic at all for this to be a problem that he'd noticed and been traumatized by. If James had an attic like this, he'd probably just stash stuff in it and never go back for it, artificially generating a nightmare for himself when he had to move next.

"Well, it's not collapsing," Alanna pointed out.

The three of them stood at the base of the stairs. Fredrick had been insistent that he show them to it and pull the ceiling panel down himself. He'd also insisted that they all remove their shoes while they walked through the house and up to the second floor, which didn't really surprise anyone in the slightest. They'd brought their crowbars out, and Alanna had her pistol worn openly on her belt. Anesh had slung his emergency bag over his shoulder, trading bulkier armor for carrying capacity. They were ready.

Ready, yes. But.

None of them was really eager to go up. It was more than just the mild trepidation that James had felt in the car; that was more than balanced out by the excitement of finding more magic, more worlds to explore. Even if it would mean more work and, gods help him, more spreadsheets. No, it was more like a gnawing unease that had taken root almost as soon as they'd hit the second floor. None of them talked about it, but they felt it mirrored in each other, getting stronger as Fredrick had pulled down the steps and then fled to his kitchen with a muttered note asking them not to break anything.

"So . . . we should go up." Anesh said it like it was a question, almost.

Up did not feel like a good place to go, and James said as much. But then he followed it up with, "I'm getting the feeling that we're not wanted here. This is like when I was a kid, looking down the stairs into the basement and *knowing* it wasn't full of snakes, but the lights were out, so how could I be sure?" He scowled at the hole that led to the attic. "Fuck you, attic. I'm twenty-eight years old—you can't fucking scare me."

A long moment passed before Alanna cleared her throat. "Hrm. Are you . . . going to go up?"

James, left foot still planted on the steps, sighed with annoyance. "Give me a second. I'm psyching myself up."

They all looked up the stairs, occasionally glancing around at the paisley wallpaper and awkward-looking family photos on the walls. Alanna wrinkled her nose at the faint scent of old shoes that permeated the air, while Anesh just looked uncomfortable, like he didn't know what to do with his hands. James took a couple of deep breaths and shifted his weight around, though still leaving his boot planted firmly on the bottom rung.

"So . . ." Anesh started, trailing off as he saw James's scowl and clenched fist.

James was escalating from annoyed, right past irritated, angry, and pissed, straight up to *furious*. He had faced endless hallways all by himself, he had fought down inhuman monsters, outsmarted traps and ambushes alike; he had stolen fire from a god and laughed about it. He had, alone or with his partners, taken to the depths of an infinite hostile labyrinth, and they had *won*, time and time again.

And now these fucking stairs thought they could scare him?

"Like hell," he hissed out between clenched teeth.

Moving felt like pulling against wet cement. But after his second foot left the floor, and his hand grabbed onto the lip of the hole in the ceiling, suddenly James had momentum. It was like someone had dumped four shots of espresso into his veins; all the fog and fear and wariness cleared away in an instant, and the clarity of reality snapped back into focus around him. And around him, he could have sworn he saw actual cracks in the air as he took that first step and ascended into the attic.

Behind him, Anesh and Alanna felt a noticeable outside shift as the unease and fear blew away. "Okay," Anesh said. "That's not normal." He glanced to Alanna for confirmation, and she nodded back at him. "Should we follow him?" Anesh pointed up the stairs at James's ascending ass and got a much more vigorous nod in response. No reason not to, really. If all the stairs could do was scare them, and James had ripped through that little enchantment, then what was the worst they could run into in the actual attic?

As soon as Anesh thought that, he shook his head. They knew of one other dungeon in the world—two if his counterpart's trip south was successful, but that didn't count yet—and it had exactly no defenses on the door. In fact, it didn't have any active defenses at all, not really. Not like this. This was the kind of thing that Anesh would expect as a home defense system for a wizard—it wasn't what he'd come to understand about how the Office worked.

It left him incredibly nervous as he followed Alanna up the steps, right up until they both stepped up behind James, who was standing there, looking at a perfectly normal-ass attic.

Unvarnished slats of wood made up the floor, a steep roof made the space incredibly claustrophobic even though there was ample room for all of them to stand, and a single circular window at the other end let in the last vestiges of light from the outside. Furniture with moving sheets draped over it lined the walls, along with decaying cardboard boxes stuffed with rusted tools, old wall hangings, plastic bags of bedding, all the things that an attic in an old house like this accumulated as people refused to give anything away or throw their junk out. It might, of course, be useful one day.

James was standing there with one hand cocked on his hip, head tilted to the side in that way he did when he was thinking. Alanna and Anesh stepped up to either side of him, flanking their partner just a half step behind him. Almost at the same time, without signaling each other, they both reached into their jacket pockets and pulled out a pair of glasses. That got a double take from James when he turned to talk to them. "Anesh, why are you wearing shades?" he asked.

"They're the infrared ones from the dungeon. I'm getting better at wearing them," he said by way of explanation as he swept his view across the room. "Clear. Alanna, anything?"

Alanna's glasses weren't shades at all; they were a thick pair of reading glasses that someone—probably Deb, if she remembered right—had grabbed off a desk in the Office last week, and she'd picked them up in trade for an orb. They were, according to probably Deb, not super useful. And, according to Alanna, insanely valuable for dungeon delving. Maybe.

Basically their function was that they let her see, as if it were a color gradient, how much time would be wasted in different spots in her vision. It was, much like the infrared shades that had just finished giving Anesh a headache, very painful until she got used to it. Mostly. It was also one of those weird things that totally changed the game on spotting traps or weird effects, because having an extra sense that wasn't common made it kinda hard to trick.

Right now, it was showing the attic in shades of sticky gray. The window lit up in a weird fluxing purple, which she was pretty sure meant that they could stand there and look out for a long time, maybe. Boxes and old shelves had similar tones to them, the potential time spent digging through them only to find old boxes of nails or moth-eaten shirts.

But off to the left . . .

"Got something," she said, pointing over to where a rectangular shape was covered in a white cloth. She pulled the glasses off her face as her vision started to sting. "Trap or something interesting—not sure."

"Do your new glasses let you see danger, potential weirdness, secrets, or something else I didn't think of?" James asked, already accepting that he'd lost track of the party's magic items by this point.

"Something else," Alanna confirmed. "Doesn't mean it's dangerous, specifically, just complicated. Do we check it out?"

James looked around again. "Someone find the light switch. I'll go take a look." He took a few steps forward, small and cautious steps, but not fearful ones. The attic was too normal now to really be afraid of it, and James had this sinking suspicion that the only actual weirdness here was the fear aura at the entrance.

There was no spatial warping, no "bigger on the inside," no monsters, no loot drops, no . . . anything that he'd come to assume was the norm for dungeon environments. Granted, his opinion of how these places should work came from *literally one example*, but, well, it was a pretty big one. Maybe they'd just hit the mother lode in the first go, and the Office was the grand mal of dungeons compared to everything else on Earth. It would go a long way to explaining why they hadn't run into anyone else who had anything even remotely close to the marginal powers they'd acquired.

At the same time, it left James feeling both disappointed and wary. He'd been looking forward to diving into something totally new, forging another path through a hostile realm, not just poking around an attic. But then, a normal attic didn't have a barrier that terrified adventurers into a standstill, even if it didn't last forever. So he kept on guard as he advanced.

Anesh hit the lights as James approached, giving him a better view of the thing Alanna had pointed out. It was a dresser, that much was now clear through the sheet covering it; the knobs on the drawers left their imprint after god knew how much time sitting up here untouched. He shuffled closer, taking small steps around it to change the angle of his viewing. Alanna stood a safe distance to the side, watching as backup, while Anesh poked his way through a shelf of jars with curiosity.

After a couple of tentative pokes that gave no reaction, James finally took the plunge and whipped the sheet off... to see the perfectly normal dresser. Dark brown-stained wood, a few scratches that looked deep and old, wrought iron knobs to pull the drawers out. "Yup," James said, looking over at Alanna with a nod. "Sure is furniture."

"Glasses said it would take time to interact with," Alanna said. "Maybe it's a self-fulfilling prophecy and the specs are useless? Like, by seeing this, it makes us take it slow, and so it uses time?"

"I'm starting to think this isn't a dungeon at all," Anesh told them. "This feels like just a wandering random effect. I'm honestly kinda sad." He set the jar of tacks back on the shelf and sighed. "Well, it's still better than literally every other attempt, right? At least we know that there's other weird stuff out in the world."

James gave a head-tilted nod at that. "Yeah, yeah, that's true. And opens the door to me getting to use my wizard résumé. Still, you two should back up; I'm gonna try to open this thing up and see what happens. If it's nothing, well, I guess this is still a place worth keeping an eye on, but..." James reached out and placed his hand on the handle of the top drawer.

The world went black.

The football coach was a wide man. Not fat, just big. Over six feet tall, bald head, broad shoulders. He held a clipboard with some laminated papers that casually ignored the sporadic light drizzles the night was giving. His face was unhappy, not because he was unhappy with anything in particular but because he himself was an unhappy man. Or, if not that, then a man who did not express anything beyond smug satisfaction at what he saw as a job well done. In other words, to Sarah's eyes, he was kind of a goober, and not someone she wanted to interact with.

Currently, Sarah was interacting with him. She, along with her backup of Team Two, was standing on the sidelines of the local high school's football field as they got ready for tonight's home game. And the coach was not being helpful.

"Why?" he demanded, brusquely. "Be fast about it."

Sarah almost wanted to be insufferably slow about it just to be a donk. But, instead, she followed the flow of enthusiasm that flowed through her veins. "Oh! We're just friends of his," she said. There had been a number of potential lies that she could have used, but she had settled on this one because it was, really, not that much of a lie. After all, what was a friend if not someone who would warn you about potential assassination attempts? *Much* easier to get the details straight compared to telling the coach she was from the student newspaper or something.

"Hrmph." The football coach scowled at them. "Well, you're too late. Idiot quit the team last week." His face looked like the words were made of something sour. "Some friends," he commented venomously.

Sarah put a look of flustered surprise on her face. "Quit the team? He didn't say! Why would he do something like that?" Behind her, she could almost feel Momo rolling her eyes as Sarah placed a hand on her chest like she was some 1930s debutante.

The coach didn't stop frowning at her, and for a moment she had that sinking feeling that she got sometimes when adults were monsters, before remembering that *she too was an adult* and that being sassy would usually work out with no repercussions.

Fortunately, the man was on a timeline, and before the kids behind her could crumple into scowled-upon piles of anxiety, the coach just snorted and turned away. "He spends all his time in the library now. Thinks he's better than his teammates," the man said by way of parting words before stomping off. In his world, Sarah and the others had already ceased to exist; there was a game, after all.

Sarah bit her lip and gave a little sigh before turning around, only to catch sight of Momo and Other James giving the finger to the retreating back of the coach. "All right, all right, cut that out." She laughed at them. "Well, we could walk over to the library. It's only"—she checked her phone—"seven p.m." They're still open, and it's, like, two blocks away."

"How do you know that?" Momo asked her, incredulously.

"I've lived in this area for a while. Before James and Anesh and I moved into the other place, we actually lived right down the street. Also I know where all the libraries are because I am great." Sarah stuck her tongue out at Momo. "We can drop in there, at least check."

"He could have meant the school library," Simon suggested in a low voice.

A snap of her fingers and a grin was Sarah's response to that. "Yes! Good thought! Okay, gang, let's split up!"

"No. No. Please no," all three of them said in a chorus.

Apparently, Sarah mused, they'd all seen episodes of *Scooby-Doo* at some point. No matter. "Great!" she told them. "Simon and James, you take the school. Momo, you're with me!"

"We said no!" Momo protested as Sarah took her hand and started dragging her off through the small groups of actual students making their way into the stadium stands, displaying a surprising disregard for physics as she pulled Momo along against the other girl's resistance. "Sarah! Saraaaaahhh!"

Her voice trailed off as she was pulled away, leaving Simon and Other James standing there. The two of them looked at each other and shrugged. "School library?" Simon asked.

"Yup," James replied. He had to make a real effort these days to not think of himself as Other James; the nickname was weirdly catchy, but he refused to be pushed to sidekick status. Even if it was looking more like Momo was the leader of their fire team.

Ah, well. Library it was. He and Simon turned away from the gathering of normal high schoolers, each nostalgic for a different part of that world, and headed off to try to find a potential murder victim.

James floated in a black void.

This was, as he thought about it, less than ideal.

There was a universe, he decided, where this had gone as expected, and nothing had gone wrong. That universe, along with all the other ones where his life was if not easy, then at least normal, perhaps even mundane, was somewhere so far distant that James knew he'd never find his way back there again. Not that he really wanted to. But it was good to keep in perspective that his life choices had led him here.

Just as he'd run over a list of his victories to surmount the stairs, he now had a clear picture of all the things he'd deliberately *chosen* that had brought him and his hubris to this point. He'd decided to open the door again. To go exploring. To *keep* exploring. To befriend Rufus, to drag Anesh into it, to tell Alanna, to enperson Secret, to fight monsters and save innocents, to do all that shit. And yes, that was all very cool, but at the end of the day, it may have left him feeling a little too cocky, such that he felt comfortable touching the one object in the "oh it's probably not a dungeon I guess" that showed up as a point of interest on a scan.

And now he was here. Floating, in a black void. Not even black, really, just nothing at all. Just empty.

He tried to take a deep breath, but it didn't quite work. He couldn't breathe. He wasn't here, really, was he? His hand, he knew, hadn't moved, but he couldn't feel the dresser knob in his grip.

Don't panic. Think this through. If this was a physical trap, he was in trouble, but if he was only here in his mind, then Anesh and Alanna would get him away in case of trouble. So what kind of trap was it?

James took a *mental* deep breath and tried to focus. There was something here, just under the surface of the void, that he felt like he could almost recognize. It was like . . . the smell, from outside. Was that it? The smell of rain? He lost his train of thought for a second and had to shake himself to stay on track.

Rain. What kind of rain. A drizzle? No. A downpour? No, no. It smelled like . . . like . . . ah! Spring rain! Not this winter stuff that was happening outside at all.

The instant James thought it, he could *smell* it. For real, as if he were standing in a grassy field while a warm shower fell on the wet grass around him. The scents took off from there as his mind made connections. The smells of water, of mud, of blooming flowers. With each thought he called to mind, he felt the physical smells burst to life.

So now he was floating in an empty void, smelling wet dirt. *Great. That's an improvement?*

James turned the thoughts over in his mind. The scents weren't going away, so . . . why? Why any of this? What was so important about the smells?

He tried to close his eyes before giving a mental sigh as he realized he couldn't tell either way. Still, he was making progress, and it was helping him keep the panic at bay for now, though the inability to move was starting to trigger James's anxiety. So, holding that back for a minute, he turned to think about the rain.

James had been in a spring thunderstorm before, which was why he sort of faintly recognized the feeling of the smell before it had really kicked in. But maybe it wasn't just the smell itself. He tried to picture how it had looked when he was staring up at the sky watching the rain fall. Gray, yes, clouds, but also bright bars where the sun punched through.

Yes, that was the ticket. He could almost *feel* the texture of the thought as it came close to something. A little less gray, a little more blue, no cloud *there* . . . and then James could see.

Well, he could see the sky. He could see the rain falling, the explosion of gray clouds overhead, the blue sky behind them promising the summer. But it still wasn't enough; that feeling James had barely grasped at the start told him there was more here.

He rotated his vision around it, peering from different conceptual angles. His head started to hurt as his thoughts overran each other, and he constantly lost his focus on any single path that he tried to go down. Over and over, his headache would creep in, and he'd have to try to do the mental equivalent of taking deep breaths until he could make another attempt. At this point, he'd been here for what felt like an hour, and it was clear that the others wouldn't be able to get him out alone.

If only he had somewhere to stand, that would at least give him a frame of reference. Why *couldn't* he feel the rain, anyway? He'd felt rain before. *This* rain, even. This warm spring shower that brought life and soggy pants. He'd felt that moment when a few drops clustered together on a bare arm and started rolling down, he'd felt drips off his glasses onto his lips, he'd felt . . .

And just like that, he could feel. The texture of the rain had always been there, and now it was kinetic, drumming against bare skin, matting his hair.

From there, the nature of the puzzle revealed itself to him in a flash of inspiration.

The feel of mud underfoot. The tickle of grass on bare feet. The sight of that grass; the sound of water splashing into puddles; the view of flowers blooming; the noise of a single duck's quack, a permanent note that sat in the still image of the scene; and, finally, the taste of a single drop of clear rainwater as it splashed across open lips.

It was exactly the impression that he'd gotten at the very start, but now made manifest. Each individual part James had pulled from his memories, or created from whole cloth, carefully matching the mental puzzle pieces to where they *belonged* in the tableau. A single slice of a beautiful rainy spring day, brought to life and kept in perfect preservation, just waiting to be uncovered inch by inch.

As soon as it was done, James felt and heard a lock click open.

He opened the drawer on the dresser.

Intellectually, Sarah knew that this wasn't what books smelled like, really.

Libraries were more than just a collection of books. This was the smell of summer camps and public computers, of free DVDs and community theater. And also books, yes, but it wasn't exclusive.

But that was still how she described the scent of a library when she thought about it. Like books, old and new, all mixed together and shared around.

There were six people in the library, including two librarians at the front desk who seemed to be gossiping away the end of their day, and Sarah and Momo themselves. One other person was plugging away at one of the public PCs, rocking out to whatever was in their headphones; he wasn't important, though, since he was roughly fifty years old and looked like he had been to every single Burning Man that had happened in that period of time.

The last person was Javier Lopez. He was seventeen years old, a senior in high school, formerly a member of the football team, tanned skin and those wiry muscles that only high schoolers seemed to ever have. The kind of guy who could, if his football career fell through, probably get a job with a moving company, spend eight hours every day hoisting couches, and then fuel this work by annihilating roughly three feet of sandwiches.

Of course, his football career had fallen through, it seemed. Because he was here, instead of at the game, sitting on the second floor and reading a book on gardening. Next to him, on the table, Sarah counted six other books stacked up in no particular order, along with a couple comics. Fiction, biography, how-to, didn't seem to matter to him. He just had . . . books.

Sarah pulled out one of the wooden chairs with the thick cushions that she'd literally only ever seen in libraries and plopped down across the table from him. He didn't look up at first, but as she sat there, hands peaked in front of her face, leaning back like she lived here, watching him, he eventually noticed. It probably helped that Momo was standing behind her, like some kind of punk-rock bodyguard.

"Did...uh...you need the table?" he asked, a little aggressively, before sweeping his vision across the empty tables around them. "Or...?" The kid left the question open, probably because the whole thing was unexpected.

"Oh, don't mind me," Sarah said, gazing at him carefully. "I'm trying to figure something out." She played up being a little flippant, but really, she was watching his reactions.

He was wearing a school sweatshirt and jeans. Nothing weird on his person, but he did have a duffel bag next to him. Course, he used to be a football player, so that wasn't weird on its own, but it could be hiding any number of things. But right now, he was just sitting in a public library, reading his books, and sometimes glancing up at Sarah with a nervous expression.

Eventually, he set the book down and started with, "Hey, I dunno why you're here, 'kay? But..."

"I'm trying to figure out why someone would want you dead," Sarah said, the words sounding incredibly out of place in her happy voice. "It's puzzling me. But then, I should know that a lot of powers don't show on the skin, right?"

"I don't...!"

"To be clear, I'm not here to kill you," Sarah informed him, still smiling. "But someone totally tried to." She glanced back at Momo, who shrugged back at her, not really sure what Sarah was doing but willing to trust her on this. "I spent about half the ride over here, when I wasn't trying to get Momo to tell me what kind of hair dye she uses, thinking up all the ways this could go. How I could lie to you to get information, that sorta thing. But then I remembered a friend of mine." Sarah let out a small sigh. "He's big on the whole blunt-honesty thing. So, I'm just telling you. Something wants you dead. We intercepted one attempt, but there might be more, and I'd like to know why."

There was a long pause. The silence of the library hung heavy in the air, like a physical presence, stifling and thick. Sarah and Momo could practically *see* the gears turning in the head of the kid across the table as he flicked his eyes between them, then over to the stairs, then to the picture windows that overlooked the parking lot behind the library, before coming back to land on Sarah again. There was a feeling rolling off him, like silent contemplation, that Sarah couldn't remember ever seeing on anyone that young before.

Eventually, he closed the book, leaned back in his chair with a slouch, and asked, "You're not here to arrest me? And you know about . . . the thing? Is it yours?"

"No," Sarah said, noting that Javier kept his eyes locked on her face as she answered. "Yes, and no. In that order."

He nodded and then leaned forward, lowering his voice to a whisper. "I got trapped in it under the school. All those tunnels and pipes and, well, you know, right? I 'unno if there's other ways in, but the only other person I met down there . . . died." He swallowed hard but didn't flinch or look away. "When I got out, I got this . . . it tells me how good I'm doing, you know? Do you have one like that?" Sarah shook her head. "Well, whatever. Mine tells me how I'm doing at reading." Now, Javier did glance to his side and reached out a toned arm to tap the books next to him. "I thought it was kinda stupid, like . . . like this was just some crazy fucked-up way to get people to do homework or some shit, right?"

"But it wasn't?" Sarah prompted.

"I used to joke that reading was kinda gay," he told them and gave a slight nod at Momo when she tensed up at the words. "I know, right? Fucking shitty of me. I get that now. But that's the thing. I had to read for class, right? And that progress feeling was always there. And one day, I figured, fuck it, why not? Right? So I really got on what I was doing, and it ticked over. And it asked me what I wanted."

"What you wanted?" Sarah was rapt now.

"Understanding, memorization, or, like, resistance or something? I don't remember the third one. I picked understanding, 'cause I didn't really get it, and I needed it to go away before the teacher noticed." Javier grabbed a book off the stack and pulled it open in front of him. "And then . . . I *got it*. It wasn't some big change or anything; I'm still me, but . . . I dunno, I feel like when I start reading, it actually matters. Have you ever wanted to know more about Vikings?" he asked them suddenly. His pattern of speech was getting smoother, like he was thinking less about what he was saying, maybe relaxing just a bit because he finally got to talk to someone about this.

"All the *time*, man!" Momo answered before Sarah could say anything, making the other girl huff out a quiet laugh.

Sarah caught her breath and then shrugged. "Yeah, okay, I'll bite. What about Vikings?"

"Well, I didn't. I didn't care. But then that was what our history teacher was talking about, and I just . . . It's . . . But now, it's like . . . yo, it's like I was starving, and didn't know, and then someone cooked a steak and I smelled it and then *all I could think about* was how hungry I was." He stared at them like he was trying to pull information out of their minds just by watching. "My coach doesn't get it. He thinks books are for nerds and doesn't get why I'd rather be here. My parents just think I'm growing up, but I can't even be mad at them, because I *get what they're seeing*. But . . . man, every day I'm here, I get a few points closer to that again." He closed his eyes. "No one gets it. But how the shit could I explain it, yeah?"

Sarah leaned back, taking it in. After a couple of deep breaths, she turned to Momo. "Okay. Okay. Momes, get in touch with the others, pass it on. Tell Anesh to look for missing persons rates among high school students. Hey"—she turned back to the kid—"who was the other guy you ran into? The one who . . . didn't make it."

"He was, like, my age. But I didn't recognize him. I don't think he was from my school," the young man replied, confused at how well

Sarah was taking this. His words were less certain this time, though she wasn't sure if he was just unsure what she was asking, or if he was lying.

"Okay. Check the school, check the records—you!" She pointed a finger at Javier, who jumped. "Give me your phone number. Are you okay on your own? We'll be keeping an eye on the thing that tried to kill you, but I can't promise we'll always be around if you need protecting."

"Who *are* you?" Javier asked, puzzled expression painted on his face and in his words.

Sarah grinned. "Imagine you could go back into the tunnels and get another, I guess, skill, that you could get perks for improving. Would you?"

His face hardened into something angry in an instant. "No, and you can't make me," he practically growled. If Sarah hadn't been tempered by actual combat, the overly aggressive teenager might have actually felt threatening to her, but sadly for him, no such luck.

She waved a hand at him. "Oh, don't worry about that. We're not some weird conspiracy like from one of the young adult dystopia books I'm really hoping you haven't read yet. I'm just trying to tell you that we're the people who keep going back." Sarah pushed her chair back and stood up, accepting the piece of paper from Momo that Javier had written his phone number on. "We'll be in touch. Probably to introduce you to Secret so you have a last line of defense against any out-of-context problems."

Javier gave her a horrified expression. "I got that reference," he said. "I don't like that reference!"

"Yeah, the world is really cool, and possibly lethal," Sarah told him as she and Momo started walking away.

"No, wait!" he called after them, ignoring the quiet of the library. "Yo, I got questions!"

"We'll talk later!" Sarah replied before whispering to Momo, "Hey, hustle. Don't let him catch up to us." She nodded at one of the librarians with an apologetic smile as they rushed out the side door, jogging across the darkening parking lot in a blatant disregard of pedestrian safety.

"Why are we running?!" Momo whispered to Sarah when they were across the street and ducking through the parking lot of a church. "Why aren't we talking to him? He was telling us stuff!"

Sarah held out a hand, stopping Momo as she peered around the corner, making sure they weren't effectively being followed. "Okay, two reasons. One, I didn't actually expect him to just tell us everything like that, and he was giving me a really weird feeling. The whole thing felt like it was kind of a trap?" Sarah glanced over her shoulder again. "Also, my original plan was to try to entice him or something, and then have the second meeting be on ground we could control, if it turned out he was kind of problematic."

"That's weirdly manipulative of you." Momo sounded kind of sad that her image of Sarah as a sparky cinnamon roll was being shattered.

"Yeah, well, I got a weird feeling from him, and not just because he's a decade younger than me," Sarah told her friend. "If he's being honest, like, I think we should help him. Even if he was lying. I think we should help everyone. But flip's sake, I'm not gonna just invite him to our secret base."

"It was the dead guy, wasn't it?" Momo asked.

"He didn't seem like he cared, and not just in a tough-guy sorta way," Sarah agreed. "That's weird. I don't think a single person in our group doesn't care about the people we've lost."

Momo pouted a bit. "Okay, I get it, it's a safety thing. Boy, if only we'd brought two strapping young men with us to be bodyguards or something." She cleared her throat, pivoting her head to gaze at Sarah. "Oh, wait."

"Hey, I know you're armed. You coulda taken him."

"If he wasn't lying about his power. Also, holy shit, that power." Momo bounced on the balls of her feet while Sarah kept peeking out around the corner, keeping watch. "Think I could get one for Smash Bros.?"

"Think we could get one for . . . oh, for any of the skill orbs?" Sarah asked.

Momo let out a long "ooooooooooh" as her brain caught up to it. "Oh, man, that's gonna be broken!"

"Yeah, it . . . oh, yeah, it would." Sarah rapped her knuckles into her palm. "Um . . . hey, so, Momo. If you were a dungeon, and there was a different dungeon, and your superpowers and its superpowers synergized really well . . ."

Momo got it right away. "Oh, you think? Marked for death for being too useful?" She frowned. "Does that mean the other one is gonna try to have us killed? Or even more we don't know about? Also, hey, does this mean that there's *two* dungeons in *this town*?"

"Oh, dear," Sarah said in her best Mary Poppins voice. "Okay, now I *really* need you to call the others."

"I've been trying. They're not answering." Momo said.

"Oh, dear."

James was currently being berated. "You've been out for *four hours*!" Alanna shouted. "We couldn't move you, we couldn't wake you up, we thought you died!"

It was hard to not notice that her eyes were a little red. Anesh's too, now that James thought about it. The two of them were kneeling next to him on the rough wood floor, ignoring the risk of sharing the splinters that were currently digging into the back of his coat. He was lying flat on his back, his legs having suddenly spiked in pain after four hours frozen stock-still in the same position. If Anesh hadn't caught him, he might have cracked his head on the dresser he'd just popped open.

The two of them had given him water and a snack from the survival bag Anesh had brought, and James had been shocked at how thirsty he'd been. After all, he'd just spent about four hours experiencing rain.

"This is the second time this has happened," James croaked out. "I'm starting to feel like I should stop touching knobs that don't belong to Anesh."

The off-color joke caught Alanna so off guard that she stopped her panicked yelling in shock, a look on her face like she was unsure if she should punch him or crack up. Anesh solved the problem by flinging the bag at James's face, flushing a dark blush on his skin. James flailed back, sputtering, and then there was another round of him picking himself off the floor and the others making worried comments.

"What happened?" Anesh asked after everyone had composed themselves. "Did you just freeze?"

"No, no," James told him, taking a deep breath of the dusty attic air. "It was a puzzle lock. I had to get a mental image just right to open it. I dunno what those glasses of yours actually see, Alanna, but it was weird."

"God, I shoulda just told you. It's potential time wasted. Or spent, maybe." She pressed a hand against her eyes in shame. "Fuck, we need to stop being cute about this. That could have killed you."

"Probably. But I'm not mad," James told her. "We know now, yeah?" He shook his arms, trying to clear away the lingering feeling of raindrops. "But yeah, it was intense. If you ever get in one, try to find the background feeling of what it really wants to be. You need almost everything, too. How it looks, smells, sounds, feels, even the pressure and texture of the ground."

"How'd you get it all?" Anesh asked, curious.

"I think it's like an actual lock, where if you get close enough, you can force it. And I just got a lot of it right because I had actual memories of scenes like that. Well, one good one, I guess, from when I was a kid." James shrugged. "What's in the dresser?"

"This." Alanna handed him a stick.

"You are shitting me." James looked at it. "No magical loot? Just... a stick?" To be fair, it wasn't exactly a stick. It was a flattened piece of wood, with a thin groove in the middle of it, and whorl patterns on each end. Shaped like a Popsicle stick, but maybe a foot long and rather thin.

"Sorry. Just a weird stick," Alanna said.

"Okay, hang on." Anesh stopped her as she went to toss the stick away. "That's irresponsible, given that we know how stuff like this works at least a little bit. Alanna, let me see that." She handed it over with a shrug and went back to making sure James wasn't about to have a heart attack or anything.

Anesh fussed with the stick for a couple minutes, turning it over in his hands, looking at the markings, and eventually did the obvious and tried to break it in half. James and Alanna watched with amused expressions as he tried to snap it and it failed to even budge. His face transformed briefly into a frown, and then he pressed down again with a lot more power, making as if to leverage the small piece of wood against his knee and shatter it.

It didn't even warp a little bit.

After that, James had to contain his laughter as Anesh went through a series of motions to try to twist, stomp, crush, and at one point *gnaw* the stick in half.

"Okay," Anesh panted out. "This is frustrating."

"Give it here," Alanna said, reaching out a hand.

As soon as Anesh passed it to her, she took a grip on her end and broke it cleanly in half.

"Huh," James said, curious. "That's weird. How'd you do that?"

But neither of them heard him. Both of them were listening to the message in their heads.

<| Connection Open : Anesh Patel—Alanna Byrne : One Corridor Established : One Corridor Empty |>

"AAAAH!" "FUCK, OW!" James scrambled to his feet as the two of them dropped back to their knees, clutching their hands as a burning hiss filled the otherwise quiet air. He raced over to them, grabbing at the hands they were clutching just in time to see the completion of the burn that left a lightly glowing green circle inscribed on the back of each of their hands. It sat just below the index finger, above the thumb.

"What the shit?!" James yelled as the other two regained their composure.

"Ah... ah..." Anesh panted for breath, holding up a hand to wait while he clutched at his chest with his other arm.

Alanna, meanwhile, took one shaky breath and let it out slowly, trying to let the memory of the sudden pain go. "We're connected," she said. "Give me a paper or something. I gotta write that down." Rustling through the emergency bag, James passed her a notepad, and the three of them took a minute to make sure that it was recorded, with Anesh verifying the notice he'd seen pop through his head.

"So... what does it do? Are you two connected somehow now? I mean, obviously, yes, but in what way?" James asked.

"Well, we're dating now," Alanna told him.

James blinked and almost tripped as he repacked the bag. "Are you... are you just messing with me, or is this a time-travel thing I should be worried about?"

"She's messing with you. I can't feel anything different," Anesh said. "Hang on." He closed his eyes and tried to feel for the link. He could certainly feel the mark on his hand, and he could... he could almost feel that it *went* to someone. But there was nothing else there. No extra information, or location data, or feelings. Just that it was connected. "I got nothing," he said, looking at Alanna, who pursed her lips and nodded in agreement.

"Okay. We need to get out of here for now," James said, and they agreed. "I wanna come back, though. We should talk to Fredrick about it." He looked over at Alanna, who was rolling her eyes sarcastically. "Okay, you guys go to the car. *I'll* talk to Fredrick about it, and you don't have to put up with him, okay?"

"He annoys me," Alanna bluntly informed Anesh, who was watching the byplay with interest.

The instant their feet hit the bottom of the stairs and alighted in the hallway, two things happened. The first was that Fredrick was instantly there, stuttering his way through asking James if they had solved the problem. The other was that Anesh's phone blew up.

"Hang on, I've got about eighteen missed calls," he said. "And about fifty texts from Momo and Sarah. And... hmm. We should go." Anesh tapped Alanna on the shoulder and motioned them outside while James negotiated terms of access with Fredrick. "Hey, look." He showed her his phone.

"That's a lot of messages," she agreed.

"No, the time. Look. We were in there for about five hours, all told. It's been maybe one out here. The attic is time compressed, but not like the Office. Unless that entrance sometimes closes and we might get trapped there. We're going to need to seriously test it before we risk more exploration."

"What was there to explore?" Alanna asked. "We checked—there were no hallways or corners or anything."

"I don't . . . know . . ." Anesh admitted. "But I have a worrying feeling from these texts that we're going to want to double-check basically everything within a hundred-mile radius from now until the sun goes out." He threw the bag into the back seat of the car, while Alanna stored their crowbars and unbuckled her unused armor.

"Why?" she asked him, turning to look for James and tapping her foot on the curb in impatience as he stood in the doorway, talking to the balding man who owned the house and their latest source of problems. He showed her the phone and the string of increasingly worried texts. "Ah, fuck. Another one?" Alanna thought for a second. "We need to actually have a defense force. Like, for real. We need better training, bigger guns, and more resources."

"I was thinking the same thing," Anesh said as James joined them and casually slid into the driver's seat.

"Aw, that's cute," he said, only having heard the back half of their conversation. "Is that part of the link you guys have now?"

"No," Alanna told him, "it's because we're both not idiots. And by the time we tell you what's up, you'll agree."

". . . We're gonna have to cancel anime night, huh?" James asked morosely.

They nodded. "Oh, yeah."

"Fuck."

CHAPTER 18

"Okay, so, I didn't make a PowerPoint for this," James said, standing in front of a truck-size whiteboard. "For obvious reasons. But I just wanted everyone to know that I thought about it and chose not to, so you're welcome."

"Boo!" Alanna called from the back of the crowd.

Crowd was increasingly becoming an applicable term to what James had thought would be a pretty quick briefing and strategy meeting. The parking lot in front of the base had filled up rapidly as everyone from all four teams, as well as a number of the nondelver members, filtered in. Even Karen was here, her decision made when she'd walked in, taken a steadying breath, and nodded once to James.

Dave had showed up early, which had caught them all off guard, because they'd been looking for *cars* and not a drake-shaped object dropping out of the sky and onto the building's roof. Momo was here, of course—it'd be hard for her to get out of it since she was living in the basement—along with her two teammates. Alanna and one Anesh sat at the corners of a cleared desk off to the side of where James stood, ready to help field any extra questions. Sarah wasn't in the room right now; she was out front talking to Lua, who had taken up a role as the guild's full-time therapist, but they'd both be back shortly. Daniel hadn't been able to weasel out of work like James had and so had sent Tyrone as a representative, and James was pretty sure that Pathfinder was watching through him. Theo was also there, leaning back in a rolling chair, feet up on a table, because she made the rules, apparently, and if she was letting James take a two-hour lunch for this, then you could bet she'd take one, too. And Karen's team were all here, too, though they were split around the room. Karen was right up front, either to better pay attention or to try to hold James accountable for small mistakes; it was yet to be seen. Deb was sitting over with JP, who was himself off to the side on a couch that he'd dragged in here from the front room. Alex was . . . around. James had seen her; he knew she was here. Even the survivors whom Anesh had been outsourcing a variety of orb-based experiments to were here, Ryan and Reed, a pair of brothers who had been mostly coincidentally taken by the Office at separate times.

Everyone was here, he realized. There were all these people now, delvers and support team and even fucking Pendragon occupying a bus-size empty corner of the room. Hell, there were so many faces in the crowd he didn't recognize all of them. And all of them, except maybe Pendragon, were here to listen in on what would have been, over the past few months, a private conversation between him and Anesh, or him and Alanna, with maybe one or two other people joining them at the coffee shop to shoot around ideas.

Things changed, James thought.

"Okay, I'm gonna run over some points as fast as I can, and then we'll discuss long-term plans," James told the crowd. It wasn't like he didn't know what he was doing; he'd even made *notes*, which his high school self surely would have scoffed at if the older version of him could see him now. Well, okay, no, that version would have questioned the reality of the situation. But the attitude would be the same.

"First off, we've got two known dungeons now," James started with. "Now, one of them is just an attic—that is, normal attic size. But we're going to be doing regular checkups there, and we're going to start accumulating the cash to make Freddy a rather handsome offer on the house, because we'd like to keep it secure."

"Fredrick!" Sarah and Harvey called from the middle of the crowd.

James rolled his eyes. "Yes, him. Okay, okay, you know what? I should know better than to make fun of names. Fredrick. Any other interruptions?"

"What part of the budget will the money be drawn from?" Karen asked from the front. There wasn't any hostility in her voice, and it was a legitimate question, but it was basically the same point she always harped on, and it was starting to bug James.

Fortunately, *this* time, he'd come prepared. With spreadsheets.

"I'm glad you asked," he told her with an unnervingly smug smile. "We've got budget printouts here for anyone who wants them. Just take a folder and pass it on. There isn't enough for everyone, but that's why we liberated multiple printers out of the dungeon, anyway."

"I thought that was to see if they were magic?" Dave asked, like he didn't already know.

"No, that . . . okay, yes. And we're pretty sure they're normal. But if you get hypnotized by spreadsheets, please let an expert know so we can break that printer." James pointed to where his partners sat. "It's Alanna. Alanna is the expert on breaking printers."

Anesh held a hand to his chest and gasped theatrically. "Not me?!"

"We are getting off track." James rubbed his eyes in frustration. "Again. Karen, we have a budget, and we'll talk more about that in a second. Now, second point! We're not using enough blues! The powers from absorbing blues are often incredibly situational, inflexible, and absolutely broken. So, everyone, especially anyone on the active roster, should have at least one slotted all the time. We still don't know why some people can't, so no pressure if that's you, but if you can, there's no reason not to have one. And we *do* have a stockpile of about two hundred small blues on hand for that. Though I think Anesh used a bunch of them to get this place set up?"

"They basically replace contractors if you get lucky, yeah," Anesh acknowledged, looking wistfully around at the warehouse space as if that explained anything.

James nodded in appreciation. "Great. So yeah, see Anesh or JP afterward to requisition your blue. Moving on, third point . . . Anesh, did you change my notes?"

"We just finished getting one to work and wanted it brought up."

"Why not at the *end*, then? Why . . . oh fuck it. Okay. Third point, our tech team has gotten a functioning Wi-Fi adapter to work with the skulljacks. Anesh, wanna take this one?" James waved Anesh to his feet.

The younger man showed signs of apprehension as he was called to speak in front of even this small collection of friends. "All right, ahem. Yes. So, we've figured out how to make a sort of series of adapters, Bluetooth devices, and a cobbled-together network card that has what we're tentatively calling full connection functionality." He stepped up to the table in front of the presentation area and laid a series of five braids of cable down. They had a lanyard on one end with a strap to pull it tight against the back of the neck. A small plastic box held a microcontroller, with the different cables wrapped tightly and zip-tied to each other as they connected to the tools the device used to send and receive data. They were wrapped in black electrical tape to keep them as tightly put together as possible but still had that jury-rigged feeling. "One of them has some connectivity issues over Bluetooth, which is annoying, but they all work."

Hands went up *instantly*. Anesh sighed at the number of people waiting to ask questions. Resigned, he first pointed over at Momo, who was frantically waving her hand in the air.

"Can I have one!? Or three?! Right now?" she asked, excitement bubbling out of her.

"No," Anesh replied. Then sighed again when her face turned into a comical display of disappointment. "Okay, wait, no. Maybe. We've got five of them, like I said, so until we can make more, that's our supply, and the microcontrollers that hold the whole mess together are still on order. It's up to James who they go to, but over the next week, we want everyone to take a turn training with them in small groups in at least basic fighting situations."

Hands went down. Only a few people had anything to ask beyond that. Anesh called on James next, mildly exasperated and wanting to get it out of the way.

"Who came up with the term? Because I have a complaint," James stated, projecting his voice to the audience and earning a few grins.

"No," Anesh replied. "Next question. Karen?"

"How do we know these are safe? Also, is it possible for the skulljacks to spread through them if someone is intentionally broadcasting to one?" Karen went straight for the question that everyone should have probably started with.

Anesh took a deep breath before replying. "Yeah, we've done some testing on that front, actually. No, they can't infect through Wi-Fi. As near as we can tell, the biggest risk is that we still can't figure out a hardware or software solution to the loss-of-self problem. If one person in a link is acting in bad faith, it may be possible for them to just arbitrarily force a hive-mind situation on the others, and we can't really stop that. So yeah, that's a huge problem, but not one that *should* be an issue with those assembled, yes?" Anesh glared at the audience, as if daring anyone to cross that line. "Good. Any further inquiries?" He looked around and spotted the one hand still up. "Yes, Nei... *Neil?!* What the hell are you doing here?"

"Wait, what?!" James and Alanna exclaimed simultaneously from the desk they sat at to the side of the presentation zone, both of them scrambling slightly to turn and spot the uninvited guest. "Neil, what the hell are you doing here?" James yelled over at him.

"I don't know!" Neil kept his hand up as he yelled back, voice cracking into a slightly squeaky tone. "I was just here to drop off a bunch of drones Anesh bought, and then it looked like you guys were doing a game thing, and then the dragon showed up and I didn't want to move!"

James lurched to his feet, slamming a hand into the desk as he leaned forward. The different delvers around Neil scooted away from the formerly unaffiliated kid, trying to put some distance between him and James's yelling. "Why didn't you say something?! Also, who even let you back here?!"

"Why didn't *you* say something?" Neil yelled confusedly, slinking down into his seat. "What are you guys even doing here?! And why didn't you invite me?!"

There was a tap on James's shoulder, and he turned to see Alanna giving him a resigned expression, mouth in a flat line. "I mean, we coulda told him. No harm now, right?" she asked.

James sighed. "Neil, there's weird shit going on, and you're just gonna have to catch up. Fortunately you snuck into the one meeting where that can probably happen. Sit down, shut up, and don't reveal our secrets to any government agencies or I'll have Pendragon eat you."

"She doesn't . . ." Dave started to say, before JP calmly clapped a hand over his friend's mouth at the prompting of a glare from their irate leader.

"Got it?" James asked, face set in an exasperated glare.

"Got it! Yes, sir!" Neil saluted, in a way that a lot of the other delvers around saw as a little too mocking. Especially since a lot of them had been doing that and actually meaning it.

"Good. Anesh, sit down." James waved a grateful boyfriend back to his seat as he himself stood up again. "Okay, we've got weirdly a lot to cover, so I'm gonna try to make a few things quick. First off, two new job appointments. Harvey, you're now in charge of operational security. Not for the dungeons, just for the mundane stuff. So what that *means* is"—James threw a meaningful look around the room, lingering on Dave in particular—"if you have a dumb idea that might compromise us entirely, run it by Harvey first. Harvey, what this means for you specifically is that we need you to keep Dave from flying Pendragon past news cameras, and also it's now your job to make sure that we don't get another Neil incident."

"Hey!"

"Neil, shut up, you are not in good enough standing with me right now to object to that." James sighed. "The other one is Karen, who is now in charge of survivor services." He nodded to the older woman, who looked legitimately shocked to be acknowledged. "We've disagreed about a lot of stuff, but you honestly care, so you're in charge of it officially now. See JP after this; he'll hand over the contact information we have on everyone, and also our budget. We've got a business account set aside for it, and it's absolutely not enough, but we're working on it." He addressed the room as a whole, looking up from meeting Karen's eyes. He'd talk to Karen in private afterward and let her know that it was probably safer if she didn't go actively delving with them, given how she wasn't very good at it. "She's also gonna be in charge of coordination of things like the support group and scheduling for private conversations. I think Anesh actually made printouts of the update, which makes me feel weird. Why is this weird?" he quietly asked Alanna.

"It's too real," she told him bluntly.

"Yeah, that." James sighed. "Okay. Now, for less real business. Anesh mentioned training with the links, and that's great, but we also need training in general. The orbs aren't reliable, and even then, practicing with those skills that help us in a fight is important. So, we're repurposing one of the basements into a place where we can work on moving and fighting together. Karen is going to be surprised to learn that she's going to be scheduling groups of people to spend a few hours there a week, to get us all . . . well, better."

There were nods from the crowd at that. Momo piped up, "Yeah, we don't get stronger, and I don't wanna get blindsided by a cat again."

A few people looked more confused by that sentence than they should have. "By a what?" Deb asked.

"No, impossible. We hung out after that one. Did no one tell you about the cat?" JP asked her. "Oh, man, that's a problem."

"Yeah, no kidding," James mused. "Okay, we need to stop relying on word of mouth. Who wants to be in charge of, fuck, I dunno, keeping a private wiki updated?" A few hands went up, more than he'd actually expected. "Wow, really? Okay, how about . . . Tyrone, I guess? Okay. So, that covers the links, the training, the jobs . . ." James muttered to himself as he looked down at his notes. "All right, last thing I've got to mention is that we need to start looking for the theoretical dungeon that Officium Mundi is putting assassination orders out on, and oh god what a sentence that was."

Hands went up again, with a few murmured conversations starting up. "I have a really important question," Dave said.

Alanna replied without waiting for anyone to actually ask anything. "We tailed a couple suits that Daniel tagged leaving the dungeon, found a dead drop with a briefcase full of cash and a request to murder some kid, tracked down the kid, and learned about the existence of something underneath the high school." Hands went down as she spoke, mostly to be replaced by shocked silence.

"Which one?" Simon asked. "Which high school, that is. There's a few around here. Was it the one we went to?"

"It's not clear yet, but I'm also curious if I went to school on top of a dungeon," Alanna told him. "Sarah's person intuition says something is kinda fishy about it. *I* think we should place one of our younger members in the school to poke around and try to figure out if this is an open-secret thing or not." She raised her eyebrows at Simon, Other James, and Momo.

Momo held her arms out in front of her body in an X shape, frantically shaking her head and letting her neon-green hairstyle dance around wildly. "Oh, hell no," she said. "If you try to make me go back to high school, I will burn this entire place, the Office, and half of the city to the ground. Then I will use my magic to bring it all back and do it again, just to prove how serious I am."

"Momo did not like high school," James made a dry joke out of explaining to the rest of the crowd.

"Yup!" Momo verified once the laughs died down.

"Also Momo is . . . twenty-five?" Simon pointed out. "I'm thirty. Do I actually look like a high schooler to you?" he asked, and Alanna tried to avoid making eye contact with him to skip having to give an answer.

"This is so fucked up!" Theo yelled from the back. "And exactly what I warned you about!"

Alanna fired back before James could respond, "This happened when we weren't even there, to someone who we don't know! Think, you dumbass! The Office is clearly capable of acting without our permission!"

"Okay, what else." James tapped his upper lip as he thought out loud, speaking firmly over the potential argument that was brewing before nodding and rattling off the remaining points. "All right, so, work on totemizing reds continues. I'm told that there's progress. The grand list of skills gained has been updated—thanks to everyone for helping track that. *Apparently* our delivery of drones has come in, so everyone who wants to take one home to practice piloting should do so. Anesh, am I forgetting anything?"

"I think that's all that's relevant?" Anesh told him, and James nodded with satisfaction.

Now addressing everyone with a small smile on his face, James got their attention again. "All right, all right. So, that's basically all the big updates. I now, against my better judgment, open the floor to discussion and questions. Just so everyone is aware, we do have a door open tomorrow night, and we will be going in. This whiteboard here . . ." James took the time to dramatically flip the whiteboard around to its opposite side. ". . . is for team assignments, and also our intentional objectives. Don't just write your name or other stuff here, but do come up and ask things. I'll be up here, but really, take some time and just talk among yourselves." He nodded at everyone. "I feel like we should do this more often. Information makes it a lot easier for us to stay alive, and also, I dunno about you guys, but I find this rad. Anyway." James cleared his throat, suddenly awkward about the number of eyes on him as he spoke. "Presentation over. Thanks for coming."

He stepped away from the front of the room, drifting over to where Alanna and Anesh sat, watching as the assembled group started to pick up their own conversations. The noise of a room full of people each having their own discussion, even a large room like this, began to pick up.

"Well, that went well," Alanna said. "And you didn't snap under pressure!" She slapped James on the back, turning the almost aggressive gesture into the pleasant pressure of a friendly hand on the shoulder. "But really, good job. This is a good idea."

"Yeah, mostly," James said. "Except for this part, though." He raised a hand in greeting as someone approached their table. "Hey, Neil."

Neil was, as James had observed before, a big kid. And he meant both of those words in a generally friendly way. He stood at about seven feet tall, wide shoulders and a soft face. One of those people that loved their hobbies in a way that was almost too devotional, but still had this weird effect of making normal people stop and think to themselves, *Do I have anything I care about that much?* He had been one of the people James and Anesh had gone to when they'd first needed some stuff for the dungeon, because he was *really* into the whole drone thing, and so it was from him that Ganesh's body had come. James briefly wondered how that meeting would go if Ganesh was introduced to Neil, and then he realized that Ganesh was here today, so it wasn't like it was some outlandish hypothetical. Especially since they'd already shattered the veil.

At the end of the day, they'd decided not to add Neil to their original small group because he was . . . well, he was a kid. And not in the way that the rest of them absolutely were when they saw the amazing sights that the Office had to offer. More that he was just a little bit unreliable and kind of a derp, as Sarah always described him. And now that they were building an organization, it hadn't really occurred to any of them to invite him on board, just because he never really felt like someone who belonged on an adventuring team.

James felt mild guilt over that. Guilt that was assuaged by the fact that Neil had just accidentally snuck into a secret meeting.

"So, uh . . . what the hell?" Neil opened the conversation with. "Dude! I know we haven't talked in a while, but what, uh, happened?"

"Well, I found a hole in reality and started my career as a professional adventurer," James said. "Then things got weird. Look, I don't really want to explain this all to you. Maybe go ask around or something?"

Neil frowned. "Wow, rude," he said. "Is this why you wanted all the drones?"

"Yeah. Actually, one of them is alive, if you wanna meet him?" James said, realizing that Neil didn't deserve this current level of dickishness and trying to be a little friendly.

"Oh, hell yeah!" Neil exclaimed. "So, what's it take?"

A cocked eyebrow from James. That was a skill he was developing all on his own. "Take to what?" he asked, like he didn't know.

"To join up," Neil asked.

James pinched the bridge of his nose while Alanna and Anesh watched expectantly behind him. "Okay. Okay! Fine!" He eventually bit the words off. "Look, we're trying to actually keep the weird shit secret, so if you wouldn't mind just keeping that trust? Actually, that's a good test, yeah." He glanced over at Anesh. "You're with Secret right now. Can you ask him if he can do that?"

"Sure," Anesh said. "I think I see where you're going with this."

"Yeah, me, too." James turned back to Neil. "Okay, that's the deal. Keep this a secret for a week, and you're in. Can't promise that you won't die if you try your hand at the adventuring part, but, well . . . we've got some rad toys."

Neil looked at him with narrowed eyes, tilting his head back like he could somehow get a better angle on James. It was strange that even though he was the taller person in the room, James seemed to tower over the proceedings. "What's the catch?"

"I'd tell you, but you wouldn't remember anyway," James said. "Anyway. If you want a detailed explanation of what's going on, go talk to Dave. He'll get you up to speed and probably won't be rolling his eyes as he has to explain it again." James made a "move aside" motion with a flat hand. "Now, someone else has a question for me. I'll talk to you later, okay?"

Neil checked behind him and was kind of startled to see a few people just waiting there. "Wait, are you *in charge*? You hate being in charge of things!"

"Times change. Move yer ass," James snorted out. "All right, JP, what's up?"

"There's a problem with the bathrooms, and I think it's your fault."

James opened his mouth, then closed it, thought about what JP had just said, and then erupted in laughter. "Okay, explain," he said, once he'd composed himself and Alanna had more or less stopped her own fit of giggles.

"So, you used a green orb on the bathroom, yeah?"

"Not on purpose, but that did come up, yes." James turned and scanned the arrayed whiteboards before tapping one of them. "Right there. Bathroom value plus forty-six K. Why, what's gone wrong with it? Toilets too complex for us to understand?"

"No, though that's going on the list of potential problems." JP pulled out a small notebook and wrote that down. "What's actually gone wrong is that a lot of that value actually was tied up in this wall plant thing. According to someone who had the luck to get a botany skill orb, it's this weird-ass fern that's mostly extinct now. So, we *wanted* to pass it off to someone who could actually use it, but when we tried to take it out of the bathroom, it just turned to dust."

"Well, that sucks. So the value is specific to the bathroom?" James asked with a disappointed click of his tongue.

JP held up a raised finger. "Ah, that would be bad, yes. But as soon as that happened, the bathroom got new silver-plated fixtures and a water feature."

"What."

"Yeah, I did some googling, and some math that I really should have passed off to Anesh, and I'm pretty sure that *specifically* that forty-six thousand of value is localized to the bathroom. As in, it has a permanent minimum value of forty-six thousand dollars, and we can only remove any value that was outside of that."

"*Do people have value,*" James immediately asked.

JP gave James a look that clearly indicated that James had fallen for a rhetorical trap. "All life has value, *James*. But in this case, no, it doesn't count people. I think because people aren't part of a bathroom, if that makes sense. Anyway, no one has disintegrated or anything."

Anesh sighed from behind James. "I told you using all the greens here was a bad idea."

"You did not! Also, we have two basements. That's worth it," James retorted.

"Worth possible disintegration? No," Alanna countered. "Just . . . buddy, no. Have some perspective."

James thought about it for a few seconds before agreeing. "Yeah, okay. I admit, perspective is hard to come by these days. Anything else?" he asked JP.

"Not really. It wasn't even a question, honestly, just keeping you apprised."

James grinned. "You know, that's the first time someone's said that. I appreciate it." He stretched himself out, arching his back over the desk he was still leaning against. "I'm gonna go wander around and talk to people. You guys need anything?" he asked Anesh and Alanna.

"A minifridge," Alanna said. "We don't have any drinks here, and I can't believe I only just noticed."

"I'll put it on the list," Anesh acquiesced solemnly, intoning the words like they were an oath.

James wandered. He meandered, strolled, or perhaps even prowled. He had no real goal in mind; he just wanted to see what people were discussing and make himself available for anyone who had specific questions.

Okay, scratch that, he thought as he noticed something. His first goal was to go check in on Pendragon.

Pendragon, when James had first seen her, had been a pen, a few of those plastic alligator clips, and a manila folder that had a few strategic tears and folds in it. Pendragon, when James had next seen her, had been a cobbled creation roughly the size of a VW bus, a composite mass of paper and office supplies formed into a drake-shaped creature. Pendragon now was very similar to that, though she'd undergone some grooming.

Her wings were made up of paper, with folders for the pinions, and if Dave was to believed, then the laminated coating on them was something done recently. Her talons were larger than before, made up of a pair of what looked like the bases of rolling chairs. Ribs made of bands of pencils and pens curved around her torso, and paper clips adorned her papery hide like decorative armor.

She was kind of magnificent and was currently curled up into a corner, warily eyeing the group of people who were equally uncomfortable with the massive dragon in the room.

Normally, Dave was the only person who really approached their resident tank. And that really was kind of the role that Pendragon was meant to fill; not much else could match her for durability, for all that she was literally made of paper. For not the first time, James pondered that it really was kind of weird how the act of turning something into a dungeon life-form really warped it in a strange way. He couldn't swear beyond all doubt that the striders hadn't started out as weird bug things, but he knew that Ganesh hadn't had chitin before being brought to life. And Pendragon's leathery wings were a testament to how seemingly common materials could take on an organic texture all too easily.

"Hey there, big girl," James said as he approached Pendragon, who gazed at him suspiciously through glittering ballpoint eyes. "Has Dave been treating you nice? Oh, yes, he has! Look at how shiny you are!" James tentatively reached out to run a hand along the side of Pendragon's folded wing and was only mildly surprised when she started purring like a garbage disposal that was doing its best impression of a cat. "I wanted to say thank you," James told the world's biggest softie. "For saving my life. For saving Alanna and Dave, too. For . . . all of it. You really came through for us. So, thank you. I'll get you some fancy-ass calligraphy paper as a real thanks as soon as I have time."

He wasn't sure if she'd really understood him, but she did roll back a bit and expose the underside of her papery-textured wing skin to more pets. And James took that as an acceptance.

After that, he just went off to eavesdrop on the rest of his growing guild.

Theo and Karen were arguing over whether the dungeon should be exploited or bricked over, and James wasn't actually sure who was on which side. Either way, the debate was turning heated, and people nearby were scooting their chairs away or finding places to talk farther away from the disturbance.

Neil was getting a crash course in dungeoneering, courtesy of Dave. Additional input, mostly contradictory, was being provided by JP, who it seemed was mostly trying to scare the new guy off. A side comment JP muttered to James as he went by was that if they were going to be this casual about recruiting, then he knew an actual network engineer who would be happy to be part of their anarcho-utopian vision for the future. James filed that away under "maybe."

Sarah was busy trying to fill Momo in on her theory that each orb had four uses, which were shared across all orbs, while one of the two brothers in the research department tried to convince her that each orb only had *three* uses, chosen from a list of five. To James, it looked like nothing so much as like an angel and a devil sitting on someone's shoulders, except in this case, he couldn't tell which was which and Momo was desperately trying to pawn the entire conversation off onto Other James.

Other James was having none of it and was currently testing the new links out with Simon, the two of them having gotten permission from Anesh to give it a try. They looked like they were having fun, the two of them running through a martial arts routine in literally perfect sync. Well, maybe not quite perfect. It looked like small missteps every now and then, and James suspected it was because they were of different heights and not used to being each other. Which was both terrifying and super rad.

On another pass, the conversation between Neil and Dave had expanded out, with a half dozen people now giving input on what seemed to be a debate over whether or not either of the two of them should take up a skulljack. Neil seemed one million percent on board, but JP was holding back, and James absolutely wasn't interested in being part of *that* debate.

He fielded a dozen small questions as he walked, too. How had he found the dungeon in the first place, anyway? What was the best way to deal with the flashbulbs? How did you make friends with a strider? Or with anything, really? What was the dollar value of a yellow orb? What was their *goal*?

What *was* their goal?

James had to think about that one pretty hard.

Halfway through his second loop around the room, Alanna caught James's attention and he slid up next to her at the desk. "Sup?" he asked as he knelt down to conversation level.

"Okay, so, that whole thing JP mentioned is something a lot of people were talking about," she started, and James nodded in acknowledgment. "So, Harvey came up to us, and asked me a really weird question that I wanted to know if you had some deeper answer to."

"That's worrying. You guys tend to be the ones who have the good answers." James pointed back at Alanna and Anesh. "What is it?"

"What do the green orbs do?"

James blinked. "Oh, that's easy. They upgrade spaces. I'm not sure exactly what that *means*, but they give, like, buffs. Better internet, more closets, sometimes really weird shit like making certain activities easier or something."

This time, it was Anesh who replied. He nodded at James, and said, "Right, okay, the more closets part is the problem. So, question part two—what do the *orange* orbs do?"

"Well, they . . ." James closed his mouth and blinked. "Huh. Okay, weird. They both do space things."

"I mean, I'd find it hard to argue that Penrose steps would be an *upgrade* to a house. Especially if you actually want to go downstairs." Anesh shrugged. "Still, is it weird that they have overlap? I kind of thought they were . . . discreet."

James let out a long breath. "Some of them are pretty obvious. I wouldn't call Secret discreet, no matter what his name is."

"Not that . . . oh, you know what I meant." Anesh sighed.

James gave him a little huff of a laugh to let him know that it was all in good fun. "But yeah, that's weird. Maybe ask Sarah about it?"

"I shall," Anesh said. "How's the crowd?" he asked.

"Not bad. We should have gotten pizza or something." James shrugged. "Now we know for next time. Anyway. I think we're about ready to wrap up the official part of this. I want to talk to everyone

one last time, though. Do you mind doing that thing where you get people's attention?" Alanna shot him a thumbs-up and then stuck two fingers in her mouth and whistled so loud it echoed through James's skull. "Ow," he murmured to himself as he stood up and faced the room again.

Everyone quieted down quickly when they realized that James was standing there, waiting for them. It was probably never going to really click with him that he had earned authority here. It just didn't feel right. All he'd done was save their lives; he wasn't a leader. But now he felt like he had to step into that role anyway.

And Secret wasn't even here this time to tell him he was doing all right. That was a bummer. But if he was going to be standing here speaking, he'd at least give it his best.

He opened with, "What are we doing here?" projecting his voice across the warehouse floor. James stood at parade rest, his hands clasped behind his back as he looked over everyone who had showed up today just to be part of this. "What's our goal? More than one person asked me that tonight." He took a deep breath. "We're all aware now of something that's so much bigger than we are. Not just Officium Mundi, but also more. More places, more phenomena. And more danger, as well. There's all these weird little hints that things are bigger than us. So what are we doing?" James met their eyes as they stared back at him. "Well, we know we're not going to stop. Now that we know, how could we? So that's the first point of our charter. We are going to explore. We are going to steal fire and take these weird little shards of power when they are offered."

There were smiles now, and James smiled back at them. But his smile wasn't quite a happy one. "Second, we're going to protect people. I don't think anyone will have a problem with that. But there's a lot of people out there to protect, and that's kind of a broad mandate. So we'll start with what we're getting good at. We're going to shut down any of these assassination attempts. We're going to, if needed, beat the dungeons back into their own territory. And we're going to rescue any victims we can and take care of them as long as they need us." Nods from the crowd. If anyone could understand the need for that, it was these people. Now for the part James was unsure of. "And then we're going to use that power we're stockpiling. Unused power, a friend of mine once said, is a travesty. So our third point is going to be changing the world." There were frowns from a couple people at that. Mostly Karen and Theo. "It is almost inevitable that we're going to stumble across solutions to some problems in there. Major ones. The kind that I don't think anyone will miss if we kill them—things like diseases or famines. And I refuse to let those solutions sit idle." James punched one hand into his open palm. "We are, almost certainly, going to piss some people off. Make enemies, even. And at some point, at least one dungeon is going to try to kill us all." He clenched his fists. "And we are going to win. Got it?"

They got it. James nodded at them all, and he felt pride and approval radiating off Anesh and Alanna behind him.

"I'll have a draft of our charter available for anyone over the next week. If anyone has any specific points they want to add, or suggestions on language use, let me know. If anyone doesn't want to sign, maybe because they don't agree with the long-term goals, well, let me know anyway and we'll talk. Oh, and if anyone has any suggestions for pun names for our organization, *please* let me know. I'm stuck on 'Official Channels.'"

The tension shattered as James did what he did best—turned the start of a new age for the world into a joke.

CHAPTER 19

"Why is the building so empty?" James asked Daniel as the guard held the door open for their procession.

The younger man looked at James like he wasn't sure if this was a test or a trick of some sort. It was like he had watched James build a trap, step back, admire his work, nod, and then point to the trap and say, "You should walk into that—it could be fun. Daniel blinked slowly before inhaling deeply. "Are you . . . joking?" he asked, tentative.

"No?" James looked puzzled as he got into the elevator with a few other delvers who were all going up. He was personally carrying a box of replacement parts for their body armor sets, but everyone had at least a small bag of stuff in their hands. The constant influx of gear and supplies into the dungeon continued unabated.

"You must be joking," Daniel said, looking around at the others in the elevator. "Right?"

No one answered him. James just shook his head in growing frustration and shot a glance at the ceiling. "Daniel. Come on."

"It's, like, the twenty-sixth? Literally the entire company has the week of Thanksgiving off. Did you not wonder why the schedules changed?" Daniel felt a little bad. He should have just assumed James was being earnest.

"Well, shit!" James said with an enthusiasm that did not mirror his feelings. The elevator doors opened, letting the group spill out into the landing area around the door, where the others were already mustering. James stepped off after the people in front of him, swept his eyes around to find where Alanna and Anesh were talking, and strode over to them, tucking the box under his arm. "So, hey, what are we doing for Thanksgiving?"

"What?" Anesh asked, confused.

Alanna took up the slack in the conversation. "Did you forget about it?" she asked confidently. Not waiting for the answer she knew she was going to get, she shook her head and continued. "It's fine, I expected it."

The words *stung*. James was, very often, a forgetful person. For example, now that he thought about things he'd been forgetting, he remembered that he still hadn't actually called the Anesh that was down in California. Especially when he had something else to focus on, like, say, the world outside of time and space that contained an endless gray and beige expanse of cubicles, for example. But even so, even knowing that he had a bad tendency to let critical details slip from his mind, it was a pretty awful feeling to hear Alanna say it like it was *expected*.

"God, this is why I hate the holidays." James bit the words off. "It's just a million stressful things to do, everyone expects things, and even when people say it's no big deal, it always *is* a big deal out of nowhere at the last minute. I should have known this was going to come up."

"Sorry, hang on. When's Thanksgiving?" Anesh asked awkwardly. "I've been in this country for years now, and I still don't really know. Isn't it the last day of November?"

"Last Thursday of November," Alanna told him, Anesh's look of annoyance fueling the small smile on her face. "And buddy, don't worry. Sarah already bought a turkey and everything; the stuff's in the fridge and ready to go. I wasn't trying to be mean—I meant that I expected that you'd be, you know . . . *that*." She pointed a gloved finger over to where the stairwell door had been thrown open and delvers were pouring into the Office. "Or, wait, did you have family plans or something? Shit, now I'm the asshole. I should have . . ."

"Ah," James said, mollified. "Sorry, I assumed . . . Never mind. And no, no family plans. I'm sure my parents want me to come over for dinner, but they haven't called or anything. I dunno what Kayle is up to, but I'm okay with it being not joining us if you are."

"Yeah, it's cool," Alanna said as they marched in behind everyone else. She didn't mention her family plans for Thanksgiving. James and Anesh were already well aware that they were it for her; now that she'd gotten out from under her mother's roof, she wasn't exactly thrilled to go back. "Hey, isn't it supposed to be our job to throw the doors open? Who's stepping in my limelight?" she demanded as they came upon JP and Dave, who were clearly the guilty parties, waiting for them just inside the door.

"You looked busy," Dave said bluntly by way of explanation.

The five of them took a look around as the group began to get down to business. Tonight definitely confirmed it; the dungeon was resetting when they weren't in it. The cubicles around here were all reset to pristine condition—or at least, as pristine as you could get rough tan carpet over flimsy drywall.

All their fortification work from last week was once again undone, and Anesh was already running the odds in his head that it might be not worth it to put it back up. This little field of low-walled cube clusters wasn't exactly defensible, but it did leave a lot of open space and clear lines of sight around the base of the tower.

The tower, as Sarah confirmed as she joined them, was sacrosanct. Nothing in there was touched, except by whatever the odd shellaxy or two that had moved in had done. All their gear was safely stored this time, and the others were already starting to pull on armor from the growing supply of riot-control bodysuits and attach flashlights, flares, radios, and crowbars to their persons.

James, much to his dismay, saw a lot more people with swords.

"This is your fault," he told JP without bothering to explain. JP, of course, just smirked back and let his hand come to rest on the hilt of the blade he was personally wearing on his waist. "It was useful once. There's *one* thing they kill; this is just extra weight."

They stood there for a while in companionable quiet, either watching the flock of paper in the far distance flutter by, or eagerly eyeing the tower, or just taking slow breaths of the now-familiar scent of recycled air that nowhere on Earth ever really matched.

After a few minutes, Alanna broke the silence. "Everyone is watching us," she said.

"All right." James opened his eyes and nodded. "Time to get to work." The stress was gone, the worries about holiday plans or budgets or other dungeons all gone, replaced only by the thrill of the adventure.

That feeling lasted exactly until James started to walk forward and got hit with questions from five different people.

"What's our goal tonight?" Karen brusquely demanded.

"Do we have, like, rotating team assignments?" Alex asked.

"Who's on door duty, my dude?" Tyrone chimed in.

"Have you seen my laser pointer?" The question from Daniel was more general, but it still joined the noise of everyone piling responsibility onto James, and it didn't help.

James jammed his eyes shut for a heartbeat, closing out the world and its distractions for just a moment. This was, he reflected, going to be something he had to deal with eventually. But right now, he just needed to compose himself briefly before . . .

"Dave and JP are taking first door shift; we're looking for, alternately, a decision tree, or for one of the cubicles listed on the two briefcases we have in the tower; third desk in on the left side of the tower is our useful xenotech reliquary, and your laser pointer is in the top right cupboard; no." The answers to all four questions exploded out of him in rapid-fire succession. "Team assignments are with JP, since we have a few different people than normal. Also, just so everyone knows, if she didn't tell you, this will be Karen's last dive for a while, so we'll be splitting her team up today so that we can start getting everyone used to each other." He looked around and tried to remember anything else he had to say. "Um . . . Neil's here today; he'll be with JP and Dave, who are apparently our new-guy wranglers. That's nice. Neil, I'm sorry we don't have any armor that fits . . . okay, Neil is distracted." James nodded in understanding as the new guy still stood in the doorway, staring off into the distance. "Aside from that . . . yeah, I don't think I have anything. Oh, Theo. You're with Daniel and Tyrone; suck it up."

James nodded as he watched everyone start to reorganize themselves. The more they did this, the less hand-holding it took to get things moving. And now it was time for *him* to get moving as well.

He made a pass through the tower's ground floor, appreciating the camp lanterns that had been set up to give the whole place an almost gloomy orange atmosphere. His first stop was where his personal set of armor plating was waiting for him, and it took a few minutes to change into it. As soon as the plastic beetle shell was in place covering his joints and limbs, James unclipped the shredded arm where the displacer cat had gotten its claws into him and anxiously slid one of the replacement parts they'd made from the box he'd brought into its place. It was with a sigh of relief that it snapped in like it was made for it. Which, technically, it was. It just woulda been pretty silly to go through all this work for something that didn't fit or clip quite right.

After that, he grabbed his PS90 and slung it over his chest, adding their last spare magazine of ammunition to a pouch at his side. Adding to that, he clipped two of Anesh's thermite lances to his back and then spent three minutes trying to get them to settle in a way that didn't keep thumping him in the ass as he walked. A flashlight, an empty pouch to carry orbs in, and one of the fresh canteens full of coffee finished his getup.

He also stopped by the useful item desk to see if there was anything . . . useful. He'd considered the pen, of course, or maybe the laser pointer, but those had both been pawned off on other teams. And really, James kinda felt *ready* in a way that made him want to just leave the weird stuff to people who needed it more. Still, he looked at the labels on a pair of headphones that let you hear intents, and a stapler—a real one, sort of—that shoved organic matter away from itself when clicked. He didn't end up taking them, but he *did* look.

And then, of course, his hatchet. They'd gone through so many weapon iterations over the months. But James still just felt most comfortable with this solid piece of cold-edged metal in his hands. Not even the crowbar compared, especially when he wasn't wearing gloves and didn't want to hurt to hit things. Crowbars just *weren't weapons*, no matter what nerdy media told people.

"All right," James said as he emerged to find Alanna similarly adorned. "I'm set. Where's everyone else?"

Alanna shrugged. "Well, JP and Dave are staying near the door to start with," she said, and James nodded in acknowledgment. "Also Sarah already left with Momo and one of the guys who I cannot keep track of."

"Simon," James informed her. "Because I see Other James over there. With Anesh."

"Right. So she's got her own little thing going on. And then Anesh is staying in the tower today."

"Whaaaat." James let out a disappointed whine. "I haven't gotten to really spend time with him at all this week. Fuck, I keep forgetting to call his counterpart, too. I'm being a bad boyfriend. And now we aren't even delving together?"

Alanna made a sympathetic expression. "Yeah, I get it. But he apparently has six hundred dollars in coffee grounds and a bone to pick with conservation of matter." She shrugged. "So, you okay with it just being the two of us?" she asked.

If there was any hesitation in her voice, James plowed through it like a truck. "Yeah!" he said enthusiastically. "Just like old times! And by 'old times' I mean 'a couple months ago when we were just so fucking cool.' Remember being so fucking cool, Alanna? Those were good times."

She smiled at him, his joy infectious. "I was kinda worried. It seems like you're spending more time with Anesh these days. Or just on your own," she said as the two of them rounded the tower's base and started walking toward where the cubicles began to rise up above head height.

"And . . . and you're worried I was avoiding you?" James asked, partly puzzled but partly understanding. "Aw, fuck. I'm sorry. I've got a lot of excuses, but the short version is, I'm sorry. I'm not ignoring you, I'm just . . . me."

"Figured," Alanna said. "But that's still good to know. I'll be honest, despite the fact that it's my fault, I'm not used to a relationship like this."

"What, with three people?" James asked, waving at Momo's party a few rows of cubes over where they were poring over a copy of the dungeon map.

Alanna joined him in signaling the other team as their path diverged from Momo's group. "No, one where everyone cares."

"Holy shit, that's bleak." James wanted to laugh but opted to choke that back instead, not wanting to be an accidental asshole. He had some more to say about how he didn't want to betray Alanna's trust, how he promised this thing they had wouldn't be that way, but as with so many things in his life, the dungeon interrupted him. This time in the form of a strider trying to cut into his ankle.

[+1 Skill Rank : Bureaucracy—Medical—Nursing]

"All right, here we go," he said as they approached the "tree line" of cubes that made up the more common labyrinthian hallways of the Office, the distraction pulling their attention back to reality. "Ready? Any other relationship woes I should know about?"

"Nah, I'm good." Alanna stepped up next to him, pulling the Velcro on her gloves tight. "Let's do this."

They stepped forward together.

The more organized they got, as a growing group, the less work James had to do to keep that organization going.

Tonight, they'd come in, he'd answered a few questions, and everyone had spun off into their own roles. They certainly had factions in the guild now. The people who watched the door. The people who explored. Karen's group, who focused on making sure the people themselves were *doing okay*. But those factions took a back seat to small group dynamics and the individual missions each team had set.

Also, preplanning was amazing. Before the meeting the other night had wrapped up, they'd more or less settled who was going where. Everyone was keeping an eye out for the cube numbers that were listed on the "delivery orders" on the two briefcases they had; after all, the value of a single case would put them in the black for a month. And everyone was also on the lookout for more briefcases. And more anomalies, orbs, cash, and magic items. Of course.

But they had gone over the map, and everyone had a certain place they were searching. And beyond that, a place they were mapping. Especially Daniel and Tyrone, who were carrying Pathfinder through large unexplored swaths of dungeon and blazing a trail for those who would follow and give it a thorough look.

Dave's team was starting to specialize in big-game hunting, preparing with blades and thermite and a not-insignificant skill with snare traps that didn't come from an orb at all, but rather, a lot of practice in the secret base. They were on the lookout for tumblefeeds and cats, ready to react and learning to track the bigger beasties of the Office.

Momo and her team attracted those who were interested in trying to figure out the dungeon's secrets, looking for places where things were different, where orbs were weirder, and where they could maybe steal a few little facts. Tonight, they were on the hunt for as many reds as they could get their hands on.

And James and Alanna? Well, they were here for one thing this time.

"How many do you have in there, anyway?" James asked Alanna as they took a short break in one of the cubicles that didn't have a ceiling and wasn't dark. They'd had a run-in with a pissed-off shellaxy, and while neither of them was hurt, they both needed some time to let the surprised adrenaline wear off.

James was pointing at Alanna's orb bag, where she'd been apparently stashing just about every yellow orb she'd gotten. With a shrug that was too casual, she answered, "Oh, a few. Forty-eight, I guess."

"You . . . guess that specifically? Oh, don't look at me like that. I'm just kind of impressed. I would have snacked on some of them by now," James told her as he rose back to his feet, stretching his fingers out in front of him as he got ready to move again and taking a break from idly snapping pencils in half. "Like, you could have gotten a skill point in, I dunno . . . anything!"

Alanna turned a laugh into a soft grin, not wanting to make too much noise. "That is how the skills work, yeah. But no, I just think it's gonna be way more valuable to turn them in with a tree." She shrugged as she idly flipped through the desk drawer in front of her, pulling out a couple pens, an overly fancy paper clip, and a candy bar. "Hey, check it out. Baby Things."

"Oh, man, I miss those," James said. "Any wallet here?"

"No, and the computer won't turn on, either." Alanna shrugged. "Ready to move on?"

James nodded decisively. "Yeah, let's do it." He tapped the drone they'd brought along that hung from his armor's webbing. "Scout first?"

A short look of thought crossed Alanna's face before she shook her head. "We're not that deep. Let's keep moving. I want to make good time."

"All right. Just don't forget we've got expendable eyes here," James told her as the two of them stacked up at the door. He peeked out to both sides, sighing a little at the surreal look of the hallway that went on for well over a hundred cubicle doors. "Clear," he said, stepping out and moving with expert steps to the right side of the hall to give Alanna room.

She moved out a second later next to him, and once again, they started walking.

It was strange how time flowed in Officium Mundi.

For long stretches like this, a half hour of walking could feel like a few minutes. But then, a trap would spring or a fight would explode into violence, and a minute would be a whole hour. Right now, James was employing one of the most valuable skills he'd learned in his time here—being alert without being paranoid.

Every step was planned, quiet, and well placed to make sure they were never stopping right in front of a potential ambush point of a cubicle door. Every corner, every overhang, every lip of the walls around them was a potential danger. James knew they had to be watching everywhere, but he also knew that watching everywhere would exhaust them rapidly.

So he let his brain click to autopilot. His feet moved, his eyes were open, but he wasn't expecting anything. He was coiled and ready, but not tense. Beside him, he felt Alanna trying to do the same, though she wasn't quite able to make the mental leap like he was. James was pretty sure it was a combination of a couple orbs, his time with Secret, and also just a lot of yoga classes on the company's dime that let him do it. Not to mention the experience of the dungeon itself.

And this hallway was far longer than it would need to be to make all that effort worth it. Because while they'd initially assessed it at a few hundred cubes, James was starting to realize it was more like a couple thousand.

"We should make this a main corridor. Get the bikes in here," he told Alanna. "Think it's worth turning back for them?" he asked.

She shook her head. "There's no intersections," she said, suspicious eyes watching the doors up ahead. "We'd have to make some."

"We could do that." James hefted his axe. "I'd be *happy* to..."

"Too loud," Alanna told him. She was firm, but grinning while she said it. "You know we've been having more problems with loud noises lately."

James winced. That was true. There'd been a strider swarm last week, and a nervous moment with a small column of masks taking to the sky a few hundred feet from another incident, and he wasn't keen to learn if the other things in the dungeon had similar reactions to loud noises.

The duo took a few more steps forward, and then both of them halted at the same time. The ground underfoot had *crunched*. Alanna took a rapid step back, one hand on her weapon just in case they needed it, the other tapping James on the shoulder. He took the signal and looked down at what they were getting into.

The carpet here was a kind of dark blue that looked somehow unspeakably boring. James hadn't been paying much attention to it, so when it suddenly decided to make a new sound at being stepped on, he felt a little stupid. When he looked down, he saw that what he'd just stepped in was also dark blue, so he felt a little better.

A whole patch of the floor was covered in ballpoint pen lids. The blue ones that showed up in every office and got lost as rapidly as the cheap pens they supposedly protected did. Wait, no. *Covered* was the wrong word. A thin strip of the floor was *replaced* by them. That was weird.

"Lids," James said to Alanna. "Maybe some kind of quicksand thing? I dunno. Looks like a few more patches up ahead. We can probably avoid walking on them, though. Keep going?" He voiced the standard question.

Alanna glanced to the side, where the looming, curved face of a cubicle offered shelter behind a curved doorframe. "Let's stop here for a second. Get the drone up."

"Good call," James said, carefully pulling his foot off the offending surface, a little worried something was going to burst out and grab his leg as he did so. But nothing went wrong. It was just different, and around here, different often meant dangerous, so he kept his eyes open as they stepped back and Alanna swept the cube for threats.

One overly aggressive computer mouse later, James flopped back in the padded chair in front of the horseshoe desk and set the drone on the flat surface, ready for takeoff. While Alanna added the yellow to her burgeoning trade stock, James powered up the drone and clipped the controller into the skulljack on the back of his head.

Without a word, the drone launched itself skyward. James had gotten pretty good at this over the last couple weeks of practice, and now he turned that training time toward ensuring them a safe path forward. He saw through four wide-angle eyes, he pushed at the air with a pair of main-body fans, and he became a hard plastic and metal shell wrapped around a radio receiver.

Alanna watched James's second body zip away overhead, humming to herself softly. She was keeping watch, yes, but this hallway felt safe to her. Sure, they'd had a couple run-ins with striders or the odd shellaxy, but nothing threatening. Which was, itself, kind of odd. They'd come a loooong way, compared to their previous delves. The hallway stretched behind them a fair handful of miles, and it felt strange to have come so far and encountered basically nothing of note.

Well, there were a few things of value, at least. They were still stripping easy cash out of the cubicles they stopped in, but they were more going for time than anything else, and a few hundred bucks wasn't anything to write home about. Alanna considered that they should maybe turn back and backtrack a mile or so to where there was an intersection. Maybe another path was what was in order; they could update their map that this area was a boring zone and move on with their lives.

She snorted into the empty air. *Boring.* What a fucking word. Alanna was staring down a hallway that went so far that she couldn't see the details at the end, only a sort of haze. Overhead, in the gaps in the fifteen-foot-tall cubicle walls around them, she saw swarms of razor-sharp self-directed printer paper flying by. And hell, even just ahead of them, there could be something amazing. Sure, so far, it was just that the dungeon had discovered how to make the world's most annoying gravel, but later? Who knew?

Alanna needed an unreality check every now and then, or she got super jaded about how great this all was.

"Okay!" James's voice behind her sent a small shock through her fingers as he snapped his eyes open and instantly started talking. "I think you're gonna like this."

At no time in the history of mankind had anyone ever taken that statement at face value. "Why?" Alanna drawled.

"Because it's rad. Come on, you'll see. I parked the drone a ways down; let's go grab it. I didn't see any wildlife on the way, and it's only a quarter mile or so," James told her.

With narrowed eyes, Alanna followed James out of their little cube refuge. She noticed that, while he said he hadn't seen any angry wildlife, he was still smart enough to keep his senses sharp to their surroundings. The perception skill Alanna had picked up on their rescue delve tickled in the back of her skull, pointing out to her the ways James tilted his head and eyes that were correct to her senses. It felt strangely intrusive but also reassuring that her tied-for-favorite boyfriend wasn't being an idiot.

They slid back into their alert positions almost by accident, taking short bursts of steps down the hallway, past innumerable cubicle doors on either side. James avoided the growing number of patches of pen-cap ground at first, and Alanna mimicked him, but eventually there was less hard carpet than there was hard plastic, and the two of them found their boots crunching with every other step whether they wanted them to or not.

And then the walls around them began to degrade.

Bit by bit, as they walked, the walls were less solid. Dustier, but in a way that felt like delicate and accidental patterns in the fallen dust, and not just that the walls were covered in the stuff. Alanna had this suspicion that if she tapped one, it might crumble away.

Some of them *had* crumbled away. There was a good ten-foot section of the left-hand facade that had the top five feet broken off and tumbled in decaying chunks into the walkway itself. They skirted around it, more out of convenience than worry, though Alanna did step on a mostly intact chunk of wall panel that had gone fuzzy at the broken edge. It turned to powder under her boot, ground into dust against the blue caps that made up the floor now.

"What is that *smell*? It's like a chemical factory exploded," Alanna commented to James in a quiet voice as they pushed on a large piece of fallen wall, caving it in through the middle and opening up their path more clearly.

"Oof." James waved a gloved hand in front of his nose. "Wow. Couldn't smell that through the drone. Maybe we should invest in filter masks if we plan to come back here."

"Back *where*? Where are we going?"

"Hang on, almost there. You'll love—or hate—this."

They pressed on, just a bit farther. Around them, the walls that had survived were pitted and ground down, looking more like beige rocks than anything else. The chemical smell got stronger in the air as the space around them got more and more open, the walls worn down to shorter and shorter heights. There was no fancy architecture or distortion here, just normal cubicles that had taken some serious weather damage. There was also ivy, of some sort.

The plant was the bright green of a highlighter and seemed to glow under the fluorescent lights. Vines crept along the walls around them, their roots seemingly buried in the mounds of sandy dust from the ruined structures. The vines had dozens of blades of razor grass growing off them, mixed with strange, clear bulbs full of some kind of fluid that never seemed to flower. They didn't move, but they created an alien atmosphere in this last stretch of hallway.

Alanna and James stayed clear of those.

And then they passed one more row of cubicles, and suddenly they saw the *sky*.

No, that wasn't right. Alanna peered upward at the ceiling here. Now that the cube walls had worn down to under waist height, her vision was unobstructed. It wasn't a sky, it was just thousands of paper birds, fluttering against the backdrop of the overhead lights, moving in such large flocks they looked like clouds.

James, taking the lead, kicked down a decrepit dusty wall to the sand and plastic floor, making them a path around a larger wall ivy. It fell with a soft sound, whatever it was made of muffling the impact. Alanna noticed him stoop down as they moved to pick up the drone he'd landed here. And she understood why he'd wanted her to get the full experience of seeing this place for the first time.

It was a beach.

Ahead of them, curving outward to the left and right for what seemed like *miles* was rocky beach. The sand from the crumbled edifices of the walls behind them mixing with the hard plastic pen-cap gravel of the floor, making a surface that crunched and drifted in the strange air currents. The hum of air-conditioning hovered omnipresent over the beach, from somewhere hidden directing the flow of air. They were in the center of a bay, with the arms of it reaching out on either side. The left side rose up into a hill in the distance, and through a flock of paper, Alanna could see a massive tower perched on it, a perverse lighthouse watching over the place.

And about twenty meters ahead of them, the sand met the waves.

Lapping at the shores of this absurd, impossible place was a sea of dripping, acrid black. The scent of it was overpowering, and it suddenly made sense why it was such a powerful chemical stink.

Printer ink. A literal ocean of it. Hundreds of thousands, perhaps millions, of gallons of the stuff.

"This is *insane*," Alanna gasped. Beside her, James wiped sweat off his forehead as he took in the scenery, too. The view through a drone camera didn't even begin to do this place justice. "Okay, this was worth the surprise," she told him. "But I want you to know, I am already trying to figure out how to pipe that entire ocean out into our world."

"Is this because printer ink is a bizarrely expensive commodity or something?" James asked with a smile aimed off into the waves. The ocean kept moving somehow, despite the lack of tides here, and the sticky noise of each individual splash against the shores was dissonant and novel all at once.

"It would literally solve all our money problems if we could pipe this out. We could buy the building, the land it's on, the entire *company you work at*, and just sell printer ink at slightly below market prices. Forever. And we could be *heroes*, James. They'd make us king. They'd make us *god*."

James shot a disbelieving glance at Alanna, then another, more worried double take as he saw the enthralled expression on her face. "Ooooookay. First of all, I don't think that's how divinity works. But fuck, I may be wrong; I have provably been wrong about a lot of stuff regarding the nature of reality. I also thought offices didn't turn into oceans after six miles. Also, holy shit, who hurt you? Was it inkjet? I bet it was inkjet."

Alanna scowled, lost in memory. "They charge more to recycle used printer cartridges than to buy new ones," she said, as if that explained everything. "I was in *high school* and I couldn't afford printer ink, James."

"I'll add them to the list," James said cryptically. "Anyway, if you want to get away from your *clearly* very traumatic memories of trying to make a printer work, I've got one more bonus for you." He pointed down the beach.

About six hundred feet away, leaning out over the sand from where it was rooted in the crushed, dusty remains of a cluster of cubicles, was a decision tree.

It wasn't like the others they'd seen. It had a curved trunk with terraced loops of cable hanging off it like vines. It felt all at once looser than the original and also more solid. Like it could weather a million storms and never complain. Large oval leaves came off its crown, each of them bouncing a neon-green, blue, and black screen-saver pattern. Monitor lizards scampered across the surface of the massive piece of flora, going about their strange symbiotic business.

"Want to go have a loot?" James asked Alanna.

"I'm not gonna rob them, dude," she told him, offended.

"I actually meant 'look,'" James said sheepishly. "I keep slipping up on words lately. It's getting frustrating. Anyway. Let's go trade."

They approached cautiously, but when they were about halfway there, a mild interruption stopped them.

James had placed his foot down on what seemed like a perfectly fine patch of sand, but as soon as he began applying weight to it, the ground underneath shifted. It wasn't quicksand and didn't try to pull him in, but in the span of a couple seconds, a shellaxy had erupted from the ground beneath them.

Dust and small runners of underground ink ran off the thing's case in waterfalls, making it look like a majestic old turtle even as it lunged forward. Alanna, reacting with worryingly precise reflexes, yanked

James back a half step by his shoulder, and the snapping mouth of the shellaxy closed on air instead of leg. Their armor was tough, probably even tough enough to survive being gnawed on for a few seconds. But a full-on chomp would still bruise and cause damage.

James retaliated with a kick, finding his balance on the ground and lashing out as soon as Alanna let go of him. His foot connected with the side of the ambulatory computer monster, but while he snapped one of the latches off, he hadn't expected the thing to keep half its leg coils rooted in the sand. The shellaxy didn't *move*, and all the force of James's accelerated kick that had to go somewhere instead went back up his body, sending him sliding back on unstable ground.

The shellaxy made a second lunge, this time going for Alanna, who deftly stepped out of its range. It might be stable, but it was leashed in the sand like this, and she just kited away from it like she'd done it a thousand times. Then, while its attention was on her, James regained his footing and hit it from behind with his hatchet. It snapped its head around toward him as he added a screeching gash to its side and another nick to his weapon, and Alanna took the opportunity to slam the point of her steel-toed boot into the same dent James had made before.

By the time the shellaxy realized that it wasn't getting an easy ambush meal out of them, it was too late. The duo dismantled it rapidly, and James pocketed the yellow orb without any remorse. He was perfectly happy to negotiate or make friends with the life-forms here, but not if they kept trying to *eat him*.

"'Kay," he said with an exhalation of breath. "So, that's something to watch out for. I wonder if they bury themselves to hunt striders or something coming down to the water? Like a massive oasis?"

"We need a nature documentary in here," Alanna said, agreeing with James in a roundabout way that this was all fascinating. "Wanna see if we can recruit David Attenborough?"

"Yes." James didn't even have to think about it. "But for now, the tree."

The monitor lizards were wary as they approached, hiding among the leaves. The little shards of still-flickering glass or plastic formed into skittering shapes that still showed a lot of curiosity. James and Alanna didn't instantly try to make their trades, instead sitting down on the sandy ground to relax for a minute and let the little shards of screen get used to their presence.

"What should we do after this?" James idly asked Alanna while the two of them stared up at the dancing colors of the leaves overhead. Decision trees were still just the coolest thing here, to him, and he could enjoy their shade all day.

"Go home." One of the leaves switched to words at his words. "Go for a swim," said another. "Look for shells," a third offered.

"I think we head back," Alanna said, causing that frond to glow brightly before the words all faded. "We've got plenty of time, but we should take a turn on the door and make sure everything's okay. We haven't had any radio contact, but we are kinda far off, and these things don't have infinite range."

"Agreed," James said. "Wanna see if they'll give us a good deal?" He motioned up to where a cluster of monitor lizards was watching them, curious but fearful.

"Yeah," Alanna said, rising to her feet and pulling out the now-bulging sack of orbs she'd collected. "Let's see what we can get."

The lizards, in fact, did *not* give her a good deal. In fact, they gave Alanna and James a deal that was about a third as good as they'd gotten from the previous trees. It felt kinda awful, but at the end of the day, there were really only two known sources of purple orbs, and one of them required ambushing stuffed shirts that happened to have orbs before they could use them. So, this time, for now, they took what they could get. Maybe, if James was being charitable, he could believe that the tree just didn't have that many orbs and it was getting the most it could out of its supply.

And what they could get was two orbs for James and fifteen for Alanna. All of them the size and color of large grapes, each one of them a delicious treasure.

They agreed to use them when they got back, in a safe place. And as they brushed themselves off and prepared to leave, Alanna casually slipped a few of her own orbs into James's hand.

"Here," she said. "I'm gonna give a handful to Anesh, too. You can owe me or something. But we've gotta keep up with each other, you know?" As if that explained away her almost automatic generosity.

James smiled nervously. "Man, sometimes I never know what to do with you," he told her.

Overhead, the leaves lit up. Only this time, the tree just had a single message for them, unified across all its different screens.

"Kiss her, you idiot."

Alanna, glancing up at the change, glared at the tree. "Now, hang on. I don't know if I'm okay with a piece of digital vegetation shipping us, and . . ."

She was interrupted as James casually pulled his gloves off, placed his hands on either side of her face, and pulled her down slightly to give her a passionate and lasting kiss.

The tree overhead resumed its dance of colored lights, though maybe a bit brighter this time.

After half a minute or so, James and Alanna pulled away from each other. "All right," Alanna said, blushing uncharacteristically. "Fucking fine, I guess the tree was right."

James's laugh echoed louder than the sound of the waves for just a minute. "Okay," he said, "let's go home. For now."

CHAPTER 20

James and Alanna made it back to the breach to find it more or less exactly as expected—kind of a chaotic mess, but otherwise fine. JP gave them a wave as they walked up, standing up stiffly from his seat to greet them. A few rows of low cubicle walls over, Dave was pointing off at different things on the horizon and regaling Neil with tales of the cool shit they'd done there. It was an almost quintessentially Dave thing to do; he wasn't really bragging, but he also wasn't shutting up, and it was looking like the new kid was getting frustrated with it.

That was a feeling James could relate to; he'd been there.

"Yo. Welcome back, guys," JP greeted the duo. "Find anything good out there?" he asked casually. When Alanna opened the pouch at her side to reveal the gleaming purple orbs, dully shimmering against the black fabric, his eyes went wide. "Oh shit, nice. Found a tree?"

"Yeah, a palm top," James commented offhandedly.

It took Alanna's brain a second to process the nineties-flavored office pun he'd just made. When she did, she bit her lip and let out a low groan. "Oh, that's bad. But yeah, hey, you know people, right?"

"That's a loaded question," JP told her. His words were guarded, but his smile was curious. "What's up?"

"We found a literal ocean of printer ink, and I'm wondering how easily we could build a pipeline," Alanna told him.

What followed was about ten minutes of explaining to JP that yes, they were serious, and yes, printer ink was actually a weirdly expensive product, but not actually a valuable *commodity*. At first, he didn't believe them, and once he did, he was actually kind of angry about it. After that, James waited patiently while he and Alanna commiserated together about how unfair modern technology was. By the time they were done, he had the impression that extracting that ocean was a literal pipe dream, but he'd honestly kind of spaced out in the middle of it. James hadn't really gotten any reasonable amount of sleep in the last twenty-four hours, and it was starting to show.

"So, when are you using the purples?" JP asked, snapping James back to reality. "Are you gonna share with Anesh?"

"Anesh has expressed mild discomfort with the level of transhumanist upgrading that James and I are so ham for," Alanna told him, rolling her eyes. "Though we're gonna offer him some, yes."

JP mouthed a confused *what* before glancing at James, who gave him a shrug. "How?" he asked. "He's literally two people. I don't . . . how?"

"Hey, man, I'm uncomfortable with the skulljack, and I'm . . . me," James said with another light shrug, which mostly just illustrated to himself how sore his shoulders were. "Look, I wanna go drop my gear off and sit for a bit. Are you guys ready to head out?"

"Yeah, Neil's ready for some action, and I've been staying out of earshot of Dave. Love him like a brother, I do, but he can talk."

"I hear that," James agreed. He raised a hand as they walked by and gave JP an overhand high five. "Tag ya in," he said with a grin. "Have fun out there. Good luck, Neil! Don't die horribly on your first go!"

"What?!"

"Don't worry about it."

James and Alanna made their way through the pattern of low walls around the tower to where the day's base was set up. *Base* was a strong word for what they were working with today, really. Mostly, the tower itself was becoming their base, but no one really wanted to put in too much time to remodel it, and they didn't *need* that much space here. Most of their gear was stashed on the lower level, and the only point of interest was the top floor, where Anesh was currently running his mad science experiments.

It felt good to strip off the armor. James still wasn't really used to wearing it; even though it'd literally saved his life more than once, it wasn't exactly comfortable to be in. It didn't help that, even with the machinery to make swappable replacement parts, the fit wasn't perfect and there were still a few points that had some rough edges.

The two of them, as they unloaded their finds and their tools, kept up a companionable quiet. It wasn't that they had nothing to say—most of their trip back had been in relative uninterrupted safety and they had spent the majority of it arguing over whether or not using their newfound power to destroy Walmart was an ethical thing to do—it was more that they were just *tired*. So exhausted. From the constant planning and resupply of the guild, from the hunt for and discovery of not one but *two* dungeons, from the fact that James *still worked his day job*, and ending on the fact that they'd just spent two hours effectively going on a hike where every fifteen minutes something tried to kill them.

Not, like, effectively or anything. But the life here still tried.

"We should go see what Anesh is up to," James suggested after they'd sloughed off the majority of their stuff. He still had the hatchet on his belt, and Alanna had the revolver in an underarm holster, because they were still in a hostile dungeon and they'd never really feel safe if they went totally unarmed. But this area near the door had always been pretty empty, and it felt even more so today. Alanna grunted in agreement, rolling her shoulders before stooping over to duck into the lower floor of the tower.

"Wonder if he made it work," Alanna thought out loud as the two of them navigated the tight hallways and sloped ramps between floors. "Have you put any thought into it?" she asked James.

He panted slightly as they surmounted the eight floors; going up stairs, or things that were basically just harder to use stairs, was way more tiring than just walking in a straight line. "Oh, I was mostly thinking on what the projector was," he admitted. "Like, I'm pretty sure it's a magic item, right? It's gotta be a blue thing. But the weird-ass coffee pentagram is . . . is . . ."

"Is bullshit?"

"Yeah, exactly," he agreed with Alanna. "It doesn't fit anything else we've seen. It's almost like totemizing a red. Like this is what happens when you make an item out of a blue and *also* a red."

Alanna nodded before giving a slight sigh as she realized they'd gotten turned around and missed the ramp up again in the weird looping interior halls. "Yeah, okay. Is it okay to say I'm pretty sure Sarah is wrong about the orb uses?"

"No, I think that's fair. I'm not sure we're right, either, though. We're acting like they all have parallel use cases, but that's kind of assuming a lot of this place," James agreed. "So, like, what if you can make an item out of any orb color? Like, okay, we know some can make life, of varying sorts. Some can make totems. Maybe some can make items? This thing could be a red item, a focus for a ritual in the same way that . . . no, that doesn't make sense, because traps."

"Traps could be red life," Anesh greeted them as they got to the top of the ramp. "Also, cheers. How was the delve?"

"A long walk to a short dock," James replied instantly.

"We found a beach and an ocean," Alanna filled in, taking pity on Anesh's poor, confused face. "So, how's the experiment going?"

Anesh sighed. Alanna sighed, too, because she was coming to intimately know the look on Anesh's face when he was about to start talking about a problem that was over her head. James did not sigh; he'd gotten used to that look a long time ago.

"Okay, here's the deal," Anesh started. He paced while he walked, pointing out coffee on the floor and table, notes on his confiscated whiteboards, and papers covered in mathematical theories that most humans would find insane. Even the mathematicians. "The thing works. I don't know how or why it works, though, and that's bugging me. Now, don't get me wrong; I've seen the 'data' from the red orb totems, and I'm aware that while it is out of my expertise, there's probably a perfectly valid theory that ties their function together. But this? This doesn't feel like it follows any rules at all, except what it personally comes up with on the spot. It's a bad magic item from a D&D game where the GM forgot something and had to cover his ass." Anesh pointed an accusatory finger at the projector, sitting innocent, and also inanimate. "This fucking thing doesn't follow any predictive rules. It mocks calculus. It is *distressingly* immune to chaos theory. It does not fit any usable model I can come up with." He stopped with a huff of air and a stamp of the foot.

"So..." James ventured, "it works?"

"I'm not done complaining about this yet, hang on," Anesh groused, looking between James and Alanna's faces as he paced. Then he rolled his eyes, sighed in a deeply offended way, and spoke again. "Yeah, okay, it works. Sort of!" He tapped the long conference table that held the projector and some stray coffee grounds. "So, the stuff from in here? The knockoff Starbucks bagged grounds that show up in the towers and only in the towers? That stuff works perfectly. And now I'm gonna be annoyed again because *that does not hang together*! No other dungeon tech that we've run across comes in two parts, except this thing, which suddenly has both two parts and those parts suspiciously close to each other." He noticed his partners losing focus and snapped back to his point. "Anyway. The dungeon coffee works fine. Coffee from outside? It also works. Sort of. But it can't copy orbs, magic—anything reality-warping, basically. And, now get this, you can *blend them*, and different combinations copy different things. Oh, and when I say, 'different combinations,' I mean, like, this Kona dark roast can copy orbs if it's up to twenty percent of the mix, but this French blond roast caps out at five percent. I can copy a magazine of bullets at about seventy percent of anything, though."

"You can copy orbs," Alanna flatly stated, ideas already sparkling in her eyes.

"I can copy *anything*," Anesh told her with a note of pride. So speaking, he plucked the slim remainder of a yellow legal pad off the table and tossed it over. James caught it and looked down to see the top page contained the words *the base of the cubicle tower, closest to the door to Officium Mundi, from the stairwell.* "I made a mistake with the teleporters, though. Each one has six pages, but the first page is always gonna be a recall to here." Anesh shrugged. "But yeah. What do we want more of?"

He said it like it was . . . nothing. Like he didn't understand the doors he'd just opened.

"Money," James said, without thinking about it. "Fund our operations. Literally all our problems are bottlenecked by money."

"No, orbs and the consumable items like this," Alanna replied. "We don't know how hard it's gonna be to get more coffee. We should make it count. Replicate *this*," she said, holding up a purple orb that glittered in the low light of the top floor of the tower.

"If conserving mana-coffee is our goal, then we should totally go with money. That and ammo, or explosives. Anything that would get us noticed by a government," James rebutted.

Anesh nodded. "Good point. I can stretch the resources we have. I'm not calling it mana-coffee, though."

"The problem is that our growth, as a trio and as a whole group, is just too weirdly haphazard. Like, we get all these random skills, but only every month or two do we figure out how to use one to *do* anything." James tapped his chin. "We should really be having everyone meditate on their orbs. Have you guys ever done that?"

"Please never say 'meditate on your orbs' again," Anesh said.

"I meditate on your orbs all the time." Alanna spoke simultaneously.

James blew a raspberry at them. "No, I mean, it's this thing I started trying to do after the whole card-counting thing. Which, by the way, I did not enjoy but am willing to do again if we need a bundle of hundreds to feed to the projector. Anyway, you just kind of focus on the orb and roll it around in your head. It helps to feel everything that you know now, since normally skills don't actually trigger unless you're using them."

"Weird. I like it, though, and I can get on board," Anesh said. "Doesn't solve our problem of what to spend the mana-coffee on."

"I thought we weren't calling it that?"

"It's a placeholder."

"Anyway. Jumping back a second. What *does* give us the capacity to accomplish our goals? Like, the real ones. Not just trying to claw through whatever new challenge is slammed in front of us by either dungeon or poverty, but actual goals. Can we, feasibly, make enough money to *buy the world?*"

Anesh and Alanna looked at the small size of the projector screen for a long, *long* moment before turning back to James. As one, with utter confidence, they answered, "No."

"Okay. Orbs, then. Yellows we can, probably, keep getting. I don't think we need to copy those. Ditto blues, though they're a higher priority. Oranges . . . we can't use yet."

"I can," Anesh interjected. "I think I know how to teach you, too. Maybe."

"Not yet," James continued. "Reds, no. Greens, maybe. Purples." He stopped and looked at Alanna. "Purples?"

She nodded. "Purples are a good start." Alanna rolled a few of them around in her hand before awkwardly dropping one, swearing curtly, and having to get down on her knees to find it under the table. "But what do they *do?*" she called up from the floor.

"Good point. I guess they get us closer to, like, being able to covertly destroy the oil industry?" James shrugged. "I feel like we need to start getting more used to the fact that the dungeon is the foundation of our abilities, not the point of them. Like, Alanna, we were just talking about this. We need to be doing something with all this, or what's the fucking point? It's heartless."

Alanna opened her mouth, then closed it again and tilted her head sideways, a look of puzzled thought on her face. James and Anesh watched her patiently, waiting for the idea to manifest, and, eventually, were rewarded by their partner saying, "Okay, this might be crazy. But. What if I could . . . get a heart?"

"Wat," James barked out.

But Anesh already got it. "Oh. Ooooh. A human heart. Because we have enough space on the projector to abuse exponential growth a bit. Oh, so you know, the projector's size is a bit cramped. But we can make most small objects work." His eyes got wide. "We could . . . I mean, the demand for organs is big, but *limited*. That is actually somewhere we could make a serious dent. Or, you know, remove the problem. Assuming the coffee holds out. Which it *could*, because organs are mundane, weird as that sentence sounds."

"Do you know organ facts just by coincidence, or is that a skill?" James asked him.

"Not everything is a skill," Anesh said cryptically.

"Okay. Okay. So we can solve the global wait list for heart transplants." Alanna held her head in her hands, like she was just now coming to terms with the fact that they were about to bend both physics and the scarcity-based economy over the table and have their way with them. Which she was coming to terms with. Rapidly, and with relish. "This is amazing. What else can we do? Can we kill hunger?"

"Logistics says no. We're looking for high value, low size. Diamonds?" James suggested.

"The value of diamond is artificial," Alanna told him. "And that solves no problems. What about . . . what about . . . goddamn, this is too much." She stole a chair, brushing Anesh's leftover coffee onto the floor.

"Okay. So we're bad at this. And our ideas cap out at 'give everyone superpowers,' or, more likely 'give ourselves, who we trust, *more* superpowers,' and also 'solve a medical shortage.'" James hummed. "That's not a bad list?" He glanced at Anesh and asked, "How much coffee do we even have left?"

Pulling a cardboard box over, the noise a harsh scraping against the smooth wood of the table and the rough leftover coffee grounds, Anesh peeked inside. "Maybe three uses if we do mundane stuff. I've been doing this for the whole three hours you were gone."

"No way we were gone that long," Alanna protested before trying to check her phone and realizing there was no way to tell if it was still keeping proper time. "Okay, maybe we were. I'm so tired. I feel like I've been up all day."

"Alanna, you wake up at seven a.m. every day. You literally have been up an entire day. It's just . . . some of it took place outside of time." James shrugged from where he was pacing in front of one of the tower's windows. "Take a nap. I'm okay with us staying on guard duty while everyone else has fun. Oh! We should use the purples now, though, before we forget again. I don't know if I've mentioned this, but it's *too* easy to forget about orbs if you don't use them right away. I think it's a dungeon curse thing, but Secret isn't here for me to pester about it."

Anesh accepted a few orbs from Alanna, less grudging than James had expected him to be about it. "Have we considered using one or more of these to make another memetic life? Something like Secret, but, I dunno, more focused?"

"We'd have to feed it," James said. "And that would mean using these up. And I've got plans for myself once I'm a supersoldier. So!" He balanced his whole half dozen purple spheres in his palm and then brought his hand together in a fist.

[Shell Upgraded : Stable Platelet Count +62,000]
[Shell Upgraded : Synapse Signals/Second +0.8]
[Shell Upgraded : Left Eye Vision 20/+5]
[Shell Upgraded : Neuroplasticity +4%]
[Shell Upgraded : Life Span +1.3 Months]
[Shell Upgraded : Comfortable Bladder Volume +3 oz]

There was a staggering amount to unpack in those six burning lines of thought that coursed through James's brain. The first of which being just how much thinking *hurt* all of a sudden.

His vision sharpened, he could feel his blood strengthening, and even the small urge to use the bathroom lessened. But mostly, his thoughts *raced*. They pounded through lines of thought like liquid electricity, simultaneously exhilarating and painful. The world came into sharp edges and harsh tones, very suddenly and very unexpectedly.

It took James a few seconds to get what was happening. He wasn't thinking faster, not really. He wasn't thinking smarter, either, which was something of a blow to his ego. No, what was happening was that his human brain was being absurdly human, a lot more than normal, at high velocity.

Your eyes don't process images; your brain does. Same for sounds, smells, tactile sensations, everything. Your mind inputs massive amounts of data from organic devices vastly superior to its own abilities. Then those live feeds are filtered and turned into something your personality can actually handle. Unless, of course, you turn the safeties off and roughly halve the input lag your brain experiences, perhaps through some magical effect that no one saw coming.

"Ow," James said, listening to the shape of the word reflect off the floor where he now lay. He could hear the carpet. It didn't matter. He'd just realized that he'd increased his life span. That was it; the key to everything. A path to immortality, his greatest fear done away with by magic and grit. The pain didn't feel so close anymore.

He focused on dialing it back. The purple orbs in a lot of cases gave you something like an extra set of muscles. And those muscles could be trained, honed, and, if you focused—and this was the important part—*relaxed*. Fortunately, this one was one of those, and James tried to let the amplification of his brain meats ease off a little bit.

"Ow," James said again and didn't crack his skull open with the sound this time. "Okay, yeah, I'm okay." He waved off a concerned Alanna and Anesh, who were hovering around him. "Just some mild brain upgrades. Hooooly shit, that feels weird." He swept his hand through the air in front of him, feeling and hearing the thin differences in the air currents as he moved. "I think I can, without hubris, say that it might be possible for me to literally dodge bullets now."

"That"—Anesh pointed accusatorily at him, finger cocked like a gun—"is hubris."

"That is probably true, and I'm probably wrong," James conceded. He blinked a few times as he tried to get his eyes to refocus. "Oh." He realized why his left eye wasn't focusing correctly and popped his contact lens out, blinked twice, and watched the world come into focus. "Neat. Okay. Do yours next."

Anesh sighed but didn't hesitate. Unlike James, he'd never gotten into the dramatic flair of smashing whole handfuls of orbs and instead used his one at a time, feeling the changes as they took effect.

[Shell Upgraded : Oxygen Requirement -.2 in^3/second]

[Shell Upgraded : Tooth Regrowth—+1/month]

[Shell Upgraded : Visible Spectrum Range +12 nm]

"I like how some of these are always profoundly dumb," Anesh commented after he waited to make sure none of his own purples were going to send him to the floor. "Like, my brain already knows yellow exists. I don't need to be able to actually literally see it."

"Of course yellow exists?" Alanna half asked, half stated. "I look forward to reading the email recap of everyone's gains from this week, because that is a weird statement to make."

"Humans can't see yellow," James explained. "It's your brain tricking you. Which is *weird*, now that I think about it, because we can totally see the yellow orbs, right? And Theo, who is color-blind, can *also* see the colors in them. Ooooh, yessss, I like this."

Anesh chuckled. "You like this." He gestured around at their penthouse tower floor, complete with a magical coffee-powered cloning device. "The colors, out of everything?"

"The colors are weird. They feel like actual magic. And in the spirit of ruining that joy, let me know if the yellow orbs look different now, 'kay?" James's words got that confused laugh out of Anesh, where his boyfriend wasn't entirely sure if he was kidding or not—or, more accurately, wasn't sure which part was the joke. "Alanna. You've got a giant pile of these. I wanna see you get even taller than me and grow a tail or something."

"Pass," she said bluntly. "Though I am kinda curious if I can get extra eyes, maybe. I think I'd look cool with four eyes."

"You would. So, not gonna use all of them?" James inquired, pointedly.

"I'm gonna give one each to most of the others. I think team Animal Magnetism could really use it, if for no other reason than as encouragement to explore more. Though that might be dangerous, and now I worry I'm pushing them too hard."

"Team wat."

"Because of the . . ." Alanna started to say.

But Anesh cut her off, slapping his forehead. "Because of the dog made of the magnetic distortion thing. Of course. James, how could you miss *that* as an obvious name for it?"

James harrumphed. "I was mostly asleep when I named it. Don't judge me. Alanna, use your orbs and save me from this."

"Yes, sir!" she exclaimed with too much enthusiasm and perhaps a little too flirtatiously. Much like James, she preferred smashing big heaping handfuls of the things, but unlike James, she didn't want to induce sensory overload *too* fast. So, rapidly but not all at once, she shattered the little motes of power that she'd assigned herself.

[Shell Upgraded : Comfortable Carry Weight +38 lbs.]

[Shell Upgraded : Wrist Joint Range +1.4 cm]

[Shell Upgraded : Skin Elasticity +13%]

[Shell Upgraded : Extremity Friction Control +/- .2 μ]

[Shell Upgraded : Organ Rejection -1/Year]

[Shell Upgraded : Ingrown Toenail -1]

"Did you *have* an ingrown toenail?" James asked her after she relayed the information that had carved a path through her brain. "I've seen your feet, and while I don't, you know, *pay attention* to things like that, I'm pretty sure you don't."

"I don't. I didn't. I still don't?" Alanna looked down at her boots like she was considering taking them off. "I'm pretty sure that didn't do anything. Does this mean I have one free one banked, or . . . ? No, you know what? I don't care. I'm way more into the friction-control thing. Also, skin elasticity? Do you guys think that works with the basically bulletproof thing? Oh, man, this is gonna get ridiculous fast."

"Assuming we keep finding trees to trade with. And that we focus the orbs on a few people. Which, you know, we *are* doing," Anesh pointed out.

James nodded as he added, "It's also relevant that some of these are kinda garbage. We actually need a whole batch of them to make sure we actually get at least one super-useful thing. But we *do* eventually get super-useful things. You still plan to give one each to everyone else, yeah?" Alanna nodded, and James returned the gesture. "I don't think that's bad, but we can't expect everyone to get something good. There's gonna be imbalance pretty rapidly."

"We just need more of them." Alanna sighed, then slapped her forehead. "Shoulda saved all of these for the copier!"

"Oh, dammit. Well, it could be worse. We can get more," James said. "And, like, holding on to them until we have enough coffee, we'd just be sitting on them for who knows how long. Way better to do this now, before we forget, and make use of the ability. Though maybe that's just me justifying not being efficient."

"Don't you still have a grade-two yellow as a night-light?" Alanna asked with a comical frown. "And you're commenting on sitting on things?"

"I don't sit on my night-light," James told her. "Anyway. We're burning time here. Let's head downstairs—this whole project will keep for a while. Anesh, c'mon. Let's go place bets on which of our neophytes gets the silliest upgrade."

Anesh rubbed his nose while he stacked up notes on the table before following James. "I bet the other me isn't having to deal with this," he mused. "No trying to fix global problems, no hazing the new kids. Just a good old stupidly long American road trip. I shoulda gone instead, if that would have been any different."

The parking lot of Aile's Diner and Lottery was mostly empty, but for a tow truck, an old RV that hadn't moved in years, and Anesh's car. All three vehicles sat together, unlikely companions brought together under dim orange streetlights by their owners' need to be, for some reason, here at this ancient diner at eleven p.m. on a Tuesday. If Anesh had been in a better mood, and not fresh off another answer of "no, nothing weird here," maybe he would have found some kind of artistic statement to be made in the mental image of these three misplaced vehicles looking like reunited old friends. But he was, so instead, he was irritated.

"This town is abso-bloody-lutely cursed," Anesh said as he got back into the car. "There's weird street art everywhere, which was cool at first, and made me think we were onto something, but now it just feels like a distraction. And everyone is either given up on life or wired on some illegal drug, and it's like this is just a place that people get dumped and forgotten to die. I hate it."

The door slammed behind him, pulled shut not too hard, but exactly as hard as was needed to get the old sedan to cooperate. From the back seat, under the half dozen blankets they'd collected on the trip, Secret poked his head out of his nest. "Curses are not real," he informed Anesh.

"Secret, you're great and all, and this has been a great bonding experience. So, don't take this the wrong way. But are you not essentially a curse that has come to life?"

"No. I am life that was, briefly, a curse," Secret told him matter-of-factly.

Anesh turned the engine over, giving the old vehicle a moment to warm up before he turned on the lights and the radio. "Well," he said, waving his hands in front of the air vent, waiting for it to start dispensing heat to ward against the frigid night outside, "that makes no sense. But I appreciate you confiding in me."

The two of them sat in the peaceful interior of the car as the sharp edge of the cold was slowly pushed away by the heater. Eventually, Anesh felt like he'd relaxed enough and leaned forward to throw the car in drive and take them to their next destination.

"Have you had any luck yet?" Secret asked from the back seat.

"No, nothing concrete as of yet," Anesh replied. It was, he realized, too easy to fall into Secret's mannerisms when he was talking to the infomorph. "The woman in the restaurant did tell me that there was a witch living in the town, so we can go see about meeting them. But after that, we're dry on leads."

"I am surprised your military was so accommodating in letting you photograph their underground tunnels." Secret let out a rustling hum that made Anesh's teeth hurt. "Hardly are they good keepers of their secret."

"Not *my* military. Also I think it's a tourism thing—they don't really use the base for anything, and advertising the town as having secret tunnels is a good way to attract sightseers on road trips. Better than what they attract now, which is mostly people who look like they're trapped here, or people who keep trying to sell me meth." Anesh glowered over the steering wheel. "Anyway. Last stupid rumor for the night, then we can grab a hotel somewhere. This whole thing has been a wash."

He sounded angry. Secret's eyes flowed into sympathetic shapes as he wrapped his body around the passenger seat. "Are you angry that they have found two more relevant spaces, stumbled into by accident, when all your true efforts have led to nothing?" Secret asked, worried.

"Yes," Anesh said. "Exactly that. But I want to feel justified in it, even though I know it's stupid. Honestly, I don't even want to be angry at all. I just want to, you know, go to this 'witch house,' learn that it's just some old lady who sells bizarrely potent marijuana, sigh deeply, and then go home." He looked out his side window, using the pretense of checking for cars before switching lanes to break eye contact with Secret. Secret was flatly intense to talk to, and it could get exhausting, fast, for someone like Anesh.

Secret understood, though. He didn't mind. Instead, he pulled himself up to the passenger seat, enjoying the play of the orange overhead lights through the dirty windshield. He rotated himself so that fewer of his eyes gazed at his driver and friend. Secret hadn't been taking too many naps on this trip, hadn't been diving into the dreams of his sleeping friends. Instead, he'd been enjoying being present, being here with Anesh, talking to him and being treated like a person.

Having a body was a transformative experience. Secret chuckled to himself as he thought that; James would approve of the pun. But that wasn't how he meant it. Instead, it was that he simply felt more grounded to a place that wasn't familiar to him. To reality, to this shell he wore. He could leave it if needed, travel back to the nowhere and everywhere that was the mental space that conceptualized him. But for now? It was nice to just be in a car.

Nothing was going wrong. Nothing here needed to be fought, though he did keep a close eye on the men and women who approached Anesh carrying concealed weapons and nudged them to not notice his travel partner. This was *not* a nice place, Secret was learning. But nothing demanded his attention except for enjoying the ride.

Which was why it came as a mild shock when they pulled up to the old, rusted barbed-wire fence that constrained the farm just outside town where the supposed witch had been staying.

Tall grass overgrowing splintered wood posts. The smell of a lot of cows, and the noise of a herd rustling even at this late hour. A half dozen rusted old vehicles, silhouettes visible in the light from the car headlights by the road. In the distance, a farmhouse sat dark and foreboding, waiting for nothing in particular but the passage of days.

The old farmer who owned the place, according to the woman from the diner who had turned Anesh on to this one last clue, fancied himself a friendly guy. And he'd been letting this traveling witch stay here in exchange for help with his car, which was a sentence that Anesh felt was maybe a little bit out of place. But then, things being out of place was kind of par for the course for this place, even if none of those things had turned out to be more dungeons.

Of course, nothing really felt as out of place as the ten-foot-tall pane of sheet metal buried in the dirt by the farm's front gate. It sat next to the wooden arch with its closed gate, next to a few posts with waving flags that didn't belong to any country, a dozen handmade wind chimes dangling from the gate itself, and a bronze wire sculpture of a bear on the opposite side of the opening of the fence. A whole welcoming arrangement of the kind of art that people made when they had access to knives, blowtorches, spray paint, chunks of wood, and a scrapyard.

And then, this one piece of sheet metal, with a mural sprayed across it in harsh strokes of a paint can.

"Well. That's probably not good," Anesh said in a studied, flat tone as he let his eyes adjust to the low light and start making out the shape of the painting. "Secret," he called back to the car. "Secret!"

It took a minute for the infomorph to manage to open the passenger door from the inside and wind his way over to settle next to Anesh. "Yes? What . . . Ah." He stopped as his own eyes made out what it was Anesh was looking at.

Nine feet tall, the piece of art showed a simple thing. A creature, some might say a monster, but Anesh and his people would know better. It was a series of looping coils, like a snake or some ancient sea serpent. A riot of blues and greens with a backdrop of a fiery red sunset. The creature reared up over the highway stretched below it, fanged mouths dotting its hide along with a number of furious eyes.

"Secret," Anesh said with a stern voice as he pointedly kept his eyes forward on the farm's collection of welcoming art. "Can you explain why there's a portrait of you here?"

"Ah." Secret sounded apprehensive in a way that Anesh had literally never heard before. "Oh, dear," the infomorph said as he peered forward at the spray-paint rendition of himself. "I may have made . . . a mistake."

CHAPTER 21

"Oh my god, it's good to see you again!" James greeted Anesh as he came through the door. He threw his arms wide for a hug, waiting politely in a frozen pose for Anesh to set down his bag, slough off his coat and shoes, and toss his keys into the bowl on the counter. After making a bit of a production of it, and also letting Secret roll off his shoulders to be greeted by the affectionate ball of fur that was their dog, Anesh finally let out a sigh of releasing tension and started to open his arms to let James in for the hug.

He got maybe two inches up before his grinning boyfriend enveloped him in a warm embrace, pinning his arms back at his side as James planted a long kiss on his lips. Sputtering in amusement, Anesh laughed and pushed him away. "What the hell! I'm glad to see you too, but what's with the grand welcome?"

"I missed you," James stated. "Am I not allowed to miss my dearest companion and lover?"

"Oh, no," Anesh deadpanned. "I took Secret away for too long, and you forgot how silly it sounds when you talk like you dropped out of a Robert Jordan novel."

James grinned. "Thanks." He ruffled a hand through Anesh's hair. "Anyway, I just wanted to greet you when you got here. You've been gone for a week, basically."

That comment bounced around Anesh's mind for a few seconds while he tried to figure out what was wrong with it. Fundamentally, it seemed fine, but there was just something off about how James had said it. Perhaps James was having an affair. Perhaps he was under duress. *Perhaps* it was the perfect duplicate of Anesh who also lived in this apartment and who regularly merged his thoughts and memories with this Anesh.

It was probably that last one.

Anesh declined to comment on that, though. Instead, knowing that shortly he would go back to being one person with two bodies and sets of memories, as opposed to two bodies with divergent sets, he opted to try for an extra perspective.

"So, how'd the delve go?" he asked James, absolutely derailing his boyfriend's joke.

The two of them flopped down on the couch as they talked, while James regaled Anesh with stories of adventure and bravery and mostly a lot of sitting around, all things considered.

"It's honestly just really been an exhausting week," James confided. "That hike Alanna and I took kinda wiped me out, so we took backup duty while everyone else went off exploring."

"Did anyone get any good skills?" Anesh asked almost out of reflex.

"That's the weird thing. There were way fewer creatures than I'm used to. No swarms or anything. I've been assuming it's a migration pattern or something, since there's no *way* it's overhunting on our part. But the short story is that we didn't get the deluge of orbs that I was hoping for." James draped himself backward over the arm of the couch and sighed dramatically. "It's not all bad, though. Neil got a skill for the taxonomy of urban European pigeons."

"How is that a good thing?"

"Everyone's first skill should be stupid," James asserted, nodding to himself. "It's a rite of passage."

Anesh wanted to say something about how silly that was, but James was currently running his fingers through Anesh's hair, and actually forming that thought was challenging at the moment. After a week going cold turkey from the affection he'd gotten used to, it did feel good to get back. Even though he'd be back to his full self shortly anyway and feel like he didn't miss anything, that didn't make this less nice.

Instead, he broke the comfortable silence a different way. "So, any major revelations while I've been gone?" Anesh asked. "I know I've got one, but I wanna hear yours first." He cast a short glance down at Secret, who was pointedly hiding under a dog. "My own messages mentioned something about orb theory."

"Oh, yeah!" James perked up, eager to not have the awkward conversation right now. "Wait, you message yourself?"

Anesh nodded as best he could while his head was pushed at an awkward angle into the couch cushions. "I maintain a series of documents on our file server. Both iterations of me update it with notes on points of interest and the general moods of the people we interact with. I'm calling it emotional triangulation."

It took James a few long seconds to parse that as he tried to blink the confusion out of his eyes. "Creepy," he settled on. "Anyway. Should I not repeat the orb thing?"

"No, no, go ahead. It's actually really interesting to have the same conversation multiple times with fresh perspectives," Anesh assured him.

"Ooookay." James cleared his throat, a little uncomfortable about repeating things. It was that feeling you got when someone missed a word in conversation; you knew that saying it again was important, but if you said it again, it wasn't conversation anymore, it was performance, and that was awkward. But he tried anyway. "So, the general thought we've got is that each orb color can make life, in the same way yellows do. Like how we know Rufus made Ganesh, or Dave making his pet dragon. That was something we never really experimented with, because of the ethics of it, but we know it works. Thing is, we've seen dungeon life that clearly uses orange orbs, and most of the boss types are greens. I suspect that Lily and the iLipedes are reds. Secret and his ilk are absolutely purple."

"Okay, makes sense." Anesh nodded. "What's it mean for us?"

"Well, that's the thing. It explains a lot of holes in our theories up to this point." James ran a hand through his hair, trying to get it out from where the long strands were trapped under him and against the cushions. "We've been assuming that blues make items, but I think that it's the same way. *Any* orb can make an item—it's just that what comes out changes based on the color. The blue ones are . . . varied and weird. The red ones are the traps. I doubt we've seen any purples or greens, but—"

Anesh cut him off. "The briefcases," he said.

"What?"

"The briefcases. Bet you a Baby Things those are the green items."

James stuck his tongue through his lips in consideration. "I'm mad you've been hoarding the good candy. I will forgive you, and admit you're probably right, if you give me one."

Their deal concluded swiftly.

"So, this really spreads out what each orb can do to a staggering level, doesn't it?" Anesh asked. "What's the list now?"

James rattled off the concepts off the top of his head. "Crack, absorb, life, item, totem. Not that many."

"'Totem' covers a lot, doesn't it?"

"Yeah, but I think it's a reasonable spread of ideas. See, this place acts *way* too much like what we think of a 'dungeon,' as in the game sense. It's almost pathologically dungeony." James pushed Anesh off and sat up, stretching out his stiff arms. "I think the fact that we can crack orbs is the dungeon's mandatory required 'reward.' Or maybe it feeds off rewarding us, which makes more sense. The absorb thing is what we see Rufus and Ganesh do with the yellows, so that's clearly how it's pushing power to its minions. And then it can make minions. And traps, and also other 'rewards.' Totems round out its ability to create unique environments."

"That's well thought out," Anesh admitted. "What about the items that are useless? Does it get points for giving us those?"

"Good question," James said with a nod.

Some time passed with him nodding to himself.

"And?" Anesh asked.

"It was a good question," James reaffirmed. "That doesn't mean I have a good answer."

Anesh barked out a laugh. "All right, mate," he said. "Well, it's a cool theory. I hope it pays dividends. But yeah, how've you been while I was gone?"

"What do you mean?"

"Well, I mean, I read the draft for the charter you published for us. You clearly put some thought into it, but it's also the kind of thing I know you're gonna be worried about. Also, you look tired. Have you been sleeping?"

A few nights earlier, James lay in bed, staring at the ceiling.

His room had become more bed than anything else, lately. Furniture had been transferred to closets or the other free room, and two mattresses, a king and a queen, occupied the lion's share of his floor. This was because there were sometimes four people sleeping in here, and none of them shared blankets well.

Right now, James lay between a fast-asleep Alanna, heavy breaths steady and quiet against his skin, and Anesh, who was snoring lightly and curled into a small ball around the stuffed dragon James kept on his bed.

Other Anesh was still on the road. That wasn't why James couldn't sleep, though.

The world was so big, he thought as he eyed the blank plane of his ceiling. There were too many people, too many problems. How could he hope to make a dent in them?

Guilt. That was the feeling eating away at him. Guilt over not doing enough, guilt over misuse of his power, guilt over not being able to see the way forward.

And he did feel like he had power, for a change. All those times he'd sworn to himself that if he could, he'd change the world. And now he was in a position to do so, and he didn't even know where to start. There was just so *much*. So many interlinked systems and issues. To tamper with one thing would have ripples on the other side of the world, and he couldn't even begin to predict a lot of them.

Alanna called it the utopia fallacy. The idea that if you couldn't fix everything, it was hard to feel like it was meaningful to fix anything. James had always thought the solution to that was simply starting with one person and going from there. But now that he could do that, it didn't feel like enough. Like it would ever be enough.

He needed to build systems. New ones. Better ones. The dungeon enabled rapid education, an end to scarcity, an end to *death*. He just had to figure out how to crack it open to share with everyone.

His mind raced feverishly. And then, without realizing it, he found himself looped back around. The world was too big for him to know where to start.

How could anyone ever expect him to be the leader, the ethical heart, of an organization, if he couldn't even keep himself on track while lying awake and insomniac at nine in the morning on a Sunday?

James considered abdicating his position, fleeing to the mountains, and living in a snow cave.

Shortly after that, his thoughts drifted again.

He didn't fall asleep for a long time.

"I've been sleeping fine," James flagrantly lied to Anesh. "Don't worry about me." He flapped a hand. "Tell me about your trip."

"No, hang on. That's not an answer. You look exhausted. How have you even been getting stuff done if you're so tired?" Anesh asked him, pointedly.

James glowered. "I put Eminem's 'Lose Yourself' on loop and listen to that while I write ethical manifestos on how to use superpowers. Please, don't worry about me. Just . . . I wanna know about your trip. It's more important to me. We can talk about the other thing later, okay?"

It wasn't okay, not really. But Anesh didn't want to pressure James, especially since his counterpart had made a few notes to the point that he'd already been doing so, and the last thing James probably needed was *two* boyfriends nagging him.

"Oh, it was interesting," Anesh said instead. "Didn't find a single dungeon, but I did get to spend some time with a bunch of drunk old bikers who were convinced they knew the lair of the Sasquatch." The comment got a snort of laughter from James. "Aside from that, not much to talk about, really. Ate some terrible diner food, ate some decent diner food, drove a lot. Saw some *art*." Anesh emphasized the last word, looking down at the table. Or, more specifically, the guilty party under it.

"I apologized," Secret muttered, uncharacteristically subdued.

"Look, there's really no unawkward way to do this. Just tell me what's up," James said with a sigh.

"Secret's not been doing a great job keeping secrets." Anesh cryptically failed to explain anything. He followed up, trying to clarify, "Apparently, when he's embodied like this for a long time, he needs to sleep. And when he sleeps, he dreams. But for him, dreams pull him into the shared subconscious with people who've got some idea of him."

"Like he did with me, originally," James half asked.

"Right. Except these are just random people who caught glimpses of him in our back seat. Or, in one case . . . who saw him as a whole, somehow." Anesh grimaced.

"As a whole?" James asked.

Anesh nodded. "It's how he described it. He doesn't know her name, only things about her. She's a traveler, a driver, an artist . . ." Anesh winced again. "She's a long way from home. She's scared. Of him, and of *us*. Like, us specifically." He shook his head. "I think she's someone like we are. Someone who found a dungeon and then mistook us for the Wizard Police when we were out scouting locations after the exodus. And now she's trying to find us."

"The painting, of Secret . . ." James prompted.

"A bread crumb. Maybe intentional, maybe just cool art she wanted to make. But the guy she was staying with, who she traded it to, said she left a few days ago. Said she was headed to Oregon."

"And that was before you turned back," James mused. "So . . . she's here. Somewhere in the state."

"Unless she's moved on. But yeah." Anesh nodded. "Probably still here."

"And she found us . . ."

"Through Secret. Through his dreams, and him trying to make friends."

James sighed. Secret had tensed up through the conversation, and Aberdeen had moved off him, as if sensing that the serpent form needed space. She was a good dog. Looking down, James patted the couch cushion next to him. "Get up here," he said, voice tired but not angry.

Secret sheepishly glided into place. "I . . ." he started to say but couldn't finish the sentence. For once at a loss for words.

"I know you can't actually read my mind," James said. "Which is probably why you didn't want to tell me about this earlier. And it's almost certainly why you're afraid now." He reached out and laid a hand on Secret's snout, a human hand on an azure-scaled maw with enough teeth in it to terrify the most adamant dentist. "But I'm not mad at you."

Secret seemed to ripple at the words. "Why?" he asked. "I've caused you another problem. When you least need it."

"You've been making friends. Exploring, in your own way. Meeting people, which isn't gonna be common for you otherwise, I'm afraid." James shrugged. "You tried to do good. We try things," he told the snake. "Sometimes those things don't work. Doesn't mean we don't try."

Anesh let out a small cough. "I, ah, I should apologize," he said. "I was kinda hard on you, Secret. I didn't really think. Sorry." The words felt awkward but real. "Also, James, who died and made you a mature adult?"

"A few dozen tumblefeeds," James admitted. "Now. With that resolved, Secret, go take a shower. You have a body—you get to *bathe*. Aberdeen smells better than you!" His words caught both of them off guard, and Anesh let out a long string of barking laughs. "And

Anesh! Kick back and let me tell you of our own adventure in an *attic* and how our state has too many dungeons in it."

The apartment was mostly dark when JP walked through the front door.

"Sup, nerds!" he exclaimed to the warmly lit living room and the single person and dog residing in it.

Sarah looked up from her book on information theory, peering over the lineup of colored orbs sitting on their table. "Hush!" she stage-whispered at JP. "It's the first time in a week James is actually sleeping; don't shout."

"Oof, sorry!" JP's reply might have read as sarcasm to anyone who didn't know him. To Sarah, though, it was . . . well, maybe not genuine, but at least polite.

"Why are you here, anyway?" she asked. Sarah loved people, Sarah was friends with everyone, Sarah always had her smile on, but Sarah would maybe not mind if JP didn't show up announced at her residence, which was only just becoming a safe space for her again.

"I wanted to touch base with everyone," JP said. "When we went over skill lists last week, James caught one of mine and set me to work building an investment portfolio for the guild. We're up three percent right now, and it's going well. Oh, also, there's some notes on the server about the charter, a couple spell-check things. And I also had the minutes for a meeting from the hideout about recruiting strategies. Just business stuff," he told her.

"Business?"

"Dungeon business." He nodded. "The recruiting ideas especially. I know James likes to be involved in that, but this was mostly a brainstorming thing. Momo thinks we should make a Reddit thread with the specific language the dungeon uses for skills and see who bites, but that seems way too obvious. I honestly just like the idea of finding . . . well, people like us. Disillusioned twenty- to forty-somethings who want to fight the world's problems. We've got a big pool to draw from," he rambled on, mostly ignoring Sarah rubbing at her temple. "We need more engineers, though. More people to . . . hmm?" He trailed off as he finally noticed Sarah's constant sighs.

"JP." Sarah didn't hide her annoyance as well as she maybe wanted to. "We have a *secret* base. We have a shared chat server. We also have a file server with enough encryption on it that I think it actually is illegal to transport across state lines. There are so many ways to share this information. Why are you at my apartment?"

"I . . . wanted to hang out," JP admitted. He withered a bit under Sarah's disciplined gaze. "We don't hang out anymore!" He fought back. "We promised! James fuckin' *promised us* that the dungeon wasn't going to change our friendship!" JP jabbed an accusatory finger at the floor. "But we don't do D&D anymore, we don't do anime nights, we aren't even doing that thing where we hang out here and talk shop while James gets irrationally good at cooking!" He puffed out a shaky breath of air. "I miss everyone."

"Even me?" she asked, surprised.

"Well, no," JP bluntly told her. "I mean, don't get me wrong. You fit into our group perfectly; of course you do. But I don't have that connection to you yet."

He was, Sarah realized, oblivious to the fact that the two of them had never had that connection. But then, a thought struck her. JP wasn't bound by the past. He didn't know that they'd gotten off on the wrong foot so many years ago. So, maybe . . .

"Hey, you wanna go for a walk?" she asked him. "There's a coffee place that's open way too late around here. We can go caffeinate ourselves, and you can tell me why three percent is a big deal."

"It's because of how much money James gave me to put into it," JP explained instantly, nodding smugly. "But . . . yeah. Yeah! Sure, that sounds good." He looked down the hall to the closed bedroom doors. "Want to see if they want to come along? Actually, I'm okay hanging out here, too. I can be quiet."

"Oh, I'm sure you can," Sarah told him with a toothy grin. "But they can't. And at some point, they're gonna go back to having really loud sex, and I'm being magnanimous and sparing you that experience."

JP was generally a very composed kind of guy. He knew how to keep cool while bluffing or haggling or in a dozen other situations. Sarah's blunt words, though, and whom they were about, *really* caught him off guard, and he cleared his throat while hoping he didn't look stupid as his face flushed red. "Ah. Well. Ahem." He was suddenly glad he'd kept his shoes on as he stepped back to the front door. "Yes, let's go," he agreed. "Wait, if you know that . . . doesn't it bother you when they . . . you know . . . ?"

"Oh, muffin!" Sarah giggled. "If you had any idea how long I've been shipping James and Anesh, you wouldn't ask that at *all*." She quickly threw a coat on, glad she hadn't changed out of street clothes for the night when she'd gotten home. "So! Recruiting?"

"Yes. Recruiting. God, yes, let's talk about that instead," JP agreed, the two potential new friends descending the steps of the apartment together. Both of them hopeful they could fix something that never was into something new and whole.

CHAPTER 22

"Oh, cool, those guys are playing Pokémon."

James and Alanna were currently lurking—though both of them would object to the other using that word—around the campus of one of the several local high schools. They would object to being called lurkers mostly because that was way more likely to get them arrested, although at this point, there was a general feeling shared between at least the two of them that any attempt to actually handcuff them wouldn't stick.

It was, James mused, a good thing they were all trying to be ethical. Because having superpowers sure would make it easy to be the bad guy. Comically easy.

They were here, going back to school, because they were looking for signs of a dungeon. It wasn't going anywhere just yet, because they hadn't gone inside yet, and they were reasonably sure that the point of entry would be in the basement. But neither of them wanted to just walk in, get in trouble with the staff, and lose their easy chance to poke around below the building.

So instead, James was watching students play Pokémon.

"I never got Pokémon," Alanna said, tapping her fingers on the lip of the open car window. It was December now, and winter had slammed down on them hard, but she wanted fresh air more than James wanted to feel his fingers, so the car window sat open for now. "Like, it's weird, right?"

"How is it weird?" James let his brain sidetrack into the conversation, dropping some of his worries about the dungeons, Secret, the skulljacks, everything else, just for a few minutes. "I mean, aside from the animal abuse thing," he conceded. "Is it because it's always fights, when, like, a Pokémon Olympics would be way radder? Just trying to get a Charmander to wobble through an obstacle course?"

"No, it's the animal abuse thing, mostly." Alanna waggled a hand, making a "well, on balance" gesture. "They aren't really animals, are they? They've clearly got sophancy. That's sorta what I mean; it's not animal abuse; it's just slavery. Also . . . not cannibalism, but something like it? What's the word for eating a sentient thing?"

"Gross!" James supplied helpfully with a cheerful lilt. "Or evil?"

"I'll take either. I just don't get why people like the games so much if the underlying premise is just so hurtful." Alanna shrugged. "I get that it's not how people look at it. I just don't understand why no one ever sees it my way." She sounded weirdly morose about it.

James hummed as he thought about it, a low tone that helped him focus his thoughts. "Well, a lot of the way the games and show and manga phrase the . . ."

"Manga?"

"Yeah, there's actually a few of them. The good one is *Pokémon Adventures*. This is unimportant. Don't sidetrack me *that* far. The point is, they frame the Pokémon as friends and not tools. The people who use them as tools are the villains, so the kids who make friends with their Pokémon are the good guys and how everyone wants to think of themselves." James took a deep breath of the winter air flooding the car, craning his neck for another look around to make sure no one was approaching while they sat in the parking lot waiting for school to get out. "Everyone wants to be the hero, right?"

Alanna nodded. "Okay, that makes sense. What about in the porn, though?" she asked with a sharp grin.

That got a choking cough out of James as his brain struggled to recover from that. It turned out, even having a purple running through his metaphysical veins that doubled his brain's perception of reality, he still couldn't deal with his partner's weirdly raunchy comments sometimes. "I'm sure I have no idea what you mean," he eventually said, playing it cool.

"Oh, come on! You've been on the internet. I know you know how much erotica there is of—"

"Wow, hey, look! School's out! Let's go!" James threw open his door and stepped out without hesitation, eager to both take the time to see if they could uncover the tunnel to unreality that they knew lurked within at least *one* of the educational buildings in the city, and to also get away from Alanna's toothy grin at his discomfort.

Another dungeon. That was their goal. Secret had called them "relevant spaces" once, and Anesh had passed that term along to the group. No one knew if that was just Secret being dramatic and handing out cool naming conventions or if he had some insider knowledge; James was prone to forgetting that Secret was actually a child in a lot of ways and that his nature didn't actually give him an intrinsic look into the inner workings of Officium Mundi.

This dungeon, supposedly, was pipes and concrete and damp. They didn't know much from their one informant, whom Sarah had a dark suspicion about but no one had been able to confirm had ulterior motives. But what they did know was that the place was lethal. So, naturally, James and Alanna planned to barge into it and trust their concealed weapons and powers to get them out. They'd both absorbed a fresh blue orb before heading out, with Alanna getting *[+6 Activations—Create Asphalt]* and James picking up *[+14 Activations—Break Electronic]*. They were trying, really hard, to make use of every tool at their disposal, and the blues and the powers they offered were a large part of that.

Or they would be, if they could reroll them to get something more useful than the ability to spawn a road.

The other thing they knew about the dungeon was the reward it offered. Sort of. From the sound of it, you got an actual skill tagged in some way, and as you yourself progressed in that skill, you were granted growing rewards that changed you as a person.

And the instant Sarah had briefed the guild on it, James understood where the assassins came in.

The dungeon could solve a lot of problems within its own walls. But its track record outside its boundaries was abysmal. Also, a large-scale fight with camracondas and tumblefeeds and shit would be instantly noticed, deployed antimemes or no. So it made perfect sense that when Officium Mundi found another dungeon that gave rewards that were shockingly synergistic with its own, it would work to eliminate the competition. And by competition, James meant "delvers that posed an escalating threat."

Theo had filled in the missing piece there. Javier, the kid who'd been targeted, had had a scheduled job interview at James's company not even a week prior. The Office had eyes, apparently, and it had spotted the potential issue, and it had acted. Rapidly, and harshly, with human weapons and tactics to eliminate someone who didn't even know it existed.

The theory was sketchy at best, but it filled in a broader picture. It highlighted a few points that suggested a world where dungeons weren't just real, but almost common. Which had made Anesh all the more frustrated that his intentional search for weirdness zones had led to nothing of substance.

Still, that was enough to get James wading through a sea of high schoolers on a Friday evening.

"Can we talk about the antiwar themes in the first game that got dropped in the later ones?" Alanna asked James. "Right up until they *really* came back, I guess. Pokémon is weird, huh?"

"Can we pretend I didn't mention Pokémon and just find the damn basement?" James grumbled. "It feels weird to be back here."

"We didn't go to school here," Alanna commented idly.

James shrugged. "High schools are all the same," he said. "It's the feeling of them, not the place itself."

That sentence rattled around in Alanna's brain for a minute while she tried to figure out what James was actually saying. Something about the emotional texture of locations, probably; he'd been on that a lot lately, when he and Anesh went on long, rambling tangents about the nature of the dungeons. "I think your feelings are weird, in this case," Alanna said. "Valid!" She backtracked a bit, "but weird."

"Oh, man, speaking of feelings." James spoke up a bit to be heard over the crowd of younger boys and girls flowing around the two of them. They stood like islands in the sea of education, if that sea was in a rapid hurry to make it to the beach. "Neil got to meet Secret yesterday."

"Oh, man, that's a hell of a trip." Alanna shook her head as she smiled. "How'd he take it?"

"Badly! The scales got to him. Also the potential for memory eating."

The two of them were not unaware of the crowd around them while they spoke. Quite the opposite, actually.

Secret could discreetly visit dreams for anyone who'd experienced him, even briefly. And this was a good test to see if that applied to secondhand knowledge, while also being able to test for anyone who had been into the school's dungeon. Also, Secret really did seem to gain some form of power from his hosts speaking open secrets aloud in crowded places. Secrets hidden in plain sight, or, in this case, Secret hidden in plain sight. James didn't know what metric of power they were using, but any edge could help.

The two of them stood in the entry hall for a brief minute, scuffed linoleum underfoot and a wide-open space around them. There was an easy door to the front office off to the left, partly obscured by the trophy case for the school's many sports teams. An open staircase to the second floor, the opposite direction they were headed. Across a round space that would be clear if not for a pack of cafeteria tables to their right there was the library, and beyond that, a sort of tunnel-ish hallway that had a distinct downward slope.

"Well." James pointed. "Down?"

"Down," Alanna agreed with a nod and a crack of her knuckles.

They were politely unarmed for this exploratory venture, modern times being what they were, but that didn't make Alanna any less bulletproof or give them any hesitation to dive into a good scrap.

They passed down the ramp, and while they didn't descend a whole floor, the atmosphere changed rapidly. It was cooler here, a little stuffier. James constantly second-guessed himself as they walked, wondering if the air was getting damper because of the dungeon or because of his imagination. It was a surprisingly long time before they passed the doors to classrooms, a pair of art classes set into either side of the hall.

James suspected some kind of space warping in effect. Alanna suspected he was being paranoid, but they retraced their steps twice to confirm she was right. Which she was.

The hallway curved left after another pair of classrooms, one of them a pottery class with a full-on kiln in it. It kept going down, too, though this one ended at a pair of those large metal fire doors that the school kept locked tight after hours.

They were unlocked. When James tugged on the handle, a wad of folded paper fell out of the latch. He replaced it as he and Alanna walked through; always be courteous to whatever juvenile delinquent made it easy for you to break into places.

"I think this leads backstage to the theater, for the plays and stuff," Alanna said. "Man, I remember actually performing here, like, a decade ago. Back when the drama club did *The Laramie Project*, yeah?"

"Oh, yeah, I remember that whole thing. That was before we were friends, right?" James nodded as he checked through the window of a darkened band classroom. "You were in drama then?"

"Briefly. I was a stagehand because I was one of, like, three people who could move the sets around." Alanna chuckled to herself, mock flexing her muscles.

James smirked at her. "Yes, yes, you're an Amazonian beauty. I know," he said and was pleased to see his words landed with a flush of embarrassed pride on Alanna's face. "Hey. This door is locked," he said, getting them back on track. "Boiler room. Think it's worth checking?"

"For this? Absolutely. Want me to punch the lock open?" she said, with way less sarcasm than that statement might have carried a year ago. "Or do you want to just luck through this one, too?"

"On it," James said, taking a knee and pulling a slim black case out of his coat pocket. "Keep an eye out for me," he said as he withdrew a thin, bent metal bar.

Alanna glanced down at him briefly in surprise before leaning against the smooth gray brick of the wall and throwing glances back up the ramp and around the corner. "You got an orb for lock picking?" she asked.

"Not everything is . . ." James got out before Alanna flicked him on the head. "Ow! Sheesh, touchy." He hammed it up, but he had a smile on the whole time. "But actually, no. JP got the orb. And then he taught me."

"Wait . . ." Alanna rubbed the bridge of her nose. "That's a thing we can do?"

"I was going to bring it up at the strategy meeting on Sunday," James said. "I don't have, like, superpowers. Not the way the orbs give them. But things *can* be taught. The knowledge, once exposed to reality, sticks."

"That's such an overdramatic way to say that." His partner snorted. "Sometimes I really want to know how your head works."

James hopped back to his feet, dusting off his knees and pocketing the lockpicks again. "Well, hey," he said, forcing a casual tone as he pulled the door open. "Get a skulljack and let's find out."

Alanna blinked in shock. "What, really?" she asked dumbly.

"Yeah," James said simply, quiet word belying the hammering of his heart in his chest. He turned to face her as he pulled the door. "I've gotta start somewhere productive, right? May as well be you and Anesh."

"Holy shit," Alanna whispered.

James made a rumbling noise in his throat. "Oh, come on. I'm not immune to trying to be mature now and then. Also it'll probably be fun," he said half-jokingly. Then he realized Alanna wasn't talking about him and followed her pointing finger to look behind him, into the boiler room.

There was no boiler. There were pipes, yes; several of them, in fact. They led out into the walls, where you'd expect pipes to go as they delivered hot water. The only thing was, they weren't leading away from a boiler. They were leading away from a hole in the wall.

It was a yawning black gap. Pipes snaked in around its edges, making it look like they were pulling the wall apart. But there was no sign of the concrete or dirt that should have been behind the outside edge of the lowest level of the building. Just darkness, and the feeling of a breach. But also a gateway. It was a rising wave of anger, and a cold and calculating razor-sharp dismissal. It curved downward out of sight; James could just barely see as he flicked his phone's flashlight on and pointed it inside, though he was careful to avoid getting too close to it.

Because there were a half dozen backpacks scattered around it, all of them with the straps dangling where they'd been cut away by something. A ripped coat lay on the floor off to the left. The shattered remains of a whole host of smartphones littered the ground as well. The hole had a pull to it, a gravity that neither James nor Alanna expected they'd be able to back out of if they crossed the invisible line.

"Hey!" a voice yelled from up the ramp behind the two stunned delvers. It was low, aggressively masculine, and very pissed off. "You're not supposed to be down here!"

As soon as they acknowledged the voice, the spell was broken. The cut in the world snapped closed so hard it was surreal that it didn't make a sound doing it. The boiler room was just a room again, no discarded bags or broken phones. No traces of anyone having been here for a while, judging by the layer of dust.

"Fuck," James muttered under his breath.

"What're you doing here?!" the security guard bellowed at them as he strutted down the ramp with confident steps. He was an older guy, midforties maybe, with a bald head and a bit of a gut. He was exactly the kind of person they should have brought JP to deal with, James realized. Because he and Alanna both responded poorly to this kind of authority.

Fortunately, he could respond by lying his ass off.

"FBI," James said, stepping forward and pulling an absolutely fake badge wallet out of his pocket, holding it open at arm's length to show the man. They'd rehearsed this, slightly, and Alanna just kept looking forward. James had to smoothly pull back to keep the school security officer from snatching the badge out of his hand. "Sir, don't do that," he said confidently as Alanna backhandedly showed off her own "credentials." "Are you staff for this school?" James asked sharply, going on the offensive.

By this point, the guard's thoughts had caught up to what he'd just been told. Part of him, the part that thought of itself as an adult, railed against the idea of a couple of children being in a position of authority over him. He wanted to throw them out, call their bluff, and call the cops, maybe not in that order. But another part of him recognized something in James's tone, false as it was, and he found himself nodding. "Yeah, I'm the afternoon and evening building patrol," he said, using his official title. "Sorry 'bout that. Didn't get word that there were, um, feds here."

James put the badge away. "No worry," he said, clipping the word from how he normally spoke it. Professional, and to the point, that was his character, he had to remember. "We weren't announced. My partner and I are looking into a possible bomb threat and didn't want to alarm anyone," he said.

"A bomb?!" The man was shocked. Here? In *his* building? Impossible. But all too possible, wasn't it? "Shouldn't we evacuate? Is it safe?" It was rude to demand answers of a federal agent, he was aware of that. But he'd been here for half his life; he'd earned a little leeway.

In response, James just gave him a reassuring smile. "Not to worry. We've swept the location"—he kept it vague; no sense giving things away—"and it looks clear. If I didn't know better, I'd think this was all just to keep the new guy on his toes." He gave a harsh chuckle.

When James had asked JP how to fake being an authority figure, he'd gotten an alarmingly detailed set of instructions. First, confidence. Not just in yourself, but in the world around you. Be sort of cold; be assured that your will is going to manifest. It was the sign of someone who was *used* to getting what they demanded. Be brief, don't overexplain, and respond to questions with questions.

And if you meet another person used to authority, don't try to override them. Work around them, and then, when they start to buy your story, give them an exit.

In this case, James telling this proud man that, hey, the too-young kid with a badge *wasn't* the top of the food chain.

James was more than a little insulted it worked.

Twenty minutes later, he and Alanna were back in the car, headed back to home base. Even after the guard had walked off, they hadn't gotten the breach to uncurl again.

"Okay, so, that one was different than the others," James said, knuckles white on the wheel. He was still feeling the slight rush of exerting authority over another person, and also his brain still hurt from looking at the hole.

"No shit," Alanna replied. "What now?"

"Now? We keep moving. There's no time to camp out here. We'll assign someone to it," James said. "For the moment. And we'll check back when we have time. Right now, though, we've got meetings to attend."

"Ah, fuck, I am not looking forward to this," Alanna told him.

James blinked. "Are you kidding? Holding interviews for dungeoning hasn't been a fantasy of yours for the last twenty years?"

". . . Has it been for you?"

"Absolutely! The most fun part of D&D is the part where you role-play recruiting new people!"

"You are joking."

"Only a little!" James laughed and let some tension flee his body. "Man, this is gonna be so much fun. I'm not sure what kind of fake jobs Anesh was offering to draw people in, but I am super psyched for this." He punched the air over the steering wheel with an enthusiastic fist. "I'm just concerned about how many people Secret can wipe, as contingency, you know?"

"I'm worried about the ethics of that." Alanna's voice was hard.

"Me, too. Which is why I'm considering not doing it at all," James agreed, losing the smile. "But we do need more people." He shrugged as he took the turn onto the main road that led back toward their fortress. "We need to be doing a better job exploiting our opportunities. And that means multipliers, like green orbs."

"I *know*. I wrote that briefing," Alanna said. "I guess... I guess I'm just being weirdly nostalgic for *good god it's only been six months* ago."

"I know how you feel." James nodded. "Hey. I promise you, me, and Anesh can sortie out this week and kill something dangerous together. 'Kay?"

Alanna gave a sheepish laugh, turning away from him as she rolled a guilty smile on her lips. "I'm kinda awkward about the fact that I'm into that," she said. "But also, that sounds good. I love you guys, you know?"

"I know," James said, happiness in his veins. "Now, since we're done *impersonating the FBI*, let's go rustle up some new friends!"

He put the pedal down and guided them back to their secret lair.

"James!" Sarah greeted him with a smile as he and Alanna came through the door. "Alanna!" She threw her arms up in the air. "You're back! You're late! I'm so glad to see you!" She wrapped herself around Alanna in a comical hug, arms sticking straight out to exaggerate how large the taller girl actually was.

"That's a weirdly cheerful greeting for people who are late," James said, slinging his bag onto the floor by the lockers that they'd installed near the front door of the hideout.

The lockers were a concession to the fact that everyone who came in here did so with kit on them these days. Every delver was now briefed on the fact that the dungeon could send out minions, and basically everyone walked around all the time with a bag of tricks and armaments. Half the support staff did, too, but theirs were a little more geared toward problem-solving and less toward mortal peril.

"Anesh is here already," Sarah pointed out to them as she backpedaled into their lair. The front room looked nice today—everything cleaned up, a couple long tables and some chairs making it look like a pleasant shared workspace or community room. They had the heat turned up to combat the winter chill, too. The only concession to their weird reality was a motivational poster on one wall that read, "Embrace Eternal Efficiency."

James was not a fan.

"Where is Anesh, then? I wanna say hi before we start the thing."

Sarah clicked her tongue rapidly in a show of mock regret. "He's doing the thing," she told him. "Your first interview showed up, and Anesh is handling them. Oh! Also! Alanna! Momo wanted to talk to you about something."

Shooting a glance up at his partner, James raised his eyebrows questioningly. "Do you wanna go do . . ."

"Yes," Alanna said flatly, eyes forward, gaze betraying no trace of her thoughts on if she wanted to conduct interviews. "Yes, I *shall* go visit Momo." Her words were overly emphasized and robotic. "I am sure it is important. Have fun." Without pausing in her walk, she veered away from the two of them and made a beeline for the elevators. "Oh! Don't forget!" She turned back to James and made a motion with one hand to tap the back of her neck with a pair of fingers, not waiting for a response before she was off again.

James watched her go for a minute before shaking his head with a grin. "Yup," he said simply, glancing at Sarah.

"Yup," Sarah agreed with a matching smile and nod. "That's pretty much what I was expecting, too." She looked over at him. "So . . . skulljack things? Is that too personal for me to ask about?"

"You were literally my best friend for my whole life and kinda still are in a lot of ways," James said, causing a lump to form in Sarah's throat at the words. "It's not too personal. And yeah, we're gonna try . . . try getting me over my fear of that later. And also gearing up Alanna, now that we know these things are pretty much entirely safe."

"I . . ." Sarah didn't have easy words, for once. "Yeah. Okay. Good! Yes, good!" She slapped James on the shoulder with an open hand, curling fingers around his arm. "Good luck, okay? It's not easy, but it is worth it, I think," she said, pulling him into a warm hug.

"You're getting to be a real good therapist," he told her, genuinely reassured as he hugged back. "Now, let's go save Anesh."

As if on cue, the door to the "office" they'd been standing outside opened, and Anesh led a young man out. "Yes, yes, thank you for your time," Anesh was saying. "We will be in touch. Thank you again." He waved kinetically as the younger man maneuvered around James and Sarah and headed for the door, his ruffled button-up shirt poking out of the back of his belt. "Thank god you're here," Anesh said with relieved eyes as soon as he took a breath and looked at James. "I have no idea what I'm doing."

James laughed. "Okay, how long until the next one?" he asked.

"Literally that person walking in right now," Anesh said, pointing to a thirty-something guy walking up to the door. He was fairly short, even more fairly bulky, bald head and tattoos clashing with the thick framed glasses he wore. "Save meeeee," Anesh whispered.

With an open handshake and a roll of his eyes, James greeted the guy. "Hey. Thanks for coming out today. Where're you comfortable, office or out here?" he asked.

"I'm fine here," the man said. His voice was a scratchy smoker's tone, but not unfriendly. Hard, not mean.

"All right! Well, I'm James Lyle, and this is . . ." He looked to his left only to notice that Anesh was walking off with Sarah, both of them deep in conversation as Anesh showed her something in a manila folder that he'd made a slew of notes on. "Okay, *never mind him, I guess*. I'm James."

"Nate," he said bluntly.

"All right. So, what're you interviewing for today?" James asked.

Normally, he'd know. Normally, he would have had far more time before being thrown into this. He had a feeling that Anesh and Alanna were really less into this whole thing than he was, and Sarah was teasing him by not leaving his notes. *Normally* also wasn't a really good word to use, because James had conducted exactly zero interviews before.

"You don't know?" Nate asked with an expression half angry, half amused. "The listing was for a chef."

"Oh, yeah?" James was interested. "Yeah, that makes sense. So! Let's get this started," he declared with more conviction than he felt.

Twenty minutes later, he had a picture of the man in front of him. He was a navy cook, worked in a retirement home, liked heavy metal music, was used to taking shit from people and was pretty sick of doing so ever again. He didn't overshare, but he did have a lot of stories that came close from his navy days. He also informed James that he had, to quote, "seen some weird shit." He also had a fairly solid grasp of ethics, in his own way. The ethics questions were ones that James and Alanna had insisted on, and here they mostly served to sound out the fact that Nate was the sort of person who would be honest, helpful, and absolutely unwilling to accept anyone doing less than their best. He didn't get political, he said, which James assumed was a lie, but yeah, he wouldn't mind the world being kinder.

James liked him.

"Okay," James said. "We could use a chef. We have a full commercial kitchen here, but no one really uses it fully. We expect to be adding a lot of staff. Want to be in charge?"

"So, a sous chef or exec?" Nate asked.

"Whichever one of those means you have a blank check to make food for the full staff, including any off-site trips," James answered.

"Exec." Nate nodded. "Just like that? You don't want to know if I'm good at it?"

"Are you?"

"Yes."

"Good enough." James nodded. "I don't know what Anesh put down as our offered pay, but it's . . . probably higher. There is one thing we need to check on first. Would you follow me?" He stood and started walking to the elevator.

Nate followed. "Higher than twenty-eight an hour?" he asked. "What kinda start-up scam are you running here? Also, this is a single-story building. Why's there an elevator?"

"I'm glad you noticed that!" James gave a sly grin, stepping in and waiting for Nate to follow. A few days ago, they'd put sticky notes on the two basement buttons, just to finally eliminate confusion. James ignored the one marked "quarters" and chose "lab" instead. "So, you've seen some shit." He reiterated Nate's words. "The job has a few . . . I'm not gonna say 'duties,' but more like 'opportunities,' in addition to the normal stuff. It's not gross, I promise." He tried to placate the man next to him, who was shooting him suspicious looks. "It's just that, before we hire you, we need to know if you can deal with certain things."

The elevator doors opened. The two people currently in front of a whiteboard filled with possible exploits for the headphones that were always plugged into your phone looked up.

"Oh, hey. Interviews today?" Reed asked.

"Ah. I suppose this is where I must take my leave of the testing," said Secret.

Next to James, Nate stared for a second, then nodded twice, solidly, jaw clenched. "It doesn't eat people, does it?" he asked James.

"I do not, no," Secret replied. "Hello. Pleasure to meet you."

"Yeah," Nate said. "Likewise." He turned back to James, who was unashamedly wearing a huge grin on his face. "I think I can handle cooking for him," he said, voice steady.

James hit the button for the first floor and watched the doors close, clasping his hands behind his back. "You start Monday at midnight. You haven't seen the start of it yet." He tried to contain the smile and found he couldn't. "Also, Secret likes hamburgers."

The next interview was cut short almost instantly when the guy couldn't answer some of James's initial barrage of questions about work experience without lying.

"We won't call you!" James waved as he showed him the door. He was a firm believer in being candid about that in interviews; too many people had scorned him the same way.

The one after that was a girl who said she was here because her parents were "making her get a job," which . . . well, it wasn't the worst reason. The follow-up comment of "I don't really wanna actually, like, have to do anything, though" led to her getting shown out as well.

The next person actually had his wife come in with him, and she answered some questions on his behalf, without any hesitation. It wasn't a translation thing, either; he spoke English, she just didn't want him embarrassing himself, she said.

That plan didn't work for them.

One girl, a barista and part-time acrobatics instructor, actually made it past the normal part of the interview, to where James started asking probing questions about how she'd do as an adventurer. She'd seemed like the perfect fit for it, too. But it had all been bluster, or maybe she just thought it was an elaborate joke, because when she'd seen Secret and later had been brought in on the whole story, she hadn't been able to handle it. At all. There was screaming, and denial, and eventually, when they gave her the option, she said she'd rather that Secret scour her memories of everything from the moment when she saw him up until she would remember being politely denied the job.

James rubbed his eyes. Anesh had walked by at one point and given him a super-sheepish smile, teeth and sorry eyes, making up for abandoning him. Alanna hadn't come back at all, and Sarah was mostly just showing new victims back to the desk James was now using in the office itself.

It was easier to surprise people with Secret here. The elevator thing was dramatic but a waste of time when he only had twenty minutes per person.

Then Virgil sat down across from him.

Skinny kid. No, not a kid, though he sorta looked young at first glance. This twig of a dude with longish hair and eyes that seemed like they never stopped moving. His hair wasn't like James's, where it was meant to be a full ponytail or braid. It was more like he'd just gotten caught up in something for a few months and forgotten to get a haircut.

He had a suit jacket on over an offensively orange Hawaiian shirt.

"How do you feel about life-and-death situations?" James asked him by way of greeting.

Virgil Thomasi, latest in what James assumed would be a string of disappointments, tilted his head, leaned in conspiratorially, and asked, "Are you planning on having me fight to the death with the other interviewees?"

"Maybe. It would weed people out faster," James said, perking up. "But no. In general, what would it take for you to risk your life? Actual question—we're starting knee-deep in the interview."

"I thought this was for a software development job," Virgil said. "Is this a military thing?"

"No," James said. "But you know how software development is."

"I do." Virgil nodded. "It's not that."

"You're avoiding the question."

The programmer cleared his throat. "I thought it was clever. Ah. No. I don't want to risk my life for money," he said. "Maybe something else. Something worth it."

That piqued James's interest. "Worth it?"

"Like, changing the world. Fixing things. I think a lot of the evil decisions in the world are just sorta dumb. I'd risk my life to help everyone be smarter," he said.

Well, that was different, James thought. And enough to make him pay attention for the rest of the interview.

He was a software engineer, a programmer, really. Knew five different programming languages well enough to improvise with them. He'd gotten into it right out of high school with nothing but a lucky interview at a tech company and knowledge of how to ask questions on forums and spent a year writing user manuals for apps that didn't exist—James had initially thought that meant something totally different than it actually did. He'd been in a dozen clubs through school, from amateur rocketry to the debate team. James asked him if he had something against sleep; Virgil said he just had things to do that were more interesting.

James didn't really like him.

He was an overachiever. Razor-sharp smarts, but maybe not the best at applying etiquette. Also he said things that sounded like jokes, but without the smile. It was uncomfortable to James. But he knew that was a personal bias.

He was also one of those people who would forget to eat if he got too into a project. And he had a clever answer for everything. James was no stranger to being a wiseass, but this was more than that; Virgil was pretty far up his own ass about how smart he was, and he really needed to show it off.

But fuck, he could be useful. And it didn't hurt that he wasn't evil. Honestly, he'd probably be good for the world, given a little power.

"Okay. Before we move to the final stage of this interview," James said, "I'd like to share Secret with you."

"You mean 'a secret,'" Virgil corrected him. It was like an automatic response. James winced.

"No," he said and kicked open the door to the supply cabinet.

"Hello," said the bright-blue, multi-eyed serpent coiled up in the impossibly small space of the second shelf, between the sticky notes and the extra pens. "My name is Secret. A pleasure to meet you."

"Huh," Virgil said. "Is that a hologram, or an animatronic?"

"Close enough," James said, not at all actually in answer to the question. "Last question—do you want to be project lead and head programmer for designing a UI for a mind-to-machine-and-sometimes-other-mind interface? The pay is pretty good."

"Yes," Virgil said without hesitation.

"Your first day is Monday. Show up at eleven p.m. Wear boots," James said as Secret slithered out the door, his role in this over.

"That's weird, but okay. And that's a really good hologram," their new programmer said.

"No," James told him. "It's really not."

Lance was the next interview candidate of the day, a bear of a man who showed up wearing a T-shirt that was a D&D joke. James asked him what his character's alignment was and spent fifteen minutes letting the dude explain why lawful good was the only correct choice if you actually wanted to be a hero. He may have been overly defensive about a perceived reaction from James.

James let him go for a bit, then told him that he had literal magic items in the basement and did the dude want to join their adventuring team?

He had some concerns. Why him? Was this some sort of chosen-one bullshit? Why him, really? He was kinda fat, wasn't he? Also, was this an elaborate practical joke? And would he be expected to kill in something other than self-defense?

James found the questions surprisingly refreshing and gave honest answers. No particular reason, because he was here, because he answered the job listing. Random chance, really. Fat was a problem, but James hadn't exactly been the apex of human potential when this had started; they had a gym here.

Then he tossed the dude a tiny yellow orb and smiled when their new recruit leveled up in beekeeping.

He'd show up on Monday, around eleven p.m. He had vambraces he could bring, he told James.

James was unsurprised and yet somehow fine with it.

"How're the interviews going?" Anesh asked without a trace of shame as James wandered into the back of the building for a brief break.

James scowled at him. "Not bad, honestly," he said, packing away the glower. "I've picked out a few people. Only had to wipe one person with Secret, and he says that it was more of a nudge than a full blackout. Whatever that means." James shrugged, brushing stray strands of hair out of his face. He frowned as he did so; he was loath to get a haircut, but it was getting in the way of looking professional *and* his ability to keep his eyes alert in the dungeon.

"What kinda people?" Alanna asked, overhearing a bit as she walked in.

"Not exactly people like us. A couple of them are ridiculously good at things; a couple others just have the right outlook. No one evil, I think. Except maybe the chef, but I think that might just be because he's dead inside from working in restaurant kitchens," James said, accepting a quick hug from Alanna as she wrapped her arms around him from behind. "What've you two been up to?"

"Do you have time?" Anesh asked. "Or any more interviews?"

"A couple more," James said. "The last guy I sent out early, so I have a short break. He used the same racist dog whistle phrase three times, like I wouldn't fucking notice." His scowl this time wasn't for dramatic effect at all; it was real, and ugly. "Fucker," he punctuated.

"Okay, well, my thing is honestly mostly just gonna be numbers, which I can skip and get right to the choice bits. Did you know that JP got a skill in investment banking a long time ago?" Nods, which prompted Anesh to continue. "Right. Well, he set us up a stock portfolio, and I've been mostly channeling extra funds into that."

"How's it doing?" Alanna and James asked in unison, curious and slightly worried.

"Well, skill ranks apparently can't account for outside information or random chance or whatever the stock market is. But between that, and all the weirdly connected people JP knows, he *can* still make us a 355 percent return on investment."

"What," James said, incredulous.

"What?"

"*What?*" he repeated.

"I don't . . . what's wrong?" Anesh was starting to look worried.

James exfiltrated himself from Alanna's hug to snatch the papers out of Anesh's folder. "Are you fucking kidding me?" he exclaimed. "Anesh, this is . . . insane. This is the kind of thing that gets us on the suspicious list of the SEC, rapidly." He looked up at his boyfriend. "This is a good profit—basically, it's too good," he said with a wince. "You need to tell JP to back off on the frequent daily trading. I know he knows more than he lets on, and the orb is probably giving him some insane instincts for good picks, but this looks like insider trading, man." James paused. "You said he *knows people*. Wait, *is* this insider trading? Is the only thing that's been stopping JP from cheating at the stock market just been that he didn't feel like needed to this whole time?"

"Wait, too good? How do you know?" Alanna backtracked to something he'd said at the start of his complaint.

"I have a degree in this sorta thing," James muttered, looking away in mild shame. "And yes, before you ask, I am aware that I work in tech support. I know. Thank you."

"Okay," Anesh said, concern on his face. "So, what happens if they catch us?" he asked James.

"Well, . . . 'catch us' doing what? I mean, the thing is, it's suspicious as all fuck, but it's not actually illegal to be good at day trading. And for a while, that's what it's gonna look like. Hell, now that I think about it, it probably won't even get noticed until we start hitting the range of millions of dollars." James shot a look at Anesh, glancing up from the documentation of their accounts. "We aren't doing that, are we?"

Anesh pulled a notepad out of his pocket, tore a page off, crumpled it up, and overhand flung it into a wire trash bin two desks down. "Nope," he said.

"Woulda been nice," James said. "Maybe we can start a finance consulting firm at some point and mask our devious plan to be 'too good at money.'" He shrugged. "Again, it's not actually illegal to be good at it. Like it's not illegal to count cards in Vegas. It's just that, with how we're doing it? It won't look like he's *just* good at it."

"All right, all right," Anesh said, a little annoyed James was harping on it. "I'll have JP step off for a bit." He gave ground on that point. "Anything else?"

Now seemed like the best time to bring it up. "Alanna... and I... want to try using the skulljacks tonight," James said, trying to get the words out before his weird sense of embarrassment caught up to him. "Like... together."

Anesh's eyes met Alanna's, and then James's. "You sure?" he asked, though he wasn't sure whom he was asking.

"Yeah," they both said together, with Anesh chorusing in for the second half of the expression, rolling his eyes as he did so. Of course they were sure. If he'd learned one thing about them in his time with his partners, it was that they really didn't ask things they weren't already sure of.

So, "Okay" was all he said with a shrug and a quirk of a grin. "I'll see you both tonight. James, I think Sarah's wild flailings over at the door mean your next interview is here."

"Great," James said, stifling something that was half yawn and half sigh. "I'll see you two in an hour, after these wrap up. If you finish up here, just meet me at home, okay? Don't stick around on my behalf."

"'Kay!" Alanna cheerfully patted him goodbye, while Anesh gave James a short peck on the lips. "Now, Anesh! I've been talking with Momo about the reds..."

James smiled as he walked over to where Sarah was giving an exaggerated tapping of her foot, feeling good about his night. Conversations with his partners always left him feeling hopeful. Maybe the next interview would be exactly what they wanted.

It wasn't.

At roughly two a.m., the elevator doors dinged open on the ground floor of the structure that Momo had started calling home.

She lived in the basement, which was also her own personal lab space. In theory, the other rooms down here that had been cleaned up and furnished served as guest rooms or permanent quarters for anyone who wanted them, but Momo was kinda it for now. She didn't mind, though. Quite the opposite.

Momo took the solitude and contemplation parts of being a goth seriously. Or at least, that's what she told herself.

Also it gave her more leeway to try dumb things with the red orbs, just to see what worked. She hadn't been able to do anything with the theory that you could make a kind of life with them, but she *was* getting better at designing totems.

Like, to the point that she was actually designing them now.

She was pretty sure that her next big breakthrough was right around the corner. Maybe with this one, she'd figure out how to transmit information in a way that didn't hurt as much.

Momo was . . . not doing great, if she was gonna be honest with herself. Sure, she had a place to stay, a hobby and/or job that she loved, and a lot of friends. But her parents didn't remember her, she was probably never gonna finish college, and she hadn't really slept in two days. One of the perks of no longer having a real job.

There were bags under her eyes. The kind you only got from prolonged lack of sleep, sleep that left you functional but never really rested.

Momo was losing ground and didn't know how to take it back.

What she did know, though, was that Harvey had taken in a delivery for the kitchen today. She also knew that James had interviewed twenty-eight people, and hired six of them. That first fact she knew because she wasn't a total isolationist, and the second she knew because the shell-and-bottlecap totem she had rolled up in a Pringles can in her pocket had just enough range to reach a few feet around her and told her the allegiance of every human in the building.

That one had taken a lot of work to make, and she was pissed that the only settings she could work out were "all living things," which included *ants*, or "human," which was . . . fine, but not as all-encompassing as she might have hoped.

It also hurt like hell to have on, but she left it running basically all the time anyway. The nosebleeds were barely noticeable anymore, anyway. The point was, she'd come upstairs for a two a.m. sandwich. And she'd taken the elevator because stairs were for chumps, and spatial violations were hilarious.

What she wasn't expecting was to see someone outside the large glass panes of the front windows.

It was a woman, or a girl, or whatever. Maybe a little older than Momo herself and looking . . . kind of like in the same shape, honestly. She stood in the rain, hoodie and tangled blond hair dripping wet as she peered through into the mostly dark interior of their little semiprivate space. Her eyes also had the look of a member of Club No Sleep, and her shoulders sagged in desperate exhaustion as she tried to find something through the glass.

Momo ignored every security protocol that Harvey had laid out to them over the last two weeks and went over and unlocked the door.

The woman nearly jumped out of her steel-toed boots when the lock clacked open. And Momo had the impression she was prepared to fucking book it back to the rolling trash heap shaped like a car that she'd parked on the far end of the otherwise empty lot.

"Hey!" Momo called over, sticking her head out the door, voice raspy and thick from lack of use and equal lack of staying hydrated. "You want a sandwich?" She very carefully did not step outside. She didn't want to find out what the totem thought "in the building" meant if she was outside.

The other woman made nervous eye contact with her before looking around at the empty parking lot, the dark building, and then back to Momo herself.

She'd come a long way to be here, Momo thought. She had that feel to her. The weight of a long trip. Only she didn't get to the end to find a place to prop her feet up and relax. She just ended up . . . here.

Momo watched the woman think, watched her steel herself to answer. If she came into the building, Momo could tell in an instant if she was a threat. She didn't think this was that kind of situation, but if it was . . . well, she hadn't lived here for a month without coming up with a few paranoid plans. And if she wasn't, then the kitchen could support two sandwiches.

She held the door open for what felt like half an hour, wind sweeping the occasional sheet of cold rain just across the threshold at a right angle to the door itself. Momo was becoming a lot more patient than she ever expected, she realized, as she waited for the answer.

Finally, after what felt like a small forever, the wanderer made her choice.

"Yeah," Eleanor called back, striding to the door. "I'm fucking starving."

"It's not the same, from what I understand," Anesh was telling them, the trio plus extra Anesh seated on the bed in a ring of crossed legs and small touches. "Simon is better at describing it, but basically, what I do is more of a refresh. I'm reminding myself of things I haven't known yet. What they do, what we . . . we're going to do . . . it's more."

James tried not to whip his head back and forth as both Aneshes spoke. It had been a while since they'd all been in the same room, and he had forgotten how easily his boyfriend slipped into that pattern of teamworked speech.

"What about for me, since I don't have a . . . ?" Alanna tapped the nape of her neck.

"It forms when someone plugged in brings an ethernet cable near your neck," James said, suppressing the urge to start shivering as he remembered having his own forced onto him. "It'll be fine," he reassured Alanna. "I'll be *fine*!"

They had, between each of them, an ethernet cord and a single router, which was plugged into the outlet in the least obtrusive way possible. The lights in the room were off, with the exception of the constellation of lights from James's PC and the glow of the first size-two yellow orb that the madman *still* kept as a night-light–slash–lava lamp.

It was a tense feeling, but a warm and comfortable one, too. They were together, and kinda worried about what was gonna happen, but they were here, with each other. Kinda sleepy, kinda excited, and none of them knowing exactly what to expect.

"Okay. Okay," James muttered as he picked up his cord. "Just like flying a drone, right?"

"Do not pilot me." Alanna stuck her tongue out at him. "At least, not right nooooooow!" Her last word turned into a yelp as both Aneshes on either side took the opportunity to poke at her sides.

"Be serious here," James tried to say with a straight face, but failed. "Or not." He laughed as his partners engaged in some kind of tickle-based skirmish.

"Oh, fuck it," Alanna said, gasping for breath and giggling as she held off a snickering Anesh. "Just shove it in already."

James almost rolled his eyes. But then, he realized, maybe that was just what should happen. Just . . . one last push over the edge, and trust that they'd catch each other as they fell.

Anesh's were already plugged in. So James reached over, grabbed the spare cord, and with a fluid motion and a leaned-in kiss, brought it up to the back of Alanna's neck.

Flesh and bone reshaped themselves, or were themselves reshaped, into something new. Something human and not, technological and yet totally irrational. A path of almost ultimate trespass, and also, a gate to a greater future.

And then James slapped his own into place before he could second-guess any more.

It wasn't instant, like with Monster Karen. It wasn't slow and awkward, like trying to learn to pilot a drone, either. Human minds quested, when presented with new things. They poked at holes they weren't supposed to; they explored down the strange paths unless taught not to. And now, there were two and a half paths for James's mind to follow.

He closed his eyes as the feelings rushed in. Impulses, at first, small snippets that he knew weren't him, but he could taste the familiarity of.

Here was fear, here was worry. Here was surprise, and satisfaction, and curiosity. Here was compassion.

He followed the feelings and felt the others doing the same. James realized he could feel the others. And they realized it, too, as he shared the thought. They were sharing, almost without meaning to. More fear, from someone, or all of them. What if they shared what they didn't mean to? What if they gave up secrets that were meant to be kept private? What if they hurt each other?

But it was too late. They were linked, and they *wanted to be*, and they couldn't pull back now.

James had thought that he'd be afraid. But now, tumbling over the precipice, he found that he wasn't. They trusted each other, ultimately, and so they would never let themselves fall. And also, it didn't feel any different. Once their minds were pulled together, the new thing they were was normal to itself.

They'd never been sure what it would be like to be three people and one person all at once. They'd not had the words for it, individually. Even now, together, they didn't quite grasp what they were. The emotion resonated with each piece of their new self, different thoughts all thought together and amplified across four platforms.

They were together, as fully as a lover ever could be. They were the next human. They were an opportunity. They were something brand-new. They were who they always were. They were terrified, and excited, and so many other things, all at once in a way a single human could never be.

They opened their eyes, and four angles of vision each saw the different parts of who they were and knew the truth of each other more powerfully than almost anyone ever had before.

And then there was only love.

CHAPTER 23

It was morning at the shared apartment. James, Anesh, Alanna, Anesh, Sarah, and Secret were all seated around the main living room table, just . . . pleasantly existing together. A comfortable breakfast was being quietly consumed while calm sunlight poured through the glass doors of the patio.

Well, okay, some of those things were true. Those people were present, and there *was* certainly a table. Some people were even seated at it. But it was about eleven a.m., so it wasn't quite morning anymore, except for the most ardent of insomniacs like James. Also the breakfast—James had made pancakes, classic blueberry—was being eaten alongside an argument regarding putting maple syrup on blueberry pancakes. And one Anesh was on his way out to classes, so he was less sitting and enjoying a meal and more cramming an entire pancake in his mouth while muttering about American breakfast foods. And Secret, more solid than normal, was coiled under the table sharing bites of bacon with Aberdeen.

Oh, and it was early December, and the sun had forsaken them entirely. What light there was was cold and gray. James scowled at the glass door, wishing it was a wall instead.

"Are you sure you guys are going to be okay today?" Anesh asked for the third time, his mouth crammed full of pancake.

"Stop asking!" Sarah and Alanna chorused back at him.

This had been going on for a while. They'd woken up today, trickled into the living room, and started making plans for what to do with their evening. When Anesh had finally made his way out, he'd been presented with a group of people who had a list of ideas on how to try to communicate with a haunted house.

He'd been unhappy with that, to say the least. Both of him. Mostly since each of him had something going on today, and neither of him was available to tag along.

The house that the human-shaped ball of nervousness named Fredrick inhabited was part of a larger picture that was starting to come into focus. The dungeons were, obviously now, not unique. And the house, while it seemed to be just weakly haunted, had the same pattern of challenges, rewards, and a confusing entrance. Getting to know it, James insisted, was going to be part of the key to understanding dungeon ecology as a whole.

Going inside it, Anesh countered, was a great way to possibly get stuck in a mental bear trap.

There'd been a small argument. Which, honestly, wasn't that much of a fight. By this point, the idea that they were putting themselves in mortal danger was kind of, weirdly, *fine* for everyone. Even Sarah, who had literally seen companions die in front of her, seemed to more or less accept the risks they all took together. Anesh seemed more concerned that he wouldn't be there to help than any overt worry that anyone would get hurt.

"All right, all right. Cool off," Anesh said through his breakfast. "I'm just trying to help. Maybe another me isn't a bad idea."

James hissed through his teeth as he flipped another pancake in the skillet. "Anesh, I love you like . . . well, like I love you. But we *cannot* get a bed large enough for five people. They don't make those."

"You take up too much space!" an Anesh protested. "And you hog the blankets! I barely have a profile on the bed!" the other Anesh chimed in.

"Rude." Secret echoed Anesh's thoughts from under the table.

"Right. And if my selfish ass isn't going to cede any territory, imagine how cramped you'll be with a whole other body," James pointed out with good humor. "But really. We might need to devote more cash to our expenses anyway—more so if you keep adding to our group. I think we just need better time management instead of more people."

One of the Aneshes, the one in a hurry, took the opportunity while James was talking to wave shortly and slip out the front door. The other one, who wasn't going off to class, picked up the whole burden of conversation. "James, I love you like we're in a long-term relationship, but you're objectively wrong."

"What? How do you figure?"

Alanna chimed in. "I mean, you took time over the last couple nights to actually hire, like, six-plus people, because we don't have enough people."

"Also, we now have *three* known dungeons. Two of which we haven't even really started to explore," Anesh said. "Wouldn't it be nice if we had someone who was, in a sense, expend—"

"No," James shortly cut him off.

"I'm just saying, I can—"

"Nope!" Sarah added to James and Alanna's voices. "You already spilled the beans when you told us each iteration of you is a whole person, Anesh!" she exclaimed at him. "You can't back out on treating yourself right now, you honk!"

Anesh fumed a bit. Honestly, it didn't *feel* like it should be a big deal to him. He could make more bodies. And yeah, those bodies were whole people, exactly like him, with their own copy of what made him Anesh running on their hardware. And yeah, he didn't *want* to die, or be hurt. But . . . well, if he *did* lose this body, it wasn't actually death, now was it? Because everything but the last hour or so would live on in another iteration of him.

That everyone else was so protective of him was a good feeling, true. It made him feel like he was more than just another tool in the box of options. But he'd always felt that way since he'd been pulled into this strange group of friends, and more so since James had shared the dungeon with him. He'd never felt like anyone would ask him to throw his life away, spare or otherwise.

And that's why he was willing to do it, without question.

"Fine," he said out loud, in a tone that reminded them all that this conversation wasn't over. "But I would—"

Now, once again, he was cut off. But this time by the front door bursting open.

Before anyone had processed that the form standing in the entryway was actually just JP, taking panting breaths from having sprinted up the stairs, they'd all started moving. James had dropped the pan and was reaching for the closest knife the kitchen offered, Sarah was flexing her hand with a motion that would compel her magnetic field to rip anything vaguely related to iron away from the intruder, and Alanna just *had a gun*. Where she'd pulled that from, they weren't quite sure.

Everyone instantly dropped their guards back when they realized it was just JP.

"Good afternoon," Secret announced to him with a dour voice. "James wishes to offer you breakfast," he said, shattering the tense atmosphere.

"Jesus Christ, JP, don't you knock?" James asked. "Also, want a pancake? Oh, also, did you get my messages about the suspicious day-trading thing?" he followed up as he slid the blade back into the knife block.

JP, leaning forward with his hands on his knees as he breathed heavily, held out a hand to wave off James's breakfast offer, ignoring the weaponry and the slight at his potential trade violations. "Don't you fuckers answer your *phones*?" he demanded of them.

All of them, on reflex, reached into pockets or picked phones up off the table. Except Secret, who basically was a phone in a weird way, and Aberdeen, who was a dog, and too smart to need an extra leash.

"Um . . . no one called me?" Sarah asked. "Alanna?"

"Nope." The other girl shrugged, the firearm she'd been gripping a second ago already vanished again. "Anyone else?"

None of them had anything, and they let JP know.

"Holy fuck, you guys. We've been calling you all damn morning. I thought you had died." He pulled his own phone out and, out of curiosity, dialed James.

Nothing happened.

James raised his eyebrows and waited while JP tested their numbers and, eventually, tried calling anyone who wasn't in the apartment. "Okay!" he eventually announced. "Your apartment is a dead zone for service! I'll just blame Secret and move on. Whatever! There's a thing you all *need* to see!"

"Do not place this on me undue," Secret protested, still coiled up around the chair that faced the door, his bacon forgotten and long since swiped by the dog.

"Dude, what's going on?" James asked. "We're just about to head out to the haunted house. Can this wait?"

"No." JP made eye contact and shook his head. "Not this time. Momo met someone you're gonna want to talk to."

James and Alanna sat in the front seats of James's defiant old Subaru, thinking and talking through the twenty minutes of road time it took to get to the secret base. They'd left Sarah behind because she was driving Anesh to a doctor's appointment, and Secret had wanted to finish his breakfast, so he planned to tag along with her.

On that note: "Secret's been weird lately," James announced.

"Lately?" Alanna raised her eyebrows as far as they'd go.

"Okay, weirder, then. And since . . . last night." James felt like he should be feeling awkward here, but he couldn't find it in himself to do so. For a brief window, he'd known literally every speck of emotion Alanna felt, and he knew damn well there was not a single thing to be embarrassed over. "Did you notice this morning? He's *solid*," James fretted, worried like a parent with a maybe-sick kid.

Alanna nodded, absently watching out the window as their route took them past a specific high school. "He's a lot less ripply than normal. Makes sense, though." She caught James's question in the air before it was asked. "Because he's still just . . . well, not *just* . . . but he's an *idea*, not a body. So, when we all hooked up . . ."

"We cannot call it that."

"... we took all the different ways we thought about Secret and connected them. And now he doesn't leak smoke as much!" Alanna concluded.

It took James a few seconds to put that together, but when he did, it made sense. Nodding to himself, he replied, "Yeah, I suppose so! I mean, it seemed rude to ask for some reason. Like, it felt so personal and I didn't want to bother him, so I just kind of forgot to bring it up. But your thing makes sense."

Biting her lip, Alanna tapped the armrest of the car. "Is it possible that Secret keeps his own secrets? Like, by default, we just find reasons to keep things secret because he has that sort of effect?"

"It's never been clear to me exactly *how* magic Secret is," James mused. "Like, I kind of assumed that he was less magic now that he had a body, but that might be a lie as well. We've seen him eat the ending of secrets, burn out communications technology, live inside forgotten dreams, and, apparently, he is fully capable of blanking memories that include him. And half of those come from *after* he turned into a not-so-endless snake." He sighed loudly. "I'm starting to think that I'm in over my head with this weird-ass adoption thing that I've got going on."

"You're a good dad," Alanna quipped offhandedly, not realizing just how much her words impacted James. "You know what *I'm* disappointed about, though?" She tried to change the subject.

"Do tell." James grabbed the segue like a drowning man after a plank.

"Our atrocious time management," she said with a barely contained grin as she brought up the morning's conversation again.

James sighed. "Okay, look," he started with consternation. "I'm gonna say something that might catch me some flak from everyone, and also possibly my own past self." He glanced at Alanna and waited for her to give a quick nod of acknowledgment of his social sacrifice before continuing. "I don't think the haunted house is that important," James announced.

"Whaaaat!" Alanna gave him a betrayed look. "James, dungeon! It's literal magic!"

"Look," James repeated himself, "the Office, Officium Mundi—which I guess is its official designation now, thanks, Sarah—it gives us things that are life-changing. World-altering. And from day *one*, I could see the way that the yellow orbs could be something more than they seemed. The sorts of skills they could offer, you know? And the reality is even more than just that." He tapped his fingers along the wheel in a nervous beat. "But the house? It's ... I mean, it's more convenient. Telling one nervous guy that his family's ancestral house is haunted and he should probably move is way easier than sneaking past corporate security every week. But it doesn't give us anything of value. You and Anesh *still* don't know what it means to be connected!"

He wasn't *wrong*, but Alanna still had a counterpoint. "Yeah, but it's cool, dude," she told him bluntly. "Like, it's magic. You're doing exactly that thing that you said you hated, where you're treating magic as just another tool in the box instead of something awesome and amazing for us to explore."

"I know." James gnashed his teeth. "I *know*! But there's so much to *do*, and the Office offers us the most in terms of power right now. The house is just a fancy escape room."

"You realize that this is literally the kind of thing that we used to go out to do on the weekend together in our free time, right?"

"Yeah, but we've had our free time surgically replaced with firearm practice, small unit tactics, and suddenly learning more than we ever wanted to about ducks."

"Touché." Alanna sighed as they pulled into the parking lot of the lair. "Lotta cars here today," she said, offhand. "It's not support group day; are these the new people?"

"I dunno, it might be a church group using our parking lot to go to the diner across the street again. But I can easily see myself having hired the kind of person who spray-painted a desert sunset on their hood, so that checks out," James said, looking over at the beat-up clunker of a car he'd parked next to. "You up for meeting new people today?"

Alanna scoffed. "Please," she said. "I'm *always* up for meeting new people."

"One of them is ex-military."

"I'm *almost* always up for meeting new people," she corrected. "Also, that's kind of out of character for you."

James turned off the car, killing the heat and making getting out and going inside a bit more necessary before he and Alanna spent half an hour bantering here. "He's a cool guy, honestly. If he's here today, maybe he can make us lunch. I'm hungry."

"We just—"

"Yeah, I didn't really get a chance to eat before JP interrupted." James gnawed at his lip in frustration. "I mostly just snacked on some bacon before Secret absconded with it."

"Damn."

The two of them traded words as they moved toward the front door, the tinted front windows not giving a good view into their secret base. The place was growing on James a lot. The short pine trees out front, the little patch of gravel around the bike rack, the way the door made a goofy *wonk* noise when you opened it out instead of in—all of it built up to a place that was just enjoyable to walk up to.

It also helped that James's modifications to it via green orbs made it exponentially more valuable than whatever building their landlord thought they were leasing.

The use of green orbs on a central location was something that had resonated with James since he'd started idly doing it. And when his brain had caught on the idea and puzzled out *why* it felt so useful, he came to a satisfying conclusion.

Yellow orbs would, sporadically, make one person more powerful. Sometimes in ways that could accumulate wealth or resources that could then be shared, but usually personal ways. Blue orbs could give powers or solve problems, but they were even more focused on personal power. Green orbs, though, were for everyone.

Every single green orb that they used at the lair would be experienced by twenty, thirty, forty people. Over and over. The whole guild made use of this central place, and it was here that their power could start to multiply. *Especially* now that they knew that some of the greens changed time itself to their benefit.

And sure, nice bathrooms or proper water pressure weren't huge deals. But if you wanted to sew a pair of pants at the lair, you'd find yourself finishing a lot sooner than you *should*. And if you needed a place to stay for the night, or space to test out potentially dangerous xenotech, or just a secret firing range to practice with the growing arsenal? Well, they had a basement. They had *two* basements.

"You know, there's a bet going around on what happens if you dig up from one of the basements," James told Alanna as he held the door open for her.

"Don't," she said. "Just don't. The basements are awesome, and they work, and somehow we haven't gotten dinged by the city for building permit violations. Don't ruin this for us by trying to backhoe your way through subdimensional space."

James snorted. "You made that term up."

"Subdimensional or backhoe? Oh, too late. Hey, Momo!" Alanna changed tones in a hot second as their younger friend came up to the duo. "Is JP here yet?"

The young woman looked up at the two of them. Her eyes were ringed with dark circles; her hair, even as short as she kept it, looked frazzled. The normal goth look she cultivated had fallen away, despite her wardrobe still being all black. But for all that she appeared like she hadn't slept in a week, her face beamed as she looked at them.

"Hey, guys. I felt you come in," she said, wiping at her nose slightly with the long sleeve of her sweatshirt. "You got here fast."

"Yeah, JP made it sound like a big deal. Where is he, anyway?"

"Not here yet," Momo said, unhesitatingly. "I'll let you know when he makes it in. Did he tell you what was going on?"

James shrugged. "He said you'd met someone, that they knew about a dungeon, and that they were on the run from the Wizard Police. I dunno if any of that is true, but I'm always open to new friends, so fuck it, let's say hi, right?" Alanna nodded agreement;

there wasn't much more to say than that. Sometimes James was oblivious, sometimes he was outright dumb, but no one in the world would ever be able to accuse him of not having compassion.

"That's what I figured. I didn't talk to her much before she snoozed," Momo admitted. "She was *tired*. Like, tired like I was when we left the Office the first time, you know? She's eating now. Oh, and your new chef is here."

James had actually kind of assumed that Nate would be here today, because he'd gotten the impression that was just the sort of person Nate was, showing up literal days early to work to poke around in the kitchen. But to hear he was actually here was still a nice, amusing confirmation.

Momo led them through to the back, where they'd set up a few round tables and sets of padded chairs so that anyone who wasn't actively working out could watch the other half of the room that was devoted to the small gym they had. *Gym* was a strong word, honestly; they had some equipment, but they mostly just used it for the mats so that Simon and Other James could kick the crap out of each other as they pushed the limits of martial arts while connected via wireless skulljack. That was why the tables were here, less for lunch and more for the show. Turned out, when humans started to pick up increasingly supernatural powers, it was fun to watch them do just about anything.

Sitting at one of those tables, eating a goddamn masterpiece of a burger, was a woman about James's age. She had blond hair, a sharp nose, and eyes that never stopped scanning the area. Over against the back left wall, the gruff ex-sailor stood half in the door to the kitchen, idly rolling a towel in his hands and keeping an eye on the room. Whether he was just making sure she was okay or making sure she wasn't stealing their punching bags, James didn't know, but either way, it gave the place a strangely familiar feeling. Like a home, not just a business.

The instant James walked in, and Momo had started to say, "This is El—" the girl had already kicked the chair backward as she lunged to her feet. As James's brain caught up to the fact that she was moving and he started to flex the limits of his enhanced synapses, she had already half drawn a small pistol from a holster mostly hidden under her arm.

Time didn't slow down, but James experienced so much more of the world in those few seconds. Crisis crystallized thought into truth. He saw with perfect clarity the emotions running through the girl. Eleanor, he knew the name; he'd seen her before. Connections fell into place at a rapid clip. She was here being hunted by the Wizard Police? No, she was here following Secret. She thought *he* was the Wizard Police. She was going to shoot him. She was afraid, felt betrayed, felt lost, felt *tired*.

James saw it all. He could feel the currents of the air-conditioning, smell the cooked food from the test run of their kitchen; he knew so much, had so much information crammed into his mind all at once. And it didn't hurt; he just went with the flow of it and experienced the world.

None of this was going to keep him from getting shot, he realized suddenly. He didn't have the time to move, couldn't actually react faster. He could move faster, think faster, but his reactions were as human as ever.

Eleanor pulled the trigger. Once, twice. The gunshots were like audio poison to his unfiltered perception. They crackled across the metal of the ventilation overhead, broke against the walls and floor, rippled off the human bodies in the room. James could feel them, more than he'd ever like, and he dreaded the feeling they precipitated. But he couldn't move to stop it.

The bullets slammed into the arm Alanna had thrown out, drilling neat, low-caliber holes in her coat, bowing her flesh inward before surrendering to the twisted physics of her body and clattering to the floor. James blinked. He'd been able to see so much, but he hadn't noticed that. Awkward.

Two and a half seconds later, three hundred pounds of chef slide tackled Eleanor, pinned her to the ground with callused hands, and kicked the gun into the center of the room.

There may have been yelling happening.

James took a deep breath. The people in the room kept yelling, but he was silent. He felt adrenaline pounding in his ears, but he didn't speak just yet. He had to get this right, and he didn't want his voice to shake.

Alanna was swearing, Momo was protesting that she hadn't known this would happen, El was screaming about her rights, Nate was telling someone to stop yelling, though James had no idea who. All of them were caught up in the moment. So James just waited for them to run out of words.

One by one, the parties present fell silent as they noticed him standing there, fingers steepled in front of his face. Even Eleanor, writhing on the ground in a vain attempt to break away from their far-more-combat-ready-than-expected cook, paused when she noticed the room going still.

"Don't," James said softly, "do that again. It's very rude to shoot at your hosts." He paused, waiting for the words to sink in. He spoke calmly, clearly, making sure not to stumble over the words. "Nate, let her up. Momo, please take that gun to the armory."

"You have an armory?" Nate asked, rumbling voice showing concerned surprise.

"*We* have an armory, comrade," James corrected him in a joking Russian accent. He glanced sideways, checking on Alanna. His girlfriend was rubbing her arm but not actually hurt, it looked like. "Regardless. I think there's been a misunderstanding. Eleanor, sit down and eat your food. You came to the right place; you just got the wrong person through the door first."

The young woman scrambled backward along the ground as Nate released his iron grip on her wrist and throat. "Wh . . . what. Who the fuck *are you people?!*" she demanded.

"Ah," James said, smiling sadly. "I wish I got to say this under more fun circumstances. We're you, you know? We're you, with a little more of a kick."

Twenty minutes later, after Momo let him know that someone had come in through the back war room area, James had met up with Secret and Sarah. He didn't ask exactly how Momo was keeping tabs on everyone in the building, but he made a note to check later. That was something they should probably look into.

He filled them in, especially Secret, on what had happened. And, more importantly, who it was that had shown up on their doorstep.

"She has been coming here for a long time," Secret said. "I knew that, and now I know that. I kept the secret from myself, somehow. She kept something secret, too; Eleanor is not what you would call baseline. There was something else that let her track us to this point."

"Good to know," James said. "Do you want to go say hi?" he asked Secret. The infomorph was sitting on his coils, rising up to just under James's shoulders. It was, especially for Nate, who had been given an open invitation to tag along for this sort of thing from now on, still unsettling to see a creature with that many mouths and teeth and eyes. But James had gotten used to it; he loved Secret, in a very protective way, no matter what he actually looked like.

"I would, yes," Secret said, bobbing his head in a nod.

They descended the elevator, the two of them. Sarah and Alanna stayed up top to talk to Momo, to discuss what had been said between her and El during the night, to figure out if they should even trust her at all. Alanna didn't know James was going down to the basement where they'd stuck their visitor; she'd protest if she did. That was why James left Nate upstairs, too. A brief distraction, and also because it was considered bad form to bring someone your conversation partner had just lost a fight to to a polite chat.

"I'm still not mad at you," James informed Secret as the elevator zipped downward. "So you know."

Secret rolled the piece of information around in his maw, tasting the myriad of little secrets in it. He settled on "Thank you."

They'd stuck Eleanor in one of the guest rooms in the more normal basement. Or rather, Momo had last night. But El was pacing the floor like she was a prisoner when James knocked and cracked the door open.

"So, this is my cell, then, huh?" she demanded in a pissed voice as he opened the door to say hi.

"Um . . . no? This is a bedroom." James went for the humor approach. Because he was James, and he could only really hold on to the serious tone for so long before he started to break down. "You can leave whenever; the door wasn't even locked," he told her.

"What about the elevator?" she demanded.

"It . . . *is* an elevator, yes." He punctuated the words with a slow nod. "There are also stairs, if you don't like elevators? Though I've been conditioned to be worried about stairwells in office spaces."

"What . . ."

"I'll show you later. Hey, so, why did you come here?" James cut to the chase. "Like, here. You came to our place, to the heart of our little operation. I'd say 'home,' but this isn't really where I live, but it is important to me. Why here, Eleanor?"

"I was looking for someone," El said. "And my name is El, not Eleanor. How do you even know that name?" she demanded.

"That's a Secret thing." James quirked a grin. "Looking for someone?"

"Not like it matters. I didn't see him on you earlier when I . . . fuck it, when I cast the spell. So maybe he got away, and I wasted my time, or maybe you've already killed him," El spat out. "Still not really doing a good job of convincing me to trust you."

"Yeah, so, full disclosure? I already know what you mean—being cryptic isn't helping. You're talking about someone who's pretty important to me. The reason your spell didn't see him on me was because he stayed back at our apartment to *eat my pancakes* while I came here first. So chill. Also, that is not a euphemism." James glanced sideways to Secret, who was still standing just out of view of the doorframe, looking absolutely unashamed for getting breakfast. Sighing at the theatrics, James casually reached over and hooked a hand around the part of Secret that was closest to being shoulders and pulled the serpentine creature into view. "Say hi," he commanded whichever one of them would listen first.

El froze. So did Secret, too, amusingly. The two of them stared at each other for a long moment. Eventually, El broke the silence. "I . . . um . . . I've seen you in my dreams."

"That is very flattering!" Secret responded cheerfully. Whatever trepidation the meme felt was gone in an instant as he found his voice.

James didn't know whether to slap his face into his palm or beam with pride.

"No, I mean . . . we've talked. You're why I'm here. I followed you, through the dreams," El said, gasping. "I thought you could help me. I was . . . goddammit, I was so fucking *afraid*." She sat down on the edge of the room's bed, one hand coming up to splay fingertips against her face. "What is even happening." It wasn't really a question.

"I do not remember my dreams very well," Secret admitted. "But I believe that, if I helped guide you here, it was because I thought of you as a friend. And I can feel that secret half of myself reminding me of that." He looked up at James, then back to El, and nodded in his bobbing way. "Do not fear," he said. "I remember telling you that. You don't need to be afraid. There are no monsters here. There is nothing to run from. Perhaps there never were, but, even so, your running has brought you to us. And we can, and will, help you."

"It's kind of what we do these days," James admitted with a shrug.

"Help me *what*?!" El demanded, angry. "I threw away my whole life, on, what, a comic misunderstanding? Are you fucking kidding me?"

James was starting to get annoyed, and he barked out his response in a tone that made both other presences in the room ripple in shock. "Hey! It's not my fault you decided to go on the run! If cheap suits and one excitable infomorph is all it takes for you to think someone is the goddamn magic gestapo, then I can't really help how skittish you are, can I?" He tried to take a deep breath and rein in his anger, but El cut off his moment.

"I gave up my car! My fucking *mom* doesn't even know what happened to me! And you think it's not your fault just because you didn't realize you'd look like feds while you were *pretending to be fucking feds?!*" she half yelled at him. Or full yelled, really.

Weirdly, her yelling crystalized his own calm. *This*, right here, was something that he could *fix*. You couldn't just tell people to not be afraid, but problems? Especially problems of logistics? James had people for that. Specifically, he had a boyfriend. "Well, first off, lemme tell you that we have the money to undo most of the basic problems," James said. "If you want to go home, we can absolutely get you a plane ticket. If you need a new car . . . holy shit, why haven't I bought a new car yet? Whatever, ignore that. But, beyond that?" He tapped a hand against his leg before deciding on how much to divulge to their potential new recruit. "How do you feel about a little more magic in the world?" He grinned what he hoped was an inviting smile, mirrored by Secret a dozen times. "Because all anger aside? I've got a job offer for you."

It didn't seem to reassure Eleanor, but that might have just been all the teeth in his smile.

CHAPTER 24

Saturday.

Alanna was off with an Anesh, checking up on the high school, sussing out the boundaries of the breach. Anesh had wanted to tag along, and James lost the coin flip for which "actual FBI agent" would be escorting a consultant around the building.

Other Anesh was off doing private tutoring. During a round of best skill pays for dinner last night, he'd scored *[+1 Skill Rank : Mathematics—Calculus—Vector Integral]*, and after that, there was no getting the grin off his face. Anesh had come a long way from "this is woefully unfair" to get to "I will absolutely take free math knowledge." He'd also come a long way in terms of drawing knowledge out of the skill orbs, turning it over in his mind until he had something he couldn't just use, but could understand. And teach. For money.

The secret lair wasn't empty, but James was avoiding it a little while longer. Today was group therapy day, and they were doing a lot of connectivity exercises. James felt like he'd taken too long; his fumbling attempts at a nascent hive mind would, for sure, not measure up to the experiences of the thirtyish people who rotated through learning to master their implants. Also, Sarah was there. And while he wanted to talk to her, he also wanted to do it when there was no risk of one of a million different people interrupting.

Secret was asleep. So was Auberdeen. So were Ganesh and Lily.

D&D night had been canceled—or rather, moved to next week. The installation of new hardware at the base's kitchen was being overseen by the guy James had unintentionally given dictatorial control over it. And it was one of his days off work.

And, most importantly, James had been ordered to "fuckin' chill" for a little while by Alanna. A mandated day off from the endless series of tasks he'd set for himself, which she seemed exempt from for some reason, at least temporarily.

James sat on the couch, listening to the almost silence of the apartment. The only noises were the constant hum of the fridge, the ocean's roar of cars passing outside, and the scratching of pen legs as Rufus scrambled to get himself up onto the table. It was a good day. A day with no expectations, no obligations.

For the first time in three months, James actually had a day off.

He made eye contact with Rufus as the little stapler finally made it up to James's level, theatrically rolling his head around from where it had been staring at the ceiling.

"Hey, friend," James greeted the strider, who waved back with his front leg, clicking a greeting. "I've got nothing to do today," he said, casual.

James looked around the room as he casually scratched Rufus's back. He could play some video games, though nothing had really been on his radar for a while that he was interested in trying, and he worried that if he sat down at his computer, he'd just end up sinking a million more hours into old favorites that didn't make him think or even excite him anymore.

He could take a damn nap, finally catch up on all the sleep he was missing. But then, he'd kinda gotten used to the nonstop pattern of living on five hours a night. Six, if he slept at the apartment and you counted the magical bonus hour. And napping now would just leave him feeling unpleasant later.

He could clean the apartment, but, well . . .

"Why is the apartment so clean?" He directed the inquiry toward the only other conscious being in the apartment, but Rufus didn't have an answer for him. Or rather, he did, but James didn't understand it. "Okay, calm down, buddy. I'm not Anesh; I can't speak your sign language." James waited patiently as Rufus walked him through a game of comically frustrating charades. "Okay. You, and the . . . others. Lily and Ganesh, right. You three . . . circles . . . oh, polishing? Wait, cleaning? Hang on, you're the one who's been doing the dishes?"

Rufus nodded enthusiastically. James asked him, "Why?" and he made some more motions. After a few minutes of the game, James came to a new answer. "Work for checkmark? Wait, check. Paycheck?" Rufus bobbed out a nod again, thrilled his friend understood. "You know we'd just give you yellows, right? You aren't our servants."

Of course Rufus knew. He had some complex thoughts on the nature of reciprocal good, though. If one did you a service, it was in your best interest to do a service for them in return. Both because it respected the gesture of friendship, and because it made for longer-lasting bonds. Rufus was very much a philosopher of the office world.

He didn't know how to say that, though. So he shrugged at James, tilting his front legs in a flat W shape and flattening his frontal eye in a similar gesture of resignation.

"All right. Well, thanks?" James settled on. It was actually kind of reminiscent of the old myths of brownies, those clever sprites that traded a clean home for a bit of hospitality. Except now James had the delightful mystery of how an ambulatory iPhone could manage to load anything into a dishwasher.

And he still didn't have anything to do.

"I think I'm gonna take a walk," he told Rufus, who nodded sadly at him. "You wanna come along?" he asked the strider.

Rufus perked up instantly.

There was, to him, a sort of magical nature to the outdoors, the same way the dungeon called to James. There were things that he didn't understand, life that didn't work the way his own knowledge of Life said it should, and so many new things to see. But he also knew that his existence was a well-kept secret, that his creation in the crucible of the Office was not something many humans, maybe most humans, would ever accept. But even still, when James offered him an arm to climb and a shoulder to perch on, how could Rufus ever say no?

"Just pretend you're inanimate if anyone asks," James told him as he put on his shoes, almost dislodging Rufus already. "Maybe hide in my coat or something."

And then, with all the gravitas needed from someone who did it a few times a day, they were out the front door. Only a slight pause for James to pet the panting dachshund on the doormat.

"I've been thinking a lot about the nature of our guild lately." James spoke out loud, and to anyone who didn't know the stapler on his shoulder was a person, he probably looked crazy. Fortunately, he was walking down a winding black asphalt trail that cut through the roughly tamed fields that separated shopping centers from residential areas. And, as it was a cold, gray winter day, there was no one here to even come close to overhearing.

"Guilds in general, really," James continued, ignoring the fact that Rufus was more mesmerized by the soggy grass around them than anything he was actually saying.

"See, the thing about a guild is that it's part of this economy of violence. Not literal violence, but, like, metaphorical violence." James gesticulated helplessly. "The idea of forcing your will or your plan or your rules onto someone else," he tried to explain. "All those old mercantile guilds that sprang up around the time that Europe was mastering the concept of trade? They existed to exercise power. 'Join the guild or don't work,' right? If you join, you get access to their support, their client list, their pool of potential buyers. If you don't, then they make sure no one does business with you if they ever want to do business with the guild. Oh! Like a union! But also kinda not, since the unions were about retaking power from authority, and the guilds were about establishing monopolies, establishing unassailable power. Like the literal opposite of a union."

James paused briefly when Rufus tapped his cheek and pointed, getting him to kneel down next to where the pathway crossed over a small creek. Rufus hopped to the ground and spent a few minutes investigating the flowing water. It was like a drinking fountain, only huge and wild and out in the open.

"So, the thing I'm worried about," James continued as he balanced on the balls of his feet and watched Rufus explore, "is that when we start calling ourselves a guild, and we start acting like what we think a guild is, we open the door to that kind of behavior. And I mean, a lot of us? We do *not* know the history of trade guilds. We're thinking of it in the video game term, like, a collection of tactically compatible individuals who want to run the same raids. And we are that! But we're also not in a video game." He shrugged at Rufus's inquisitive look before plucking the strider up and depositing him back on his own shoulder.

"I mean, the skill levels are like a video game. Kind of. A really weird one," James conceded. "I've always wondered if you actually get levels when you eat the orbs." Rufus gave the crossed-legs gesture for no pretty quickly. "Oh? Is it the time thing?" James asked, getting a nod in return. "That makes sense. It's food for you guys."

The two of them stopped at a crosswalk, and James waited the customary few steps back to signal to the one oncoming car that he had no intention of speeding up his walk to cross in front of it. It was hard enough to get Rufus to balance without jogging.

"So, the thing about our group." James tried to pick up his thoughts as they crossed and continued. "I don't want to be a guild. An economic one, at least. But I don't really know what else to go for. I just know that I don't want us to fall into this pattern of using force or control. I can see it really easily, too, you know? Karen is the big example."

On his shoulder, Rufus dug pointed legs into James's coat and shuddered.

"Person Karen, not dungeon Karen," James clarified, to Rufus's gratitude. "So, her philosophy and her political outlook differs from the majority of our group. She and at least one or two of her teammates would prefer to operate differently, use the powers for different things, and the big one: kill the dungeon if needed. And *yes*, I am aware that I was on Team No Dungeon for a while there." James tapped a chittering Rufus on the snoot. "But then, through an exercise in control of the dungeon's door, I cowed her into going along with my plan. And that's . . . worrying. Like, I think my plan is *better*, for us and for the world, but I don't like the idea that I would absolutely going to have to use force, in various ways, to implement it."

James sighed and looked up at the gathering gray clouds. "So, economies of violence. Hurt earns hurt. Control earns obedience. We end up acting out of fear, out of need, and not out of respect and mutual agreement to build the best society we can." He winced as a raindrop impacted directly on his nose. "All right, enough of that. You wanna get coffee?" he asked Rufus. "You'll like coffee. Not dungeon coffee, but the good stuff." James tilted his head to give Rufus a glance; the strider was looking at him with a mix of confusion and suspicion. "Okay, maybe we'll get you some fancy paper clips or something."

Rufus could live with that.

They sat at a café table, watching the rain pour down outside. One of the perks of living in a suburb that James could only barely afford before the beginning of his delver career was that there was literally always a coffee shop open somewhere nearby. And this time, it also wasn't Starbucks.

James sipped at his cappuccino. He was trying something different from his usual coffee-with-training-wheels that most people called a mocha. Partly, he was just enjoying something different, but he also partly liked looking the part of a modern bohemian, drinking from an oversize ceramic cup filled with foamed milk and staring out at the Oregon rain.

Rufus was eating a piece of cake on the table in front of him. The barista hadn't asked about the stapler on James's shoulder, and James wasn't prepared to volunteer the information. But he and Rufus had both come to the conclusion that if anyone had a problem with the little strider eating his legally purchased cake, then they could take it up with the guild. He still thought *guild* was the wrong term, but James was *pretty* sure a stapler wasn't anything that was wrong or illegal to keep as a pet, or take into coffee shops, or feed cake. Especially not feed cake, judging by how quickly Rufus was demolishing the strawberry and cream concoction in front of him.

And he was tired of hiding.

It was strange, to James, how quickly he fell into patterns of what was normal. It had been not even a year since he'd discovered the semisacred geometry of the Office, since he'd stepped through that tear in normality and into a world of wonder and nightmare. And already, he was so used to it. Not bored, but accepting, adapting. To the point that when the girl behind the counter asked him if he had any plans for the weekend, he had to catch himself from talking about engagement tactics for illusionary cats.

His life had literal magic in it now. From the things El had told him about her dungeon, there were a lot of things out there that hewed closer to mana pools and spell lists than their own use of blue orbs. But beyond that, he fought monsters. He hoarded knowledge and experience and small powers that added up to him being something a lot more than human right now. He spent eight hours a week that didn't exist in a place that wasn't accessible by normal space, exploring sentient geometry that should not be.

It was so goddamn cool, it hurt. But it was also becoming normal. Not just normal, but part of him, part of who he was. And his circle of trust wasn't wide enough to contain his desire to share.

He didn't know what normal meant. But he knew that, for him, it was stifling and choking.

He couldn't tell his parents that he wasn't wasting away in a dead-end job anymore. He could barely tell his sister—and James had some serious concerns there, too—and she was more or less a cool person sometimes. She seemed to have accepted that it was real; she'd *been there* for the last stand. But it was like the impact of the information had just leaked out of her. Super worrying.

Still, it wasn't like James could go to a therapist or a counselor or anything. Or rather, he *could*, but it had to be Sarah or Lua, people who were in on it. He couldn't see a normal-ass, boring, baseline human to talk about his problems.

He could maybe write a blog. Actually, he could maybe just start turning his life into a narrative and write a book. But, as cool as that sounded, it still wouldn't give him the connection he craved. At most, it would get the actual Wizard Police on his head. At least, it would give him a laugh to hear that his life was too unrealistic. All James wanted was to be able to tell someone, anyone he wanted, that he planned on taking a hatchet to a hostile ball of CAT-5 cable tomorrow night.

"What do you think about what normal means?" James idly asked Rufus as the stapler tried to jam more cake into his metal maw.

Rufus froze midbite and slowly pivoted to look up at James, his large central eye glittering under the frosting stuck to it. With deliberate, meaningful gestures, he stuck his forelegs out to indicate the cake and then tilted them back to indicate himself. Then he gave a forward bob, prompting his friend to really *think* about the question he'd just asked.

"Yeeeeeah," James drawled out, leaning back in his chair with his cup. "Yeah, I'm with you, buddy."

"Um . . . excuse me." James looked up at the sound of a young man's voice. The kid was wearing a damp T-shirt with a printed image of a banana on it, dark cloth over slightly less dark skin. He pushed up his glasses nervously, fidgeting as he got James's attention. "We were curious . . ." He pointed over his shoulder at a table on the other side of the main room of the coffee shop, where a duo of other obvious nerds sat, stacks of cards visible on the table indicating a game in progress. "Um . . ."

James blinked once, then looked back down at Rufus, who hadn't paused in demolishing his dessert. "Oh. Yeah, I was wondering if anyone was going to ask," he told the kid.

"Right. So . . . what is that?" the teen asked, pointing a somewhat accusatory finger at Rufus's cake-covered form.

"It's a stapler," James answered, desperately trying to keep a straight face.

The answer was delivered so directly that it caught the kid off guard. He nodded a couple times and turned as if to leave before he paused, pulled together his courage, and turned back to James. "Really?"

"Nope," James said, absolutely failing to hide a smile.

"Okay. So what is it?"

James raised an eyebrow. "What if it's a secret?" he asked.

"I wanna know, though. We have a bet."

"Weird thing to bet on. Are you guys playing Magic?" James redirected, enjoying the hell out of himself.

It was not lost on him that literally the one thing he was just pining for had dropped into his lap, but that didn't change the fact that he still had to at least pretend to have a veneer of operational security. Also, now that he was actually presented with the option . . . well, a group of high schoolers wasn't exactly James's first choice for people he wanted to talk to. He was young enough he still remembered high school, and hindsight had showed him that almost no one was really a good person at the time, himself included.

"No! I mean, yes!" the kid stammered. "Wait, no, come on! You gotta tell us what that is. Is it a robot or something?"

At this point, James was starting to feel a seed of actual irritation that the kid wasn't taking the hint. James was sitting here, politely being a lone old goat, staring out into the rain and musing on the nature of what it meant to be different, and here comes someone who was . . . actually instantly curious about the weird, instead of repulsed by it.

James made a decision. "This is Rufus," he said, waving an open palm toward the strider. "He's a species of Life we call striders. Capital *L*, lowercase *s*," James explained, absolutely failing to clarify. "Honestly, I'm probably not going to go into detail on that. This really is something that I shouldn't probably be doing. *But!*" He held up a finger, forestalling the protests. "If you've got an extra deck over there, I promise to be suitably cryptic to your friends so you can win your bet, and we can see if Rufus can learn to play Magic." He cocked an eyebrow at the high schooler, who stared at him like he'd just grown an extra head.

The look the kid gave him made James realize that, whatever the nature of normal really was, he was still at that age where teenagers assumed that he was an adult. And that adults didn't make jokes.

That stung more than not being able to tell his mom he was learning how to kill things with an axe.

But then, after a few seconds of puzzling it out, like he'd just been presented with a dry British panel show for the first time, the kid's face cracked into a smile and he burst out laughing.

"Yeah!" he said. "Sure! I've got mono red, if you want?"

James nodded back, bobbing his head to the invisible beat of the world around him. "I bet Rufus could puzzle that out. You know how to set people on fire, right?" he asked the strider rhetorically.

Rufus shrugged before miming firing a gun. The movement got a flinch of motion out of the teenager still standing by the table. He looked at the strider like it was a particularly egregious tarantula.

"Good enough for me," James said. "Grab the cake and let's go say hi to your friends. What did *you* bet on?" he asked, standing and stretching his legs.

And for just a little while, the rain and the worries were forgotten.

"I've been less afraid of things lately," James spoke aloud to Rufus.

They'd left the café and James's ephemeral friends behind and were out walking again. The rain had picked up, but despite the chilling air and the oncoming storm, James wasn't cold. He had to raise his voice to be heard over the sporadic traffic as he and Rufus walked down the sidewalk, passing by apartment complexes interspersed with shopping centers as they made their way home.

Rufus had absolutely no time for the rain. It had been interesting at first, but it turned out that cold *was* a sensation that striders could feel, and Rufus had decided he'd rather stop feeling it. So he was huddled, as best he could, inside the hood of James's jacket. He was also trying to be a good listener, giving James taps to the back of the head as prompts to continue talking.

James felt a tap on the back of his head and startled alert. He'd trailed off again while eyeing an oncoming truck, making sure it wasn't about to send a curbside puddle airborne and into James's face. "Oh, right! Less afraid." He wiped rain off his forehead. "I think it's a side effect of knowing there's a path to immortality out there. Seriously, I dunno how much staplers think about existential dread, but for me it's . . . often. Really often. And just having the knowledge that there's an orb out there that adds to life span is kinda *the* game changer for me, even beyond the dungeons themselves."

He went quiet for a minute as they walked past a couple in reflective vests pulling bikes up onto the sidewalk; the rain was coming down so much now it was starting to turn the bike lanes into more rivers than road. James nodded at the duo as he walked past, and then continued with a grin when he felt Rufus tapping at his skull again.

"Thing is, a lot of it isn't even stuff I should have been afraid of. Just things like talking to people, social anxiety, that sorta thing. I guess it always felt so immutably permanent before, but now? Now I could have a million years to fix that. So why stress it? But by *not stressing it*, it turns out that there was never a problem, and everything could always have been fine, and I wasted a decade of my life worrying about things that literally did not matter." James snorted, droplets of rainwater splashing off his soaked face as he shook his head in annoyance. "And all I needed to learn this secret of human interaction and mental stability was literal real-life magic. Rad." He laughed bitterly to himself.

He paused at a crosswalk, mentally tallying the distance back to the apartment. It wasn't that far; his walk hadn't taken him more than the required distance to get coffee, after all. It was just that being dripping wet was starting to wear thin. James leaned on the corner's light pole, stretching out his legs while he waited for the light to change. He was silent for a long time, stewing in that own internal bitterness, before there was another light tap from his jacket.

At first, he didn't respond. It wasn't something he had words for at the moment.

He *was* bitter. He was angry and frustrated. But unlike so many other things in his life, this time it was intensely personal. This wasn't like the resentment of having an inescapable job change his schedule on a whim, or the sour taste of having to put up with a high school's worth of bullies. It wasn't even the anger at the dungeon, thinking it got to take lives like a bored god. It was something else, something that simmered in his chest and with a dark whisper reminded him that *he could have fixed this whenever he wanted.*

James was mad at himself. Because it had always only been himself, not being as good as he wanted to be.

He jolted back to alertness as Rufus half crawled out of the hood and pulled his attention to the changed crosswalk light. Patting the strider back to slightly less soaked safety, James started moving again, in silence this time.

He was almost back to his front door when his good mood for the day caught back up to him.

"You know," he said to Rufus, "the one thing I don't think I'd ever have been okay with before was this. Taking you out on a walk, the coffee shop, that sorta thing." He smiled as he started to climb the apartment stairs. "I've spent basically this whole time being afraid of the Wizard Police or something like it. Or of just being too weird for people to handle. But now, I dunno. I feel pretty good."

James opened the door then and took the two of them inside just as the rain started to die down.

"Thanks for listening," he told Rufus as he slung his coat off and helped the strider extricate himself from the back of it.

Rufus nodded heavily. *Of course*, he wanted to say. Of course he'd listen. They were friends, after all.

"James, what is all this?" Anesh asked as he came back through the door. Alanna wasn't with him, so either she'd met a terrible high school–induced fate or this was the Anesh who'd been doing math tutoring. "Also, hi!" he added cheerfully.

James looked down at the table, currently covered in piles and piles of expensive cardboard. "This is what remains of my Magic card collection. Rufus learned to play today, and we're building him a deck."

Anesh looked down at the table sadly. "Ah. And here I thought we'd buried this so deep that no man or god could once more dredge it up."

"No, we're not doing dredge. It's more of a control shell, but we're seeing what I've got before committing to anything." Rufus bobbed his torso sagely, pushing forward James's worn and ancient copy of Upheaval for consideration. "Yes, perfect. I was looking for this," James said, adding the card to one of the many piles in front of him. "So, how's your day been?" he asked Anesh casually.

"Normal," Anesh replied, still hovering, as if afraid that sinking down onto the couch would drag him into the card game on display here. "Yours?"

"Not bad, not bad." James let the words roll casually off his tongue. "Went on a walk with Rufus. Met some people in a coffee shop that taught him to play *this*. Well, I say 'people,' but I mean 'teenagers.' Wandered around for a bit longer, came home, started a YouTube channel, and now I'm doing this."

Anesh blinked at him, slowly and deliberately. "Sorry, what was that middle part?"

"The YouTube channel?" He didn't wait for Anesh to confirm that this was absolutely not what he'd meant. "Remember that aux cable I bought off Momo that converts things into nineties power metal? I've been using that to make covers of things. For the internet!"

"That's a terrible idea from an operational security perspective," Anesh said without breaking stride. "And also not what I meant. The *other* thing that's a terrible idea from an operational security perspective was what I was talking about. You just randomly introduced Rufus to people?"

"I think they thought he was an especially advanced robot," James said, nodding. "I didn't really tell them much. Just like I didn't put on my channel 'made with extranormal technology' or something." He snorted. "I'm not, like, inviting trouble. I just feel like we can afford to be a little less afraid of the consequences of enjoying our position."

"Our position being . . . ?"

"I'm still deciding on a title," James admitted. "But, you know. Being delvers. Going into the dungeon, coming out with the fun stuff. We put in the work, we should enjoy the reward."

Anesh sighed. "You know, I don't even disagree with you, really. I do wish you'd at least talked to Alanna before doing the YouTube thing. She's gonna have words for you about that."

"Long and profane words, I'm sure!" James said with good spirits. "But this is something that we need to test," he insisted, switching to a serious tone. "We need, before we ever start spreading around skulljacks and green zones and totems and whatever to know that we can start spreading these innocuous things without attracting attention. And I'd rather get a polite warning from a shadowy government agency than an assassination attempt from the same."

"Big assumptions," Anesh mused.

"I'm mostly backward justifying the fact that I wanted to share the totally rad power metal cover of the first half of *Hamilton*."

"And what happens when you get an assassination attempt over blatant copyright violation?" Anesh asked.

"Overwhelming retaliation," James deadpanned back.

"Good to know."

James stood, weaseling his way out from between the couch and the table, leaving the deck-building process to a hyperfocused Rufus. He wormed his way out to the living room floor and gave Anesh a quick, warm hug before sliding past. "It'll be fine!" he promised as he headed down the hallway. "We were already planning stuff like this anyway. I'm just stepping up the tempo."

"I'm worried about this," Anesh said.

"Me, too!" James told him. "Now do you wanna hear how many electric guitars the xenotech fit into that one song about George Washington, or not?"

There was a moment where Anesh considered, in however a small capacity as he could, if it would be better to just stop this now. To put his foot down, demand they keep their lives secret, and delete a YouTube channel before the greater internet culture found it.

Then he shook his head, rubbing at the port for the skulljack on the back of his neck. "Yeah, yeah, all right!" he called after James's retreating back. "Hang on, I'm coming!"

And for just a little while, it was the best day off ever.

"That's him."

The words were spoken by Alanna as she and Anesh sat in Anesh's beat-up old sedan out front of the local high school. It was a cold, rainy, *ugly* day, and the lack of normal classes had not stopped the place from being busy with students. There was a basketball game tonight and a slew of after-school clubs besides.

The him that Alanna was pointing out was Javier, the young man who'd turned them onto this dungeon in the first place, however unintentionally, when *their* dungeon had tried to order a hit on him. He was walking through the rain toward the school, hood pulled up around his face, but Alanna had caught a glimpse of him and had enough observation skills and Skills to keep track of the student.

"I thought he dropped out. No one's heard from him since Sarah first contacted him. And we still don't know why she got bad vibes from him," Anesh responded, peering through the rain-slick windows toward their new point of interest.

"Well, he's back. And he's armed." Alanna's mouth was a thin, unhappy line.

Anesh did a double take. "Armed?"

"Armed." She nodded once. "He's got two knives, and a handgun in the back of his pants." Weapons were almost comically easy for her to pick out on the person of the untrained student, the Skill that let her keep track of the flow of combat making it child's play to spot.

"Should we stop him?" Anesh asked. "He's probably here for the dungeon, but I don't want to sit by while a school shooting happens."

"Sarah didn't say he was unstable or anything like that, just that he gave her a bad feeling. That said, we should follow him. I bet he knows a lot that we need to know about the breach and the other side. We'll just have to hope that everyone's in the gym and no one stops us in the halls." She popped the door of the car open, letting in the sound of rain and the smell of muddy grass. "And call James," Alanna ordered. "His day off is over. Time to check this place out."

CHAPTER 25

"All right, we're here. What's the sitch?" James asked as he and Anesh strode down the stone ramp toward Alanna and Anesh.

"First off, just because we're in a high school doesn't mean you get to revert to slang," Alanna started, ticking off the point on her fingers like she had a whole presentation prepared about how James wasn't allowed to say "sitch."

She didn't get to go that far; Anesh cut her off. "The kid went in earlier, we assume. Didn't catch up in time, so we've been waiting here for you. The breach is open, we don't know how long for, but if he's in there, we can always follow him out. Or just ask."

"So you want to go in? Now?" James asked, eyebrows raised. He turned to the Anesh at his side, who was currently pulling a coiled ethernet cable out of his pocket and tossing one end to the other Anesh. "I know I was saying we should up the tempo, but this is a bit much."

"The breach seems to be open at pretty random times," Alanna said. "We haven't been able to catch it when it's convenient to us, and I'm starting to suspect that's the problem."

The four of them shut up as a couple of students in band uniforms rounded the corner behind them and walked past chatting. One of them did a double take at the two Aneshes, but neither of them said anything about the four adults hanging out in front of a high school boiler room. Quite the opposite, really—their eyes just seemed to slide over the group, or maybe just the space around the door.

James set his mouth in a thin line. There was definitely an antimeme here. He wanted to say he could feel it, but the problem really came down to the fact that he *couldn't*. None of them could except Secret. That's what made them so damn dangerous.

"Secret, you feel that?" he asked the open air.

"Hmm." The low humming noise came back from his ethereal passenger. Secret was a strange thing to James sometimes, only loosely associated with the act of having a body. James had actually assumed that the infomorph had locked himself into a physical form, but when he'd asked Secret to come along on this one, the half-asleep serpent had simply shed his physical form and looped a ghostly tail across James's chest. "I feel nothing. It is hiding."

"So there is something," James prompted.

"There is nothing, which is hiding from me," Secret said cryptically. Perhaps as punishment for being woken up. "I cannot find it. I know it is there. It is bad at hiding. It is not hiding itself; I do not think it understands that it is not alone."

"Antimeme." Alanna half spat the word out, and the others nodded. Anesh nodded in time with himself as the two bodies synced up their minds. "I'm getting sick of these," Alanna admitted. "No offense, Secret. But it seems like we keep running into 'don't look at me' fields."

"Dungeons gotta dungeon somehow." James shrugged. "Can't do that if literally everyone stumbles in. I guess? No, that actually doesn't make any sense, unless they're all actively aware of the threat of, like, military intervention. Okay, put that on the list."

"Which list?" Anesh asked in unison.

"The list of worrying thoughts. Are we going in or not?" James asked. "I brought a bag full of machetes if we are." He hoisted aloft the duffel bag in his left hand.

It didn't just have machetes in it, but that statement wasn't too far from pure truth. They'd had a bit of fun making up what James called "starter packs" of dungeoning equipment for all the new people they'd hired, and so there'd been a whole lineup of duffel bags just sitting there at their secret lair. Perfect for an improvised trip to a new hell dimension.

"We absolutely should go in," Alanna said. "We don't know what schedule this thing is on, we can't reliably find the kid who apparently does know, but now he's in there, and also, have you guys noticed the number of broken phones and backpacks strewn around here? These things are covered in dust or water damage; people aren't coming back to pick them up." She flicked her eyes at the rift in space before them. "That means it's eating people. And that makes it our problem."

"We absolutely should *not* go in." Anesh spoke simultaneously with himself. "For exactly that reason. Grade schoolers aren't exactly what I'd call 'ready for a fight,' but some of these people must have been in athletics. Track and field or American football or something, right? That marks this place as dangerous. Clearly more obviously lethal than the Office."

"Also, what happened to these kids?" James asked quietly. "There isn't some massive missing-persons case or serial killer manhunt. Which means this place just totally blocked everyone out of being remembered. Maybe being recorded, too. I hate that."

"Exactly why we should scope it out," Alanna insisted. "Look, we're probably the people in the best position to do this, and I include calling the police in that list this time. We've got more enhancements than ever. We've got Secret with us. We can do this."

"What could possibly go wrong," James stated dryly.

Anesh and Alanna both grimaced, while Secret simply flatly replied with a "Do not say that. It is a curse."

There was a pause. "What, really?" James asked.

"No, but do not say it regardless. It makes me nervous," Secret replied.

James sighed theatrically. "Fine, fine. Okay, so, one vote for, one vote against."

"Two," both Aneshes chimed in.

"Oh, that's not fair. Well, I vote for. I want to explore this place, and Alanna's right. We don't know what schedule the breach is on, scouting the place is a good preliminary goal, and we absolutely need to find out if anyone is still alive in there."

"Oh, shit, I hadn't even thought of that," Alanna said. "I just assumed they'd already be dead."

Anesh begrudging shook his head. "We've seen a few times now that dungeon spaces seem to have a habit of taking prisoners, in one way or another," he said with a sigh as he ran a hand through his wiry black hair. "Okay, fine. I change my vote."

On James's shoulders, Secret bobbed his head. "That is good, as I would have voted for regardless," he admitted. "And so we are united in purpose."

"I forgot he got a vote," Anesh admitted sheepishly in a quiet voice when Alanna shot him a smug look.

"All right, sanity check," James said, cracking the door to the boiler room open and leading the group of them in. The air was hot, dry, and warped in that strange way that the breach here caused. This was no subtle door that displaced the real door, or a staircase that led farther than it should have. This was simply a hole cut in space, hostile and angry. "Secret, any outside influence on us?"

"No," the memetic life replied. "We are, as you say, in the clear."

"I don't say that. Alanna, Anesh, gear?" James knelt among the scattered backpacks and unzipped the duffel bag, pulling out the thick blades of machetes and passing them around, along with gloves. "I don't have armor with me, but I did get something for you." He handed Alanna a pair of gloves made of a thicker black cloth. They had a raised rectangle on the back of each hand, which was filled with lead shot. "Riot gloves, for when you inevitably need to punch something."

"Aw, I love you, too," she said, pulling them onto her hands with a strangely soft smile. "What else?"

"Blues slotted?" Anesh asked. Alanna and James answered at the same time. They both still had charges on making asphalt or breaking delicate electronic devices. "Okay, good. I've got three shots left of 'melt copper,' so maybe." Anesh eyed the metal of the piping around them.

"How *do* blues absorbed work with you?" James suddenly thought to ask.

"They sync up when we do, just like the yellow orbs. But the charges are shared when I do, and I can't absorb new ones past my limit. I haven't tried it, but I suspect that if we let ourselves drift too long, one of us would just lose it. Or maybe not—maybe it copies. It's a mystery."

"I need to figure out how to absorb an orange," James grumbled. "I want more of me."

"One of you is plenty." Alanna tapped him on the head. "Anything else?"

There was one more thing. James tossed a controller adapter to Anesh, who slotted it into his skulljack and quickly assumed control of a small camera drone that buzzed into the air next to them. And *then* they were ready.

James rose to his feet, hoisting his own weapon, a heavy metal baseball bat. "Are we sure we want to do this?" he asked.

He wasn't really asking. It was more of . . . seeking consent. Seeking affirmation. Not so much making sure that his partners were in this with him but that they were ready for it. Willing to take the plunge, yes, but also assured that they were in it together.

Two Aneshes nodded, Alanna gave him a "Absolutely," and Secret tightened around James's torso in assent.

"All right," he said, hoisting the duffel in one hand and the bat in the other. "Let's fuck it up." James went first, slipping through the hole in the wall and dangling his feet over the edge, bracing his hands on the sides of the slick pipes that lined the walls. It felt like dropping down a throat. "Well, it's familiar at least," he grumbled, remembering a similar plunge into the Office.

He let go, and he and Secret fell, heart pounding, as Alanna and Anesh hurried to move in behind them.

"I figured out how to soak up the yellows today," Momo casually dropped into the conversation she was having with Sarah.

The two young women were sitting at one of the cafeteria tables, eating expertly made shoyu chicken from their new resident chef, and watching that same chef along with three other delvers get their asses collectively handed to them in unarmed combat by Simon and James. The two friends were linked up wirelessly and had expanded their martial arts training from fighting each other to challenging everyone in the building to bouts. At once, if possible.

When Nate had seen it, he'd handed off keeping an eye on tonight's soup to Harvey and gone over to try to instill some leadership into the losing trio.

"You! Neil! You're huge! Don't scowl at me, you pussy, *use it!* Keep on their sides; go for grabs and pins. Make them *work* for it if they want to hit anyone! And you, Debby?"

"Deb," the now-licensed nurse replied. "Just Deb."

"Great. Stop trying to kick them. You're overextending! Go in when they're pinned and keep them down, or focus on being a problem they can't take their eyes off!" The tattooed man had plucked his glasses off, tossed them onto the table where Sarah and Momo were sitting, and rolled up his sleeves like getting in a fight with internet-enabled black belts was just another day for him. "They can read each other's minds, but who cares? Marines can do that, too! And you can still punch marines!" He'd thrown the first punch in the next bout, and Simon and his James suddenly had a hell of harder time.

They seemed to be having fun, though.

"Good job on the yellows. Have you slept at all?" Sarah asked Momo as the two of them watched the devolving brawl in front of their table.

"Pssssshaw." Momo tilted her head back before whipping it back down as she ended the drawn-out dismissal. "Sleep is for people who didn't collect a whole strider nest worth of tiny orbs!"

"That's not true at all." Sarah tried to play it off, but she was a bit worried. "When they run out, you'll crash. Sleep is good for you, spookypants!"

Momo spoke around a mouthful of chicken. "Bah. I need more time. I'm close to figuring out limiters on the totems, I think. Also I want to absorb the orange Simon gave me, but I don't know how yet, and I need time. *Also* I still haven't seen El do magic! And I wanna do magic! I wanna be a war witch!"

There was a turn of phrase that made Sarah giggle. "Oh, please. You're much more of a science witch," she told the younger girl. "War is for boys." Sarah casually gestured to the scene of their head chef getting his knees kicked out from under him by two perfectly timed strikes from each side, courtesy of a localized hive mind.

"That's weird to hear you say. Like, weirdly sexist, kinda? It makes me feel not great, anyway." Momo quirked an eyebrow as she waved toward the ongoing spar. "Also, Deb is there, too! Look, she just hit Simon!"

"Holy shit, she hit him with a chair." Sarah almost choked on her drink. "Is that allowed?" She looked around, like she was waiting for a ref or something to step in and inform Deb that yelling at someone you'd just cut down at the backs of the knees with a piece of furniture to "stay down" was unsportsmanlike. "That shouldn't be allowed."

"The *point* is that I want to do magic." Momo pouted.

"The point, young lady, is that El is . . . not sharing much." Sarah sighed. It was a tired sigh. The kind that crept out when you were trying really hard to not be mad at someone who was trying your patience. It was a sigh Sarah made a lot these days. "We know what three spells she has: indexing, speed boost, and . . . well, she said 'repair,' but she said it in the voice that means she's hiding something. We know, if we can believe her, that her mana pool is based off velocity. But we don't know how she learned them, and they don't seem to have rituals attached that we can replicate." Sarah called out a sudden "boo" toward the gym mats, cupping her hands around her mouth as Deb stood triumphant, holding her chair over her head like a broadsword. "She likes you—maybe you can get more from her. But you've been busy, and she's been sleeping or 'out.' And we *aren't* keeping her prisoner."

"I'm pretty sure she just goes out to remind us that she can leave if she wants to," Momo said timidly, a bit put off by Sarah's tone.

Sarah rubbed her face with one open hand, realizing how harsh she sounded. "Yeah, you're probably right. I don't *want* to keep her here, either. It's not that I don't like her, it's just that she seems so angry all the time, especially at James, and over something that was an accident."

"I'll talk to her about it," Momo promised. "We're supposed to go bowling tonight!"

"Wait, seriously?" Sarah questioned. No one had asked her if *she* wanted to go bowling.

Momo read Sarah's face, narrowing her eyes as she sent out her empathic feelers. "Do . . . do yooooou want to come . . ."

"Nah, I'm good." Sarah grinned. "You have fun. Really! Be a normal teenager for a while."

Momo glanced around at the walls and high windows of the back area of their literal secret lair, a building that had two basements occupying the same space, where she lived with her dog made out of a magnetic field and did half research half arcane guesswork on condensed balls of information and power. But only the red ones. Nearby, her teammates, who were plugged into each other's brains, were being pulled off the gym mats by a nurse, a drone enthusiast, and a chef, and that last guy was someone who'd literally been hired not even a week ago and somehow had adapted to this like it wasn't a bizarre fever dream.

"Yeah, too late. Also I continue to be twenty . . . something. Fuck, I don't even know how old I am, with the . . ." She rubbed at the skulljack on her neck; the thing was useful, but a constant reminder of a violation. "So hey, what are you up to with the rest of the night?" Momo asked of Sarah, casually turning their conversation back to normal things.

"Eh. Waiting for James to drop by, mostly. We're gonna go visit Pendragon."

"Where'd he go, anyway? He was here earlier, grabbing a bag or something," Momo asked, curious, as she collected their empty plates to go pile in the kitchen.

"Hardware store, I think?" Sarah tapped her chin. "Hmm. I actually don't remember what he said. Maybe ask JP?"

"Nah, it's fine, I was just curious. I'm sure he's all right. He's an adult." Momo casually mocked her guild leader and personal—secret—hero.

The two made eye contact as they thought about it for a second, and then both stood up at the same time.

"We should really go ask JP," Sarah stated.

"Yeah. Because he's fine, but . . ."

"Yeah."

James hit the ground on his hands and knees, coughing up a sour liquid. It took him a second to realize he was vomiting, spilling orange stomach acid onto the pitted and marked concrete floor below him. The sudden transition had left his stomach reeling, his brain feeling like he'd been struck repeatedly in the head, and when he'd dropped out in midair, left to fall to the floor with no warning, his lunch had come back the way it had gone.

Something had gone wrong. Something had been ripped away from him as he was falling, a sharp tugging in the dark like things were being plucked off his person at high speed.

Next to him, there was a tooth-grinding *crunch* as an Anesh landed, stumbled, and slammed shoulder first into the sharp concrete of the wall. The walls here were that awkward jagged texture that schools used to love so much, crystal spires of unpolished rock jutting out, just waiting for a student to trip into it. Or be thrown there by sudden, violent teleportation.

Alanna landed mostly upright and half caught the other Anesh, but that Anesh was in a similar state to James, spilling the contents of his stomach across the floor.

Secret was fine. Already alert, perched protectively above his father's prone form. A blue guardian mantle, ready to snap at anything that approached. He had no stomach to empty, no lunch to lose.

There was a vile smell in the air, and not just from two people puking in the last minute. It was sour and wet. The kind of wet you get when you leave a leak dripping for far too long and the mold and mildew build up until it's just not worth it to clean it with anything except a flamethrower. And under all that, the iron bite of old, spilled blood. Not fresh, but not dried. How could anything dry down here, in the damp and heat?

The four humans blinked as their eyes adjusted to the gloom. It wasn't dark here, not at all. But it wasn't well lit, either. The light didn't come from anywhere in particular; it was more like everything had been rendered just so that no one would trip on anything.

A concrete floor surrounded them, with drainage grates at a handful of seemingly random spots around the room. The room they were in was broad and mostly empty, maybe twenty-five feet or so across. Mostly featureless, except for the set of rusted showerheads sticking out of the wall at odd intervals.

Well, that, and the graffiti. And the body.

As soon as James was on his feet and looking around, he spotted the huddled human form by the back wall and rushed over as best he could on wobbly feet. His motion drew the attention of Anesh and Alanna, who were still looking around, gazing at the stacked rows of piping overhead that made up the low ceiling. They came to join him, with one Anesh keeping his eyes on the only door that led out of the room.

As soon as James knelt over the still form, he knew he wasn't looking at someone alive. Something in his gut told him so. But he still checked for a pulse and jerked his hand back as several long, flat beetles crawled out of the coat of the deceased. With an angry snarl, he flattened the three of them with his gloved hand, watching a few strange red sparks jump out of the squashed carapaces before going back to verify that this person was, in fact, dead.

With sad eyes and a pang in his heart that had nothing to do with the disorientation of their arrival, James turned the kid over. He couldn't stop himself from needing to know.

He had been maybe fourteen, tops. On his head, there was still a cloth wrap, askew and rotting but clearly in the Sikh style. His eyes were wide-open, though one of them had been gnawed out by something vile; the other one showed a terrified kid who didn't understand what was happening to him. In one hand, he was clutching a notebook, torn in half and soaked in some brown liquid.

James pried the text out of his hands like it was a sacred object and flipped it open as best he could. Most of it was empty, but on a random page in the middle, written in red ink, was the line "Tell my dad I'm sorry. I will die before I . . ."

James closed the book and pressed his hand over the boy's eye, closing it for the last time.

Then he stood up and turned to his companions. "Okay," he started to say, before looking down at his hands. "Where the fuck is my bat?"

"Our machetes are gone, too," Alanna noted. "So's the bag." She checked her pockets. "Swiss Army Knife's gone. Wallet's still here, but phone is gone, too. I felt a bunch of stuff getting dragged off me."

"In retrospect, we really should have just piled our phones up by the entrance. I hope they didn't break when they got flung back out," Anesh said. "Drone is gone, too," he said, rubbing the controller still plugged into his head. "But not . . ."

"Yeah, that's not what I'm worried about right now," James growled out.

He was angry. He was beyond angry. He'd known, in the abstract, that this place was dangerous. But here, right here, in the *entry hall*, was a dead human *child*. Covered in bugs, on a stained floor, surrounded by rusted metal and concrete and graffiti. He had died alone and afraid and James had already thought of six different things to try to see how much structural damage a dungeon could take before it *fucking died.*

But he didn't let that show right now. Instead, he took as deep a breath as he could, given the damp and disgusting air, rose to his feet, and swept his eyes around the room.

"The graffiti is human," Alanna muttered.

"Hey!" James tried to muster up some of a humorous mood despite his simmering rage. "You don't get to make cryptic statements about reality! That's *Secret's* job."

Secret decided to ruin James's fun, chiming in with "I am not the authority on humans. That is your job. I am here to safeguard your identities. And perhaps to make a different category of crypticism."

"Thanks," James huffed dryly. "Okay, what's up with the graffiti?"

It was all over the walls, disorganized and drawn in scratches of rust and concrete. Messages left by those who had come before.

"No one is going to help." "First right leads to . . ." "Was here" "This room isn't safe." "Don't run."

"Huh," James said as he scanned it, running his gloved fingers over the space in front of the words *was here*. "This one feels weird."

"Something is there," Secret said, snapping several of his eyes onto it. "A worm. I shall simply . . ." His coils rippled, and he darted forward through a direction that hurt James's eyes to watch. A second later, there was the impression of a pair of leviathan jaws closing around an unsuspecting minnow. And then . . .

Just like that, there were more words.

"'Mike Yager was here.'" Anesh read the name that had been there the whole time. "I wonder who that was," he asked softly as one of him pulled out a pocket notebook and made a note of the persona. "Um . . ." He held the paper up a second later by two worried fingers as the very name he'd written was concealed again. On the wall, similarly, the graffiti was once again partially hidden.

There was a deep growl from Secret, whose myriad eyes darted around the room, seeing things kept unknown from the others. "They cluster like grubs. So many of them here, waiting for a name to feed upon. This place is disgusting."

No one had ever heard Secret call something disgusting before.

"Okay. No names. Super." James spat onto the floor, clearing the taste of bile from his tongue. "Let's get the hell out of this place," he said. "Who's on point?"

Alanna took point, followed by Anesh, then James and Anesh bringing up the rear. Secret didn't stick to any singular one of them, instead looping his ghostly coils around their feet intermittently. Occasionally, he would lash out to snap with one of his many rows of teeth at something none of them could see but was presumably one of the small buggish antimemes here.

The only exits from this room were a few gaping hallways. Though calling them *hallways* was generous at best and a flagrant lie at worst. They stood around one of the gaps, looking into the tube leading into the blackness, concrete floor occasionally broken up underfoot by random encroachments of pipes replacing the stable ground. The pipes were made of a dozen different substances, some metal, some ceramic, some plastic; there was no order to it.

The piping also surrounded them on all sides. The rock of the walls was barely visible through small gaps in the tubes that covered it, and overhead, the ceiling was completely concealed by those same liquid routes. They could all hear fluids moving through the spaces from time to time, water, or worse, flowing around them in random intervals.

The strange, pervasive light that had let them see in the room they'd dropped into was absent here. Instead, there was just the light from behind them, the pitch-black of the hallway and its tripping hazards ahead, and the pale, unreal glow of Secret as he drifted in and out of actual space.

"I hate this," James caught Anesh muttering to himself as they steeled themselves as a group and began to walk slowly down into the abyss, picking a tunnel. Not the first left, though. James decided to trust the graffiti.

"No phones, so no easy flashlights. No bag, so no flashlights," Alanna griped. "I don't suppose anyone has a flare in their pants?"

"No, I'm just happy to see you," James responded, almost by reflex.

Alanna made a face like she'd just eaten an entire lemon in one go. Not that the boys appreciated it in the darkness. "Stay close, then," she said, "No getting separated here."

No one had any arguments about that.

They trudged on, shuffling footsteps probing uncertain ground as they walked. Every now and then James felt a draft from one side of their group, what he was pretty sure were side passages. But they weren't ready to start taking twists and turns yet, not until they had a little more of a picture of the place.

Time started to lose meaning as they walked. They were going slowly, so everyone knew that they hadn't gone that far, but it was so easy to forget that. To feel like they'd descended into the bottomless pit and had been falling for years and years.

Then Alanna broke the spell by letting out some kind of startled barbarian yawp ahead of them, sending electric adrenaline coursing through the veins of Anesh and James. The two of them heard bellowed swears and the sound of boots smashing into concrete and chitin with equal vigor. In the off-color light of Secret's passing, they caught glimpses of Alanna pulverizing the fist-size beetle that had made the fatal mistake of skittering across her foot, the creature's death accompanied by a small spray of red sparks that lit up the darkness far more than the serpent form of Secret did. Briefly.

"Jesus Christ, are you okay? Don't fucking scare me like that!" James didn't wait for a response to the question before chastising Alanna, holding one hand to his suddenly aching chest while he clapped the other on her shoulder.

"I hate bugs," she explained, in a way that wasn't an explanation at all, crushing another fleeing insect underfoot and generating another burst of red light that briefly lit up the corridor.

"Why do they keep sparking when they die?" Anesh asked as one of him caught his breath, trying to distract from the shock of the moment.

James made an annoyed face that continued to go unseen, but his tone conveyed how he felt just as well. "Probably the dungeon giving us some kind of radiation poisoning for breaking its toys," he guessed. "Also, stomp on another one of those," he directed Alanna.

"I don't want to find more of them," she grumbled, but she started sweeping her eyes across the floor. Secret hovered nearby, a gloomy spotlight on the stone and pipes poking up underfoot, his light only extended a foot or two around him in the dark. A second later, she spotted another of the palm-size bugs and brought the heel of her boot down on it.

In the flash of light that followed its death, James didn't watch the sparks, but instead the walls around them. And in that moment of light, something stood out to him.

"There's a door here," he said, holding out his hands and running them across the pipes on the wall. There it was, a small rectangle of space where the pipes sank into the wall at ninety-degree angles before emerging again a short distance later. No doorknob, but the lines around it were clear. This was a point of entry. To *somewhere*. "Someone give me a hand here. Secret, can you light this up?"

"Barely," Secret said. "But I shall try."

"Would it help if someone shared some deep secret with you?" James asked. "I could tell you I don't like *Star Trek*. Would that help?"

Secret rippled with a blue gleam as he brought his serpentine body up against the pipes surrounding the strange door. "No, as that is not exactly a well-kept gem of information. But I appreciate the thought."

In the thin glow he put off, they clustered close and looked at the doorframe. It was set back in the wall, but it was clearly meant to open; the rectangle of lines cut into the concrete and the texture of smooth metal gave that away.

"I don't get it. What opens this?" James asked, reaching out a hand to feel around where the doorknob should have been.

As his hand got close to making contact, there was a fiery shock to his skin, even through the glove. And in the space where he'd reached, light bloomed, a red slash of illumination, clearly shaped like the number ten. It sat there in midair for a brief second before fading back again.

"Ten *what*?" Anesh asked. "Key number ten? Ten minutes of waiting? Ten . . ."

"It's the same color," Alanna said. "As the sparks."

"Oh, fuck no." James looked around, meeting the others' eyes under the glow of Secret. All of them pressed so close like this almost made him feel a false sense of safety. "It means ten kills," he said, "Ten sparks. Are we supposed to be collecting them?" He looked down at his hand, where some of them had landed earlier when he'd smashed the small bugs crawling on the kid's corpse. "Can we see how many we have?"

As soon as he said the words, there was a brief flare of light and heat; a red three scarred into the air above the back of his hand. He felt his blood cool noticeably, as if all the energy it took to ask that was pulled out of him with a brisk force.

"I'll find more bugs," Alanna said, resigned.

Five minutes of crushing the slimy shells and stinking insides of the beetles that crawled between the floor pipes later, Alanna had amassed ten of whatever this place "awarded" them from their kills. After doing her best to wipe the worst of the rapidly solidifying goop off her boots, she stepped over to the door where James and an Anesh were standing to keep track of it and pressed her hand toward the doorknob.

It was a feeling like something being yanked out of her. Like her veins or muscles being pulled out through the palm of her hand, though it wasn't physical. Instead, a string of red light lit up the surrounding space as it streamed forward, coalescing into darkness, and the form of a door handle.

Alanna grabbed it, impetuously, and yanked the door open on rusted hinges.

The inside was a bathroom stall in absurd proportions. It was lit, though, and she and James stepped in while Anesh waited by the door, his back to the two of them as he and Secret kept an eye out for anything coming for them.

There was one toilet, though if anything in the *world* could remove the urge to take a piss, it was this one. Chunks of it were broken away, leaving jagged plastic covered in rotten, damp toilet paper, mold, and scuttling insects. It sat, strangely isolated, on the opposite side of the room from where the broken toilet paper holder was mounted on the wall. The walls were blue tile, with a host of thin black Sharpie lines or dusty white gouges leaving messages that, this time, had absolutely not been left by passing humans. The floor clung to their boots, and every step felt like walking across hot asphalt, a sticky suction feeling that pulled them down. Steam rose from where the sink ran against the wall to their left, boiling hot water splashing down into a broken ceramic basin, flooding down to the floor and the drainage grate there, a host of green and black growths feeding off the moisture.

At the corner where the far wall met the floor, there was a hole. The tile was shattered away, more so than normal, and behind it was mud and dirt, looking like it had been scooped out in a ball. Small scraps of cloth and bone sat in the dark recess, but it was otherwise empty.

The whole room smelled like someone had pissed on it. James nearly gagged on the stench, but Alanna just cupped a sleeve against her mouth and stepped farther in.

They each analyzed the space in a different way, but both of them came to the conclusion that unless the toilet was a mimic—something they would *never* rule out, or ever test, either—then there was nothing here that was going to try to kill them right away. Instead, at roughly the same time, they started looking around at the writing on the walls.

A lot of it was banal: names inside hearts, though the hearts were accurate human anatomy; phone numbers, with the wrong number of digits or wrong characters to actually work; random symbols that might have been gang tags or maybe extradimensional hate symbology. But some of the things written were weirdly composed sentences, and those stood out to them both.

"All right, here's a weird one," James said. "'Two trains are a hundred miles apart, traveling at fifty miles an hour. How long until everyone on board dies?'" He shook his head. "Kinda grim. This one, too, actually. It's asking what the original fourth horseman that killed people was. That's a biblical question."

Alanna poked a finger suspiciously against the ink on the tile wall where she stood. "This one says, 'two idiot children die to poison and impatience.' What the hell does that mean?"

"Oh, that's easy. Romeo and Juliet," James answered. "It's like a rough overview of the plot of the most annoying romance ever."

As soon as he finished speaking, the words began to burn with a sickly green fire. Alanna yelped and shuffled backward, falling into a smooth combat posture in case this was something hostile. But it wasn't, and instead, a couple seconds later, the writing was scoured from the wall and replaced by a scorch mark. And a burst of green sparks that fell from the scarred tile and onto James's arm. He jerked back, shaking his coat, but the small flare of light had already vanished, drawn in just like the red sparks.

"Fuck. I hate that," he said.

Anesh, watching from the door, added his own opinion to the mix. "It doesn't help that the colors look poisonous. Did you guys notice that? The red ones look like an infection, and now this green looks like toxic waste."

"This place is intentionally gross," Alanna said, glaring at the nest of scuttling, clicking bugs around the toilet bowl. "And it took our weapons away, so we have to interact with our hands."

"At least we have gloves," James said, turning his attention back to the other writing. "We should solve all of these. If answering the questions get us sparks, we will absolutely need them later. May as well stock up."

"That's RPG thinking." Alanna shook her head. "This isn't a game."

James agreed, in the abstract, but . . . "Tell that to the place that charges us in souls to open doors," he said. "This one is one hour. This one is sulfuric acid. This one is, I think, the word *conquest*." Three flares of green sparks accompanied his answering of questions, and a sweep of the surroundings showed no more of the graffiti quiz show to play. "All right. Let's go. If I get radiation poisoning, someone make sure that my casket is solid lead," he joked without a smile.

Alanna followed him out of the room, scowling in perfectly rational concern. "Don't do that! We don't know if that's dangerous!"

"Yes, we do," James said. "Nothing here has shown us that this place doesn't have the same base rules as the other dungeons we've seen. The prizes can't kill us. They might hurt, like the 'connection' thing you two have, but they never kill us. El and Sarah both agreed with that. I'd bet that if we find food here, it'll be gross as fuck but still edible."

"I will never eat anything in this place," Alanna grumbled as they stood in the thin line of light, preparing to head back down the dark tunnel.

Secret coiled himself around the group's legs once again. "I wish that I could state the same," he said sadly, spitting *something* slightly to the side.

"Please don't actually eat the antimeme bug things," James pleaded with the infomorph as they started walking into the darkness again. "I know that they're trying to feed on names and things, and that's great, but, like . . . don't chew them?" He dropped the volume of his voice unconsciously as they stepped farther and farther from the source of light they'd discovered.

Secret declined to answer, and once again, they were moving in silence. Shuffling along to keep their feet from catching on any loose pieces of pipe or rock, a steady but quite cautious pace.

It was when there was a scratching noise from the pipes near their head that they all froze. Even Secret, who snapped dozens of eyes up to look into the dark, stopped his rotation around their feet.

The noises wasn't like the sloshing of liquids that they'd been hearing intermittently, though those noises too would often stop them for a minute or two at a time as they waited to make sure they weren't a threat. This was more like something sharp scraping against the stone and plastic of the pipes overhead.

They all waited, eyes pointed into the dark overhead, before they moved on again. But it wasn't more than thirty seconds before the noise came again, from slightly behind them but getting closer. Catching up. But there was nothing they could do except be on their guard and keep moving as best they could.

Five minutes of that, of suffering under the unknown, before James had a thought. "Hey, I just realized something," he said softly. "I've got a light source, though only a brief one. Want to see what's tailing us?"

"What . . . Oh." Anesh made the connection. "Okay. I'm ready if you are. Alanna?"

"Do it," she said, tensing up, her gloved hands balled into fists.

"How much green do I have?" James whispered aloud.

And in a flash, a number spiked into existence over the back of his right hand. He was surprised to see it was twenty, and not four like he'd expected, but he was more surprised to see the thing that had been stalking them perched in a gap in the pipes just overhead to their right.

It had a snout like a cone, tapered to a blunted point. Fur that was dull metal wire, eyes that were nothing more than hateful black beads. It had two mouths, one stacked on top of the other, two parallel rows of teeth that dripped with a grim liquid. James had never had a problem with the fact that Secret had more than one maw, but now, in this moment, he realized that was mostly because Secret had never screamed at him in a hissing voice and tried to eat him.

The thing was like a rat, if someone had taken a rat's general shape, scaled it up as far as they could, and replaced every part of it with something painful and disgusting. Exposed muscles through patches where it had no fur or skin, places where the bones poked out through its hide, and a glossy sheen where it oozed some kind of substance as it moved, a trail that glimmered across the pipe it had been stalking them on.

The burst of light didn't leave any of them with much time to adjust their eyes. But it startled the rat thing even more, and in a fight-or-flight moment, it decided to commit to an assault.

Lurching out from where it was wedged between the piping, it screamed in a horrifyingly human voice as it dived downward. It was a high-pitched wail, feminine and young, and it absolutely did not stop James from slamming his fist into the right side of its snout as it fell through the air toward him.

Momentum warred with itself for a brief moment as James's acceleration-enhanced fist and the monstrous rat's fall met. And then, a tipping point, and James felt his arm move like there was no resistance at all, sending the rat thing into the wall at high velocity.

It left a gooey splat mark against the pipe it hit, a blast of that secreted liquid that also splattered droplets onto the exposed skin of the four delvers. As it rolled to the floor, it was already landing on its feet, trying to regain control, trying to snap out with either set of fangs to dig into soft flesh and hard bone. It didn't hesitate at all to continue its violence.

Then Anesh jumped on it with both feet. And it kind of burst open.

"Oh god," he muttered with a low noise from his throat as the blood and viscera of the creature coated the wall and floor and his pant legs. "I didn't expect that. Oh, I'm gonna be sick." He didn't notice it, but his counterpart did, as did James and Alanna, that the fountain of red light coming off this thing was far stronger than those from the bugs they'd been running into.

"That seems to be the theme of this place," Alanna said, slowly lowering her guard as the sparks faded from their vision. "Was that the only one?"

"Only one I saw," James said, his blood still cold from calling up his score. "We should move faster. I want to find a way out of this fucking place." He tried to sigh, but it turned into a cough instead as the smell of the hallway and the steaming blood of the rat caught in his throat instead. "Let's go." He took the lead this time, wiping his hand on one of the stone pipes as he walked, trying to get as much of the slime from the thing off him as possible. Anesh didn't even have that option; the legs of his pants were thoroughly soaked by the blood from his aggressive maneuver, and while he didn't complain, it quickly became clear that this was a place where no one was going to be enjoying themselves tonight.

As if they hadn't known that already.

"Should we try one of these side passages?" Alanna asked, ten minutes and a few dozen beetles later. The bugs were a near-constant irritant. And while they probably weren't dangerous, they kept trying to crawl on the delvers, and they actually probably *were* quite dangerous if they dropped their guard.

"I don't want to lose track of where we are," James replied. "If we need to turn back, we know exactly how to do it. That said, if we see light coming from any one of these intersections, we should take it."

"I'll keep an eye out," Anesh said. James wasn't really surprised; Anesh had been on high alert for the last two hours. If he didn't know better, James would have assumed that Anesh hadn't even blinked.

Time once again started to blur together as they walked. They found another door, but this one demanded a hundred red sparks, which none of them had, even with the constant trickle of beetles onto their legs. They heard more sounds from farther in, the noises of steam screaming and some beast letting out a feral roar, but nothing that approached where they were. And with the tunnels so tight and echoing, it was impossible to know how far away something might be except that it wasn't close.

But eventually, after a fork in the hall and some backtracking after a dead end, they came upon something different.

"Light up ahead." Anesh had the best low-light vision out of all of them, Secret included. Even James's purple-upgraded eyesight didn't let him see in the dark. "Fan out?"

James and Alanna moved without speaking, stepping to either side, letting Anesh take a forward-facing position between them while another Anesh stood at an angle to their left, watching their backs. Secret formed into a cowl around James as they approached, ceasing his constant looping motions as his light became less needed.

The noise started to trickle in as they got closer to the arched shape of light at the end of the hallway. It was a rhythmic clacking, something beating on the floor in poorly timed unison. Every few seconds, a wave of noise washed over them, getting louder and louder as they approached. By the time they were maybe twenty feet from the glow of the room they were nearing, James could make it out much more clearly; it was the sound of plastic on stone, or stone on stone. A series of claps as objects were slammed together every ten seconds of so.

He shot a glance at Anesh. "Ready?" he asked his boyfriend. Anesh just narrowed his eyes, not wasting words on it. More than the other two, he'd been getting thirsty, and with all their supplies in the bag that hadn't come with them, a few hours of marching wasn't his idea of a good time. "All right." James tilted his head up at Alanna. "Let's do this," he said as he stepped forward.

The room resolved in their vision as they walked into it, the barrier of sharp light in the darkness pushed aside as their eyes adjusted rapidly. The floor and walls were much like the room they'd fallen into originally, but it was wider around, and more of a circular shape. Across the walls, protrusions of stone and brass extended, looking like stadium seating that was designed to trip and slice at the ankles. The floor was splattered with dark stains, angry wet patches that stank of old iron and blood. At the base of those jutting spaces around the walls, off-balance school lockers sat. They were in a variety of styles, but they all had gleaming padlocks holding shut rusted doors and bent metal grating.

The first thing Anesh saw was the hole on the far side of the room. That angry, gaping black maw, like pipes were pulling apart the wall, looked *very* familiar to how they'd gotten down here. It was most likely their one exit from this nightmare of pipes and concrete. The first thing that *James* saw was the gate built across the thing. More of a portcullis, really. It was made of splintered pipes, jagged metal welded together to form something that looked like a tetanus shot waiting to happen. There were no chains or pulleys attached to it, no obvious way of opening it. It just sat there, showing them the way out but barring the way.

The first thing Alanna noticed were the creatures here. To be fair, James and Anesh saw them, too, just a half second after her.

They were bipedal, four feet tall, five at the max, and many of them carried clubs or crude spears made out of the piping material. Maybe two dozen of them in total; they lined those jutting sets of seating around the walls, looking down on the floor of the rounded room. Every few seconds, they would clumsily bang the butts of their weapons into the floor, letting out a rattling din that echoed through across the pipes and down the halls.

They had fur. Fur that looked mangy and unkempt, but real fur. It jutted from their skin in patchwork patterns, multiple colors adorning each of the creatures. Brown, black, some even a pale cream, though all their colorations were tainted with mold growths and a sticky red substance that no one assumed was paint.

Where they did not have fur, they had chitin. Brown beetle shell like a cockroach that covered most of their bodies, especially their joints. It glistened in the light, dripping secretions running down it and matting their fur where the two met. They would frequently itch at the lines between their materials, as if they were sewn together and uncomfortable with the divides. They scratched themselves with three-fingered clawed hands, and every one of them had three arms. Though they always had at least one arm per side, where the third one sat seemed random for each of their monstrous shapes.

Their faces were wide triangles. Antennae jutted out of the back of their skulls, and sunken, mammalian eyes betrayed insectile compounding. Five eyes per face, though again not always in the same places. Some of them wore scraps of clothing. Things recognizable as jeans or blazers in the faded colors of the school above.

One of them stood in the center of what was now clearly an arena and waited patiently for the five delvers to advance to its position.

"Welllllcome," it hissed out, voice like a leaking faucet. It bubbled its words around a thick tongue, or perhaps it was some other body part. None of them looked closely into its mouth. "Yooou . . ."

It didn't get to finish the sentence before James interrupted it. "We have questions," he stated bluntly, cutting off the thing before them. "What are you doing here?" James opened with, not giving the thing time to deny that questions would be happening.

It answered anyway, waving two of its three hands to silence the crowd around them that had begun jeering as James interrupted. "Weee were borrrrn here," it spat out, droplets of liquid falling from its mouth as it spoke. "Weee serrrrve, withh deliiiight." It grinned then, a horrifyingly happy look on the face of something so obviously built to be ugly. "And weee guard thhhe passssage to your hooome," it told them.

"You're going to stop us from leaving?" Alanna asked, a dangerous glint in her eye. Next to her, both Aneshes tensed up, his hands clenching into fists as he felt his breathing speed up.

"Neeeevar!" the creature protested. "Thhhe doooor requires sssparks," it told them, grin still plastered to its face. "Hunnndreds of themm." It spread the two arms that were in front of it in a placating gesture, as if to explain that this wasn't its fault. The third arm, the one that jutted out of its back, swept into view then and tossed something at their feet. "Dooo nhat worry, though." Its grin grew even wider, showing off more and more teeth as its drool dripped down onto the floor. "Onnne of yoou sshhould be more than enough to passs."

All five delvers glanced down to see a polished and wickedly sharp knife, casually tossed at their feet.

"Sssparks demand killssss," the cockroach-rat hybrid said in a sarcastic apology as it began stepping backward. "Noowwww . . . choooooose."

"Hey, do you know where James and Anesh went? They were here earlier, but they just vanished, and they aren't answering their phones." Sarah poked her head into the office where JP was sitting.

He looked up at her like a deer caught in the headlights, one hand midway through the process of running through his gleamingly gelled hair. "What? Nothing! Wait, what?" He slammed the laptop screen shut.

"I asked . . . hang on, what's going on?" Sarah gave him a mischievous smile. "I smell a story here," she probed.

JP tried to relax, but it looked almost mechanical the way he did it, lowering his arm with surgical precision and growing a clearly fake smile across his face just a little too slowly. "No," he settled on, clasping both hands together in front of him on the desk.

"Did you do something horribly illegal?" Sarah poked at him verbally.

"Yes. Absolutely. What was the original question? Can we go back to that?" He floundered in the conversation, his usual charm fled with his brain caught off guard.

Sarah came in and plopped into one of the chairs on the other side of the desk. "Wow, you're really flustered! This is different. I feel like I should take advantage of it, but now I feel bad seeing you this way. It's like a puppy that's been told it doesn't get treats." She kicked her feet up on the desk, draping herself across as many pieces of furniture as possible. "I'm just looking for James."

"Oh, he and Anesh went to the school. Alanna said something was going on. Didn't they tell you?" JP raised an eyebrow. "Also, hey, did you have a blue a while back that destroyed suspicion?"

"It moved it around, didn't destroy it," Sarah said. "And I used a lot of that on the police, what with the active missing-persons case about me. Why?" Her brain caught up to what he'd said earlier. "Wait, did they just skip out on me and go on *another* new dungeon delve without me? Those . . . boggarts!"

"I think that's the closest I've ever heard you to actually swearing. *And* actually angry!" JP commented. "Anyway, yeah, a while back James pointed out that the investment account that I'd set up was going to look suspicious if my skill actually let me pick winners consistently, because investment portfolios really didn't ever do that. So I was just checking on it and planning to make some mildly bad short-term investments to offset the theoretically good long-term ones."

"And?" Sarah took the distraction.

"And the long-term good ones turned into short-term good ones, and it *really absolutely does* look like I'm abusing insider information, because I *am*. I'm just using the Skill to be better at it. But the orb left me with blind spots and I didn't think until now to try covering for it." JP leaned forward on the desk, pressing his fingertips into his forehead and then back over his skull. "Fuck, if I worked for the SEC and I saw this? I'd want to question me."

"Are they going to see it?"

"Probably not," he admitted. "I'm not using millions of dollars or anything. But I'm also not using nothing, and . . . you know what? It's fine. I can fix this. The Skill's already kicking in my brain showing me a few fixes. It's not a huge deal. Sorry, I didn't mean to cut you off. You were mad at James?"

Was she? That was a good question. Sarah leaned her head back to look up at the ceiling fan. The question muddled through her brain for a bit before she settled on an answer.

"Nah, I'm just worried about them. From what I understand these days, the Office is, like, 'medium well-done' in terms of lethality? So I'm kinda just concerned they'll get hurt. He's my best friend, you know?"

JP nodded. "I get that. But I think they'll be fine. He's got Anesh and Alanna with him, right? They always take care of each other."

That was reassuring. "Yeah!" Sarah kicked her feet back onto the ground and hopped up, a little of her enthusiasm restored. "Yeah, they do! I mean, I'm still worried; that kid didn't give me enough details to assuage my fear of the unknown, but yeah. You're right. They'll be *fine*," she said as she strode out of the office. "Thanks, JP!" she called back.

JP leaned back in the chair with a sigh, gnawing on his lip before he opened up the laptop again and settled in to compose an incredibly apologetic email. "Okay," he muttered to himself. "Let's fix this before Sarah realizes how full of shit I am." He started typing and got about two sentences in before he sighed and spoke again in the quiet air. "They do take care of each other, huh?"

The knife sat on the bloody concrete. Four sets of human eyes, one cavalcade of infomorph stares, and a whole host of strange compound gazes cast down upon it.

One of them would be enough. That's what the thing had said. And then it gave them a knife. A weapon, when all other weapons were taken away. Enough to get through the gate, to the breach. Enough sparks, those bits of bloody light that came from *kills*. And apparently this nightmare sewer didn't care if the kills were from its own creations, as long as they happened on its ground.

Ah. This was why Sarah got a bad feeling from the kid. This was why there were so many backpacks and phones left unclaimed. So many blank spots on the walls for names.

In the silent air that followed, Anesh took a half step forward and started to clear his throat. "Ah. I . . . can . . ."

He didn't get any further than that.

Anesh *was* the logical choice, yes. He could make more of himself. One Anesh would be, not *easy*, but *simple* to pay as the toll to pass. But this was a conversation that James and Alanna had gone over before.

They'd put together a few key things they needed to know. A sort of living will. What to do if one of them was on life support, what to do if one of them was unconscious and a decision needed to be made, that sorta thing. What to do if they were under duress or threatened. And their answer on that last one had been mutually agreeable and simple.

No negotiation with terrorists.

So while Anesh was stumbling over the words that it would take to offer himself up as a noble sacrifice, James's mind was already firing on combat mode. He flexed muscles that weren't real and felt the purple orbs tethered to his soul latch onto his physical form. His perception spiked into sharp, almost painful focus. His every motion started faster and ended cleaner. And beside him, he could almost physically feel it as Alanna did the same.

And his brain had already made a few connections. How much blood would it take to stain concrete like this, this much? This probably wasn't even the only exit. How many children had died here, scared and alone, pitted against each other? How *well-fed* were these monsters? They were wearing scraps of human clothing; they were baiting people into *murder*.

But that was the thing, wasn't it? Sure, Anesh might be worth a few hundred sparks. But so far, every kill here had given them something. And James had to imagine that a ratroach would give him a decent enough pile. And oh, look. There were a convenient thirty or so of them *right there.*

Anesh was four words into his explanation when James began moving. He burst forward in a spike of sudden momentum, Alanna already rushing in just behind him. The creature clearly hadn't expected it, and James slipped around its side without it showing more resistance than trying to slap him away with one of its claws.

That was a stupid idea. He caught the wrist as he stepped past it, pivoting at a hard angle to position himself directly behind the monster; he yanked *hard* on its arm, his other hand going up to wrap gloved fingers around the third arm that stuck out of its shoulder and angled backward. With a twist, he got that arm around the thing's neck and began to tighten it into a chokehold.

This took all of five seconds. And in that time, Alanna had closed the distance, evaluated her vulnerable and pinned opponent, and drew back one riot glove–covered fist for the hardest punch she could throw.

The strike drilled the thing in the middle of its chest, and James felt the impact from behind the creature's mass. He also felt, more than heard, the wet popping as Alanna's punch, which she had fully committed to, went through its skin and bones and sank her fist into its chest.

Then she grabbed whatever it thought counted as a heart and *ripped*.

A gory fountain of red sparks lashed at her forearm, and in the moments that followed, silence reigned in the arena.

Anesh, reading the room, stopped offering to sacrifice himself. One of his bodies picked up the knife, and the other one moved to flank James as best he could as his boyfriend dropped the lifeless corpse of a ratroach onto the concrete.

"One of us will do?" James bellowed into the still, damp air, turning around to point a threatening finger at the crowd of ratroaches around them in the stands. "Just kill one of us, and we can leave?" he shouted, clenching his hand into a raised fist. "How many of *you* would it take?" His challenge echoed off the walls, and a second later, screams and war cries assailed the humans and Secret from all sides as the motley ratroaches began pouring over the edges of the platforms like a tide to get to them, rattling weapons on the stone and metal floors.

"Let's find out," James heard Secret hiss out from his shoulder. "I look forward to this secret knowledge."

Then the first row of the things reached them.

If Anesh had been willing to sacrifice himself, it was only because he didn't see another way out. Perhaps he hadn't really thought that they could fight this whole horde. But now that it was happening, he had no reason to be sheepish or recalcitrant. Instead, the first thing that got near him, he let Alanna grab the throat of and lift off the ground before slipping in and jamming his new knife into its stomach, pulling upward as hard as he could until he hit ribs. He repeated the process again, shoving the blade in with both hands until the sparks flew and Alanna dropped the thing like so much trash. Anesh grabbed the spear out of its hand as it fell and tossed it to his other body, who quickly twirled it once to get used to the weight, and then used it to slap aside a ratroach's attack and impale it through the eye.

James slugged one of the four things that fell toward him, screaming their defiance. Secret solidified just long enough to *bite off one's arm*, a trick that he was becoming fond of, it seemed. James caught the club on the way down, a piece of ceramic pipe that was shaped, for all the world, like a crowbar. He grinned at the familiar heft and jammed it into the eye of one of the other ratroaches. The last one lunged forward, weaponless but snapping its dripping fangs, and James caught it on his arm. He could feel the teeth sawing into him as the saliva melted through his jacket, but then, before he could reach, an Anesh bodychecked it to the ground, leaving torn and bloody teeth behind in the sleeve of James's coat before putting a spear into it with multiple two-handed thrusts.

"Fuck you!" Alanna screamed her bloody defiance of their would-be killers as she punched one so hard that its neck snapped on the spot. She almost slipped on the slickening concrete under her feet as blood, or something like it, had begun to pool. He purple orbs gave her all the might she needed to be a one-woman force of destruction, breaking bones and plating with every hit she threw out, her skin stubbornly refusing to breach when spears and blades made their way to her. She could afford to be a little reckless, a little aggressive. But she wasn't. Instead, she carefully calculated each punch, each positional step. They never hit her on their terms; she let them commit to feeble thrusts with their off-placed arms that would never hurt her but always leave them ready to be ground down to nothing. But they were quickly going to be overwhelmed at this rate. Her perception skill gave her a mental layout of the battlefield, and while they'd already killed maybe a third of the monsters, the rest were all going to hit them at once, and James and Secret weren't in any position to assist.

So, she dived down into her mind and triggered the blue orb she had embedded in her palm.

With a sweep of her hand that was utterly unneeded, a three-foot-high wall of asphalt sprang up like grass in spring. It cut across the right side of their battlefield where the oncoming crowd was thickest, forcing the rats to either climb over or go around. And either way, it stalled them long enough for Alanna to grab the one that had just tried to *stab her* and slam it by the throat into her new wall a few times until it went limp, leaving a wet stain on the stone.

James had turned into a furious whirlwind of righteous anger. Every one of these things, he knew now, deserved to die. This wasn't like the Office, he thought as his crowbar caved in a skull and his arms started to burn. There were no friendly staplers or ways to make their own kind of life. These were *monsters*, and with a splatter of green and black ichor, he broke one's arm, tripped it with the backswing, and then slammed a boot into its chest and put all his weight on it as he turned his attention to another charging *thing* with a copper spear.

Apparently, Anesh had decided he'd had enough of that, and a with a dusting of blue light, a half second before it encountered James, the thing was screaming as its spear melted around its hands, all three of its claws sizzling as the red-hot metal took too long to cool.

James didn't bother putting it out of its misery. He simply waited for the spray of red from the thing to crunch under his boot and then slammed his club into the side of another one, sending it sideways.

The melee didn't last nearly as long as he'd expected. It felt like only seconds later that James found himself with nothing left to kill, a final flood of red sparks pouring into him as he stalked over to the ratroach still screaming in pain as its hands burned under their metal coating and jammed the broken haft of his shattered club into its eyes. Repeatedly.

He stood, panting, Secret draped around him with several mouths splattered with black blood and scraps of fur like a violent cloak. Alanna and Anesh, similarly, both whipped their heads around like they were on the lookout for their next target, *anything* else to kill, stolen weapons clasped tight in their hands.

But there were no more.

Every one of these things was dead. James took a second to breathe and then nodded, spat on the nearest corpse, and walked over to his friends.

"I'm going to check the lockers. Then we should go," he said. Or tried to say. His voice came out as a shaken, adrenaline-pumped squeak, and he was pretty sure the words hadn't made it out right. From the looks they were giving him, that seemed about right. Instead of trying again, he just pointed a now-jittering finger at the portcullis, gesturing for someone, anyone, to get the damn thing open, before he himself walked off to the side.

James didn't have much left in his stomach to throw up. Which was good, because the smell of rot and blood and offal spilled across the floor in wild streaks and bubbling pools was more than enough to turn his stomach. Instead, he staggered over to the back wall, where that modern-art display of lockers jutted from the ground. There were five, no, six of them. All different shapes and sizes. And while each one was damaged, they were all still locked. He reached for one of the padlocks and found to no surprise that its dial did not turn but instead lit up with a bright-green twelve.

He nodded. Ten for this one, then. He scanned the prices on the others, finding another that came in at six, and settled on that.

The feeling of the green light leaving him was exactly the same as the red was for Alanna, though he wouldn't know that until later. It was a gravitic pull on his system, like something was sucking his blood out of him, but no blood would spill. The sparks from his earlier answers dripped into the locks, and dials spun and tumblers clicked until the lock itself simply burned away, dissolving in an acid flare of green and silver.

The locker door swung open. There was a composition notebook inside, a little bit browned around the edges of the paper. James grabbed it, then did the same with his other choice of container and pulled a battered copy of a paperback novel out of it. The beaten and half-torn cover simply had it labeled as "INHERITORS" in all caps, with much of the art having been torn off, showing only the top half of a man with absurdly good abs.

"I'm underwhelmed by this reward," James muttered to himself, or tried to, as he shifted his grip around on the two books like they were closer to garbage than fought-for texts. "Which has traditionally been standard for first delves, actually." He was starting to find his voice again. His snark. The adrenaline was fading, along with the fury; it had died down to embers of hate that still sat in his chest but weren't fanned overly much when he looked at the room full of corpses.

Every one of them had deserved this. He knew that. No ethical questions this time.

"The door says three hundred!" Anesh called over to him as he approached. "Neither of me has that, and apparently you don't share it within your own hive mind. Which seems unfair," he griped, trying to insert what levity he could. The words ran over each other, though, his voice shaking and slurred as the adrenaline wore off.

"I've got it," Alanna said, stepping *through* a body with a wet splash, her boots really pulling their weight with the waterproofing as the blood of that particular ratroach hissed against them like acid. She strode up to the gate like she was ready to just start punching it apart if it didn't comply, but when she laid her hand against it, a river of red light flowed out of her and into the jagged, rusty iron.

And then it swung upward, with a sound straight out of a horror movie.

"Let's not come back here without demolitions-grade explosives," James said with dark conviction as he slipped forward into the cut through the wall and felt gravity shift so that he was suddenly falling away, back upward, hopefully back *out*.

No one argued as they followed him.

CHAPTER 26

"James, *wait!*" The shout echoed against the polished stone ramp of the high school's lower level. It echoed alongside heavy, wet bootsteps as James stomped his way up to the ground floor, away from the door to the boiler room and its vile little pit of secrets. Around him, Secret coiled like a gathering storm, a blue hurricane of equal parts fury and determination.

They were, mildly, upset.

"James!" Alanna yelled again. "No! This is a bad idea!" She caught her bearings and finally managed to stand up. She'd hit the ground with a case of vertigo that left the walls spinning and her head pounding, and she had literally no idea how James had almost instantly started moving.

Anesh, too, was still slumped on the floor, among the scattered stuff the dungeon had yanked away from them on entry. One with an arm held out to one of the suspended pipes, trying to haul himself up, the other simply curled up, clutching at his stomach and groaning. But there was no time for Alanna to be nice and try to help him up; there was an angry partner about to do something stupid who needed to be stopped.

She staggered out the door, holding on to the wall for balance, and realized with concern that she was already a few hundred feet behind James. She could just see his retreating back at the top of the ramp and realized it was too late to stop him from wading into the thin group of people in the school's lobby.

There had been a basketball game tonight—the thought wormed through the back of her head. There were a lot of students here, many of them wandering around in patterns they didn't normally use. And the dungeon was open. The dungeon had only been open when there were students here. Interesting.

The thought impacting her brain didn't stop her from also noticing the startled and sometimes outright fearful yelps and screams as James was noticed.

Alanna shook off her dizziness and lurched forward. She kept a hand on the wall for balance, but she moved as fast as she could to catch up to James. For the first time, she found herself actively wishing to have already absorbed a purple that would give her some kind of enhanced inner ear or something. But wishing things were magically better was never really where Alanna's mind lived, and she shrugged that off about as quickly as she sloughed away the vertigo and started jogging forward.

As he'd walked through the lobby, cutting a straight line past several groups of high schoolers, James had left a trail of blood and filth and panic. His clothing was soaked with the dual-color blood of the ratroaches, some of it smoking from whatever weird corrosive effect some of that blood had, splattering intermittent drips onto the tile floor. His boots left bloody footprints behind as he stalked forward. And around him, Secret continued to spiral, his form still physical enough that everyone could see him.

There were maybe a hundred people here, Alanna realized with sinking dread. Kids out to see the game, members of the basketball teams who were milling around now that they were done, a few teachers or parents. All of them now wide-eyed and staring at the late-twenties man and infant infomorph as the two of them cut a silent path across the floor toward the front office.

"Goddammit," Alanna muttered, pressing her fingers together over her nose.

It was, at this point, *far* beyond too late to slip out of the building unnoticed. Unbelievably too late to stop James from opening up a million lines of questioning from a hundred people. Stop him from carving open all those weak points in their shroud of anonymity that anyone who wanted to find them—or people like them—could exploit.

"Holy shit, are you all right?" The voice from behind Alanna was an older man, gruff but instantly concerned. She turned sharply, and her vision swam for a second before the shape before her resolved into a polo shirt and the visage of the school's security guard. "You're bleeding!" He said the words as if by speaking it would fix the problem.

Alanna looked down at herself, then back up. "I don't think any of this is mine," she said impotently. "Sorry, I have to go help my . . . partner. There's someone else down by the boiler room—can you go check on him?" she asked, remembering at the last minute that this man was at least somewhat convinced that she was a representative of the federal government.

"Wh . . . yes, ma'am!" He gave her a nod, and she saw his arm twitch like he was thinking about saluting her but decided against it at the last minute. His hustle down the ramp was almost amusing, the way he shuffled his arms in short bursts as he power walked his way into the depths of the school building.

Alanna shook her head. At least if Anesh needed anything, he'd have someone there. With a grimace on her face, she turned and followed James, hoping that everyone would still be too focused on his passing to notice her.

It didn't work.

While frightened and startled yells had followed James and the strange apparition on his shoulders, it was more like a wall of murmurs that swaddled Alanna. People pointed, stared; no one was shocked to see her follow him, only curious and wondering, perhaps, *why she was also bleeding.*

"It's not mine," Alanna told the young woman who was bold enough to have asked. Then she looked down at her arms again, turning them over and checking the drying fluid that was forming a crust against her skin. "I think. I don't think anything can actually cut me anymore," she muttered. Then she realized what she'd said and shook her head again, starting up another migraine. "Ah, please ignore that," she told the student before continuing after James.

No one else interrupted her, though whether that was out of fear of the woman who looked like she'd stepped out of a *Conan the Barbarian* comic or out of relief that she was being polite to the few people who asked her questions and was not there to kill them all, she didn't know.

When she pushed open the doors of the office, James had already made it behind the desk. There were two older women in here, the administrators most likely, somewhere below a vice principal but vital to making the school actually operate. Alanna had been friends with their counterparts at her high school when she'd still attended and was all too aware of the frequent need for them to be in on weekends, especially game days.

Right now, they were somewhat cowering back against a row of filing cabinets as James rustled around in the long desk for what he was looking for.

The main desk dominated this front of the office. Anyone walking in, from either the front door or either of the two doors that led to the school, would have to pass by this huge, curved facade. It wasn't wood, Alanna realized, just paneled with it, but it was still imposing to a student who was either needing something or sent here for a conversation. The rest of the office was carpeted, in sharp contrast to the paved stone floor of the main building. Real carpet, too, which she noted both she and James had now tracked blood onto. That would require a serious apology to the school's janitorial staff.

Alanna drew her attention back to what was going on and addressed the two women who were now looking fearfully at her. She opened with a sigh. "Excuse me. You'll have to pardon my partner, he's had a rough day." She reached into her coat, wincing as the women both flinched. What, Alanna wondered to herself, did she actually look like right now? Slowly, she pulled out the fake badge that had somehow managed to survive mostly unscathed, though it did have a red smear across the plastic cover. "I'm Agent Byrne, FBI. We need . . ." She looked over at James, and he finally looked up at her. "What do we need?" she asked him quietly, trying to draw him back out of his anger.

"Student roster," he croaked out, like he'd finally found his voice again.

Alanna nodded and raised her eyebrows at the administrators or assistants, who were now looking noticeably less afraid of *her*, but no less concerned about the neon-blue leviathan that was rotating through the air of their office. She followed their gazes, and then nodded. "Ah. It would be for the best if you didn't tell anyone about that," she said. "Government secrets, you know? But it's been a rough day," she repeated, unable to think of anything better at the moment.

It really *had* been a rough day.

James looked up like he was only just now noticing there were other humans here. "Oh," he said. "I'm . . . sorry. I didn't mean to worry you," he told the women. The older of the two, a matronly figure who looked like she'd been fifty years old for the last twenty years, scowled at him, as if by removing her fear, all that was left was annoyance. It wasn't a hard scowl, but it was filled with frustration. "I'm not going to make your day easier, though," he said as she brought him a thick, ringed book filled with pages and pages of names.

"Just keep that monster away from me," she snapped at him, leaning back away from Secret as some of his eyes turned toward her.

"He's not the monster you need to be worried about," James growled out, anger flaring up again. The woman shrank back, unsure how to react to this sudden and forceful shift of the power dynamics in her little slice of the world. Ignoring her completely, James slammed the book of student records onto the table and soon joined it with three others brought out to him for each of the students' classes. "Secret," he instructed. "Kill the bugs."

Secret flickered through the air, moving like he was diving through caverns and tunnels in reality. There was a burst of motion, and everyone in the room had the same feeling, like they were remembering the sensation of *teeth* and darkness and an abrupt ending.

James sighed in deep, exhausted sorrow as he spotted, just on the one page out of hundreds that he was looking at, three names slowly blur into his perception.

He turned to the younger of the employees here, a woman still well into her forties. "You'll need to . . ." He coughed, trying to find his words. "You'll need to check all of these," he said, choking back tears. "For names. Look for names of students that you can't find. You won't have noticed them. That's not your fault. It's . . . it's not your fault." He closed his eyes and leaned forward on the desk. Around his shoulders, Secret stopped moving and coiled up against James, butting his head against his friend's cheek. Alanna stepped over and laid a hand on his arm, casually offering comfort. "It . . ." James didn't know what to say. "They're dead." The words fell out before he could stop them. "They're dead, because we weren't here fast enough. We didn't know. We couldn't have possibly known. And they're dead. They were *kids*, Alanna." He looked up and met her eyes, and she saw tears running down his face. "They were just kids," he whispered.

"We'll be back," she told him. "We'll kill it," she promised. "Until then, we'll post a guard. No one in without us knowing. And we'll go back and make sure nothing is left in there to be a threat." Her voice was hard, uncompromising. Alanna felt the same furious anger that James did, but it didn't hurt her the same way it did him. She felt . . . she felt strange. She wanted the world to be better, of course; she wanted to help people, to build a utopia one step at a time. But when she looked at James now, she realized just how much he *felt* things like this. How hurt he was. "Come on," she said. "Let's get Anesh and get out of here. We'll need to get some stuff to deal with it. The roll of police tape in the trunk won't keep people out forever."

James nodded. "Yeah," he whispered, wiping at his eyes and nose, smearing blood from his coat onto his face and making himself look even more like a crazed killer. "Yeah. Oh, Anesh. I need to . . . we should . . ."

"Go sit in the car," Alanna ordered him. "I'll be out in a minute."

He thanked her and apologized to the poor front desk clerks who were suddenly having the worst quiet Saturday of paperwork ever. And eventually, he stumbled out the door.

"Oh, boy," Alanna muttered, looking out the glass door to the lobby and the crowd of nervously watching people. "We're really gonna have to lie our asses off about this one."

"Ow," Anesh repeated for the eighth or ninth time.

He was sitting slumped against a wall, applying pressure to the wad of bandage pressed against the hole in his ribs. It wasn't too deep, but it was bleeding, a lot. Unlike Alanna, most of the blood actually *was* his, and it wasn't pleasant. His counterpart stood nearby in the hallway, on a phone call with Sarah, and from what injured Anesh could hear of the conversation, he felt a bit lucky that he'd been stabbed rather than having to deal with that.

"Oh jeez, kid. You sure you're gonna be okay?" the security guard, a man who was ironically named Rufus, Anesh had learned, asked him. For the fifth time.

Anesh just tilted his head back against the cool stone of the wall. "Probably," he said. He didn't add that even if he was going to die, it wasn't a big deal. He'd link up with himself beforehand and lose maybe two minutes, tops. Minimal existential dread. Instead, he opted to say, "We have a . . . an agency doctor. I'll be stitched up in no time." He tried to smile, but it came out as more of a feral grin.

The older man was squatted near him, burly arms rustling around in the medical kit looking for some tape to hold the bandages in place. At this point, Anesh wasn't even sure he'd need stitches, but regardless, he'd been saving up blues for exactly this circumstance, and avoiding *another* awkward emergency room trip was high on his list of priorities. Whether it was orbs, death, or just not needing more than bandages and bed rest, he was prepared to not have to answer questions from pushy doctors again this year.

"You sure you're okay, kid? This is *bad*. How did you get this, anyway? And are you with the feds, too? You and your brother there?" The man had an endless barrage of questions. He talked methodically, not slow, but also with just enough room to answer if Anesh had wanted to fit words in there. Since he wasn't doing that, Rufus just kept rolling until he was out of stored questions, and Anesh sat and thought about it.

"I'm fine," Anesh said, feeling a sense of true relief as Alanna came striding back to them holding a roll of wide yellow tape. "There was . . . an altercation. And I'm with them, so, yes, I suppose."

"An *altercation*, eh?" The man stressed the word in that tone that adults often used when they knew you were absolutely full of shit but wanted you to come to the conclusion on your own. Anesh had found that he himself had started using that tone lately, and he expected it would only ramp up as he aged.

"Alanna, save me. Also, what's that?" he asked, curiosity pushing aside pain for a brief moment before it flooded back and made his eyes slam shut in concentration.

Alanna looked down at the roll of plastic in her hand. "Police tape," she explained slowly.

"It's the wrong color," Anesh said flatly.

"We're American," she told him, already starting to cordon off the boiler room door. "Sir, you wouldn't happen to have a key to this door, would you?" she asked Rufus politely.

"Yes, ma'am," he told her. "I think. I always forget this damn door is down here, for some reason."

"It's a hell of a reason," Alanna muttered before shutting her mouth, realizing she was being cryptic out loud and that was exactly what she'd scolded James for doing, repeatedly. When the guard handed her the key off his ring, Alanna took it, inserted it into the lock, locked the door, then *slammed* the flat of her gloved hand down on the exposed part of the key, snapping it off with a clean motion. "Ow," she said mildly, while Anesh looked over from his call at the noise before turning back to being berated by Sarah for their recklessness. The security guard had a hell of a lot more of a reaction, his eyes going wide as he glanced between the unassuming—but blood-soaked—woman in front of him, and the now-jammed door. "No one in or out," Alanna told him with an iron command in her voice. "If anyone mentions this door, you call us. You have my number. If anyone mentions too many pipes, rats, roaches, a combination of rats or roaches, red or green sparks, or having to make a hard choice, you *get their names and call us.*" Her eyes made it clear this was not up for debate. "Tell your coworkers, too. Keep this quiet, but make sure the people who need to know, know." Alanna reached down a hand and helped Anesh to his feet.

As the three of them turned to head back to their cars, the man called after them. "What happened here?" His voice had a note of urgency in it. He needed to know; this was his job. More than that, his duty. He was supposed to protect these kids; he couldn't do that if he was in the dark.

Alanna paused and turned her head slightly. She looked at this poor man with sad eyes as she tried to find the words to say. James would have known, she thought. He would have had something. Instead, all she could give him was "Something cruel and unfair. I can't tell you more."

Leaving him with that, she and Anesh carried his other limping body out of the building.

[+1 Skill Rank : Animals—American Goose]
[Problem Solved : Turned Off the Oven]
"Nope."
[+1 Skill Rank : History—Military—The Great War]
[Problem Solved : Renewed License]
"Useful, but no."
[+2 Skill Ranks : Fabrication—Fletching—Broadhead Arrows]
[Problem Solved : Medical Attention]
"There." Anesh sighed as the third orb dissipated into that glowing dust that followed the soft pop. He leaned back into the couch, the

gash in his side made by a shiv of rusted pipe now thoroughly cleaned, disinfected, stitched, and bandaged, leaving him dosed with painkiller of some kind. He knew, from experience, that the pain wasn't *fixed* by the orb. It stuck to using mundane means when it could, it felt like. And so his blood now had a little more chemical assistance in it than normal. But at least it didn't feel like he'd been stabbed.

Again.

"I'm a little concerned that you expected to be stabbed so much that you stockpiled blues for exactly that purpose," Alanna told him. She was in the kitchen, currently wearing basically nothing and making eggs and toast. The instant they'd gotten home, she'd insisted on collecting their clothing and throwing it in a garbage bag, with only the most remote possibility that anyone would ever get their blood-crusted pants back. Anesh had wrapped himself in a robe and settled down on the couch to run through blues until something fixed his wound, while the other Anesh and James had gone off to take showers and try, desperately, to purify themselves of the stains of war.

"I'm kind of concerned that you wouldn't expect me to have a stockpile of our most useful weapons." Anesh raised his eyebrows at Alanna as she wandered over and slid a plate onto the table in front of him. He quickly glanced aside as she wandered back into the kitchen, flushed in the cheeks and doing his best not to stare at her ass.

"Are they weapons?" she asked, like this was normal. Which, in her defense, it was quickly becoming.

Anesh could answer that one without any embarrassment. "Absolutely!" he said. "They say 'problem solved,' but you know what they count as problems? Certain death. Also, absorbing them is crazy useful. I'm kind of annoyed that only Dave can load three at once right now; I'm not sure if it's a state of mind thing or he's just a higher level or what. But I want it."

"Combo potential?" Alanna asked, reading Anesh's mind without the aid of the skulljack.

He cocked a finger at her, nodding. "Exactly. And now, I'm going to go shower, since I'm done with it, and I want to get the hot water before James soaks it all up."

"We need a green for that," Alanna said. She, too, had wanted a shower. But she was fine waiting. Fifteen minutes with the sink and a washcloth had been enough to get the worst of it off her hands, forearms, and face. If she'd shown up to a kitchen job looking like she did, she'd probably be cussed out of the building, but she was clean enough to make a late-night breakfast for her family here.

As soon as she said the words, she suddenly realized just how selfish it was. But also, her mind started burning with a dozen other ideas for how the green orbs could enhance their living space. And some of them were, seriously, important. What if they healed faster here, or didn't get sick? What if they had more time? They already had the bonus sleep hour. Could they get more? She let herself be distracted by it for so long that she almost scorched her toast, and by the time she'd gotten through daydreaming about what benefits their apartment could score from their next tumblefeed hunt, James had come out wrapped in his posh red bathrobe and claimed the entirety of the couch. He sat there, a blank look on his face, as a worried Rufus and Ganesh watched him from perches on the table and fireplace mantel, respectively. Even Aberdeen noticed the mood, the giant white furry beast padding over to rest a worried snout on his leg.

"Hey," Alanna said, keeping her voice calm. James had been shaken by the school dungeon. Beyond shaken. He'd been *angry* in a way that Alanna had never really seen. Even with the Office, when James had once settled on the idea that the place was dangerous and clearly it would have to die, it was with a sad kind of remorse. But here? He'd been coldly furious. Prepared to purchase a few hundred thousand bucks' worth of black-market C4 and just level the whole fucking place.

"Hey," he said in reply, hand idly scratching the dog's ears. There was long moment where Alanna considered asking him if he wanted any eggs, but she couldn't form words in a way she found at *all* satisfactory for the mood. And then, "So, uh," James said, "the books."

They were sitting on the table. One old composition notebook, and one half-destroyed fantasy paperback. No one had opened either of them. They were, blatantly, rewards. And the whole team knew what that meant.

"Yeah," Alanna said. "Who do we foist them on?"

"*Foist* is not the word I'd use," James said, with the ghost of a smile on his lips. It was gone almost as soon as it was there, and he was back to that sad frown again. "Still. We do need to choose who gets them. I could only get two, and there's four of us. Or maybe three. Depends on how you look at it. *And* how they work; they might not jump the gap like the orbs do."

"So, how do you wanna split them?" Alanna asked.

James glanced over at her and did a slight double take as he realized for the first time that she was mostly naked in his kitchen. But then he realized something else; she was looking at the two innocuous-seeming books on the table with a slightly hungry look in her eyes. And he knew it because he felt the same thing. This was the score of a lifetime, and they might never get to mine out an infinity of resources from the Sewer like they would from Officium Mundi. Oh, there'd be a few more. But they had very real plans to kill that place into oblivion, and these were a limited resource. And they knew, all of them, that these things were *powerful*. They'd taken a kid who hated learning and turned him into a scholar with a ferocious appetite for words and ethics in about a *week*. What could they do for *them*, who actually had designs on bending their power to shape the world?

Well. This was it then, wasn't it? He'd finally engineered a situation where they all wanted the power on offer, and there simply wasn't enough to go around. And now...

"What's up, friends?" the more clean and less stabbed Anesh asked as he walked out and grabbed the plate of food that his other half had already half finished.

"We're talking about the books," James said, tense.

"Oh. You two take the bloody things." Anesh waved a fork in the air before sort of awkwardly sitting down next to James. He started to reach out to lay a hand on James's arm, then paused as his brain kicked in, overanalyzing the unfamiliar gesture, before he shook that feeling off and took the plunge, offering a small moment of warm contact as a reminder that they were all in this together. "We'll get more eventually anyway, and the two of you can probably put them to better use. It sounds like they buff something kinda abstract, from what Sarah got out of the kid, and while it would be cool to think 'better,' whatever that means, I'm really pretty sure they're going to be better for you guys."

James narrowed his eyes, not in suspicion but more in exaggerated concern. "Whhhhy?" he asked slowly.

"Because I'm spending more and more time on the support team." Anesh shrugged. "Sure, skills are useful. Math skills especially make me feel like I've both wasted my life and also chosen wisely. And the location powers are super-good amplifiers. And as mentioned, blues are just killer. Actually, I like all the orbs. But the thing is, I'm not using them looking for power. I'm more using them to solve problems. It's why I like the blues. Sometimes they're problems I didn't even know I had, but that's really the goal for me." He tapped the books on the table, reaching past a curious Rufus, who was poking his forelegs onto the stacked paper. "These? We have a good forewarning on what these do. They are *power*. Personal, intimate power. And I think you two could do a lot with that. More than me."

"So you don't want one?" Alanna asked cautiously.

Anesh made a "pff" noise with his lips. "Of course I want one. But I'm not gonna be a wanker about it. We'll get more, if only because we'll go back to keep killing anything that pops up in that place. I'll get the next round; you two can have first pick."

"Welp! That solves that crisis!" James said, injecting so much false cheer into his voice that he actually started to really feel it. "I'm taking the paperback! I feel a connection to the eighties-style fantasy art."

He reached over dramatically, slapped his hand down on the book, and dragged it across the table toward himself. Now with a slightly more real smile as he caught grins on his partners' faces at his antics, he cracked it open to the first page and began to read.

James blinked.

He was done with the book. It had been hours. It had been minutes. It had some important things in it, which was a shame, because he remembered none of it. He looked up and saw that Alanna and Anesh were both staring at him. He looked back down at the book in his hands, turned to the last page, and watched in curiosity as it dissolved to dust, which itself poured into nothingness. And as his brain was just starting to restart its processes, connecting the dust of the book with the glittering smoke of the orbs, an alien thought crossed his mind.

[Lesson Begun : Basketball 0/100]

"Uh-oh," he said, leaning forward onto the table with a hand on his chin to hide the smile he wore.

"What, what's up?!" Anesh worriedly looked at his boyfriend as Alanna came around the kitchen counter to check on him. "Uh-oh" wasn't exactly what you wanted to hear after someone tampered with xenotech. "Are you dying? Is there a curse? Do we need to get Secret out of the bathtub?"

"Why is Secret . . . no, never mind. It's not nearly that important, it's just that now we're going to have to hear more from JP about how Anesh is squandering basketball." James relayed the notification to them, getting a slap on the back of the head from Alanna as her heart rate normalized.

Anesh also sighed and leaned away from James into the cushions of the couch. "Okay, that's not too bad," he said. "I can teach you basketball, and JP can never know about this."

"I like that plan." James and Anesh high-fived. "Alanna? Your sword." James offered her the remaining notebook.

She took it with a snap of the wrist and a roll of the eyes, far less gravitas than James had offered it with. But when it came time to open it, Alanna hesitated. She stared down at the marbled black-and-white cover of this unassuming little book. If she'd seen this on a desk at the library, she never would have known it was a shard of condensed power. It was a bit daunting.

A few seconds or a few hours later, depending on how you looked at things, the book was dust in her hands, flowing into directions that took it out of our visible reality, and Alanna had a new and strange thought crossing over her brain.

[Lesson Begun : Communication 0/100]

"Okay," she said. "Good. Glad we got this established." She clenched the hand that had been holding the remains of the book into a fist and held it up in a determined gesture.

Both boys nodded at her, carefully keeping their eyes focused elsewhere.

"Yup," James said. "Good. All very good," he repeated himself.

Alanna looked at them, eyebrows raised, then looked down at herself. She rolled her eyes as she tilted her head back up. "Oh, fuck's sake, you two. We've *had sex*—are you seriously embarrassed seeing me without pants on?"

"It's more that . . ." Anesh started to formulate an excuse, then thought about it for a second and changed his mind. Instead, he nodded, and went with, "Yes."

"Absolutely," James added.

"You are both beautiful and terrifying," Anesh concluded, getting James to point a single finger at him in agreement.

Alanna stared at the two of them for a good ten seconds before snorting and turning to stride down the hallway. "I'm going to take a shower. You two have fun being *you*," she told them.

It felt just a little patronizing when Rufus crawled up onto the back of the couch a minute later and gently patted James's shoulder in consolation.

Instead of getting upset, though, James just laughed. A real, happy one this time.

"You feeling better?" Anesh asked him, still concerned.

"Yeah, I mean . . ." James hummed. "It's either bounce back or drown in it, right? And I can't save people if I'm too out of it."

Anesh nodded slowly, still worried, but a bit reassured. "True."

"I mostly say true things!" James informed him. "Anyway. It's still my day off. Wanna go teach me how to play basketball? I understand it involves *hoops* of some sort." He pushed himself to his feet and hopped off the couch.

"It's almost eleven p.m.," Anesh pointed out.

James briefly froze in the middle of stretching out his arms. "Shit, really?" he asked, surprised. "No wonder I'm so hungry. And tired. And sore. Okay, wanna get dinner and *then* . . ."

His friend only laughed in response before waving a hand to try to shut James up and also show that he meant no offense in trying to shut James up. "No, no. No way! Not tonight! I'm tired, and half of me is still stabbed. No. I just want to go to bed for a day or so." Anesh thought about it. "Which is convenient, yeah? Because in just over a day, we're going back into the Office."

James groaned theatrically. "Uuggggh," he drawled out. "Do I *have* to? I'm gonna call in sick that day."

There were a few puzzled responses that Anesh instantly thought of, wondering why James would actively want to avoid the Office, wondering why he thought that anyone would actually blame him for not being there or try to force him to come in. It took him a second to conclude that James wasn't serious, but a few seconds longer than that to realize that he wasn't serious because he was trying to make it normal.

He was trying, so hard, to force normalcy onto this night. Where anyone else would have given up and collapsed into bed, James just chugged ahead, like he hadn't publicly sicced Secret on a pile of insectoid antimemes not even two hours ago. Like he hadn't dripped monster blood across half a high school. Like he didn't know how many dead kids there were buried in those tunnels.

Anesh wasn't having as easy a time shaking that off. He'd reconnected with himself, yes, taking the ten minutes needed to share memories. And that act did give him a serious amount of mental stability that most humans would never have. But he was still, somewhat, shaken. He wasn't really ready to play basketball or make jokes. Or do much of anything aside from nap. For twelve hours.

But James . . . well, what he needed was different. And still important to Anesh.

So what he actually settled on saying was less of a puzzled "what" and closer to "Listen here young man; we didn't pay for you to go to wizard school for twelve years so you could *not* dungeon delve! No sick days!"

And what he did after that, with James's genuine laugh still in his ears, was put on shoes and try to go find a neighbor to borrow a basketball from at close to midnight.

ABOUT THE AUTHOR

Argus got started writing sci-fi short stories a decade ago and has spent the majority of that time trying to capture within narrative the feeling of simultaneously not knowing what is happening and overexplaining what is happening. He lives in the Pacific Northwest, where he studied and worked at a number of unconnected things before becoming an author. He did not know if this biography should be in first or third person, and as with all uncertainty in his life, has decided to turn that fact into a joke.

www.ingramcontent.com/pod-product-compliance
Ingram Content Group UK Ltd.
Pitfield, Milton Keynes, MK11 3LW, UK
UKHW041304180426
11947UKWH00009B/667